Last Man in Tower

Aravind Adiga was born in Madras in 1974. He studied at Columbia and Oxford universities. A former India correspondent for *Time* magazine, his articles have also appeared in publications including the *Financial Times*, *Independent* and the *Sunday Times*. He is the author of three critically acclaimed works of fiction: the Man Booker Prize-winning novel *The White Tiger* (2008), the short-story collection *Between the Assassinations* (2009) and the novel *Last Man in Tower* (2011).

Also by Aravind Adiga:

The White Tiger
Between the Assassinations

Last Man in Tower

ARAVIND ADIGA

HarperCollins *Publishers* India
a joint venture with

New Delhi

First published in hardback in 2011 by Fourth Estate
An imprint of HarperCollins *Publishers*

First published in paperback in 2012 by
HarperCollins *Publishers* India
a joint venture with
The India Today Group

Copyright © Aravind Adiga 2011, 2012

ISBN: 978-93-5029-519-9

2 4 6 8 10 9 7 5 3 1

Aravind Adiga asserts the moral right to be identified
as the author of this work.

This is a work of fiction and all characters and incidents described in this book are the product of the
author's imagination. Any resemblance to actual persons, living or dead, is entirely coincidental.

HarperCollins *Publishers*
A-53, Sector 57, Noida, Uttar Pradesh 201301, India
77-85 Fulham Palace Road, London W6 8JB, United Kingdom
Hazelton Lanes, 55 Avenue Road, Suite 2900, Toronto, Ontario M5R 3L2
and 1995 Markham Road, Scarborough, Ontario M1B 5M8, Canada
25 Ryde Road, Pymble, Sydney, NSW 2073, Australia
31 View Road, Glenfield, Auckland 10, New Zealand
10 East 53rd Street, New York NY 10022, USA

Printed and bound at
Thomson Press (India) Ltd.

To my fellow commuters on the Santa Cruz–Churchgate local line

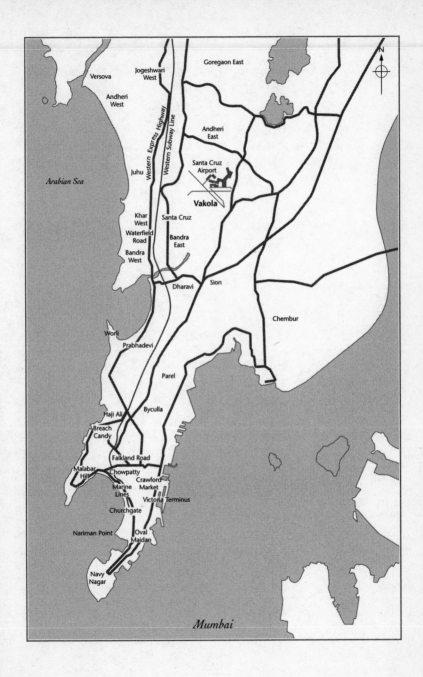

A NOTE ON MONEY

A lakh is 100,000 rupees, equivalent to around £1,400 or $2,200.

A crore is 10,000,000 rupees, equivalent to around £140,000 or $220,000.

So Mr Shah's offer to the members of Vishram Society would translate into a typical windfall of around £210,000 or $330,000 per family.

The average per capita annual income in India in 2008–9 was 37,490 rupees, around £500 or $800.

PLAN OF VISHRAM SOCIETY (TOWER A)
VAKOLA, SANTA CRUZ (EAST), MUMBAI – 400055

Ground floor:

0A   the security guard's personal room

0B   allotted to the Secretary of the Society for official work,
with an alcove for the cleaning lady to store her broom,
disinfectant, and mopping cloth

0C   Felicia Saldanha, 49, and her daughter Radhika, 20;
Mr Saldanha, an engineer, is said to work in Vizag

1st floor:

1A   Suresh Nagpal, 54, timber merchant, and wife Mohini, 53

1B   Georgina Rego, 48, social worker, and son Sunil, 14, and
daughter Sarah, 11

1C   C. L. Abichandani, hardware specialist, 56, his wife Kamini,
52, and daughters Kavita, 18, and Roopa, 21

2nd floor:

2A   Albert Pinto, 67, retired accountant for the Britannia Biscuit
Company, and wife Shelley, 64

2B   Deepak Vij, 57, businessman, his wife Shruti, 43, and
daughter Shobha, 21

2C   Ramesh Ajwani, real-estate broker, 50, his wife Rukmini, 47,
and sons Rajeev, 13, and Raghav, 10

3rd floor:

3A   Yogesh A. Murthy (known as 'Masterji'), retired school-
teacher, 61, now living alone after the recent death of his
wife Purnima

| 3B | Given on rent to Ms. Meenakshi, possibly a journalist, single woman of about 25. Owner Shiv Hiranandani (known as 'Import-Export') lives in Khar West |
| 3C | Sanjiv Puri, 54, accountant, his wife Sangeeta, 52, and son Ramesh, 18, afflicted with Down's syndrome |

4th floor:

4A	Ashvin Kothari, 55, the Secretary of the Society, occupation unknown, his wife Renuka, 49, and son Siddharth (known as 'Tinku'), 10
4B	George Lobo, 45, respectable chemist, his wife Carmina, 40, and daughter Selma, 19
4C	Ibrahim Kudwa, 49, internet-store owner, his wife Mumtaz, 33, and children Mohammad, 10, and Mariam, 2

5th floor:

5A	Given on rent to Mr Narayanswami, 35, working in an insurance company in the Bandra-Kurla Financial Centre. Wife said to be in Hyderabad. (Owner Mr Pais lives in Abu Dhabi)
5B	Sudeep Ganguly, 43, proprietor of a stationery shop in Bandra (East), his wife Sharmila, 41, and son Anand, 11
5C	left empty, on request of owner Mr Sean Costello, after the suicide of his son Ferdinand, who jumped from the terrace of the building; owner currently in Qatar, working as chef for American fast-food company

Other regulars:

Mary, 34, the *khachada-wali*, or cleaning lady; and Ram Khare, 56, the security guard; maids and cooks are employed in most of the households

If you are inquiring about Vishram Society, you will be told right away that it is *pucca* – absolutely, unimpeachably *pucca*. This is important to note, because something is not quite *pucca* about the neighbourhood – the toenail of Santa Cruz called Vakola. On a map of Mumbai, Vakola is a cluster of ambiguous dots that cling polyp-like to the underside of the domestic airport; on the ground, the polyps turn out to be slums, and spread out on every side of Vishram Society.

At each election, when Mumbai takes stock of herself, it is reported that one-fourth of the city's slums are here, in the vicinity of the airport – and many older Bombaywallahs are sure *anything* in or around Vakola must be slummy. (They are not sure how you even pronounce it: Va-KHO-la, or VAA-k'-la?) In such a questionable neighbourhood, Vishram Society is anchored like a dreadnought of middle-class respectability, ready to fire on anyone who might impugn the *pucca* quality of its inhabitants. For years it was the only good building – which is to say, the only registered co-operative society – in the neighbourhood; it was erected as an experiment in gentrification back in the late 1950s, when Vakola was semi-swamp, a few bright mansions amidst mangroves and malarial clouds. Wild boar and bands of dacoits were rumoured to prowl the banyan trees, and rickshaws and taxis refused to come here after sunset. In gratitude to Vishram Society's pioneers, who defied bandits and anopheles mosquitoes, braved the dirt lane on their cycles and Bajaj scooters, cut down the trees, built a thick compound wall and hung signs in English on it, the local politicians have decreed that the lane that winds down from the main road to the front gate of the building be called 'Vishram Society Lane'.

The mangroves are long gone. Other middle-class buildings have come up now – the best of these, so local real-estate brokers say, is Gold Coin Society, but Marigold, Hibiscus, and White Rose grow and grow in reputation – and with the recent arrival of the Grand Hyatt Hotel, a five-star, the area is on the verge of ripening into permanent middle-class propriety. Yet none of this would have been possible without Vishram Society, and the grandmotherly building is spoken of with reverence throughout the neighbourhood.

It is, strictly speaking, two distinct Societies enclosed within the same compound wall. Vishram Society Tower B, which was erected in the late 1970s, stands in the south-east corner of the original plot: seven storeys tall, it is the more desirable building to purchase or rent in, and many young executives who have found work in the nearby Bandra-Kurla financial complex live here with their families.

Tower A is what the neighbours think of as 'Vishram Society'. It stands in the centre of the compound, six storeys tall; a marble block set into the gate-post says in weathered lettering:

THIS PLAQUE WAS UNVEILED BY SHRI KRISHNA MENON, THE HONOURABLE DEFENCE MINISTER OF INDIA, ON 14 NOVEMBER 1959, BIRTHDAY OF OUR BELOVED PRIME MINISTER, PANDIT JAWAHARLAL NEHRU.

Here things become blurry; you must get down on your knees and peer to make out the last lines:

... HAS ASKED MENON TO CONVEY HIS FONDEST HOPE THAT VISHRAM SOCIETY SHOULD SERVE AS AN EXAMPLE OF 'GOOD HOUSING FOR GOOD INDIANS'.

ERECTED BY:

MEMBERS OF THE VISHRAM SOCIETY CO-OPERATIVE HOUSING SOCIETY FULLY REGISTERED AND INCORPORATED IN THE CITY OF BOMBAY 14-11-1959

The face of this tower, once pink, is now a rainwater-stained, fungus-licked grey, although veins of primordial pink show wherever the roofing has protected the walls from the monsoon rains. Every flat has iron grilles on the windows: geraniums, jasmines, and the spikes of cacti push through the rusty metal squares. Luxuriant ferns, green and reddish green, blur the corners of some windows, making them look like entrances to small caves.

The more enterprising of the residents have paid for improvements to this shabby exterior – hands have scrubbed around some of the windows, creating aureoles on the façade, further complicating the patchwork of pink, mildew-grey, black, cement-grey, rust-brown, fern-green, and floral red, to which, by midday, are added the patterns of bedsheets and saris put out to dry on the grilles and balconies. An old-fashioned building, Vishram has no lobby; you walk into a dark square entranceway and turn to your left (if you are, or are visiting, Mrs Saldanha of 0C), or climb the dingy stairwell to the homes on the higher floors. (An Otis lift exists, but unreliably so.) Perforated with eight-pointed stars, the wall along the stairwell resembles the screen of the women's zenana in an old haveli, and hints at secretive, even sinister, goings-on inside.

Outside, parked along the compound wall are a dozen scooters and motorbikes, three Maruti-Suzukis, two Tata Indicas, a battered Toyota Qualis, and a few children's bicycles. The main feature of this compound is a three-foot-tall polished black-stone cross, set inside a shrine of glazed blue-and-white tiles and covered in fading flowers and wreaths – a reminder that the building was originally meant for Roman Catholics. Hindus were admitted in the late 1960s, and in the 1980s the better kind of Muslim – Bohra, Ismaili, college-educated. Vishram is now entirely 'cosmopolitan' (i.e. ethnically and religiously mixed). Diagonally across from the black Cross stands the guard's booth, on whose wall Ram Khare, the Hindu watchman, has stencilled in red a slogan adapted from the Bhagavad Gita:

I was never born and I will never die; I do not hurt and cannot be hurt; I am invincible, immortal, indestructible.

5

A blue register juts out of the open window of the guard's booth. A sign hangs from the roof:

ALL VISITORS MUST SIGN THE LOG BOOK
AND PROVIDE CORRECT ADDRESS AND MOBILE
PHONE NUMBER BEFORE ENTRY

BY ORDER –
THE SECRETARY
VISHRAM CO-OPERATIVE HOUSING SOCIETY

A banyan tree has grown through the compound wall next to the booth. Painted umber like the wall, and speckled with dirt, the stem of the tree bulges from the masonry like a camouflaged leopard; it lends an air of solidity and reliability to Ram Khare's booth that it perhaps does not deserve.

The compound wall, which is set behind a gutter, has two dusty signs hanging from it:

VISIT SPEED-TEK CYBER-CAFÉ.
PROPRIETOR IBRAHIM KUDWA

RENAISSANCE REAL ESTATE. HONEST AND RELIABLE.
NEAR VAKOLA MARKET

The evening cricket games of the children of Vishram have left most of the compound bare of any flowering plants, although a clump of hibiscus plants flourishes near the back wall to ward off the stench of raw meat from a beef shop somewhere behind the Society. At night, dark shapes shoot up and down the dim Vishram Society Lane; rats and bandicoots dart like billiard balls struck around the narrow alley, crazed by the mysterious smell of fresh blood.

On Sunday morning, the aroma is of fresh baking. There are Mangalorean stores here that cater to the Christian members of Vishram and other good Societies; on the morning of the Sabbath, ladies in long patterned dresses and girls with powdered faces and silk skirts returning from St Antony's church will crowd these stores for bread and sunnas. In a little while, the smell of boiling broth and spicy chicken wafts out from the opened windows of Vishram Society into the neighbourhood. At such an hour of contentment, the spirit of Prime Minister Nehru, if it were to hover over the building, might well declare itself satisfied.

Yet Vishram's residents are the first to point out that this Society is nothing like paradise. You know a community by the luxuries it can live without. Those in Vishram dispense with the most basic: self-deception. To any inquiring outsider they will freely admit the humiliations of life in their Society – in their honest frustration, indeed, they may exaggerate these problems.

Number one. The Society, like most buildings in Vakola, does not receive a 24-hour supply of running water. Since it is on the poorer, eastern side of the train tracks, Vakola is blessed only twice a day by the Municipality: water flows in the taps four to six in the morning, and 7.30 p.m. to 9 p.m. The residents have fitted storage tanks above their bathrooms, but these can only hold so much (larger tanks threaten the stability of a building this ancient). By five in the evening the taps have usually run dry; the residents come out to talk. A few minutes after seven thirty, the reviving vascular system of Vishram Society ends all talk; water is coursing at high pressure up the pipes, and kitchens and bathrooms are busy places. The residents know that their evening washing, bathing, and cooking all have to be timed to this hour and a half when the pressure in the taps is the greatest; as do ancillary activities that rely on the easy availability of running water. If the children of Vishram Society could trace a path back to their conceptions, they would generally find that they occurred between half past six and a quarter to eight.

The second problem is the one that all of Santa Cruz, even the good part west of the railway line, is notorious for. Acute at night, it also becomes an issue on Sundays between 7 and 8 a.m. You open your window and there it is: a Boeing 747, flying right over your building. The residents insist that after the first month, the phrase 'noise pollution' means nothing to you – and this is probably true – yet rental prices for Vishram Society and its neighbours are at least a fourth lower because of the domestic airport's proximity.

The final problem, existential in nature, is spelled out by the glass-faced noticeboard:

NOTICE

Vishram Co-operative Hsg Society Ltd, Tower A
Minutes of the special meeting
held on Saturday, 28 April

Theme: Emergency nature of repairs is recognized

As the quorum was insufficient, even on such an urgent issue, the meeting had to be adjourned for half an hour; the adjourned meeting commenced at about 7.30 p.m.

ITEM NO. 1 OF THE AGENDA:

Mr Yogesh Murthy, 'Masterji', (3A) suggested that the minutes of the last meeting of 'A' Building be taken as read as the copy of the minutes had already been circulated to all members. It was unanimously agreed that the said minutes be taken as read.

ITEM NO. 2 OF THE AGENDA:

At the outset, Masterji (3A as above) expressed serious concern about the condition of the Society Building and emphasized the need to start repair work <u>immediately</u> in the interest of the members' safety and the safety of their children; most of the members gathered expressed similar...

... meeting was finally concluded about 8.30 p.m. with a vote of thanks to the chair.

Copy (1) To Members of Vishram Co-op Hsg Society Ltd, Tower A

Pinned behind this notice are older notices of a similar nature. After more than four decades of monsoons, erosion, wind-weathering, air pollution, and the gentle but continual vibrations caused by the low-flying planes, Tower A stands in reasonable chance of complete collapse in the next monsoon.

And yet no one, either in Vishram Society or in the neighbourhood at large, really believes that it will fall.

Vishram is a building like the people living in it, middle class to its core. Improvement or failure, it is incapable of either extremity. The men have modest paunches, wear checked polyester shirts over white *banians*, and keep their hair oiled and short. The older women wear saris, salwar kameez, or skirts, and the younger ones wear jeans. All of them pay taxes, support charities, and vote in local and general elections.

Just one glance at Vishram in the evening, as its residents sit in white plastic chairs in the compound, chit-chatting, fanning themselves with the *Times of India*, and you know that this Society is – what else? – *pucca*.

BOOK ONE

How the Offer was Made

Three o' clock: the heat at its annual worst.

Ram Khare, the guard, cooled himself with his checked handker-chief, while reading aloud from a digest of the Bhagavad Gita scarred in places by the long fingernails which he pressed down on it.

… never over a man's actions, said the Lord Krishna, but only over the fruit of a man's actions, is…

A fly rubbed its legs near the holy book; two sticks of jasmine incense burned under an image of Lord Shiva, only partly masking the odour of rum inside the guard's booth.

A tall man in a white shirt and black trousers – salesman, Ram Khare assumed – stood in front of the booth and entered his details into the ledger. The visitor put his pen back in his pocket. 'Can I go in now?'

Ram Khare moved a thumb from his holy digest to the visitors' register.

'You haven't filled in this last column.'

The visitor smiled; an upper tooth was chipped. Clicking the ball-point pen back to life he wrote in the column headed *Person(s) to see*:

Hon'ble Sec

Turning to his right upon entering the building, as directed by Ram Khare, the visitor walked into a small room with an open door, where a bald man sat at a desk, one finger of his left hand poised over a type-writer.

'… no-tice… to… the… res-ee-den-ts… of Vi-shraaam…'

His other hand held a sandwich over a scalloped paper plate brightened by comets of mint chutney. He bit into the sandwich, then typed with one finger as he ate, breathing laboriously, and murmuring between breaths: '... sub-ject... Gen-ral... Wa-ter... May-n-ten-anse...'

The visitor knocked on the door with the back of his hand.

'Is there a place to rent here?'

The man with the sandwich, Mr Kothari, Secretary of Vishram Tower A, paused with a finger over the old Remington.

'There is,' he said. 'Sit down.'

Ignoring the visitor, he continued typing, eating, and mumbling. There were three printed sheets on his desk, and he picked one up and read aloud: '... questionnaire from the Municipality. Have all the children in the Society received anti-polio drops? If so, kindly provide... if not, kindly...'

A small hammer sat near the typewriter. With the polio notice in one hand, the Secretary stood up with the hammer in the other hand and went to the noticeboard, whose glass face he opened. The visitor saw him pinning the notice into place with a nail, then driving the nail into the wooden board with three quick blows – tuck, tuck, tuck – before closing the glass. The hammer returned to its spot near the typewriter.

Back in his chair, the Secretary picked up the next piece of paper. '... complaint from Mrs Rego. Giant wasps are attacking... why am I paying monthly maintenance fees if the Society cannot hire the...' He crushed it.

And then the final sheet. '... complaint from Mrs Rego. Ram Khare has been drinking again. He should be replaced with a sober, professional... Why am I paying monthly maintenance...' He crushed it.

About to return to his typing, he remembered the visitor.

'A place to buy, you said?' he asked hopefully.

'Rent.'

'Good. What is your line of work?'

'Chemicals.'

'Good. Very good.'

14

Dark-skinned, tall, upright, in well-ironed Oxford-style shirt and pleated cotton trousers, the visitor gave the Secretary no reason to doubt that he was in a solid field like Drug & Chem.

'Nothing is strictly speaking available now,' the Secretary confessed, as the two men climbed the stairs. ('Ninety-nine per cent of the time the lift works.') 'But, I can tell you, confidentially, that the owner of 3B is not fully happy with the *present situation*.'

An eczema of blue-skinned gods, bearded godmen, and haloed Christs covered the metal door of 3B – a testament to generations of ecumenical tenants who had each added a few icons of their own faith without removing those of any other – so that it was impossible to know if the present tenant was Hindu, Christian, or a member of a hybrid cult practised only in this building.

About to knock on the door, the Secretary checked himself – his fist was going to hit a sticker with the face of Jesus on it. Shifting his hand to find one of the few blank spots on the door, he knocked with care; after knocking again, he used his master key.

The cupboard doors had been left wide open; the floor an archipelago of newspapers and undergarments – the Secretary had to explain that 3B was currently rented to a most unsatisfactory single woman, a working journalist. The stranger looked at the peeling grey paint and the water-damage blotches on the wall; the Secretary got ready with the official line given to potential tenants – 'in the monsoons the rainwater stains the walls, but does not reach the floor'. He got ready with official answers to all the usual tough questions – how many hours of water supply, how much noise from the planes at night, whether the electricity 'tripped'.

Stepping over a variety of underwear, the stranger touched the wall, scratched on the flaking paint and sniffed. Turning to the Secretary, he took out a striped red notebook and wet a finger on his tongue.

'I want a legal history of Towers A and B.'

'A what?'

'A summary of lawsuits filed, pending, or likely to arise in the future?'

'There was a disagreement between the Abichandani brothers, true,

15

over 1C. Solved out of court. We are not court-loving people here.'

'*Very* good. Are there any "peculiar situations"?'

'Peculiar...?'

'I mean: family disputes ongoing or pending, *pagdi* system dealings, illegal sub-rentings, transfers of property under the informal method?'

'None of that happens here.'

'Murders and suicides? Assaults? Any and all other things that may make for bad luck, karma, or negative energy in the *Vastu* sense?'

'Look here.' Secretary Kothari folded his arms on his chest. The stranger seemed to want to know the moral history of every doorknob, rivet and nail in the Society. 'Are you from the police?'

The visitor looked up from his notepad, as if he were surprised.

'We live in a dangerous time, do we not?'

'Dangerous,' the Secretary conceded. 'Very.'

'Terrorists. Bombs in trains. Explosions.'

The Secretary couldn't argue.

'Families are coming apart. Criminals taking over politics.'

'I understand now. Can you repeat your questions?'

When he was gone, the Secretary, though eager to resume his typing, found himself too nervous. He refreshed each day's labours with two ready-made sandwiches, purchased in the morning and stored in the drawers of his desk. Unwrapping the second sandwich, he nibbled on it ahead of schedule.

He thought of the visitor's jagged upper tooth.

'Fellow might not even be in chemicals. Might not even have a job.'

But the anxiety must have been merely digestive in nature, for he felt better with each bite he took.

The residents of Vishram Tower A, thanks to the ledger in the guard's booth, knew the basic facts about the strangers who visited them, something that could not necessarily be said about the people they had lived with for twenty or thirty years.

Late in the morning Mr Kothari (4A), their Secretary, got on his Bajaj scooter and left on 'business'. Early in the afternoon, while all the others were still working, he drove back, the rear-view mirror of his scooter reflecting a quadrilateral of sunlight on to his breast like a certificate of clear conscience. From his movements his neighbours had deduced the existence of a 'business' that did not require a man's presence for more than two or three hours a day and yet somehow funded a respectable existence. That was all they knew about Mr Kothari's life outside their gates. If they asked, even in a round-about way, how he had saved up enough to buy the Bajaj, he would reply, as if it were explanation: 'Not a Mercedes-Benz, is it? Just a scooter.'

He was the laziest Secretary they had ever had, which made him the best Secretary they had ever had. Asked to resolve disputes, Kothari listened to both parties, nodding his head and scratching sympathetic notes on scrap paper. *Your son plays music late at night disturbing the entire floor, true. Yet he's a musician, true.* When the disputants left his office, he threw the paper into the waste bin. Jesus be praised! Allah be praised! SiddhiVinayak be –! Etc. People were forced to adjust; temporary compromises congealed. And life went on.

Kothari brushed his hair from ear to ear to hide his baldness, an act that hinted at vanity or stupidity; yet his eyes were slit-like beneath snowy eyebrows, and each time he grinned, whiskery laugh-lines gave him the look of a predatory lynx. His position carried no salary, yet he was ingratiating at each annual general meeting, virtually pleading for re-election with his palms folded in a namaste; no one could tell why this bland bald businessman wanted to sit in a dingy Secretary's office and sink his face into files and folders for hours. He was so secretive, indeed, that you feared one day he would dissolve among his papers like a bar of Pears' Soap. He had no known 'nature'.

Mrs Puri (3C), who was the closest thing to a friend the Secretary had, insisted there was a 'nature'. If you talked to him long enough, you would discover he feared China, worried about Jihadis on the sub-urban trains, and favoured a national identification card to flush out illegal Bangladeshi immigrants; but most had never known him to express any opinion, unless it was related to the game of cricket. Some believed that he was always on his guard because as a young man he

17

had committed an indiscretion; his wife was rumoured to be his cousin, or from another community, or older than him by two years; or even, by the malicious, his 'sister'. They had one son, Tinku, a noted player of carom and other indoor sports, fat and white-skinned, with an imbecilic smile pasted on his face at all times – although whether he was truly stupid, or whether, like his father, merely hiding his 'nature', was unclear.

The Secretary threw his sandwich wrapper into the waste bin. His breath was now a passion of raw onion and curried potato; he returned to work.

He was calculating the annual maintenance fees, which paid for the guard, Mary the cleaning lady, the seven-kinds-of-vermin man who came to fight invasions of wasps and honeybees, and the annual heavy repairs to the building's roofing and general structure. For two years now Kothari had kept the maintenance bill constant at 1.55 rupees a square foot per tenant per month, which translated into an annual bill of (on average) 14,694 rupees per year per tenant, payable to the Society in one sum or two (in which case the second instalment was recalculated at 1.65 rupees a square foot). His ability to keep the maintenance bill steady, despite the pressure of inflation in a city like Mumbai, was considered his principal achievement as Secretary, even if some whispered that he pulled this off only by doing nothing at all to maintain the Society.

He burped, and looked up to see Mary, the *khachada-wali*, who had been sweeping the corridor with her broom, standing outside his office.

A lean silent woman, barely five feet tall, Mary had big front teeth erupting out of her concave cheeks. Residents kept conversation with her to a minimum.

'That man who asked all the questions is taking a long time to make up his mind,' she said.

The Secretary went back to his figures. But Mary still stood at the doorway.

'I mean, to ask the same set of questions for two days in a row. That's curiosity.'

18

Now the Secretary looked up.

'Two days? He wasn't here yesterday.'

'You weren't here yesterday morning,' the servant said. 'He was here.' She went back to her sweeping.

'What did he want yesterday?'

'The same thing he wanted today. Answers to lots and lots of questions.'

Mr Kothari's bulbous nose contracted into a dark berry: he was frowning. He got up from his desk and came to the threshold of the office.

'Who saw him here yesterday other than you?'

With a handkerchief over his nose he waited for Mary to stop sweeping, so he could repeat the question.

Mrs Puri was walking back to Vishram Society with her eighteen-year-old son Ramu, who kept turning to a stray dog that had followed them from the fruit and vegetable market.

Mrs Puri, who moved with a slight limp due to her weight, stopped, and took her son by the hand.

'Oy, oy, oy, my Ramu. Slowly, slowly. We don't want you falling into *that*.'

A pit had materialized in front of Vishram Society. It swallowed everything but the heads and necks of the men digging inside it, and an occasional raised muddy arm. Pushing her son back, Mrs Puri looked in. The soil changed colour every two feet as it went down, from black to dark red to bone-grey at the very bottom, where she saw ancient cement piping, mottled and barnacled. Wormy red-and-yellow snippets of wire showed through the strata of mud. There was a sign sticking out of the pit, but it faced the wrong direction, and only when Mrs Puri went all the way around the hole did she see that it said:

Work in Progress
Inconvenience is Regretted
BMC

Ramu followed her; the dog followed Ramu.

Mrs Puri saw the Secretary was at the guard's booth, reading the register and holding a hand up against the early-evening sun.

'Ram Khare, Ram Khare,' he said, and turned the register around so it confronted the guard. 'There is a record of the man today, Ram Khare. Here.' He tapped the entry the inquisitive visitor had made. 'But...' He flipped the page. '... there is no record of him in here yesterday.'

'What are we talking about?' she asked.

Ramu took the stray dog with him to the black Cross, where he would play until his mother called him in.

When the Secretary described the man, she said: 'Oh, yes. He came yesterday. In the morning. There was another one with him, too. A fat one. They asked all these questions. I answered some, and I told them to speak to Mr Pinto.'

The Secretary stared at the guard. Ram Khare scraped the ledger with his long fingernails.

'If there is no record in here,' he said, 'then no such men came.'

'What did they want to know?' the Secretary asked Mrs Puri.

'Whether it is a good place or a bad place. Whether the people are good. They wanted to rent a flat, I think.'

The fat man with the gold rings had impressed Mrs Puri. He had red lips and teeth blackened by *gutka*, which made you think he was lower class, yet his manners were polished, as if he were of breeding, or had acquired some in the course of life. The other man, the tall dark one, wore a nice white shirt and black trousers, exactly as the Secretary had described him. No, he said nothing about being in chemicals.

'Maybe we should tell the police about this,' the Secretary said. 'I don't understand why he came again today. There have been burglaries near the train station.'

Mrs Puri dismissed the possibility of danger.

'Both of them were good men, polite, well dressed. The fat one had so many gold rings on his fingers.'

The Secretary turned, fired – 'Men with gold rings are the biggest thieves in the world. Where have you been living all these years?' – and walked away.

She folded her fat forearms over her chest.

'Mrs Pinto,' she shouted. 'Please don't let the Secretary escape.'

What the residents called their *sansad* – parliament – was now in session. White plastic chairs had been arranged around the entrance of Tower A, right in front of Mrs Saldanha's kitchen, an arrangement that allowed those seated a glimpse, through an almond-shaped tear in the green kitchen curtain, of a small TV. The first 'parliamentarians' were about to sit on the plastic chairs, which would remain occupied until water returned to the building.

A small, slow, white-haired man, refined by age into a humanoid sparrow, lowered himself into a chair with a direct view of the TV through Mrs Saldanha's torn curtain (the 'prime' chair). A retired accountant for the Britannia Biscuit Company, Mr Pinto (2A) had a weak vascular system and kept his mouth open when walking. His wife, almost blind in her old age, walked with her hand on his shoulder, although she knew the compound well enough to navigate it without her husband's help; most evenings they walked as a pair, she with her blind eyes, and he with his open mouth, as if sucking sight and breath from the other. She sat next to her husband, with his help.

'You have been asked to wait,' said Mrs Pinto, as the Secretary tried to make his way around the plastic chairs into his office. She was the oldest woman in the Society; Mr Kothari had no choice but to stop.

Mrs Puri caught up with him.

'Is it true, Kothari, what they say the early-morning cat found in 3B's rubbish?'

The Secretary, not for the first time during his tenure, cursed the early-morning cat. This cat prowled the waste bins that the residents left out in the morning for Mary to collect, in the process spilling beans, bones, and whisky bottles alike. So the residents of the building knew from the rubbish who was a vegetarian and who merely claimed to be one; who was a rum-man and who a gin-man; and who had bought a pornographic magazine when on holiday in Singapore. The main aim of this cat – ginger and scrawny, according to some, black and glossy according to others – indeed, was to make sure there was no privacy in the building. Of late the ginger (or black) fellow had led

Mrs Puri to a vile discovery when it knocked over the waste bin of 3B (the flat Kothari had shown to the inquisitive stranger).

'Among young people today, it is a common thing for boy and girl to live without marriage,' he said. 'At the end, one says to the other, you go your way, I go my way. There is no sense of shame in the modern way of life, what do you expect me to do about it?'

(Mr Pinto, distracted by a stock market report on the TV, had to be filled in on the topic of discussion by his wife. '... the modern girl on our floor.')

Turning to her left, Mrs Puri called: 'Ramu, have you fed the dog?'

Ramu – his soft, pale face hinted at the presence of Down's syndrome – looked perplexed. His mother and he left a bowl full of channa near the black Cross to feed stray animals that wandered into the Society; he looked about for the bowl. The dog had found it.

Now Mrs Puri turned back to the Secretary to make one thing clear: the modern, shame-free way of living counted for nothing with her.

'I have a growing son—' She dropped her voice. 'I don't want him living with the wrong kind of people. You should call Import-Export Hiranandani *now*.'

That Mr Hiranandani, the owner and original resident of 3B, a shrewd importer-exporter of obscure goods, known for his guile in slipping phosphates and peroxides through customs, had moved to a better neighbourhood (Khar West) was understandable; all of them dreamed of doing the same thing. Differences of wealth among the members did not go unnoticed – Mr Kudwa (4C) had taken his family last summer to Ladakh, rather than nearby Mahabaleshwar, as everyone else did, and Mr Ajwani the broker owned a Toyota Qualis – yet these were spikes and dips within the equalizing dinginess of Vishram. The real distinction was leaving the Society. They had come to their windows and cheered Mr Hiranandani when he departed with his family for Khar West; yet his behaviour since had been scandalous. Not checking the identity of this girl tenant, he had taken her deposit and handed her the keys to 3B, without asking the Secretary or his neighbours if they wanted an unmarried woman – a journalist, at that – on their floor. Mrs Puri was not one to pry – not one to ask what was happening within the privacy of a neighbour's four walls – but when the condoms come *tumbling* on to your doorstep, well, then!

As they were talking, a trickle of waste water moved towards them.

A pipe from Mrs Saldanha's ground-floor kitchen discharged into the open compound; although she had been chided often, she had never connected her kitchen sink into the main sewage – so the moment she began her cooking, it burped right at their feet. In every other way, Mrs Saldanha was a quiet, retreating woman – her husband, who was 'working in Vizag', had not been seen in Vishram for years – but in matters of water, brazen. Because she lived on the ground floor, she seemed to have it longer than anyone else did, and used it shamelessly when they could not. The emission of waste water into the compound only underlined her water-arrogance.

A glistening eel of water, its dark body now tinted with reddish earth, nosed its way towards the parliament. Mr Pinto lifted the front feet of the 'prime' chair and moved out of the sewage-eel's path; and it was forgotten.

'Have you seen anyone going into her room?' the Secretary asked.

'Of course not,' Mrs Puri said. 'I am not one to pry into my neighbours' lives, am I?'

'Ram Khare hasn't told me he has seen any boy come into the building at night.'

'What does that mean, Ram Khare has seen nothing?' Mrs Puri protested. 'A whole army could come in, and he would see nothing.'

The stray dog, having done crunching its channa, ran towards the parliament, trotted throught the water, slid under the chairs, and headed up the stairwell, as if pointing out to them the solution to their crisis.

The Secretary followed the dog.

Breathing heavily, one hand on the banister and one hand on her hip, Mrs Puri went up the stairs. Through the star-shaped holes in the wall she could see Mr Pinto standing by the black Cross to keep watch on Ramu until she returned.

She smelled the dog on the second landing of the stairs. Amber

23

eyes shone in the dim stairwell; pale legs, impastoed with dry dung, shivered. Mrs Puri stepped over the sickly legs and walked to the third floor.

The Secretary was standing by Masterji's door, with a finger on his lips. From inside the open door, they could hear voices.

'... and my hand represents...?'

'Yes, Masterji.'

'Answer the question, boys: my hand represents...?'

'The earth.'

'Correct. For once.'

The bi-weekly science 'top-up' was in session. Mrs Puri joined the Secretary by the door, the only one in Vishram Society unmarked by religious icons.

'This is the earth in infinite space. Home of Man. Follow me?'

Reverence for science and learning made the Secretary stand with folded hands. Mrs Puri pushed past him to the door. She closed an eye and spied in.

The living room was dark, the curtains were drawn; a table lamp was the only source of light.

A silhouette of a huge fist, looking like a dictator's gesture, appeared on the wall.

A man stood next to the table lamp, making shadows on the wall. Four children sitting on a sofa watched the shadows he conjured; another sat on the floor.

'And my second fist, which is going around the earth, is what?'

'The sun, Masterji' – one of the boys.

'No.'

'No?'

'No, no, no. The sun is this. See—' A click, and the room went black. 'Earth without sun.' Click. 'Earth with sun. Understand? Lamp: sun.'

'Yes, Masterji.'

'All of you say it together.'

'Yes, Masterji' – three voices.

'All of you.'

'Yes, Masterji' – four.

24

'So my second, that is to say, my moving fist is –? Big white object seen at night if you look up.'

'Moon.'

'Correct. MOON. Earth's satellite. How many satellites does the Earth have?'

'Can we go now, Masterji?'

'Only after we get to the eclipse. And what are you wriggling about for, Mohammad?'

'Anand is pinching me, Masterji.'

'Stop pinching him, Anand. This is physics, not fun. Now: how many satellites does…'

The boy on the floor said: 'Question, Masterji.'

'Yes?'

'Masterji, what happened when the dinosaurs died out? Show us again how the meteor hit the earth.'

'And tell us about global warming again, Masterji.'

'You're trying to avoid my question by asking your own. Do you think I taught in school for thirty-four years not to see through tricks like this?'

'It's not a trick, Masterji, it's a—'

'Enough for today. Class is over,' Masterji said and clapped his hands.

'We can go in now,' the Secretary whispered. Mrs Puri pushed open the door and turned the lights on in the room.

The four boys who had been sitting on the sofa – Sunil Rego (1B), Anand Ganguly (5B), Raghav Ajwani (2C) and Mohammad Kudwa (4C) – got up. Tinku Kothari (4A), the fat son of the Secretary, struggled to his feet from the floor.

'Enough, boys, go home!' Mrs Puri clapped. 'Masterji has to have dinner soon. Class is over. Go, go, go.'

It was not a 'class', though conducted with such dignity, but an after-class science 'top-up' – meant to do to a normal schoolchild what a steroidal injection does to a merely healthy athlete.

Anand Ganguly picked up his cricket bat, which was propped up against the old fridge; Mohammad Kudwa took his blue cricket cap, emblazoned with the star of India, from above the glass cabinet full of silver trophies, medals, and certificates attesting to Masterji's excellence as a teacher.

'What a surprise to see you here,' Masterji said. 'I hardly have visitors these days. Adult visitors, that is.'

Mrs Puri checked to see if the lights were off in 3B – of course they were, young people of that lifestyle are never home before ten – and closed the door. She explained, in low tones, the problem caused by Masterji's neighbour and what had been found in her rubbish by the early-morning cat.

'There is a boy who goes into and comes out of that room with her,' Masterji conceded. He turned to the Secretary. 'But she works, doesn't she?'

'Journalist.'

'Those people are known for their *number two* activities,' Mrs Puri said.

'She seems to me, though I have only seen her from a distance, a decent girl.'

Masterji continued, his voice gaining authority from the echoes of 'sun, moon, eclipse, physics' that still seemed to ring through it: 'When this building first came up, there were no Hindus allowed here, it is a fact. Then there were meant to be no Muslims, it is a fact. All proved to be good people when given a chance. Now, young people, unmarried girls, they should also be given a chance. We don't want to become a building full of retirees and blind people. If this girl and her boyfriend have done something inappropriate, we should speak to them. However...' He looked at Mrs Puri. '... we have no business with her rubbish.'

Mrs Puri winced. She wouldn't tolerate this kind of talk from anyone else.

She looked around the flat, which she had not visited in a while, still expecting to see Purnima, Masterji's quiet, efficient wife, and one of her best friends in Vishram. Now that Purnima was gone – dead for more than six months – Mrs Puri observed signs of austerity, even disrepair. One of the two wall-clocks was broken. A pale rectangle on the wall above the empty TV stand commemorated the ancient Sanyo that Masterji had sold after her death, rejecting it as an indulgence. (*What an error*, Mrs Puri thought. *A widower without a TV will go mad.*) Water stains blossomed on the ceiling; the pipes on the fourth floor leaked. Each year in September Purnima had paid for a man from the slums to scrub and whitewash them. This year, unscrubbed, the stains were spreading like ghostly evidence of her absence.

Now that Mrs Puri's issue was dismissed, the Secretary raised his own, more valid, concern. He told Masterji about the inquisitive stranger who had come twice to the Society. Should they make a report to the police?

Masterji stared at the Secretary. 'What can this man steal from us, Kothari?'

He went to the sink that stood in a corner of the room – a mirror above it, a framed picture of Galileo ('Founder of Modern Physics') above the mirror – and turned the tap; there was a thin flow of water.

'Is *this* what he is going to steal from us? Our plumbing?'

Each year, the contractor who cleaned the overhead tank did his work sloppily – and the silt from the tank blocked the pipes in all the rooms directly below it.

The Secretary responded with one of his pacifying smiles. 'I'll have the plumber sent over next time I see him, Masterji.'

The door creaked open: Sunil Rego had returned.

The boy left his slippers at the threshold and entered holding a long rectangular scroll. Masterji saw the words 'TUBERCULOSIS AWARE-NESS WEEK FUND-RAISING DRIVE' written on the top.

Fourteen-year-old Sunil Rego's mother was a social worker, a for-midable woman of left-wing inclinations nicknamed 'The Battleship' within the Society. The son was already proving to be a little gunboat.

'Masterji, TB is an illness that we can overcome together if we all—'

The old teacher shook his head. 'I live on a pension, Sunil: ask someone else for a donation.'

Embarrassed that he had to say this in front of the others, Masterji pushed the boy, perhaps too hard, out of the room.

*

After dinner, Mrs Puri, folding Ramu's laundry on the dining table, looked at a dozen ripe mangoes. Her husband was watching a replay of a classic India versus Australia cricket match on TV. He had bought the mangoes as a treat for Ramu, who was asleep under his aeroplane quilt.

Closing the door behind her, she walked up the stairs, and pushed at the door to Masterji's flat with her left hand. Her right hand pressed three mangoes against her chest.

The door was open, as she expected. Masterji had his feet on the small teakwood table in the living room, and was playing with a multi-coloured toy that she took a whole second to identify.

'A Rubik's Cube,' she marvelled. 'I haven't seen one in years and years.'

He held it up for her to see better.

'I found it in one of the old cupboards. I think it was Gaurav's. Works.'

'Surprise, Masterji.' She turned the mangoes in her right arm towards his gaze.

He put the Rubik's Cube down on the teakwood table.

'You shouldn't have, Sangeeta.'

'Take them. You have taught our children for thirty years. Shall I cut them for you?'

He shook his head.

'I don't have sweets every day – once a week: and today is not that day.'

He would not bend on this, she knew.

'When are you going to see Ronak?' she asked.

'Tomorrow.' He smiled. 'In the afternoon. We're going to Byculla Zoo.'

'Well, take them for him then. A gift from his grandfather.'

'No,' he said. 'The boy shouldn't be spoiled with mangoes. You are too generous in every way, Sangeeta. I see that there is a stray dog lying on the stairs now. It seems to be ill – there is a smell from it. I hope you didn't bring it into the Society, as you have done before.'

'Oh, no, Masterji,' she said, tapping on the mangoes. 'Not me. It was probably Mrs Rego again.'

Though she had not actually given Masterji the mangoes, Mrs Puri felt the same sense of neighbourly entitlement that would have resulted from the act, and moved to his bookshelf.

'Are you becoming religious, Masterji?'

'Certainly not,' he said.

Sliding out a thin paperback from the shelf, she showed it to him as evidence; on the cover was an image of the divine eagle Garuda flying over the seven oceans.

The Soul's Passageway after Death.

She read aloud from it: 'In its first year out of the body, the soul travels slowly and at a low altitude, burdened by the sins of its…'

'Purnima's first anniversary is not so far away. She wanted me to read about God when she was gone…'

'Do you think about her often, Masterji?'

He shrugged.

For his retirement, Masterji had hoped to re-read his collection of murder mysteries, and history books of old Rome (Suetonius, *The Twelve Caesars*; Tacitus, *The Annals*; Plutarch, *Illustrious Figures of the Roman Republic*) and old Bombay (*A Brief Life of Mountstuart Elphinstone*; *The Stages of the Creation of the City of Bombay, fully illustrated*). An *Advanced French Grammar (with Questions and Answers Provided)*, bought so he could teach his children at home, also stood on the shelf. But since the murder novels were in demand throughout the Society, and neighbours borrowed them frequently (and returned them infrequently), he would soon be left only with history and foreign grammar.

Mrs Puri claimed one of the last Agatha Christies from the bookshelf and smiled – there were a few Erle Stanley Gardners too, but she was not *that* bored.

'Does it say on my door, Agatha Christie lending library?' Masterji asked. 'I won't have any books to read if people keep borrowing them.'

'I'm taking this for my husband. Not that I don't read, Masterji. I was such a reader in my college days.' She raised her hand over her head, to indicate its extent. 'Where is the time now, with the boy to look after? I'll bring it back next week, I promise you.'

'Fine.' He had begun playing with the Cube again. 'Just bring the book back. Which one is it?'

Mrs Puri turned the cover around so he could read the title: *Murder on the Orient Express*.

Yogesh Murthy, known as Masterji, was one of the first Hindus allowed into Vishram on account of his noble profession and digni- fied bearing. He was lean, moustached, and of medium height: in physical terms, a typical representative of the earlier generation. Good with languages (he spoke six), generous with books, passion- ate about education. An adornment to his Society.

Barely had the buntings of his retirement party (catered with samosa and masala chai, and attended by three generations of students) been cut from the auditorium of St Catherine's the previous May than his wife was diagnosed with pancreatic cancer – a side-effect, it was speculated, of years of medication for her rheumatoid arthritis. She died in October. She was his second death; a daughter, Sandhya, had fallen from a train over a decade ago. On the positive side of the ledger, Gaurav, his only surviving child, a banker, was now 'put up' in a good flat in South Mumbai – Marine Lines – by his employer (who had paid the six-month down-deposit for his flat and even took care, it was said, of half of each month's rent); so Masterji's story was, in a sense, over – career ended with retirement party (catered), wife passed away with- out unreasonable suffering, and child having migrated to the golden citadel of inner-city Bombay. What would he do with his remaining time – the cigarette stub of years left to a man already in his sixties? After the loss of his wife, he had continued to keep himself clean and his home tidy; had continued to teach children, to lend murder mys- teries, to take his evening walks around the compound at the right pace and to buy his vegetables in appropriate quantities from the market. Controlling appetites and sorrows, he had accepted his lot with dignity, and this elevated his standing among his neighbours, who had all, in one way or the other, and usually in the matter of children or spouses, been blighted by fate. They knew they were complainers, and that he, though he had suffered more than his fair share, bore it.

'Oy, oy, oy, my Ramu. Out of bed now. Or Mummy will whack your bottom harder. Up, or the Friendly Duck will say, Ramu is a lazy lazy fellow.'

Mrs Puri coaxed Ramu into a bath half filled with warm (*never* hot) water, and let him play with his Friendly Duck and Spiderman for a few minutes. Mr Puri, an accountant, left for work an hour before Ramu woke up, with a metal lunch box that his wife had packed. It was a long trip for him – auto, train, change of train at Dadar, and then a shared taxi from Victoria Terminus to Nariman Point, from where he would call Ramu punctually at noon to inquire about the state of the Friendly Duck's health that day.

'Rum-pum-pum,' the naked, dripping boy said, while she scrubbed his pale, downy legs. (Good for the circulation, according to *Reader's Digest*.) 'Rum-pum-pum.' There was a time, not so long ago, when he would bathe and dry himself off with a towel in minutes – and she had had dreams of his being able to dress himself one day.

'We should learn a new word today, Ramu. Here, what's this word in Masterji's novel? Ex-press. Say it.'

'Rum-pum-pum.'

Treading on the old newspapers lying on the floor, Ramu, now fully dressed, headed into the dining room. The Puris' 834 sq ft of living space was a maelstrom of newsprint. The sofas had been lost to *India Today* and *Femina* magazines, while the dining table was submerged under office papers, loan applications, electricity bills, savings bank statements, and Ramu's cartoon drawing books. The face of the fridge in the dining room was a collage of philantrophic stickers ('Fight Global Warming: Lights out for one hour this week') and crumpling notes with long-expired messages. There were cupboards in each room; their doors gave way suddenly to let books and newspapers gush out with traumatic force. Every few weeks, Mr Puri would scatter magazines while searching for a bank cheque or letter and shout: 'Why don't we clean this house up!' But the mess grew. The enveloping junk only enhanced the domestic glow from the neat beds and the well-stocked fridge, for (as outsiders instinctively understood) this dingy, dirty flat was an Aladdin's cave of private riches. The Puris owned no property and little gold. What they had to show for their life was in the form of paper, and how comforting that all of it was within arm's reach, even Mr Puri's old, old *Shankar's Weekly* magazines, full of cartoons mocking Prime Minister Nehru, borrowed from a friend when he dreamed of becoming a professional caricaturist.

As his mother put Ramu's shiny black shoes on her knees, one after the other, to tie his laces, he sneezed. Down below in 2C, Mrs Ajwani, the broker's wife, was spraying herself generously with synthetic deodorant. Done with the laces, Mrs Puri spat on the shoes and gave them a final polish with a thick index finger, before she took Ramu to the toilet, so he could admire his good looks. The moment the boy stood before the mirror, the toilet filled with gurgling noise, as if a jealous devil were cursing. Directly overhead in 4C, Ibrahim Kudwa was performing extraordinary exercises with salt water, designed to strengthen his weak stomach. Mrs Puri countered with some gargling of her own; Ramu pressed his head into her tummy and chuckled into his mother's fatty folds.

'Bye, watchman!' Mrs Puri shouted, on Ramu's behalf, as they left the Society. Ram Khare, reading his digest of the Bhagavad Gita, waved without looking up.

Ramu disliked heat, so Mrs Puri made him walk along the edge of the alley, where king coconut palms shaded them. The palms were an oddity, a botanical experiment conducted by the late Mr Alvares, whose mansion, full of unusual trees and plants, had been sold by his heirs to make room for the three florally named concrete blocks, 'Hibiscus', 'Marigold', and 'White Rose'.

Mrs Puri tickled her son's ear.

'Say "Mar-i-gold", Ramu. You could say lots of things in English, don't you remember? Mar-i...?'

'Rum-pum-pum.'

'Where did you learn this thing, Ramu, this "Rum-pum-pum"?'

She looked at her boy. Eighteen years old. Never growing, yet somehow picking up new things all the time – just like the city he lived in.

As they neared the church, Ramu began to play with the gold bangles on his mother's hand.

The school bus was waiting for them in front of the church. Before helping Ramu board its steps, Mrs Puri loaded him with a home-made sign: it showed a big green horn with a red diagonal going through it and the legend 'NO NOISE'. Once again, Mrs Puri made his classmates promise, as she did every morning, to be quiet; and then she waved, as the bus departed, at Ramu, who could not wave back (since he was pressing the NO NOISE sign to his chest), but said what he had to say to his mother with his eyes.

Mrs Puri hobbled back to Vishram. Walking around the big construction hole in front of the gate, which the workers were now filling up with shovels, she noticed that the sign:

WORK IN PROGRESS
INCONVENIENCE IS REGRETTED
BMC

had been crossed out and rewritten:

INCONVENIENCE IN PROGRESS
WORK IS REGRETTED
BMC

Age had accumulated in fatty rings around Mrs Puri, but her laughter came from a slim girl within. The shovels stopped moving; the men looked at her.

'Who wrote this joke on the sign?' she asked. They went back to filling the hole.

'Ram Khare! Look up from your book. Who did *that* to the municipal sign?'

'Mr Ibrahim Kudwa,' the guard said, without looking up. 'He asked me what I thought of the joke and I said, I can't read English, sir. Is it a good joke?'

'We are impotent people in an impotent city, Ram Khare, as Ibby often says. Jokes are the only weapon we have.'

'Truly, madam.' Khare turned the page of his book. 'There will be no water supply this evening, by the way. These men hit a water pipe when working and they have to shut down the supply for a few hours. The Secretary will put up a sign on the board after he gets back from his business.'

Mrs Puri wiped her face with a handkerchief. Breathe in. Breathe out. She turned around from the guard's booth and retraced her steps out of the gate.

The warning about the water cut had reminded her of Masterji's blocked taps.

Any good Society survives on a circulation of favours; it is like the children's game where each passes the 'touch' on to his neighbour. If Mrs Puri needed a man's helping hand when her husband was at work, the Secretary, who was good with a hammer and nail, helped out; just last week he had struck a nail into the wall for a new rope-line for her wet clothes. In return, she knew she had to take responsibility for Masterji's needs.

When her boy was diagnosed with Down's syndrome, Sangeeta Puri, before telling her mother or sister, had told her immediate neighbours. Masterji, listening to the news with a hand on his wife's shoulder, had begun to cry. She still remembered those tears falling down his cheeks: a man who had never wept on any other day, even when there was a death in his family. For years he had given her suggestions from medical journals and newspapers, to halt – or even reverse – Ramu's 'delay'. Everything she had done to stir Ramu's inert neurons into life, she had discussed first with Masterji: consultations with foreign-trained specialists, oil massages, innovative mental and physical exercises, shock doses of shark liver oil and cod liver oil; Masterji, despite his well-known atheism, had even approved of her trips to holy shrines to seek divine favour on Ramu's slow brain.

And there was another matter. Six months before her death, Purnima had lent Mrs Puri five hundred rupees, which she had in turn lent to a relative. Masterji had not been told about this by Purnima, who often shielded her financial indiscretions (as he would judge them) from his temper.

So, becoming Ms Responsibility once more, Mrs Puri headed for the slums.

There were two ways in which the residents of Vishram Society had, historically, dealt with the existence of slums in Vakola. One was to leave the gate of Vishram every morning, process to the main road, and pretend there was no other world near by. The other was the pragmatic approach – taken by Mr Ajwani, the broker, and also by Mrs Puri. Down in the slums, she had discovered many men of talent, experts at small household tasks. Had she not once seen a plumber there?

So now she walked down the mud road, past two other middle-class buildings – Silver Trophy and Gold Coin – and into the slums, which, branching out from here, encroached on to public land belonging to the Airport Authority of India, and expanded like pincers to the very edge of the runway, so that the first sight of a visitor arriving in Mumbai might well be of a boy from one of these shanties, flying a kite or hitting a cricket ball tossed by his friends.

Smelling woodsmoke and kerosene, Mrs Puri passed a row of single-room huts, each with its tin door open. Women sat outside, combing each other's hair, talking, watching over the pots of steaming rice; a rooster strutted across the roofs. Where had Mrs Puri seen that plumber? Further down the road, two giant half-built towers covered in scaffolding – she had not seen them before – only multiplied her confusion.

Suddenly, the roar of an engine: white and tubular and glistening, like a sea snake leaping up, a plane shot over a small Tamil temple. *This* was the landmark she had been trying to remember: this temple. Somewhere here she had seen that plumber.

A group of boys were playing cricket at the temple: a guardian demon's face painted on the outer wall (its black mouth opened wide enough to swallow all the world's malefactors) served as the wicket.

All this animal power, all this screaming from the cricketers: oh, how a mother's heart ached. These boys with their rippling limbs and sinewy elbows were growing into men. And not one of them *half* as good-looking as her Ramu.

'Mummy,' one of the cricketers shouted. 'Mummy, it's Mrs Puri Aunty.'

Mary, the cleaning lady of Vishram Society, stood up from the roots of a tree in the temple courtyard, wiping her hands on her skirt.

'This is my son,' she pointed to the cricketer. 'Timothy. Spends too much time here, playing.'

Inside the Society, relations between Mary and Mrs Puri were frosty ('yes, it *is* part of your job to catch that early-morning cat'), but the distance from Vishram and the presence of Mary's boy permitted a relaxation in mistress–servant tensions.

'Nice-looking boy. Growing tall and strong.' Mrs Puri smiled. 'Mary, that plumber who lives here, I need to find him for some work in Masterji's flat.'

'Madam—'

'There are problems with his pipe. Also his ceiling needs to be scrubbed. I'll go from flat to flat and make a collection for the plumber's fee.'

'Madam, you won't find anyone today. Because of the big news. They've all gone to see the Muslim man's hut.'

'What big news is this, Mary?'

'Haven't you heard, madam?' She smiled. 'God has visited the slums today.'

In the evening, the 'big news' was confirmed by Ritika, an old college mate of Mrs Puri and a resident of Tower B, who came over to parliament.

Their higher average income, lower average age, and a sense of being 'somehow more modern' meant that Tower B residents kept to themselves, used their own gate, and celebrated their religious festivals separately.

Only Ritika, a show-off even in college, ever came over to Tower A, usually to brag about something. Her husband, a doctor who had a clinic near the highway, had just spoken to the Muslim man in the slums, who was a patient of his.

Mrs Puri did not like Ritika getting such attention – who had beaten whom in the debating competition in college? – but she sat on a plastic chair in between Ajwani the broker and Kothari the Secretary and listened.

Mr J. J. Chacko, the boss of the Ultimex Group, had made an offer of 81 lakh rupees (81,00,000) to that Muslim man for his one-room hut. It was just down the road from Vishram. Had they seen where the two new buildings were coming up? That was the Confidence Group. J. J. Chacko was their big rival. So he was buying all the land right opposite the two new buildings. He already owned everything around the one-room hut; this one stubborn old Muslim kept saying *No, No, No*, so Mr Chacko bludgeoned him with this astronomical offer, calculated on God alone knows what basis.

'Everyone, please wait a minute. I'll find out if this is true.'

Amiable and dark, Ramesh Ajwani was known within Vishram to be a typical member of his tribe of real-estate brokers. Ethics not to be trusted, information not to be doubted. He was a small man in a blue safari suit. He punched at his mobile phone; they waited; after a minute, it beeped.

Ajwani looked at the text message and said: 'True.'

They sighed.

The residents of Vishram Society, even if they kept away from the slums, were aware of changes happening there ever since the Bandra-Kurla Complex (BKC), the new financial hub of the city, had opened right next to it. Bombay, like a practitioner of yoga, was folding in on itself, as its centre moved from the south, where there was no room to grow, to this swamp land near the airport. New financial buildings were opening every month in the BKC – American Express, ICICI Bank, HSBC, Citibank, you name it – and the lucre in their vaults, like butter on a hotplate, was melting and trickling into the slums, enriching some and scorching others among the slum-dwellers. A few lucky hut-owners were becoming millionaires, as a bank or a developer made an extraordinary offer for their little plot of land; others were being crushed – bulldozers were on the move, shanties were being levelled, slum clearance projects were going ahead. As wealth came to some, and misery to others, stories of gold and tears reached Vishram Society like echoes from a distant battlefield. Here, among the plastic chairs of their parliament, the lives of the residents were slow and regular. They had the security of titles and legal deeds that could not be revoked, and their aspirations were limited to a patient rise in life earned through universities and interviews in grey suit and tie. It was not in their karma to know either gold or tears; they were respectable.

'Wouldn't it be nice if someone gave *us* 81 lakh rupees?' Mrs Puri said, after Ritika was out of earshot.

Ajwani the broker, who was punching away at his mobile phone, looked up and smiled sardonically.

The value of their own homes was uncertain. The last attempted sale had been seven years ago, when Mr Costello (5C) put his fifth-floor place on sale after his son had jumped from the terrace; no one had purchased the flat, and it was still under lock and key while the owner had himself moved to the Gulf.

'The poor in this city were never poor, and now they…' Mrs Puri moved her head to the right – Mrs Saldanha's daughter, Radhika, had entered her mother's kitchen in a most thoughtless manner, obstructing the parliamentarians' view of the TV. '… are becoming rich. Free electricity in the slums and 24-hour cable. Only *we* are stuck.'

'Careful,' Mr Pinto whispered. 'Battleship is here. Careful.'

Mrs Rego – the 'Battleship' for her wide grey skirts, formidable girth, and stentorian voice – was returning home with her children.

With a 'Hello, Uncle, Hello, Aunty', Sunil and Sarah Rego went up the stairs. Their mother, without a word to the others, sat down and watched the TV.

'Have you heard, Mrs Rego, about the 81 lakh offer? For a one-room in the slums?'

The Battleship said nothing.

'Even a Communist like you must be interested in this,' Mrs Puri said with a smile.

The Battleship spoke without turning her face.

'What is the definition of a dying city, Mrs Puri? I will tell you, as you do not know: a city that ceases to surprise you. And that is what this Bombay has become. Show people a little cash, and they'll jump, dance, run naked in the streets. That Muslim man is never going to see his money. These developers and builders are mafia. The other day they shot a member of the city corporation dead. It was in the papers.'

Mr Pinto and his wife slipped away like doves before a thunderstorm.

But it did not start at once.

The TV presenter, as if to add to the atmosphere of gloom, mentioned that the water shortage was likely to get worse unless the monsoons arrived – for once – on time.

'Too many people come into the city, it's a fact,' Mrs Puri said. 'Everyone wants to suck on our...' She touched her breasts.

The Battleship turned to her.

'And did you drop to Bombay from heaven, Mrs Puri? Isn't your family from Delhi?'

'My parents were born in Delhi, Mrs Rego, but I was born right here. There was enough space in those days. Now it's full. The Shiv Sena is right, outsiders should stop coming here.'

'Without migrants, this city would be dust. We are ruled by fascists, Mrs Puri, but everything is second-rate here, even our fascists. They don't give us trains, don't give us roads. All they do is beat up hard-working migrants.'

'I don't know what a fascist does, but I know what a Communist does. You don't like developers who make people rich, but you like the beggars who get off at Victoria Terminus every day.'

'I am a Christian, Mrs Puri. We are meant to care for the poor.'

Mrs Puri – debating champion at KC College – was about to finish her opponent off with a riposte, but Ramu came to his mother's ear and whispered.

39

'There's no water coming up the pipes, Ramu,' she said. 'No water tonight, dear. I told you, didn't I?'

Ramu's lower lip covered his upper, and bulged up towards his nose: his mother knew this as a sign that he was thinking. He pointed to the pipes that went up the sides of Vishram Society's walls.

'Quiet, Ramu. Mummy is speaking to Communist aunty.'

'I am not a Communist, and I am not anyone's aunty, Mrs Puri.'

Mrs Kothari, the Secretary's wife, put her head out of the window and shouted: 'Water!'

It was an unscheduled blessing from the Municipality, a rare kindness. The fighting adjourned; both women had to obey a higher imperative – fresh water.

Where is Masterji? Mrs Puri wondered, as she went up the stairs. He should have returned from seeing his grandson by now. After giving Ramu his evening bath, she made sure to collect an extra bucket of water for the old man, in case the Municipality, for giving them water they were not meant to have, punished them by annulling their morning water supply. That was, after all, how the people who ran Mumbai thought.

Despite dismissing the idea that the inquisitive stranger might represent any danger, Masterji woke up realizing he had spent a part of the night dreaming of the man.

In this dream, which he powerfully recollected several minutes after waking up, the stranger (whose face appeared as a black playing-card) had smelled of sulphur; posed riddles to the members of the Society (including Masterji); grown wings, laughed, and flown out of a window, while all of them ran after him, shouting, trying to knock him down with a long stick. Masterji puzzled over his dream, until he realized that some of its images had been borrowed from the book he had been reading late into the night; he picked it up and continued reading:

The Soul's Passageway after Death
(Vikas Publications, Benaras)

In its first year out of the body, the soul travels slowly and at a low altitude, burdened by the sins of its worldly existence. It flies over green fields, ploughed fields, and small dams and dykes. It has wings like an eagle's at this stage of its voyage. In the second year it begins to ascend over the oceans. This flight will take it all of the second year, and a part of the third year too. It will see the ocean change colour, from blue to dark blue, until it is almost a kind of black. The darkening of the colour of the ocean will alert the soul to its entry into the third year of its long flight...

With eyes closed, imagine a human soul with your wife's face – and with wings like an eagle... yes, eyes, nose, cheeks like your wife's, wing-span like an eagle's, suspended in mid-flight over the ocean...

In all, the flight of the soul after death lasts seven hundred and seventy-seven years. The prayers and pious thoughts offered by relatives and loved ones from the world of the living will greatly affect the course, length, and comfort of this journey...

Yogesh Murthy, called 'Masterji', sixty-one years old, distinguished emeritus teacher of St Catherine's High School, yawned, and stretched his legs: *The Soul's Passageway after Death* landed on the teakwood table.

He went back to bed. In the old days, his wife's tea and talk and the perfume from the fresh flowers in her hair would wake him up. He sniffed the air for scents of jasmine.

Hai-ya! Hai-ya!

The screams came from somewhere below, and to his right. The two sons of Ajwani, the broker, began the morning by practising tae kwon-do in full uniform in their living room. Ajwani's boys were the athletic champions of the Society; the elder, Rajeev, had won a great victory in the martial arts competition last year. As a gesture of the Society's gratitude, he was allowed to dip his hand in kerosene and leave a memento of his victorious body on the front wall, where it could

41

still be seen (or so everyone was sure), just above Mrs Saldanha's kitchen window.

Now to the left, a loud voice, flipping diphthongs up and down. 'Oy, oy, oyoyoyoy, my Ramu – come here... Turn that way, my prince, ayay...' What was Ramu going to take to school for lunch, Masterji wondered, yawning, and turning to the side.

A noise from the kitchen. The very noise Purnima used to make when chopping onions. He tiptoed into the kitchen to catch a ghost, if one was there. An old calendar was tapping on the wall. It was Purnima's private calendar, illustrated with an image of the goddess Lakshmi tipping over a pot full of gold coins, and with key dates circled and marked in her private shorthand; she had consulted it to the day she had been admitted to the hospital (12 October; circled), so he had not replaced it with a new calendar at the start of the year.

He would have to walk a bit today with his grandson; in anticipation, he wrapped a pink orthopaedic cloth tightly around his arthritic left knee before putting his trousers on. Back at his teakwood table, he picked up *The Soul's Passageway after Death*.

The bell rang: bushy-haired and bearded, Ibrahim Kudwa, the cyber-café owner from 4C, with dandruff sprinkled like spots of wisdom on the shoulders of his green kurta.

'Did you see the sign, Masterji?' Kudwa pointed to the window. 'In the hole they made outside. I changed the sign from "inconvenience is in progress, work is regretted", to the other way.' Kudwa slapped his forehead. 'Sorry, I changed it from "work is in progress, inconvenience is regretted", to the other way round. I thought you would like to know.'

'Very impressive,' Masterji said, and patted his beaming neighbour. In the kitchen, the old calendar began tapping on the wall, and Masterji forgot to offer his visitor even a cup of tea.

By midday, he was at the Byculla Zoo, leading his grandson hand in hand, from cage to cage. The two of them had seen a lioness, two black bears covered in fresh grass, an alligator in emerald water, elephants, hippos, cobras and pythons.

The boy had questions: what is the name of that in the water? – who is the tiger yawning at? – why are the birds yellow? Masterji enjoyed giving names to the animals, and added a humorous story to explain why each one left his native land and came to Mumbai. 'Do you think of your grandmother?' he asked from time to time.

The two of them stopped in front of a rectangular cage with bars, and a low tin roof; an animal moved from one end to the other. The idlers who had turned up to the zoo, even the lovers, stopped at the cage. A green tarpaulin on the roofing made a phosphorescent glow through which the dark animal came, jauntily, as if chuckling, its tongue hanging out, until it stood up on a red guano-stained stone bench and reared its head; then it got down, turned, went to the other end of the cage and reared its head before turning back. It was filthy – it was majestic: the grey fleece, the dog-like grinning face, the powerful striped lower limbs. Men and women watched it. Perhaps this mongrel beast looked like one of those, half politician and half criminal, who ruled the city, vile and necessary.

'What is its name?'

Masterji could not say. The syllables were there, on the tip of his tongue. But when he tried to speak they moved the other way, as if magnetically repulsed. He shrugged.

At once the boy seemed frightened, as if his grandfather's power, which lay in naming these animals, had ended.

To cheer him up, Masterji bought him some peanuts (though his daughter-in-law had told him not to feed the boy), and they ate on the grass; Masterji thought he was in a happy time of his life. The battles were over, the heat and light were dimmed.

Before it is too late, he thought, running his fingers through his grandson's curly hair, *I must tell this boy all that we have been through. His grandmother and I. Life in Bombay in the old days. War in 1965 with Pakistan. War in 1971. The day they killed Indira Gandhi. So much more.*

'More peanuts?' he asked.

The boy shook his head, and looked at his grandfather hopefully.

Sonal, his daughter-in-law, was waiting at the gate. She smiled as he talked, on their drive into the city. Half an hour later, in his son's flat in Marine Lines, Sonal served Masterji tea and bad news: Gaurav, his son, had just sent her a text message. He would not be coming home until midnight. Busy day at the office. 'Why don't you wait?' she suggested. 'You can stay overnight. It's your home, after all...'

'I'll wait,' he said. He tapped his fingers on the arms of his chair. 'I'll wait.'

'Do you think of her a lot, Masterji?' Sonal asked.

His fingers tapped faster on the chair, and he said: 'All the time.' The words just burst out after that.

'Gaurav will remember when his grandfather died, in 1991, and she went to Suratkal to perform the last rites with her brothers. When she came back to Mumbai, she said nothing for days. Then she confessed. "They locked me up in a room and made me sign a paper." Her own brothers! They threatened her until she signed over her father's property and gold to them.'

Even now the memory stopped his breath. He had gone to see a lawyer at once. Four hundred rupees as a retainer, paid in cash upfront. He had come home and talked it over with Purnima.

'We'll never put them behind bars, I told her. The law in this country takes for ever to do anything. Is it worth wasting all that money? She thought about it and said, "All right, let it drop." Sometimes I would look back on the incident and ask myself, should I have paid for that lawyer? But whenever I brought it up with her, she just did this' – he shrugged – 'and said that thing. Her favourite saying. "Man is like a goat tied to a pole." Meaning, all of us have some free will but not too much. One shouldn't judge oneself harshly.'

'That is so beautiful. She was a wonderful woman, wasn't she?' Sonal got up. 'I am sorry – I have to check on my father for a minute.'

Her father, once a respected banker, now suffered from advanced Alzheimer's; he lived with his daughter, and was fed, bathed, and clothed by her. As Sonal slipped into an inner room, Masterji silently commended her filial devotion. So rare in an age like this. He tapped his knee and tried to remember the name of that striped animal in the cage. Ronak was taking a nap in his bedroom. He wanted to remember before the boy woke up.

Sonal came out of her father's room with a large blue book which she placed on the table in front of Masterji.

'The boy doesn't read much; he plays cricket.' She smiled. 'It is better that you keep this yourself, since you are fond of books.'

Masterji opened the blue book. *The Illustrated History of Science*. Purchased a decade ago at the Strand Book Shop in the city, maintained impeccably, until two weeks ago given to his grandson as a gift.

He got up from his chair with the book. 'I'll go back now.'

'At this hour?' Sonal frowned. 'The train will be packed. Wait an hour here. It's your home, after all.'

'What am I, a foreigner? I'll survive.'

'Are you sure you want to take the train at this…' There was a gurgling from the inner room, and Sonal turned in its direction. 'One minute,' she said. 'My father needs attention again.'

'I'm leaving,' Masterji shouted after putting on his shoes. He stood waiting for a response from Sonal, then closed the door behind him and took the elevator down.

With his blue book in his hand he walked past the old buildings of Marine Lines, some of the oldest in the city – past porticos never penetrated by the sun, and lit up at all times of day by yellow electric bulbs, stone eaves broken by saplings, and placental mounds of sewage and dark earth piled up on wet roads. Along the side of the Marine Lines train station he walked towards Churchgate.

He tried not to think of the *Illustrated History of Science* in his hands. Was that flat so small they couldn't keep even one book of his in it? The boy's own grandfather – and they had to shove my gift back in my hands?

He opened the blue book, and saw an illustration of Galileo.

'Hyena,' he said suddenly, and closed the book. That was the word he had not been able to find for Ronak; the striped animal in the cage.

'Hyena. My own daughter-in-law is a hyena to me.'

Don't think badly of her. He heard Purnima's voice. It is your ugliest habit, she had always warned him. *The way you get angry with people, caricature them, mock their voices, manners, ideas; the way you shrink flesh-and-blood humans into fireflies to hold in your palm.*

She would cut his rage short by touching his brow (once holding a glass of ice-cold water to it) or by sending him out on an errand. Now who was there to control his anger?

He touched the *Illustrated History of Science* to his forehead and thought of her.

It was dark by the time he reached the Oval Maidan. The illuminated clock on the Rajabai Tower, its face clouded by generations of grime and neglect, looked like a second moon, more articulate, speaking directly to men. He thought of his wife in this open space; he felt her calm here. Perhaps that calm was all he had ever had; behind it he had posed as a rational creature, a wise man for his pupils at St Catherine's and his neighbours.

He did not want to go home. He did not want to lie down on that bed again.

He looked at the clock. After his wife's death, Mr Pinto came to him and said: 'You will eat with us from now on.' Three times a day he went down the stairs to sit at the Pintos' dining table, covered with a red-and-white checkerboard oilcloth they had brought back from Chicago. They did not have to announce that food was served. He heard the rattling of cutlery, the shaking of the chairs, and, with the clairvoyance provided by hunger, he could look through his floor and see Mrs Pinto's maid Nina placing porcelain vessels steaming with prawn curry on the table. Raised as a strict vegetarian, Masterji had learned the taste of animals and fish in Bombay; exchanging his wife's lentil-and-vegetable regimen for the Pintos' carnivorous diet was the only good thing, he said to himself, that had come of her death. The Pintos asked for nothing in return, but he came back every evening from the market with a fistful of coriander or ginger to deposit on their table.

They would be delaying their dinner for him; he should find a payphone at once.

A loose page of the *Times of India* lay on the pavement. A former student of his named Noronha wrote a column for the paper; for this reason he never trod on it. He took a sudden sideways step to avoid the paper. The pavement began to slide away like sand. His left knee throbbed; things darkened. Spots twinkled in the darkness, like mica in a slab of granite. 'You're going to faint,' a voice seemed to shout from afar, and he reached out to it for support; his hand alighted on something solid, a lamp post. He closed his eyes and concentrated on standing still.

He leaned against the lamp post. Breathing in and out. Now he heard the sound of wood being chopped from somewhere in the Oval Maidan. The blows of the axe came with metronomic regularity, like the hour hand in a grandfather clock: underneath them, he heard the nervous ticking of his own wristwatch, like splinters flying from the log. The two sounds quickened, as if in competition.

It was nearly nine o'clock when he felt strong enough to leave the lamp post.

Churchgate train station: the shadows of the tall ceiling-fans tremulous, like water lilies, as hundreds of shoes tramped on them. It had been years since Masterji had taken the Western Line in rush hour. The train to Santa Cruz was just pulling in. He turned his face as a women's compartment passed them. Even before the train stopped, passengers had begun jumping in, landing with thuds, nearly falling over, recovering, scrambling for seats. Not an inch of free green cushion by the time Masterji got in. Wait. In a corner, he did spot a vacant patch of green, but he was kept away by a man's hand – ah, yes, he remembered now: the infamous evening train 'card mafia'. They were reserving a seat for a friend who always sat there to play with them. Masterji held on to a pole for support. With one hand he opened the blue book and turned the pages to find the section on Galileo. The card mafia, their team complete, were now playing their game, which would last them the hour and a quarter to Borivali or Virar; their cards had, on their reverse side, the hands of a clock at various angles, giving the impression of time passing with great fury as they were dealt out. Marine Lines–Charni Road–Grant Road–Mumbai Central–Elphinstone Road. Middle-aged accountants, stockbrokers, insurance salesmen kept coming in at each stop. Like an abdominal muscle the human mass in the train contracted.

Now for the worst. The lights turned on in the train as it came to a halt. Dadar station. Footfalls and pushing: in the dim first-class compartment men multiplied. A pot belly pressed against Masterji – how rock-like a pot belly can feel! The smell of another's shirt became the smell of his shirt. He remembered a line from his college *Hamlet*. The *thousand* natural shocks that flesh is heir to? Shakespeare under-estimated the trauma of life in Mumbai by a big margin.

The pressure on him lessened. Through the barred windows of the moving train, he saw firecrackers exploding in the sky. Bodies relaxed; faces glowed with the light from outside. Rockets shot out of begrimed buildings. Was it a religious festival? Hindu, or Muslim, or Parsi, or Jain, or Roman Catholic? Or something more mysterious: an unplanned confluence of private euphoria – weddings, engagements, birthdays, other incendiary celebrations, all occurring in tandem.

At Bandra, he realized he had only one stop left, and began push-ing his way to the door – I'm getting out too, old man. You should be patient. When the train stopped he was three feet away from the door; he was pushed from behind and pushed those ahead of him. But now a reverse tide hit them all: men barged in from the platform. Those who wanted to get out at Santa Cruz wriggled, pressed, cursed, refused to give up, but the superior desperation of those wanting to get in won the day. The train moved; Masterji had missed his stop. 'Uncle, I'll make room for you,' one young man who had seen his plight moved back. 'Get out at Vile Parle and take the next train back.' When the train slowed, the mass of departing commuters shouted, in one voice: 'Move!' And nothing stopped them this time; they swept Masterji along with them on to the platform. Catching the Churchgate-bound train, he went back to Santa Cruz, where the station was so packed he had to climb the stairs leading out one step at a time.

He was released by the crowd into harsh light and strong fragrance. On the bridge that led out from the station, under bare electric bulbs, men sold orange and green perfumes in large bottles next to spreads of lemons, tennis shoes, keychains, wallets, *chikoos*. A boy handed him a cyclostyled advertisement on yellow paper as he left the bridge.

He dropped the advertisement and walked down the stairs, avoiding the one-armed beggar, into a welcome-carpet of fructose. In the market by the station, mango-sellers waited for the returning commuters: ripe and bursting, each mango was like a heartfelt apology from the city for the state of its trains. Masterji smelled the mangoes and accepted the apology.

Near the mango-sellers, a man who had his head and arms sticking through the holes of a cardboard sign that said: 'Fight seven kinds of vermin', with appropriate illustrations below (cockroaches, honeybees, mongoose, ants, termites, lice, mosquitoes), saluted Masterji. This pest control man often came to Vishram to knock down, with a long bamboo pole, an impromptu beehive or a wasps' nest on the roofing. Extending his hand through the illustrated cardboard sign he wore, he seized the old teacher's arm.

'Masterji. Someone was asking about Vishram Society in the market.'

'Asking what?'

'What kind of people lived in it, what their reputation was, did they fight with each other and with others, lots and lots of questions. He was a tall fellow, Masterji.'

'Did he wear a white shirt and black trousers?'

'Yes, I think so. I told him that any Society with a man like Masterji in it is a good Society.'

'Thank you, my friend,' Masterji said, having forgotten the pest control man's name.

So the Secretary was right, something is going on, Masterji thought. He had a vision of the green cage in the zoo again; he smelled something animal and insolent. Maybe they should go to the police in the morning.

When he reached Vishram, the gate was padlocked. Walking with care over the recently filled-up construction hole, he slapped the heavy chains and lock against the gate. 'Ram Khare!' he shouted. 'Ram Khare, it's me!'

The guard came from his room in the back of the building and unlocked the chain. 'It's past ten o'clock, Masterji. Be a little patient.'

The stairwell smelled. He found the stray dog lying on the first landing of the stairs, its body shivering, foam at the mouth. Did no one care that this dog could be sick? The animal had lost a layer of subcutaneous fat, and its ribcage was monstrously articulated, like the maw of another beast that was consuming it.

Masterji prodded at the dog's ribs with his foot; when it did not move, he kicked. It yelped and rocketed down the stairs.

Waiting for a few seconds to make sure the dog did not return, he continued up to the third floor, where, as he was turning the key to his room, he heard a click behind him. The door of 3B opened wide – light, laughter, music – a young man stepped out.

Ms Meenakshi, the journalist, loose-haired and wearing her nightie, had her hand on the young man's shoulder as he took a big step into the hallway, which caused him to bump into the old school-teacher. 'Sorry,' the boy said. 'I'm sorry, sir.'

He had bathed a few minutes ago, and Masterji smelled fresh soap.

'Can't you watch yourself?' he shouted.

The boy grinned.

Before he knew what he was doing, Masterji had pushed the grin-ning thing. The boy fell back, banged his head into the door of 3B, and slid to the floor.

As Masterji watched, the young man rose to his feet, his fist clenched. Before either man could do anything, the girl began to scream.

What is Bombay?

From the thirteenth floor, a window answers: banyan, maidan, stone, tile, tower, dome, sea, hawk, *amaltas* in bloom, smog on the horizon, gothic phantasmagoria (Victoria Terminus and the Municipal Building) emerging from the smog.

Dharmen Shah watches the hawk. It has been hovering outside the window, held aloft by a mysterious current – a thrashing of sunlit wings – and it is on the sill. In its claws a mouse, or a large part of one. Entrails wink out of grey fur: a ruby inside ore. A second later, another hawk is also on the sill.

Opening the window, Shah leaned out as far as he could: the two birds were flying in a vindictive whirl around each other. The dead mouse, left behind on the sill, was oozing blood and grease.

Shah's mouth filled with saliva. He had eaten a packet of milk biscuits in the past twelve hours.

Consoling his belly with a massage, Shah moved to the next window. He ate the view from here: the football field that occupied most of the Cooperage, the green Oval Maidan beside it, the gable and deep-arched entranceway of the University, the Rajabai Tower, and the High Court of Bombay. Amidst the coconut palms and mango trees, the red blossoms of a *gulmohar* burned like love bites on the summer's day.

A stubby, gold-ringed index finger sketched round the Rajabai Tower and dragged it all the way to the other end of the Oval Maidan. *There:* it would fit much better there.

Shah looked down. On the road directly below the window, a

woman was talking on a mobile phone. He craned his neck to see what she was wearing below her waist.

'It's a girl, isn't it, Dharmen?'

Doctor Nayak came into the room with an X-ray photograph in his hand.

'That's the only thing that would get your neck out of the window.'

The doctor flipped the photograph, and held it up against the view of the city.

Dharmen Shah's skull glowed. The X-ray had been taken less than an hour ago at the hospital. Shah saw something milky-white chuckling inside his cranium, a ghost grinning through his wide-open jaw. The doctor slid the X-ray back into its folder. He indicated for his guest and patient to use the sofa.

'Why do you think I called you here to my home after the tests? I have cancelled three morning appointments for this.'

Shah, with hands massaging his belly, grinned. 'Real estate.' He stayed by the window.

'Not this time, Dharmen. I wanted to say things that are better said in the house than at the hospital. In the hope that you might listen this time.'

'*So* grateful.'

'It is a bit worse each time I see you, Dharmen. That thing that is growing in your chest and head. Chronic bronchitis. Worse and worse each time. You have infected mucus in your lungs and in your sinuses. The next stage is that you have trouble breathing. We may have to put you in a hospital bed. Do you want things to come to that?'

'And why *would* things come to that?' Shah knocked on the window. 'Despite the fact that I take every blood test, X-ray, and medical pill that you recommend. After starving myself the previous night.'

Youthful and square-jawed, Doctor Nayak sported a black moustache above a tuft of goatee: when he grinned he looked like the Jack of Spades.

'You're a big, spoilt child, Dharmen. You don't do what your doctor tells you to do, and you think he won't find out as long as you turn up for blood tests and X-rays. I've been warning you for months.

52

It's the construction business that is doing this to you. All the dust you inhale. The stress and strain.'

'I've been at construction sites for *twenty-five years*, Nayak. The problem began only a year or two ago.'

'It's all those old buildings you're around. The ones you break up. Materials were used then that are banned now. Asbestos, cheap paint. They get into your lungs. Then these places you like going to, these slums.'

'The place is called Vakola.'

'I've seen it. Very polluted. Diesel in the air, dust. The system is weakened by pollution over time.'

'What is this, then?' Dharmen Shah drummed on his stomach. He pinched his thick forearms. 'What is this, then? Isn't this good health?'

'Listen to me. I gave up three paying appointments for this. You're picking up fevers, coughs, stomach illnesses. Your immune system is weakening. Leave Bombay,' said the doctor. 'At least for a part of each year. Go to the Himalayas. Simla. Abroad. The one thing money can't buy here is clean air.'

The fat man reached into his shirt pocket. Straightening out a cheaply printed brochure, he handed it to Doctor Nayak.

The 'King' of the Suburban Builders, J. J. Chacko, MD of the Ultimex Group, has astounded all his observers, friends, and peers, by acquiring a prime construction plot in Vakola, Santa Cruz (East) at an audacious rate that constitutes the HIGHEST PRICE ever paid for a redevelopment project in this suburb, despite the vigilant and audacious efforts of various competitors to bag the prize instead.

Mr Chacko exclusively discloses to 'Mumbai Real Estate News' that an architect from Hong Kong, the noted land of modernism, will be called in to design the world-class apartments; Mr Chacko also believes he will add a park and shopping mall to the area in a few months' time. Hotels, plazas, gardens, happy families will follow.

Ultimex Group's motto is 'The Very Best' and it has been

progressing all over the city of Mumbai. On the personal front, Mr Chacko, visionary, Ultimex Group, is not a known figure, preferring to keep away from the glamour scene of So-Bo (south Bombay) social life. He is 'mischievous', 'shy', and 'a family man with simple pleasures', says one private friend. He is nimble in his thoughts, and sly, like the man of the future; he is a great philanthropist, winner of thirteen gold medals, plaques, dedicatory poems, and paper-based awards for his humanitarian achievement in the field of social work.

He is also passionate about chess and carom.

The doctor read the brochure, and turned it over, and read it again.

'So?'

'So that's J. J. Chacko, head of the Ultimex Group. The area around the Vakola train station is in his pocket. Has three buildings on that side already. He's coming over to my side now. Know what he did the other day? Paid eighty-one lakhs for a one-room in a slum. Just so everyone would talk about him. In my own territory. Even sends me this brochure in the mail.'

'So?'

Shah took back the piece of paper, folded it, and replaced it in his pocket. He patted it.

'How can I take a holiday when J. J. Chacko doesn't? Does his doctor tell him to slow down?'

Doctor Nayak's forehead filled with lines.

'I don't care if *he* kills himself. But you can't go straight into another project. Are you doing this for Satish? What could he want more than for his father to live a long life?'

Dharmen Shah drew a line on the window with his finger.

'There is a golden line in this city: a line that makes men rich.'

Now he dotted three points on it.

'You have Santa Cruz airport there, you have the Bandra-Kurla Complex there and you have the Dharavi slums there. Why is this line golden? Air travel is booming. More planes, more visitors. Then' – he moved his finger – 'the financial centre at Bandra-Kurla is expand-

54

ing by the hour. Then the government is starting redevelopment in Dharavi. Asia's biggest slum will become Asia's richest slum. This area is boiling with money. People arrive daily and have nowhere to live. Except' – he dotted his golden line in the centre – 'here. Vakola. The Fountainhead and Excelsior will be ready by November this year. I've sold most of the units in them already. But the main show is next year. The Shanghai.'

Doctor Nayak, who had been yawning, closed his mouth shut. He grinned.

'*That* again. That city is going to kill you, Dharmen.'

'You should have come with me, Nayak. Roads as far as the eye can see, skyscrapers, everything clean, beautiful.' Shah hit the window; it trembled. 'Those Chinese have all the will power in the world. And here we haven't had ten minutes of will power since Independence.'

The doctor, with a chuckle, got up from his sofa and went to the window. He stretched.

'The experience of Shanghai being to a middle-aged Indian businessman what the experience of sex is to a teenager. You can't keep comparing us to the Chinese, Dharmen.'

Shah turned to look at him.

'How else will we improve? Look at the trains in this city. Look at the roads. The law courts. Nothing works, nothing moves; it takes ten years to build a bridge.'

'Enough. Enough. Have some breakfast with us, Dharmen. Vishala wants to thank you. You arranged that deal for her friend in Prabha Devi.' Nayak placed his hand on the fat man's shoulder. 'You're starting to grow on her. Stay. I'll cancel a fourth appointment for you.'

Dharmen Shah was gazing out of the window.

The hawks rematerialized. Still in combat, blown towards the building by a sudden gust, they came straight at the window and slammed into it, before another current lifted them, as if at a cliff face, vertically up.

'Bloody nuisance,' Doctor Nayak said. 'Leave shit on the windows, fight all day long. Someone should…' He pulled an imaginary trigger. '… and knock them off. One by one.'

*

Pressing the buttons on his mobile phone, Shah walked through the basement car park until a spectral voice began echoing under the low ceiling.

'Mr Secretary, members of Vishram Society...'

Shah slipped the mobile phone into his pocket and walked with stealth.

A tall dark man in a white shirt and black trousers stood at the open door of the basement lift. Facing its half-mirror, he raised his left hand towards it.

'Mr Secretary, members of Vishram Society, Towers A and B, all your *dreams* are about to come true.'

The man shifted the angle of his jaw: a broken upper tooth now showed prominently in the mirror.

'Mr Secretary, members of...'

A boy in dirty khaki, a tea tray in his hand, poked the man from behind, asking to be allowed into the lift.

The man spun around with a raised hand. 'Sister-fucker, *don't* touch me.'

The tea boy stepped back, shifting the tray with its leaping glasses to his left hand.

Shah cleared his throat.

'Shanmugham,' he said, 'let the boy use the lift.'

With a 'yes, sir', the tall man hurried to a grey Mercedes-Benz, whose door he opened for his coughing employer.

On Marine Drive.

Coconut palms bent by the ocean breeze and pigeons in sudden flight added to the sensation of speed on the long straight dash down the avenue. A satin patch of sun gleamed on Back Bay.

'Has everything but the deadline in it,' Shanmugham said, turning from the front passenger seat of the Mercedes-Benz to show his boss a printed page. The driver changed gears as a red light finally snared them.

'I went over it word for word last night, sir. Made sure every comma was right.'

Ignoring the letter, Mr Shah opened a little blue metal box, and flicked what was inside with a plastic spoonlet into his bright red mouth. Small black teeth chewed the *gutka*: he had lost a few.

'Don't worry about words, Shanmugham. Tell me about the people.'

'You saw them, sir.'

'Only once.'

'Solid people. Tower B is modern. Finance, high-tech, computers. Tower A is old. Teachers, accountants, brokers. Both are solid.'

'Teachers?' The fat man winced. 'What else about this Society? Has anything bad happened there?'

'One suicide, sir. Many years ago. A boy jumped from the roof. They didn't tell me, but I found out from the neighbours.'

'Just *one* suicide?'

'Yes, sir.'

'I'll manage.'

Shah dreamed of breakfast. Eight pieces of toast, sliced diagonally, piled into a porcelain dish; a jar of Kissan's Mixed-Fruit Jam; a jar of Kissan's Marmalade; a bottle of Heinz Tomato Ketchup; and, suspended in a lobed bowl of water to keep it soft, an iceberg of home-made butter.

The Mercedes drove up Malabar Hill; the ocean glinted to Shanmugham's left.

As the driver adjusted his gears, they stalled outside an old ruined mansion. Fresh saplings had broken through the exquisitely carved stone leaves and flowers on the nineteenth-century cornice, and a sign hammered into the front wall said:

Mumbai Municipal Corporation

This building is dangerous, dilapidated, and unfit for humans to be around. No one should enter it.

As the car accelerated past, light from the ocean echoed through the ruined mansion.

Shanmugham saw four massive banyan trees growing in the

compound of one grand building, their aerial roots clinging as if glued to the boundary wall: four escutcheons of the House of Shah.

The lift took them to the eighth floor.

'We'll go to the construction site right after breakfast,' Shah told his assistant, as they walked towards his flat. 'The contractor told me this morning that everything was all right and there was no need for me to be there. You know what *that* means.'

A medallion of a golden Lord Ganesha sat on the lintel above the builder's home.

The door was open. Two black leather shoes had been left outside.

In the living room, a tableau as if from a stage comedy. In front of a giant bronze image of the Dancing Nataraja, Shah saw Giri, his housekeeper, alongside two men in khaki uniforms, one of whom sipped a glass of cold water. The other man in uniform had a hand on Satish, his son, and was admonishing the boy with his index finger, as if putting on a dumb show for his father's sake.

The mucus in Shah's chest rumbled.

'Boss.' Giri, who wore a tattered *banian* and blue lungi, came up to him. 'He did it again. He was spray-painting cars outside the school; they caught him and brought him here. I told them to wait till you...'

The policeman who had his hand on Satish, appeared to be the senior of the two. He spoke. The other kept drinking his cold water.

'First, we saw him doing this...'

The policeman made a circular motion to indicate the action of spraying. Shah listened. The fingers of his left hand rubbed the thick gold ring on the fingers of his right.

'Then he did *this*. Then *this*. They finished painting the first car, and then they went to the next. It's a gang, and each one of them has a gang-name. Your son's name is Soda Pop.'

'Soda Pop,' Shah said.

The policeman who had been sipping water nodded. '... Pop.'

Plump, fair-skinned Satish exuded nonchalance, as if the matter concerned someone else.

58

'Then Constable Hamid, sir' – the policeman talking gestured to the one who was not – 'he's sitting in the police van, he said, isn't that the developer Mr Shah's son? And then, considering the excellent relations that our station has always had with you, sir, we thought…before it gets into the papers…'

The developer Mr Shah, having heard enough, wanted possession of the goods: with his fingers, he beckoned the boy. The policeman did not stop him; he strolled over to his father's side.

'His friends? Those other boys, who were doing this—' Shah made the same circular motion. 'What happens to them?'

'They'll all have to go to the police station. Their parents will have to come and release them. We'll keep the names out of the papers. *This* time.'

Shah put his hand on his heart. '*So* grateful.'

Giri went at once into his master's study. A wooden drawer opened, then closed. Giri had done this before, and knew exactly how much to put in the envelope.

He handed it to Shah, who felt its weight, approved, and handed it to the policeman who had done the talking: 'For some chai and cold drinks at your police station, my friend. I know it's very hot these days.'

Though the envelope had been accepted, neither of the policemen had left. The talkative one said: 'My daughter's birthday is coming up, sir. It'll be a nice weekend for me.'

'I'll send her a birthday cake from the Taj. They have a nice pastry shop. It'll arrive soon.'

'Sir…' The quiet policeman spoke.

'Yes?'

'Well, my daughter's birthday is coming up too.'

Giri saw the policemen out with a smile; Shah stood chafing the thick gold rings on his index finger. The moment Giri closed the door, Shah jabbed the ring into his son's nose.

'Soda Pop' flinched, squeezed his eyes closed, and held his face averted, as if preserving the force of the jab.

Soda Pop trembled; if he could, every part of his body said, he would have launched himself at his father and killed him right then.

Giri took him away to his room. 'Let's wash up, Baba. We'll go to your room and drink some warm milk. That's what we'll do.'

Returning to the living room, Giri found his employer and Shanmugham on either side of the Dancing Nataraja, examining the white thing that shared the wooden table on which the bronze statue stood: a plaster-of-Paris model of a building, which a peon from Mr Shah's office had brought to the flat two days ago.

'Will you go and speak to the boy now?' Giri asked. 'Say something nice.'

Shah ran his palm down the side of the plaster-of-Paris model.

'Bring me a plate with some toast, Giri,' he said. 'At once. And some for Shanmugham, too.'

Giri glared at Shanmugham as he went to the kitchen; he did not approve of the presence of employees during meals.

Shah kept looking at the plaster-of-Paris model. His eyes went down to the inscription on its base:

CONFIDENCE SHANGHAI
VAKOLA, SANTA CRUZ (E)
SUPER LUXURY APARTMENTS
'FROM MY FAMILY TO YOURS'

'Look at it, Shanmugham,' he said. 'Just look at it. Won't it be beautiful when it comes up?'

From the moment the car turned on to the bridge at Bandra, Shah had kept his eyes closed.

He felt his pulse quickening. His lungs became lighter. It was as if he had not coughed in years.

The Mercedes came to a halt; he heard someone opening the door for him.

'Sir.'

He stepped out, holding Shanmugham's hands. He had still not opened his eyes; he wanted to defer the pleasure for as long as possible.

He could already hear the two of them: the Confidence Excelsior and the Confidence Fountainhead. Rumbling, the way the boy had been inside his mother's womb, in the last months before delivery.

He walked over truck tyre ruts, hardened and ridged like fossilized vertebrae. He felt crushed granite stones under his feet, which gave away to smooth sand, studded with fragments of brick. The noise grew around him.

Now he opened his eyes.

Cement mixers were churning like cannons aimed at the two buildings; women in colourful saris took troughs full of wet mortar up the floors of the Fountainhead. Further down the road, he saw the Excelsior, more skeletal, covered with nets and scaffoldings, ribs of dark wooden beams propping up each unbuilt floor.

A small village had sprung up around the construction work: migrants from north India, the workers had re-created the old home. Cows swatting away flies, broth in an aluminium vessel boiling over, a small shrine of a red god. Hitching up his trousers, Shah walked up to the cow; he touched its forehead three times for good luck and touched his own.

A group of day-labourers were waiting for him.

'How is the cement pouring today?' he asked.

'Very well, sir.'

'Then why are you people standing here, wasting time?'

He counted the men. Six. They wore *banians* and white dhotis, and their bodies were filmed over with construction dust. The contractor in charge of work at the Fountainhead came running.

'They say, sir, the heat... they want to go and tend their fields...'

Shah clicked his tongue.

'I want them to speak for themselves.'

One of the group of mutineers, a small man with neatly parted hair, explained.

'We can't work in these conditions, sahib, please forgive us. We will finish the day's work honestly, and leave in the evening. Ask the contractor. We have been your best workers until now.'

Shah looked up at the Fountainhead, and then at the Excelsior, and raised his eyes to the sun.

'I know it is hot. The coconut palms are turning brown. The cows don't want to stand even if you put food in front of them. I know it is hot. But we have only a month before it starts raining, and we must finish pouring concrete now. If we don't, I will lose a month and a half – two months, if the rains are heavy. And time is one thing I cannot lose.'

He spat something thick, pink, and *gutka*-stained. He stroked the cow again, and spoke.

'You may think, looking at me, he is a rich man, what does he know about the heat? Let me tell you.'

Using the hand which had been rubbing the cow, he pointed a finger at the men: 'This Dharmen Shah of yours knows what it is to work and walk and sweat in the heat. He did not grow up in luxury like other rich men. He grew up in a village called Krishnapur in Gujarat. When he came to Bombay he had just twelve rupees and eighty paise on him and he came in summer. He took the train, he took the bus, and when he had no more money for the bus, he walked. His chappals wore away and he tied leaves around his feet and he kept walking. And you know what he found when he came to Bombay?'

Two fifty, Shanmugham thought. *Don't offer them more than 250.*

'Gold.' Mr Shah now showed the mutineers all his fingers and all his rings. 'And the hotter it becomes, the more gold there is in the air. I will increase your pay…' He squeezed his fingers back in and tingled them as he frowned. '… to… 300 rupees per day per man. That's a hundred rupees more than you are getting now, and more than you'll get anywhere else in Santa Cruz. You say you want to go home. Don't I know what you'll do? Work your farms? No. You'll lie on a charpoy in the shade, smoke, play with a child. When the sun sets, you'll drink. You'll run out of money, come back on 15 June, when it's raining, and beg me for work. Open your ears: the contractor will remember each worker who leaves now when the boss needed him most. No man who does not work for Shah when it is hot will work for him when it is cool. I will send buses around Maharashtra to pick up villagers and bring them here. It may double my expenses but I will do it. But if you stay and work, I'll pay you 300 rupees, day after day. I'm tossing gold in the air. Who will grab it?'

The workers looked at one another: indecision rippled over them, and then the one with the neatly parted hair said: 'Sahib, do you mean what you said, 300 a day? Even the women?'

'Even the women. Even the children.' Shah spat again and licked his lips. 'Even your dogs and cats if they put bricks on their heads and carry them for me.'

'We will stay for you, sahib,' the worker said.

And though none of the other men in *banians* and dhotis looked happy, they seemed powerless to resist.

'Good. Get to work at once. The rains are coming closer to Bombay every second we waste.'

When they were out of earshot, the contractor whispered: 'Are you really going to pay the women the same, sir? Three hundred?'

'How much are you giving them now?'

'One twenty-five. If they're hefty, 150.'

'Give the women 200,' Shah said. 'The fat ones 220. But the men get 300 as I said.'

'And you—' he jabbed a gold-ringed finger at the contractor's chest. 'Next time something is wrong at the site, don't tell me: "All is well, sir." Does it hurt your mouth if the truth comes out of it once a year?'

'Forgive me, sir,' the contractor said.

'They're social animals, you understand. If one complains, all will complain. I need to know as soon as there is trouble.'

'Forgive me, sir.'

Shah walked with Shanmugham from the Fountainhead to his other building.

Shanmugham felt his shirt sticking to his back. His employer's shirt was wet too, but it seemed to him that these were spots not of moisture, but of molten butter. The man who had been sick in the morning now glowed with health. Shanmugham could barely keep up with him.

They were at a group of workers' huts in between the two building projects. A stunted gulmohar tree stood here with criss-crossing branches, like a man who has got his arms in a tangle by pointing in every direction at once. A water pump dripped in its shade. A heap of sand was piled up on one side of the tree, with crushed stones on the other side. Two of the workers' children had pitched a tyre on a low branch, on which they swung until their feet dug into the sand. Another had picked up an axe, with which he attacked the sand, sneezing each time his wobbling blows connected.

The builder stopped by the water pump to read a message on his mobile phone.

'That was from Giri.' He put his phone into his pocket. 'I would have cancelled the birthday party for Satish but the invitations have gone out. The boy has agreed to be there, and behave himself.'

'Yes, sir.'

'You have children don't you, Shanmugham?'

'Yes, sir. Two sons.'

'I hope they never become to you, Shanmugham, the curse mine is to me.'

'Shall I go now, sir? To Vishram Society – to make the offer?'

'You wait until I tell you to go. The astrologer is going to call me and give me the exact time. This won't be an easy project, Shanmugham. We need every chance we can get. The stars might help us.'

Shah pointed with his mobile phone across the road. A plane went overhead; waiting until its boom passed, he said: 'Look at his guts, Shanmugham. Right under my nose he buys that place.'

Across the road, a giant billboard had come up next to the ramshackle brick houses with corrugated tin roofs held down by rocks.

ULTIMEX GROUP
IS PROUD TO ANNOUNCE THE FUTURE SITE OF
'ULTIMEX MILANO'
A NEW CONCEPT IN HOUSING
SUPER LUXURY APARTMENTS

'Do you know when he's going to start work?'

'No word yet, sir.'

'People will laugh at me if he finishes his building first, Shanmugham.'

'Yes, sir.'

Mr Shah went alone to the Excelsior. The work had fallen behind schedule here, so Shanmugham knew that his boss would have plenty to do for the next few hours.

He sat in the shade of the stunted tree, his mobile phone in his right hand.

The three workers' children sat on the sand pile, watching him with open mouths.

Showing them a closed fist, Shanmugham said: 'Mr Secretary, members of Vishram Society, all your dreams are...'

A water buffalo drew near the children.

Shanmugham left the site, had lunch on the main road, returned, and waited near the sand. The children came back to watch. He practised again on them. Taking out his blue-checked handkerchief, which his wife laid folded for him every morning on the breakfast table, he wiped his face: temples, nose, and then the back of his neck, down to the first sharp knob of his spine. He folded the handkerchief back into the square his wife had made. Then, lunging forward, he showed the children his jagged tooth: Aaaargh!

They ran.

He left the site, had tea near the main road, and returned to the pile of sand. The children came back to watch. The water buffalo moved near the sand, turning its long curved horns from side to side; a crow glided to the earth in between the buffalo's horns, and sucked a worm raw out of a hole.

Some time after five o'clock, Shanmugham reached his hand into his pocket and fumbled: his mobile phone had beeped. Mr Shah, standing on the third floor of the Excelsior, was waving at him.

The message had arrived from the astrologer in Matunga.

Leaving his group of spectators seated on their sand pile, Shanmugham sprinted from the construction site, down the mud path, past the Gold Coin and Silver Trophy Societies, past the Tamil temple in front of which boys were playing cricket (hopping to avoid the red cricket ball), and arrived, panting, at Vishram Society, where he placed his hands on the guard's booth and said: 'I want to see your Secretary again.'

Ram Khare, who had been fanning himself with his checked handkerchief as he recited from his holy digest, looked up at his visitor and dropped the handkerchief.

He followed the visitor all the way to the Secretary's office, standing outside and watching as the man put his hands on either side of the Remington typewriter and said: 'Mr Secretary: I have to make a confession to you. I am not the man I said I was, when I came to see you the other day. My name is, indeed, Shanmugham: that much is true. But I come as a representative of one of Mumbai's leading real-estate development companies, namely, the Confidence Group, and of its managing director, the esteemed Mr Dharmen Shah. Let me tell you now why I had to deceive you the other day. First read this letter that I am placing, with all due respect and reverence, on your desk; while you read it, I will wait here with my...'

The foundation of the 32-year-old friendship between Masterji and Mr Pinto was the 'No-Argument book' – a notebook in which every financial transaction between them had been faithfully recorded. In July 1975, the first time they had had lunch together, Mr Pinto, an accountant for the Britannia Biscuit company, had proposed an actuarial conscience to watch over their snacks and coffees. Realizing that petty fights, mainly over money, had disrupted his other friendships, and determined that this one should be saved, Masterji had accepted.

Mr Pinto was making his latest entry into the 'No-Argument' – the sixteenth of its kind since the original notebook of '75.

'Fill it out later. I can see the waiter.'

'Okay,' Mr Pinto said. 'But you owe me two and a half rupees.'

'Two and a half?'

'For the newspaper.'

'Which one?'

'*Hindustan Times*. You made me buy it last Saturday because you wanted to read a column by some former student of yours.'

'Nonsense,' Masterji said. 'I have no students writing for that paper.'

Mr Pinto knew that Masterji had not bought the *Hindustan Times*; a life-long accountant, he deflected a variety of worries into money talk. What he had really meant to bring up was something else: the previous night's incident. Masterji's behaviour in pushing the modern girl's boyfriend, for no good reason – the girl's screaming had brought people from around the building to the third floor – was so contrary to his usual 'nature' that people in Vishram had talked all day long about the incident, retelling and embellishing it. A man deprived in quick order of both occupation and wife was in a dangerous place, some felt. Ajwani, the broker, had even asked how safe was it to leave their children in a darkened room with him any more? Mrs Puri's stout rebuttal ('—ashamed of yourself!') had put an end to such talk.

Mr Pinto knew that it was his duty to let his friend know what they were saying about him in the Society. 'But it is best to raise such matters after dinner,' he decided.

Putting away the No-Argument book, he prepared himself for what the Biryani Emperor of Bombay had to offer.

A good biryani needs excitement. A touch of mystery. At Café Noorani near Haji Ali, the waiter comes out with a plate with an oval heap of steaming rice, speckled with yellow and red grains; the chicken was somewhere inside, true, but you had to dig into it with the fork – what aroma! – to find those marinated red chunks.

In contrast – Mr Pinto stuck his fork into his plate – look at this. Two paltry brown chicken pieces, by the side of lukewarm rice. Not a vegetable in sight.

The 'Biryani Emperor' was set in between shops selling bright silk saris, which added to the diners' awareness of the excitement missing from the food. This was a Sunday night; and for the two friends Sunday night was always biryani night. Conservative in most other things, they were reckless on biryani night, trying out a new place each week. Mr Pinto had found the 'Biryani Emperor of Bombay' much written about in the papers, even numbered among the 'the ten best-kept secrets of Mumbai' in one newspaper.

'Biryani Emperor of Bombay. What a fraud, Masterji.'

Not hearing a response from his friend, he looked up. He saw Masterji staring at the ceiling of the restaurant.

'Is it a rat?'

Masterji nodded.

'Where?'

The roof of the Biryani Emperor was held up by rafters of wood, and a rodent had materialized on one of them.

'Boy!' Masterji shouted. 'Look at that thing up there on the wood.'

The 'boy' – the middle-aged waiter – looked up. Undeterred by all the attention, the sly rat kept moving along the rafter, like a leopard on a branch. The 'boy' yawned.

Masterji pushed his biryani, not even half eaten, in the direction of the boy.

'I have a rule. I can't eat this.'

It was true: he had a 'one-rat rule' – never revisit a place where a single rat has been observed.

'You and your rule.' Mr Pinto helped himself to some of his friend's biryani.

'I don't like competing for my food with animals. Look at him up there: like a Caesar.'

'A man has to bend his rules a little to enjoy life in Mumbai,' Mr Pinto said, chewing. 'Just a little. Now and then.'

Masterji could not take his eye off the rodent Caesar. He did not notice that his arm was tipping over a glass.

As the waiter came to pick up the pieces, Mr Pinto took out the No-Argument book and added to Masterji's debit list: 'Fine for broken glass at (so-called) Biryani Emperor. Rs 10.'

Having paid for food and the broken glass, the two were walking back to Vishram Society.

'Rats have always fought humans in this city, Mr Pinto. In the nineteenth century there were plagues here. Even today they outnumber us: six rats for every human in Bombay. They have so many species and we have just one. *Rattus norvegicus. Rattus rattus. Bandicota bengalensis.* We must not let them take over the city again.'

Mr Pinto said nothing. He wished again that Masterji had his Bajaj scooter with him, so they wouldn't have to walk back on a full stomach. He blamed his wife Shelley for this. After Purnima's death, she had suggested Masterji follow the advice in a *Reader's Digest* article and renounce something to remember the deceased person by.

'For example,' she had said, 'you can give up eating brinjals. And each time you crave a brinjal, you'll remember Purnima.'

Masterji thought about it. 'I will give up my scooter.'

'No no,' she protested. 'That's extreme. Brinjals will do.'

Masterji relished the extreme: the scooter went.

A fifteen-minute walk later, the two old men reached their local market, a row of blue wooden stalls, lit by white tube-lights or naked yellow bulbs, in which the most disparate trades were conducted side by side: a chicken shop smelling of poultry shit and raw meat, a sugarcane-vendor's stall haloed in raw sucrose, a Xerox machine in a stationery shop yawning flashes of blinding light, and a barber's salon, busy even at this hour, stinking of shaving cream and gossip.

Mr Pinto finally summoned up the courage.

'Masterji,' he said, 'why don't you have yourself checked at Mahim Hinduja hospital? They do a full-body check-up.'

'Checked? For what?'

'It begins with D, Masterji.'

'Nonsense. I have perfect control over my bowels. I have always had strong lower organs.'

Mr Pinto looked at his shoes and said: 'Diabetes.'

'Mr Pinto. I don't drink much, don't eat much, I don't even have television. How can *I* get diabetes?'

'You are losing your temper. The other night it happened with the modern girl's boyfriend. Everyone in the Society has been talking. And you go to the toilet all the time. We hear it from below.'

'How dare you, Mr Pinto. Spying on me. I'll go to the bathroom when I want to. It is a free country.'

They walked back to Vishram in silence. Ram Khare, the guard, came running up to them: 'Have you heard the news, sir?'

'What news?' Mr Pinto asked.

'The Secretary is at Ajwani's office now, sir – go there and hear the news for yourself,' Khare said. 'There's gold for all of you! Gold!'

'He's drinking again,' Mr Pinto whispered. They left the raving guard behind them and walked up the stairs.

The old accountant said: 'Come to our room and have a small peg, Masterji.'

'Not tonight, Mr Pinto.'

'We have the Amaretto. Tony's gift. Let's have a peg. A peg each.'

Mr Pinto had a wonderful liqueur, brought by his son Tony on his most recent visit from America, and sipped only on treasured nights. Masterji understood that this was in the nature of an apology, and touched his friend's shoulder, before walking up to his own flat.

Vakola at night: the red neon cross of St Antony's church glows over the main road. Vendors of paani-puri bhelpuri, and gulab jamuns suspended in sugar syrup feed the tidal waves of tired humans coming in from the train station. Plastic watches, metal locks, toys for children, sandals and T-shirts punctuate the offerings of food.

Across the road, the lights are on at the Renaissance Real-Estate Agency.

Vakola is not a suburb where real-estate brokers become rich. At least four operate just along the main road. Of these, Renaissance is the most attractive; spacious, bright, its glass door painted with an image of Lord Krishna playing his flute in the magic gardens of Brindavan.

Inside, seated at his steel desk, Ramesh Ajwani, looked up from a copy of the real-estate pages of the *Times of India*. Mani, his assistant, had opened the glass door to allow a young woman to enter.

Ajwani removed his half-moon glasses, and motioned for the visitor to sit.

How nice, he thought, *to find a young woman in this modern day who can wear a sari well.*

A radiant sky-blue, cut perhaps a bit low.

Her English was better than his; he noted this with pleasure.

A two-bedroom for herself, a working woman, unmarried, with both parents living with her. One-year rental lease of the renewable nature. Range of Rs 15,000 to 20,000.

Ajwani, as was his habit, added 10 per cent to the upper range of the figure quoted, and thought at once of a set of places to show her. He put his hands on his table and leaned in to the woman.

'You seem to think I am a broker, miss?'

Ajwani's dark, pockmarked face was so unusual for his community that clients routinely mistook him for a South Indian – a good thing, he felt, because South Indians, unlike Sindhis, are known as an honest people. He was stocky, thick-necked, wore blue or cream safari suits, and smelled of Johnson's Baby Powder.

The woman in the sky-blue sari recovered. 'Yes,' she said. 'Aren't you?'

'I am *not.*'

Parallel engraved lines slanted high on Ajwani's cheeks, like facial gills, adding a touch of menace to his grin.

'I will *not* do what every other broker in this city does. I will not lie to you. Will not say a building is "virtually new" if it is forty years old; will not gloss over peculiarities in the neighbours, seepages and leakages in roof or walls. I believe in accurate information – for myself and for my clients. Please look at the wall. My three gods are up there.'

The young woman saw a full-length framed portrait of the Sai Baba and another one of the god Balaji in his 24-carat-gold costume at Tirupati.

'The third one is my most important god. Do you know his name? Please take a closer look at him. Go to the wall, please.'

The woman in the blue sari did as she was told; in between the deities she saw a small printed list.

KNOW YOUR FACTS

One BHK (Bedroom Hall Kitchen)

Two BHK (Two Bedroom Hall Kitchen)

Three BHK (Three Bedroom Hall Kitchen)

Deposit: Multiple of rent – up to six months

'Token' Money – must be paid

NOC (No Objection Certificate, from Secretary of Society) –
   must be given

Police Clearance Certificate (from local station) – broker will
   obtain.

Passport-size photo (x2) – needed. Proof of Employment –
a must

Carpet area; Built-up area; Super built-up area – know the
difference

Leave-and-Licence Agreement: who pays for stamp paper?
Decide first

Types of renters: Family, Single Bachelor, Company Bachelor,
NRI, Foreign Passport – who are you?

Standing behind the broker, she noticed that his right foot, having slipped out of its slipper, was opening and closing the lowest drawer of his desk in a clear state of excitement.

'Do you know the name of this god, miss? He is called "Information". Make him your master too. Now, please sit down.'

Waiting for her to return to her seat, he turned a framed diptych of photographs around to her.

'R and R, my two boys. Rajeev and Raghav. Just like me. R for Ramesh. Also my brokerage, R for Renaissance. And notice they are both wearing tae kwon-do outfits. Fitness is my fourth god.'

While the young lady admired the diptych, he leaned in.

'Miss Swathi, this Ajwani of yours is neat, happy, ugly, crude, truthful, mongoose-faced.' He emphasized each adjective with his hands, which were covered with cheap rings. 'And these are his virtues.'

The girl tried hard to suppress the urge, then put her hand on her mouth, and succumbed. She shook with laughter; the broker beamed.

'I also enjoy making people laugh. Especially young women. Their laughter is the sweet...'

Just then the glass door of the Renaissance Real-Estate Agency opened. Secretary Kothari walked in with another man – tall, dark, dressed like a salesman in a white shirt and black trousers.

'What is it, Kothari?' Ajwani asked. 'I'm with a client.'

'It's urgent,' the Secretary said.

Ajwani was talking to a young woman in a sky-blue sari that exposed her navel. Nothing could be more urgent right now.

'We are looking for a two-bedroom for her parents and herself. I'll come and see you in your office when we have finished our work, Kothari. And you, sir, I'm not interested in any more insurance, thank you very much.'

'Ajwani, Ajwani.' The Secretary put his fists on the desk. His voice trembled. 'All your dreams are about to come true, Ajwani.'

The man who looked like an insurance salesman sat down, and slid a piece of paper over the laminated table towards the broker.

Ajwani put on his half-moon glasses; then he picked up the paper and began reading.

A small Hindu temple stood at an intersection just beyond the fruit and vegetable market. Beggars crouched about it; dappled brown goats wandered around it; Mrs Puri prayed.

Move it, God. The stone that blocks Ramu's mind. That was how she had always pictured it: a boulder had locked her Ramu's mind inside a cave. At least stop it from rolling backwards and pushing him deeper into the cave. Who will take care of him when he grows old?

When it came to places of worship in Mumbai Mrs Puri was an expert; Muslim, Christian and Hindu, she had been to each of them for her Ramu. Haji Ali, Mount Mary, SiddhiVinayak, Mahalakshmi, you name it, she had prayed there.

She gave a rupee each to the supplicants squatting by the temple, making sure they earned their money – 'Ramesh Puri. We call him Ramu. Pray for him with all your strength' – and went to the market to buy fresh vegetables for dinner.

Curved green stems bearing yellow bananas were suspended from the ceilings of the grocery shops; glitzy plastic satchels of instant Chinese noodles and malt powder twinkled beside the bananas like nouveau-riche cousins. Two Catholic priests, head to toe in white cassocks, stood at the counter of a grocery store, learning about the Reliance Company's prepaid mobile phone plans from the owner. Mrs Puri overheard. Reliance? Oh, no. Vodafone had much better reception here. She was about to save the two holy men from being swindled, when:

'Good evening, Sangeeta-ji.'

Ibrahim Kudwa (4C) passed her on his Honda Activa scooter with a wave. His wife had her arms around his waist, and his ten-year-old son Mohammad sat in front of him in his martial-arts outfit (GOJU-RU TAE KWON-DO); inside his bulky, billowing white kurta, Kudwa had the look of a bleached kangaroo carrying its entire family in its pouches.

Mrs Puri felt lighter. She envied Kudwa his happy family life – just as she knew he in secret envied Ajwani for owning a Toyota Qualis; just as Ajwani probably envied someone else; and this chain of envy linked them, showing each what was lacking in life, but offering also the consolation that happiness was present right next door, in the life of a neighbour, an element of the same Society.

She returned to Vishram with brinjals and beetroots.

The Secretary and Mr Ajwani were standing by the black Cross with folded palms. A man in a white shirt and black trousers – she recognized him as one of the two who had come the other day asking all the questions – was grinning behind them.

'Mrs Puri,' the Secretary's voice trembled. 'Quickly. Up to your room. Your husband wants to tell you himself.'

Her heart contracted. God, what have you done to my family this time? What new horror?

Mrs Rego stood athwart the entrance of the Society.

'This is an illusion, Mrs Puri. You must understand that. The money will never come.'

'Let me go,' Mrs Puri almost pushed the Battleship aside. She ran up the stairs to her Ramu. The door to her flat was open. Her husband and her boy were sitting together in the dark.

'All of us… all of us… all of us in this building…' Mr Puri said, when she turned on the light.

'Yes?' she whispered. She soothed Ramu's brow with her palm. 'Yes?'

'We've paid our taxes, and we've helped each other, and we've gone to SiddhiVinayak and Mount Mary church and Mahim church…'

'Yes?'

'... and now all of us in this building, all of us good people, have been blessed by the Hand of God.'

And then her husband told her why the Secretary, Ajwani, and the strange man were standing by the black Cross, and why the Battleship was attempting to block the entrance.

Rum-pum-pum. Ramu, catching the excitement, walked round his parents. Rum-pum-pum-pum-pum-pum-pum.

Mr Puri watched his wife. 'Well? What do you think?'

'If this is really true,' she said, 'it will be the first miracle of my life.'

For the past three decades, the residents of Vishram Society 3A (Murthy) and 2A (Pinto) had been four people with one set of sleeping habits. If one couple went to bed early the other couple turned off their television and went to bed. If one couple chose to sing along to Lata Mangeshkar late into the night the other couple also sang along to Lata Mangeshkar late into the night.

Tonight Mr Pinto was enjoying a bout of insomnia. He stared at his ceiling. For thirty years that ceiling – with the chandelier hanging from the centre like a glowing fountain of intelligence – had been an image of his neighbour and friend's mind.

'Why is he walking about so much, Shelley? It's past ten o'clock.'

Mrs Pinto lay next to him. Because of her near blindness, she did not accompany her husband and Masterji on their biryani outings.

'Nothing to worry,' she said.

'Are you sure he has diabetes? He hasn't seen a doctor yet.'

Mrs Pinto, who could not see the chandelier, concentrated on the footsteps, which went from one end of the room to the other, then stopped (a moment's pause at the window) before turning around.

'It's not diabetes, Mr Pinto.'

'Then what?'

Mrs Pinto was wiser about men. At her age, the body has become an automatic machine that moves in predictable tics, short repeated motions; but the mind is still capable of all its eccentric leaps. She guessed, from the pattern of the footsteps, the truth about the man up there.

'The evenings, they must be terrible.'

So many months on his own, without a hand to touch in the dark. Mrs Pinto turned around in bed so she wouldn't have to listen.

'He's not the only one moving about,' her husband said. 'Can you hear? Something's happening in the building.'

A glow-in-the-dark portrait of the Lord Balaji at Tirupati, his late wife's favourite deity, hung from a hook on the wall of Masterji's bedroom. A semi-automatic washing machine sat near the god's portrait, while a cotton mattress for visitors, rolled up like a striped pink earthworm, was stacked on a small chair next to the machine. A square window with iron bars looked out on to the black Cross in the garden.

The wall was lined with built-in cupboard doors: but this was false cupboarding, meant to imitate the home of a man with more money – behind the doors were six green metal Godrej *almirahs*, where Purnima had stored everything from her wedding jewellery to the ledgers in which she did the household accounting. Masterji had only been allowed to watch as she went through a thick set of keys, found the right one, opened an *almirah*, and took out what she wanted. He knew that one shelf in an *almirah* was for her saris; one was for saris in which bundles of coins and notes were hidden; one was for saris in which chequebooks were wrapped; one was for documents relating to their children's education; one for their finances. A month after her death, Gaurav had called to ask for her diamond necklace, the one she had bought at the Vummidi store in Chennai; Sonal was eager that her mother-in-law's jewels shouldn't be lost. Masterji said he did not remember any such necklace, but promised to look in the cupboards. His son's coldness, he was sure, had started from this time.

Masterji opened one cupboard, and stared at the Godrej *almirah* inside, on which he saw himself reflected. A narrow full-length mirror had been set into the body of the almirah. Hundreds of red dots (brick red, mud red, and blood red) covered the mirror's upper half; his wife used to stick one of these *bindis* on her forehead each time she left the house. Masterji thought the mirror made him look like a man with diseased skin, or a flowering tree.

In the kitchen the old calendar began to tap against the wall: once again he had the sensation that his wife was right there, chopping onions.

A key had been left in the lock of the *almirah*; he turned it to find the shelves empty, except for one that was paved with newspaper and defended by camphor mothballs, with just an old silk sari lying in it.

Her wedding sari.

He closed his eyes and brought his hands near the gold border of the sari. He breathed in the camphor-tinted air from the shelf. He thought of the time he had not defended her from her brothers in Suratkal. The old calendar began to hit the wall faster, *tap-tap-tap*, and now he was sure that Purnima was speaking to him. *Tap-tap-tap*. She did not want to know about the past. She wanted to know about the girl next door. The journalist.

He breathed in more camphor-tinted air for strength, and confessed. A human being at sixty-one is shining lusts in between old bones, Purnima. The girl next door disturbed him, it was true. He thought his wife would be angry, but she was some place beyond anger now. The calendar tapped again: she was telling him not to agitate himself. She understood now that a man cannot punish himself for his desires, which are sent to him from another world, and she knew he must have felt the same feelings for other women – his colleagues at school, perhaps even some who lived in Vishram Society – but he had repressed those urges and stayed true to her, and this self-control was meritorious, something that helped her on her journey over the oceans. Why, she asked, now that she was dead, did he feel shame at being aroused? Shame and guilt, he replied, with a candour he could never have summoned when Purnima was alive, they had been more than half of a man's life. For his generation, or for his type of man within that generation, this was always the case. True, she said, true, beating her wings and rising over the ocean. She understood that her husband's life had bent to black magnetic poles marked 'Shame' and 'Guilt': yet one of the grey wavelengths in between must be Conscience. That faint line was the one he should find. To guide him through what was coming next.

The vapours of mothballs, old newspaper, and silk sari made him drowsy.

Instead of the image of his wife's soul, Masterji saw himself, with the body of an eagle, flying over an ocean: as if his own death, and subsequent trial, had already begun.

When he heard a loud, steady knocking on the door, his first thought was that it must be a summoner come to take him to his trial.

He opened the door to find Mr Pinto.

'Why didn't you ring?'

'It's not working—' Mr Pinto pressed the bell to prove it.

Now Masterji was conscious of voices in the compound, and feet in the stairwell. From the compound, he could hear the Battleship shouting: 'Illusion! Illusion!'

The two old men went down the stairs, to the noticeboard, where half a dozen people had gathered. Masterji saw Ibrahim Kudwa, his wife Mumtaz, Mrs Saldanha, her daughter Radhika, and Mrs Abichandani from the first floor, along with the Secretary, who was saying, 'How could I tell anyone sooner? I found out only this evening.'

Masterji asked in a soft voice that people move to the side, until he was close enough to read the notice pinned on the central panel.

General Offer of Redevelopment:
To Vishram Societies, A and B.
Proposal Made by Confidence Group
(Headquarters Navnirman Building,
Parel, Mumbai).

Attention: Secretaries, Society A and B,
and all residents

In consideration of the proposed development of a new super-luxury residential project on the current site of the Vishram Societies A and B, the Confidence Group makes an offer to the Vishram Societies (A and B Tower) for the

78

outright purchase of all flats in the said
Societies on the following basis:

It being noted that the two Societies consist
of apartments, both one-bedroom and two-
bedroom, ranging in size from 450 square feet
to 950 square feet, and of an average size of
790 square feet; also that the prevailing rate
in Vakola is of the range of Rs 8,000 to 12,000
a square foot, which may even be lower in the
case of a building of the age and condition of
Vishram Society, a generous offer is made to
all owners at the uniform rate of Rs 19,000 a
square foot.

For instance, an owner of a flat of size 800
square foot will receive a payment of 1.52
crore (1,52,00,000) rupees before tax. This is
opposed to a market-rate of likely 60 to 70
lakhs (60,00,000 to 70,00,000) maximum, and
that too only after the residents have paid for
the repair, repainting, etc of flat and Society.
Numerous other financial and tax advantages to
the offer will be stated by the Managing
Director of Confidence Group, Mr Dharmen Shah,
when he comes in person to your Society to
address the residents.

If the residents accept this generous offer,
the said sum is payable in three instalments.
One instalment upon your signing the agreement,
one upon the vacating of the building, and one
payable within three months into the nominated
bank account. In addition, eight weeks' rent,
calculated on the basis of average rental rates
in the Vakola area for a decent-quality two-
bedroom flat, will be paid to each family, so
they can stay nearby while they search for a
new home. All payments will be made by cheque.
Nominated Accounts may be in any nationalized
bank (likes of Corporation Bank, Punjab
National Bank etc.) or recognized and reputable

private bank (likes of HSBC, HDFC, Karur Vysya, etc.). Please check with Builder for list of acceptable banks.

About the Confidence Group: Our motto is: 'From my family to yours.' Founded in 1978, we are one of Mumbai's leading developers, with new projects also under development in Thane and Pune. MD of the Confidence Group, Mr Shah, is the recipient of numerous gold medals and paper-based awards for excellence. He has been cited by the Rotary Club for his charitable contributions and philanthropic vision of humanity. A family man at heart, he avoids the high society and glamorous life and concentrates on the quality of his work and accomplishments. He is also passionate about chess and carom. You may visit his numerous projects and accomplishments via the prospectus of Confidence Group, which has been left with the Secretaries of the Societies.

Important: The last date for the acceptance of the offer is the day after Gandhi Jayanti: 3 October. (Non-negotiable.) The offer will not be extended one minute beyond this date.

BOOK TWO

Mr Shah Explains His Proposal

Yawning as he emerged from the car park of the Mirchandani Manor, Shanmugham walked out of the gate – the security guard, unsure whether this was a servant or friend of Mr Shah, stood up without saluting – and went down wide stone steps, passing old men doing stretching exercises, until he stood on fresh, clean sand.

Versova beach. He took a deep breath of early-morning ocean breeze. A few fishing boats were out on the ocean; he turned to the north to see the coconut palms in faraway Madh Island. Stretching his neck and raising his arms over his head he turned to the other side of the beach: and flinched.

He had forgotten about Versova in the mornings.

Here, in this beach in this posh northern suburb of Mumbai, half the sand was reserved for the rich, who defecated in their towers, the other half for slum dwellers, who did so near the waves. Residents of the slum that had encroached upon the beach were squatting by the water, defecating.

An invisible line went down the middle of the beach like an electrified fence; beyond this line, the bankers, models, and film producers of Versova were engaged in tai-chi, yoga, or spot-jogging. Behind the exercising crowd, a woman in a billowing red dress posed against rocks as a photographer snapped. Large silver-foiled boards held up around the model reflected light on to her body; and she forced her rouged face into another smile for the cameras. Homeless men stood in a semi-circle round the photo-shoot, from where they passed loud and accurate judgement on the model's physique and posing skills.

Looking at the long waxed limbs that showed through the flutter of red cloth, Shanmugham sat, precariously, on two rocks.

He turned around to look at the Mirchandani Manor, which stood on a rocky embankment behind him: sleek, beige-coloured, with a pointed gable. The curtain was still drawn at the seventh-floor window. He had received a text message from the boss at 6.30 a.m.: he assumed that they would be leaving for Vishram by nine.

Good.

Mr Shah should have been there when the offer was made yesterday, shown his teeth, gained their trust, seduced them with smiles and handshakes, done the politician's number with their babies, and left with a bow and a quotation from a holy book. That was how it had always been done until now. Delay, and lawyers and NGOs smell you out; the vultures swoop lower.

But look at the boss, locked up here in Versova, his other home, all of last evening and night. Just because that astrologer in Matunga had told him that yesterday evening, while *auspicious* for the offer to be presented, was *inauspicious* for a personal visit. The boss was growing more and more superstitious: no question of that. A year or two ago he would have insisted that the stars give him better times. Or perhaps it was not those stars, but the fading one on the seventh floor of the Mirchandani Manor that was keeping Mr Shah here – the Versova property inside the Versova property. Shanmugham, a married man, smirked.

Ah, Versova. The ultimate 'number two' suburb of the city. Succeed in Bollywood, and you are probably living in Juhu or in Bandra: fail, and you leave; but if you have neither succeeded nor failed, just survived in that grey, ambiguous, 'number two' way, you end up here.

Mr Shah was human. He had his physical needs. That Shanmugham understood.

He just wished the boss would not keep him in the dark about his astrological appointments – he had no idea if the astrologer had nominated morning, or evening, or night, as the time for them to go to Vishram. Until the time came, he was expected to stay close to the Manor.

One of the silver foils reflecting sunlight on the model had been sponsored by a bank; on the back, bold red lettering announced:

8.75% COMPOUNDED CANARA CO-OPERATIVE BANK
365 DAYS FIXED DEPOSIT
NO PENALTY WITHDRAWAL
APPLY NOW!

Shanmugham went closer, was shooed away by the model's minders, smiled, and hurried back to the rocks.

On his way up in life, he had discovered petty finance like other men discover cocaine. He subscribed to the *Economic Times*; watched CNBC TV; and played with stocks. But he was a married man, with children, and the bulk of his money was locked away in the safety of a bank deposit. 2.8 lakh rupees, in the Rajamani Co-operative Bank, at 8.65 per cent for 400 days. He had been proud of that rate – he had forced his manager to add 0.15 per cent on top of the bank's normal lending rate.

A helicopter striped the beach with its noisy shadow. Shanmugham, on his knees, did mathematics on hot sand (8.65 per cent as against 8.75 per cent; 400 days as against 365), while the waves creamed on the shore like the extra compound interest he could be making on his principal at the Canara Co-operative Bank.

The ocean breaking below your window; a lizard on the ceiling staring at you with fat envious eyes; and in the next room, a woman, twenty-six years younger, brushing her freshly washed hair and sending waves of strawberry and aloe towards your nostrils.

Dharmen Shah yawned. He saw no reason to get out of his bed.

'Woke up?' Rosie called from her room. 'Come and see what I've bought for you, Uncle. A surprise.'

'Let me sleep, Rosie.'

'Come.'

She took him by the hand and led him into the living room; there it lay propped against the sofa; a framed three-part poster that showed the Eiffel Tower being erected in stages.

'For you, Mr Builder. To put up in your office.'

'Very sweet of you, Rosie,' Shah said, and put his hand on his heart. He was truly touched, even though the money was his.

'Eiffel,' he said, seated at the laminated dining table outside the kitchen, 'was the same fellow who built the Statue of Liberty. What would we do with him in India? Ask: *what is your caste, what is your family, what is your background? Sorry, go away.*'

The fat man stretched his hands and flexed his toes. Rosie turned from the kitchen to see him yawning indulgently.

'Rosie,' he said. 'Did I ever tell you that I was my father's first wife's son?'

'No, Uncle. You never tell me about yourself.'

'They pulled my mother out of a well one day. That is the very first memory I have.'

She came out of the kitchen and wiped her hands.

'I was four years old. She jumped into the well in our house in Krishnapur.'

'Why did she do it?'

He shrugged.

'A year later I had a stepmother. She had four sons. They got all my father's love. He would not even look at me with kindness. The worst part was this: he made *me* feel ashamed, Rosie. It was as if my mother's suicide were *my* fault. He would glare at me if anyone ever mentioned it.'

'And then?'

Then came the day he went to his father's grocery store and asked: 'May I have a bicycle, Father? It's my sixteenth birthday', to be told, 'No', even though a younger half-brother had received one. Understanding then that being second-best was what was expected of the sons of a first wife, he left home the next morning with twelve rupees and eighty paise that he had saved up. He walked, took the bus, took the train, ran out of money and walked again, till the sandals had fallen off his feet and he had to tie plantain leaves around them. Reached Bombay. He had never once returned to Krishnapur.

'Not once?'

'Why go back? In the village, a man lives as a social animal, Rosie: pleasing his father, grandfather, brothers, cousins. His caste. His community. A man is free here. In the city.'

Rosie waited for more, but he had gone silent; she got up from the table.

'I'll bring you the toast in a second, Uncle.'

'Butter. Lots of it.'

'Don't I know? That's the only thing on earth you love: fresh butter.'

In a little while he was licking butter off triangular pieces of toast at the table. Wiping her hands down the sides of her blue jeans, she watched from the kitchen.

'Did something happen today, Uncle? You're very talkative.'

'Satish is in trouble. The second time this year.'

'What kind of trouble, Uncle?'

'Go get me more toast.'

Rosie returned with fresh bread, which she flicked with the back of her fingers on to his plate.

'The Shanghai, Rosie. Did I tell you that's the name of my new project?'

'What happened to Satish, Uncle?'

'I want to forget about him. I want to talk about my Shanghai.'

'Bo-ring, Uncle. You know I don't like construction talk. Some marmalade?'

'Every man wants to be remembered, Rosie. I'm no different. Once you fall ill, you think about these things. I began as a contractor, then did slum redevelopments because the big developers did not want to get their hands dirty. If I had to kiss this politician's arse, I did it; if I had to give that one bags of money for his elections, so be it. I climbed. Like a lizard I went up walls that were not mine to go up. I bought a home in Malabar Hill. I taught myself to build in style, Rosie. The Art Deco style of Marine Lines. The Gothic style of VT station. And I will put all the styles into this new one: the Shanghai. When it is done, when they see it, shining and modern, people will understand my life's story.'

When he got to the city, knowing no one here, he had stood in line outside a Jain temple in Kalbadevi and been fed there twice a day; a store owner pitied his feet and threw him his own chappals; he began working as a delivery boy for that store owner, and within a year he was managing a store himself.

In a socialist economy, the small businessman has to be a thief to prosper. Before he was twenty he was smuggling goods from Dubai and Pakistan. Yes, what guilt did he have about dealing with the enemy, when he was treated as a bastard in his own country? The pirateering felt natural; on the back of trucks marked as 'emergency wheat supplies', he shipped in cartons of foreign-made watches and alarm clocks into Gujarat and Bombay. But then the Constitution of India was suspended; the Emergency was imposed – the police given orders to arrest all blackmarketeers, smugglers, and tax-dodgers. Even if you hated that period, you had to admire the guts: the only time when anyone showed any will power in this country. He had to get rid of his black money – *Man has risen from the earth,* he thought, *he may as well put his money back into the earth.* A construction company was formed – with an English name, of course: it was part of the new world of talent-and-nothing-else. Smuggling was for small men, he found out; the real money in this world lies on the legitimate side of things. Starting out as a contractor for another builder on Mira Road, he soon realized that much as he loved cement and steel, he loved people more. The human being was his clay to squeeze. Poorer human beings, to begin with. He entered the business of 'redeveloping' chawls and slums – buying out the tenants of ageing structures so that skyscrapers and shopping malls could take their place; a task requiring brutality and charm in equal measure, and which proved too subtle for most builders – but one he negotiated with skills from his smuggler years, allying himself with politicians, policemen, and thugs to bribe and bounce people out of their homes. With an instinct for fairness that taught him to prefer (unlike many others in his profession) the use of generosity over violence, he earned a reputation as a man who made other men rich, always preferring to entice a recalcitrant tenant out of a building with a cheque rather than with a knife, and waiting until there was no other option but to order Shanmugham (as he had done in his most recent redevelopment project, in Sion) to go all the way: to shove a man's head out of a window and indicate that the rest of him would follow in three seconds – unless a signature appeared on the appropriate document. (It did.)

Rosie fed more bread into the toaster. Shah heard the click of the toaster and thought of her with gratitude, bringer of toast and floral perfume into his life, this chubby girl from the provinces – *All the way from Ranchi, would you believe it?* He licked his fingers and waited for more bread. How little it takes to be happy in life: soft white beds, buttered toast, and plump young girls, three pleasures that are essentially interchangeable.

In the shower the hot water flowed through gilded fittings; he stood on green onyx and felt the warmth on his scalp.

His wife had died five years ago. After a year in which he kept to himself, he had started taking women to hotel rooms. Then he built his own hotel here, in the seventh floor of this Versova building. Down pillows and cushions, pure white bedsheets of 2.8 micron pore size to repel allergens. Lights that turn themselves on as you clap your hands: so you don't even have to move from bed. The flat in Malabar Hill was messier, subject to Giri's crankiness; and it was home, things broke. This place with the sea view had palace-of-sin plushness.

'How is your spit today, Uncle?' – Rosie shouted at the bathroom. It was a role every mistress sooner or later took to playing, that of surrogate mother.

'Clear, Rosie.'

He coughed and spat, then dipped his finger in the spit and inspected it. Last December it had been much darker, and sometimes flecked with red.

'Don't lie to me, Uncle. I can hear the cough. Like the thunder they use in films.'

'If I had designed the human body, I'd have done a much better job, Rosie. The materials used are not the best. Corners have been cut. The structure collapses too soon.' He laughed. 'But I'm fine, Rosie. By the grace of Lord SiddhiVinayak I'm fine.'

By the grace of the Lord. Rosie knew exactly what that meant.

By my own grace. Just like a film producer who says, once you've sucked his cock, 'By the grace of God, you'll get a small role in this film.'

She sighed, and cleared the greasy plates from the table.

Six months earlier: Shah had been waiting in a restaurant for an order of chow mein that his mistress of the time, Nannu, had wanted him to bring her, personally; she was in one of her hysterical moods. The pretty girl in the tank-top had smiled at him, walked up to him without an invitation, and stuck out her hand: 'My name is Rosie. Yours?' He had known, at once, what was on offer. This was Versova, after all. 'Thank you,' he had smiled and left. Nannu was lighter-skinned.

Next morning – one of those small things that add up to make life grand – opening the newspaper, he saw this in a side-column: 'Aspiring model arrested in Oshiwara gym. Accused of stealing from women's locker.' He read the name of the girl: 'Rosie.' A challenge thrown down to his will power. He had cancelled the morning's meetings, driven down to the Oshiwara gym; settled in cash with the gym owner; gone to the police station, freed her, and looking at her, her shoulders, hair, still, after a day in the lock-up, in good shape, had decided, 'She'll do.' Nannu was given three days to clear out of this flat; after which he moved Rosie in here, telling her she could continue to do what she came to Bombay for: try and make it in the movies. No need for petty hustling as long as she lived with him; just one great hustle and humiliation to accept. One or two mornings a week she went to see a producer about an itty-bitty role in a new production; sometimes had her hopes of success renewed, at other times worried about ageing, felt she would never make it, and asked for 'help' in setting up a hair-dressing studio of her own, which Shah promised she would receive. At the end of their relationship. But until then, if she made eyes at anyone else, she would fly head-first into the Indian Ocean.

When he came out of the shower, she was singing songs in a foreign language.

'Opera,' she shouted in response to his question. There was a new craze for Italian opera in Bollywood, and she was trying out bits of songs. They were called 'aria'.

'Ariya,' he said, rubbing his hair with a soft white towel. 'Is that how it's said?'

'Aaa-ria, Uncle. Don't pronounce things like a Gujarati village goat.'

'Ha, ha. But I *am* a Gujarati village goat, Rosie.'

Another of her moods; and he enjoyed all of them. 'Get a room with a sea view. One wall is always new,' they said in real estate. Get a woman who changes and you have a dozen women. He relished the smell of Pears' Soap on his skin; he wanted her in his arms.

'Why don't you introduce me to Satish, Uncle? I'm in his age group, I can talk to him if he's in trouble,' she asked, when he emerged, still rubbing his hair.

'I'll bring you a model of the Shanghai, Rosie. It's so beautiful, you should see it. Gothic, Italian, Indian, Art Deco styles, all in one. My whole life story is in it.'

'Why don't you introduce me to Satish, Uncle?'

He bent down and rubbed more vigorously, so the moisture from his hair irritated her face.

'I'm not your prostitute! I'm not your property! I don't give a shit about your fucking money!'

With his head bent to the floor, covered in his towel, he heard feet thump on the floor, and a door going *Slam!* He rubbed his hair and asked the floor (dark green tiles with embedded white flakes, a favourite pattern, used in all his buildings): why, when she is worried about your interest in her, will a woman do the very things that will cause your interest to drop further?

Sitting on his chair, watching his ocean, swaying from his hip, Shah hummed his favourite Kishore Kumar song. *Aa chal ke tujhe, mein...* Leaning back from the chair, he pressed down on the bed with a finger, feeling the 2.8 micron pore width bedding on the premium spring mattress: he lifted the finger with a pinprick of recharging will power.

The path to a new building in Mumbai sparkled with small stones – police, litigation, greed – and he would need every ounce of his body fat to crush those stones, one by one. Before every new project, like a religious ritual, he had to come here, to this flat, to whichever girl he was with at that moment, Nannu or Smita or Rosie, to inhale her perfume, eat toast, watch the ocean, touch the golden fittings in the toilet. In the presence of luxury his capacity for violence was always heightened.

He knocked on her door: 'I'll count to five, Rosie.'

'No. I'll never come out. You never take me to your home. Never—'

'One,' he counted. 'Two. Three. Four.'

A woman's face peeped from behind the opened door.

An hour later, Mr Shah washed his face, hands, and chest in her bathroom. From the window he spotted a man in white shirt and black trousers down by the beach, sitting on rocks and doodling on the sand as he waited for his master's phone call.

No assistant had done the job as long as this one had without giving in to fear or greed. But this Shanmugham was special. A thorough-bred Doberman.

He called Giri on his mobile phone.

'I'm going to SiddhiVinayak temple at five o'clock and then to my Society in Vakola. Tell the boy to be at the temple. On time.'

Rosie lay on her right side, her face hidden in her arms. He lay down beside her, and clapped, turning the light in her room on. He clapped again – it went off – and again – until Rosie slapped his shoulder and said, 'Stop acting like a child.'

Shanmugham, still sitting on the rock, had picked up a stone and was pounding it into the hot sand, again and again.

He had been tricked. *Tricked.*

By his own bank manager.

He remembered that greasy old white-haired man's exact words – since he was such a valued customer, he would be getting a 'little extra' on top of the scheduled interest rates ('the best rate legally obtainable in this city, I promise you'); and now he had discovered that a beach umbrella was advertising a higher interest rate!

Throwing the stone away, Shanmugham got up from the rock, and brushed the sand off his trousers.

After lunch at a Punjabi dhaba where he had to wash his hands with water from a plastic jug, he watched young women run on treadmills inside a gym called 'Barbarian', drank a fresh coconut by the side of a road at two o'clock and ate pistachio ice cream from a porcelain plate at a restaurant at three.

He divided the slab of ice cream into sixteen parts, and ate one part at a time, to prolong his stay at the restaurant. By the fourteenth piece of ice cream, he was certain that the middle-aged man in shorts was that actor who used to be famous ten years ago. Amrish Puri.

Not Amrish. He punished a piece of ice cream by squashing it with his spoon. Om Puri.

Chewing the fifteenth piece, he thought: *I am eating ice cream at a restaurant where a film actor strolls in for the same thing.*

He would never have dreamed such a thing possible till that day, six years ago, when in his dingy real-estate office in Chembur he heard that a builder was looking for a labour contractor. They had met in a nearby south Indian restaurant. Mr Shah had been pouring tea into his saucer.

'A simple question.' The fat man had shown him two gold-ringed fingers. 'Two rooms. One is four by five, one is ten by two. Both are twenty square feet. Correct?'

'Yes, sir,' Shanmugham said.

'So they both cost the same to build. Correct?'

'No, sir.'

'Explain.' Shah slurped tea from the saucer.

'The ten-by-two room is thirty-three per cent more expensive, sir. Four plus five is nine, nine nine is eighteen feet of wall to build. Ten plus two twelve, twelve twelve is twenty-four feet of walls to build. You don't build floors, you build walls.'

'You're the first man today who has got the answer right. I've fired my labour contractor. Do you know how to get me workers for a job?'

'No, but by the evening I will,' Shanmugham had said.

Six months later, Shah had told him at a construction site: 'The other day you broke up a fight between the workers. I was watching. You know how to hit a man.'

'I am sorry, sir,' Shanmugham looked at the ground. 'I won't do it again.'

'*Don't* say sorry,' Shah had said. 'This is not politics we are in: this is construction. We have to speak the truth in this business, or nothing will ever get built. Do you know what a left-hand man is?'

Shanmugham had not known at the time.

'Doesn't matter. You're a quick learner,' Shah had said. 'You can be my new left-hand man from Monday. But today, I must fire you from my company, and you must tear up all your business cards. If we ever get involved with the police, I have to say that I dismissed you.'

Pushing aside his ice cream, Shanmugham took a small black book out of his pocket, and found a clean white page. Drawing a box with seven columns and twenty rows, he made a small calendar: the last date was October 3. Next to it he wrote: 'Shanghai.'

He turned the pages. The first few pages of the book were covered with Mr Shah's wise sayings, which he had been recording for months.

When it comes to work – hurry, hurry, hurry. When it comes to payment – delay, delay, delay.

Caste, religion, family background nothing. Talent everything.

Be 10 per cent more generous to people than you feel like being.

He clicked a black ballpoint pen and added one of his own:

Do not trust connections made with bank...

When the sixteenth piece of ice cream melted, he paid his bill and left with a last glance at the actor.

He stopped in the shade of a small park.

A stray black dog loped by the park, a bright red patch of flesh shining near its left buttock. Shanmugham thought of a bank manager with grey oiled hair. Of 'a little extra'. With an eye closed, he aimed a sharp rock at the open wound.

His mobile phone began to beep.

At four o'clock, Mrs Pinto's left arm reached for solid wall. Her *chappal* found the first step.

When her eyesight had begun to dim, over a decade ago, Mrs Pinto had kept a strict count of the steps (even retracing her path when she lost the count), but that was no longer necessary.

The walls had sprouted eyes for her.

She knew she had taken three steps down when she reached 'the Diamond': a rhomboidal crevice in the fourth step. Seven steps and two landings later came 'the Bad Tooth'. Sliding along the wall her palm encountered a molar-shaped patch in the plaster, which felt like the back of her teeth when they had cavities in them. This meant she had almost reached the second floor. She angled her body again.

She sensed radiance: the evening sun blazing into the entranceway.

'Is anybody there?' she called. 'Be careful when you run; Shelley Pinto is coming down, step by step she is coming down.'

Just five steps to go now to the ground floor: she heard her husband's weak voice from the plastic-chair parliament.

'... if one person says no, you can't tear down the Society. That's the whole idea of a Co-operative Housing Society. One for all, all for one.'

I wish he had said something smarter than that, she thought.

Last night, the moment he had come up the stairs with Masterji and told her of the thing posted on the noticeboard, she had wanted to cry. Their plans for the rest of their lives were set into Vishram Society. What did they need money for? A fixed deposit in the HDFC bank's Versova branch paid them Rs 4,000 a month, taking care of all expenses; both children were settled in America – a good, Christian country – one in Michigan, the other in Buffalo. The children were far away, but they had Vishram all around them, warm, human, familiar; it was the protective keratin they had secreted from the hardships of their lives. It guided Shelley down its stairs and around its fragrant garden. How would she find her way in a strange new building? Mr Pinto and his wife had sat on the sofa, hand in hand, feeling more in love than they had in years. And when Masterji said, 'If it's no from you, it's no from me', Shelley Pinto had begun to cry. A husband by her side, and a wise man for a friend.

All day long, whether eating breakfast with Masterji or lying in bed, she had heard the buzz of discussion around Vishram. What if the others overpowered them and carried her off to a building with strange walls and neither 'the Diamond' nor 'the Bad Tooth' nor her million other eyes? Her heart beat faster. She forgot how many steps lay before her and the ground floor.

The powerful voice of Mrs Rego revived her.

'It's an illusion, Mr Pinto. I know about these builders. They won't ever pay up.'

We have the Battleship on our side, Mrs Pinto thought. *How can we lose?*

'We knew all these years you were strange, Mrs Rego, but we did not realize you were actually mad,' Mrs Puri fired back at the Battleship.

Now Mrs Pinto's heart sank. Mrs Puri is on *their* side. How can we win?

'This is a democracy, Mrs Puri. No one will silence me. Not you, not all the builders of the world.'

'I'm just saying, Mrs Rego, even a Communist must understand that when someone comes and offers us Rs 20,000 a square foot we should say yes. Once you think of all the repairs we need to make to the building, to each individual flat, before it can be sold – new paint, new doors – it is closer to 250 per cent of market value. And think of the time it takes to find a buyer in a neighbourhood like this. Mr Costello waited six months, gave up, and went to Qatar. This is cash in hand.'

'But will this Mr Shah actually pay?' Ibrahim Kudwa's voice.

Good. Ibrahim Kudwa, the cyber-café owner, was the average man in the building. If he was sceptical, everyone was sceptical.

'Look,' Mr Pinto said, when his wife came out into parliament, groping for a chair. The main item of evidence.

'How will she survive in another Society?'

Aware that people were looking at her, Mrs Pinto held her smile for all to see.

'Just wait until this man comes here and speaks to us,' Mrs Puri said. 'Is that too much to ask of all of you?'

Ibrahim Kudwa came up to Mrs Pinto and whispered: 'I wanted to tell you about the sign that I changed outside the Society. They've filled up the hole now, but there was a sign there. It said: "Work in progress, inconvenience regretted", but I changed it to "Inconvenience in progress, work regretted".'

'That's very clever, Ibrahim,' she whispered back. 'Very clever.'

She could almost hear the blood rushing proudly to his cheeks. Ibrahim Kudwa reminded her of Sylvester, a pet dog that she had once had. Always needed an 'attaboy', and a pat on the head.

'Now all of you must excuse us. Shelley and I are going for our walk.'

Masterji, who had been sitting in the 'prime' chair, pretending not to watch Mrs Saldanha's kitchen TV, got up in stages. He followed Mr and Mrs Pinto to the compound wall.

Behind him, he could hear the indiscreet Ibrahim Kudwa whispering: 'What's *his* position?'

Masterji slowed to hear the faithful Mrs Puri's reply: 'The moment his friends said, we don't want the money, he said, me too.'

Even though he had opposed the offer, she was proud of him, and wanted everyone to know this.

'He is an English gentleman. Only when the Pintos change their answer will he change his.'

Suppressing his smile, Masterji caught up with the Pintos. Shelley had her hand on her husband; he could hear her count her steps. When she counted 'twenty' she had passed the danger-zone: where the boys played their cricket game, and their smacked balls could hit her cheeks or stomach. Now she would smell hibiscus plants for twenty steps.

Mary, having done with her evening cleaning of the Society's common areas, was beginning to water the plants in the garden. Picking up the green pipe that lay in coils in the garden all the day long like a hibernating snake, she fitted it to a tap near the compound wall; sluicing the water flow with a pressed thumb, she began slapping the hibiscus plants awake. One-two-three-four-five, holding the pipe in her right hand, Mary counted off the seconds of irrigation for each plant on the joints of her left hand, like a meditating brahmin. Small rainbows sprang to life within the arch of the sluiced water, disappeared when the water moved away, then reappeared on the dripping spider's webs that interlinked the branches.

Mrs Pinto left the smell of hibiscus behind. Now came 'the blood stretch' – the ten yards where the stench of raw beef from the butcher's shop behind the Society wafted in, mitigated somewhat by the flourish of jasmine flowers growing near the wall.

'It's your phone, Masterji.' Mrs Pinto turned around.

She could pinpoint the exact cubicle within the building that a noise came from.

'It must be Gaurav again. The moment he smells money on me, my son calls.'

Gaurav had called earlier in the morning. The first call he had made to his father in months. He explained that 'Sangeeta Aunty' had told him about the builder's offer.

'I wish Mrs Puri had not phoned him.'

'Oh, she is like a second mother to the boy, Masterji. Let her call.'

Masterji winced; yet he could not deny the fact.

Everyone in Vishram knew of Mrs Puri's closeness to the boy; it was one of the triumphs of their communal life – one of the cross-beams of affection that are meant to grow in any co-operative society. Even after Gaurav moved to Marine Lines for his work, Mrs Puri stayed in touch with him, sending him regular packages of peanut-*chikki* and other sweets. It was she who had called to tell him of his mother's death.

Masterji said: 'I told Gaurav, you are my son, this is your home, you can come see me whenever you want. But there is nothing to *discuss*. The Pintos have said no.'

And then, looking at Mrs Pinto through the corner of his eye, he waited in the hope that she too would call him an 'English gentleman'.

Mr Pinto completed the circuit of the compound wall, and scraped his chappals on the gravel around the guard's booth. He waited for his wife and Masterji with his thin hands on his hips, panting like the winner in a geriatric sprint.

'Let's do breathing exercises together,' he said, and gave Shelley his arm. 'It makes you feel young again.'

As the three of them practised inhaling-exhaling-inhaling, the Secretary walked past with a large microphone, which he planted near the black Cross.

At five o'clock, 'Soda Pop' Satish Shah, recently the terrorizer of parked cars on Malabar Hill, stood by the entrance of the most famous Hindu shrine in the city, the SiddhiVinayak temple at Prabhadevi, waiting for his father.

With the latest issue of *Muscle-Builder* magazine in his right hand, he was practising behind-the-head tricep curls with his left.

He paused, turned the page of the magazine, and practised more repetitions with his left hand.

With his right hand he touched his nose. It still hurt.

It had not been *his* idea to spray-paint the cars. He had told the other fellows: the police would never allow it in the city. Let's go to the suburbs, Juhu, Bandra. A man could live like a king out there. But did they listen?

In any case, what *had* they done? Just spray a few cars and a van. It was nothing compared to what his father did in *his* line of work.

The bastard works in construction, Satish thought, *and he has the guts to tell me I am the bad one in the family*.

Thinking about his father, he goaded himself into practising his tricep curls faster. He thought about the way that man chewed *gutka* like a villager. The way he wore so many gold rings. The way he pronounced English, no better than Giri did. 'Cho-chyal Enimalz. Cho-chyal.'

Satish felt someone seize him by the arm.

'This is not a thing to be doing here. You should be praying to God and remembering your mother.'

Shah straightened out his son's arm, and pushed him into the temple. Shanmugham followed.

The temple was crowded, as it is at any hour of the day, yet the Lord Ganesha was receptive to free-market logic, and an 'express' line, for anyone who could pay fifty rupees a head, sped the three of them into the sanctum.

'You'll be seventeen in a few days. Do you know what I was doing when I was your age? Have you thought about those people whose cars you damaged? You will never again hang out with that gang. Understand?'

'Yes, Father.'

In his fat fingers his father held a cheque. Satish, by craning his neck as he moved in the queue behind his father, could see that it was a donation of one lakh and one rupees, drawn on the Industrial Development Bank of India. A petition to God to improve his moral character? No, probably for a new building his father was starting today. A Confidence Group project could only begin after two divine interventions: a call from a Tamil astrologer in Matunga with a precise time to lay the foundation stone, and a visit here, to the shrine of Ganesha, whose image was the official emblem of the Confidence Group, embossed on to every formal communication and every building.

They were in sight of the sanctum. Within gilded columns, the red image of the deity was surrounded by four Brahmins, bare-chested, with enormous light-skinned pot bellies filmed over with downy hair: a purdah of human fat around His image. This was the final challenge to the devotees – only a faith that was 100 per cent pure would penetrate through *this* to reach the Lord.

Satish saw his father joining his palms over his head. Behind Mr Shah, Shanmugham did the same. 'How cute: he thinks my father is God.' The chanting of the devotees grew louder – they were right in front of the sanctum now – and Shah turned and glared at his son: 'Pray.'

Satish closed his eyes, bowed his head, and tried to think of something he really wanted.

'Please Lord Ganesha,' he prayed, 'make my father's new project fail and I'll write you a much bigger cheque when I have money.'

At six twenty, with the builder expected at any moment, the compound of Vishram Society glowed with rows of white chairs facing the black Cross.

The event had raised the metabolism of the old Society. The lamps over the entranceway had been turned so they would shine on the plastic chairs. The microphone near the black Cross, borrowed from Gold Coin Society, had been attached to a speaker, borrowed from Hibiscus Society. The members of both Vishram Societies were filling the seats. Secretary Kothari stood by the Cross along with Mr Ravi, the Secretary of Tower B.

Looking down from his window, Masterji saw Mr Pinto sitting in the middle of the array of chairs, his hand on the vacant white seat next to him, looking up.

Masterji raised his right hand – *coming, coming*.

The phone rang again. It was Gaurav, for the second time in an hour.

'No, the real-estate developer hasn't come. Of course I'm going down to listen to him. Yes, I'll keep an open mind. Now: goodbye, and tell Ronak his grandfather will take him to the aquarium one of these days.'

Back at the window, Masterji saw the person he had been waiting for. He had guessed that a journalist wouldn't miss an event like this. She moved through the crowd, taking care not to tread on the feet of older and slower people.

He waited with his ear to the door: listening for footsteps on the stairs. He *had* to do this: *had* to apologize to the girl. What did his neighbours call him? English gentleman.

'Ms Meenakshi,' he said, opening the door. 'Would you wait a minute? Just a minute?'

His neighbour, who had already put her key into the door of 3B, did not stop.

'I'm sorry for the other night. I shouldn't have pushed your friend. The young man. Please tell him I'm sorry.'

Her face partly hidden behind her door, the girl looked at him.

'*Why* did you do it? He wasn't harming you.'

'Would you come into my room for a minute, Ms Meenakshi? It'll be easier for you to understand in here. I was a teacher at St Catherine's School for thirty-four years. My students have good jobs throughout the city. You may have heard of Noronha, the writer for the *Times*. You have nothing to fear.'

*

101

He showed her the glass cabinet, filled with the little silver trophies and citations in golden letters that testified to his three decades of service; the photograph of his farewell party at St Catherine's, signed by two dozen old boys; and the small framed photo, next to it, of a pale, oval-faced woman in a blue sari.

'My late wife.'

The girl moved towards the photograph. She wore braces, and her dark steel-rimmed glasses echoed the metal on her teeth. The frames were hexagonal. Masterji counted the number of edges a second time. An ungainly shape: why had it ever come into fashion?

Reading the date below the photograph, she said,

'I'm sorry.'

'It's been almost a year now. I'm used to it. She would have liked you, Ms Meenakshi. My daughter would have been your age. Your name *is* Meenakshi, isn't it?'

She nodded.

'Where is your daughter these days? In Mumbai?' she asked.

'She died many years before her mother did.'

'I keep saying the wrong thing.'

'Don't worry, Ms Meenakshi. If you don't ask about people, you don't find out about people. Here,' Masterji said, 'this is her drawing book. I just found it yesterday inside my cupboard.'

He wiped the dust off the book – 'SANDHYA MURTHY SKETCH & PRACTICE JOURNAL' – and turned the pages for her.

'That's our local church. Isn't it?'

'Yes. St Antony's. And this drawing is of the Dhobi-ghat, see the people washing. No, not the famous one in Mahalakshmi. The one right here. And *this* is a lovely drawing. This parrot. The best my daughter ever did. She was nineteen years old. Only nineteen.'

He could see from Ms Meenakshi's eyes that she wanted to know how the artist's life had ended. He closed the album.

'I don't wish to bore you, Ms Meenakshi. I wanted to apologize, that was all. When men grow old, contrary to what you may have heard, they do not become wiser. Are you going down to see Mr Shah?'

Her eyebrows arched.

'Aren't *you*? He's giving you all this money.'

'He *says* he's giving us all this money. You must know about developers. You're a journalist, aren't you?'

'No. Public Relations.'

'What does that mean, exactly? All the young people now want to be in Public Relations.'

'I'll come back one day and explain.'

Thanking her for her graciousness in accepting his apology, and inviting her over another day for some ginger tea, he closed the door.

Down below, the hubbub grew. The Secretary's voice boomed over the microphone: 'Can everyone hear me? Testing, testing. Can everyone...'

Masterji sat down. Why *should* he go down? Just because some rich man was coming? He hated these formal gatherings of the Society: every time they held an annual general meeting, the bickering among his neighbours, the petty accusations – 'your son pisses on the compound wall', 'your husband's gargling wakes me up in the morning' – always embarrassed him.

He expected another bloodbath this evening, Mrs Rego and Mrs Puri shouting at each other like women at the fish market.

With his feet on the teakwood table, he turned the pages of Sandhya's album until he reached the parrot. The sketch was incomplete; perhaps she had still been working on it when... He placed his fingers on the edges of the drawing, which felt as if they were still growing. Her living thought.

Where is your daughter these days?

The same place she has been for eleven years.

She had been on her way to college, when someone had pushed her out of the train. A packed compartment in the women's first class in the morning – someone had elbowed her out. She had fallen head first on to the tracks, and lain there like that. Not one of her fellow passengers stopped the train. They didn't want to be late for their work. All of them women, good women. Secretaries. Bank clerks. Sales managers. She had bled to death.

Her brains, oozing from her broken head, because the passengers

103

did not want to be late. Surely in the men's compartment someone would have pulled the emergency chain, jumped out, surely someone would have...

For three months he could not take the train. He used to take one bus after the other, and walk when there was no bus around. His revolt had to end eventually. He was helpless before Necessity. But he could never look again at a women's compartment. *Who said the world would be a better place run by women? At least men were honest about themselves*, he thought.

He turned the page.

She had drawn the hibiscus plants that grew by the back of the compound, and the little spider's webs between their leaves, shiny and oval and gliding over one another like parallel Milky Ways. Father and daughter, in the old days, had often stopped in the garden to look at the webs and talk of the differences between men and spiders. He remembered one difference they had agreed on. A spider's mind is outside him; every new thought shoots off at once in a strand of silk. A man's mind is inside. You never know what he's thinking. Another difference. A spider can live without a family, all alone, in the web he makes.

A smattering of applause from below; the builder must have arrived.

Mr Pinto is holding a chair for me. With Sandhya's sketchbook in his hand, he stood by the window.

A fat man with a gold necklace stood by the black Cross between the two Secretaries.

'... to me you are now members of my own family. I say this, and the proof is in the motto of the Confidence Group: from my family to...'

Poor Mr Pinto had given up his fight to protect the vacant seat. Someone from Tower B had taken it.

Standing at the window, he turned the pages of the sketchbook back and forth. Parrots, churches, washing, trees, Sandhya's school dress, her face, her brushed and shampooed hair, as if they were corpuscles of sunlit water, bobbed up and down around him. Every now and then, in the distracted way that a man busy at the office might overhear the odd snippet of cricket commentary from a colleague's desk, he heard voices from the meeting.

'... I speak for everyone here, Mr Shah, when I ask: are you serious about this offer? Will you honour it in all its details?'

'... it is normal for developers to offer members of the existing Society units in the new building. Why are you not...'

'Why are the residents of Tower B, which is newer and in better condition in every way, not getting a higher rate per square foot than...'

He turned to the last page. Here she had scribbled in pencil: 'Je tien. Vous tenez. Il tient. Vous Tenez. Nous...' Practising the French that he had been teaching her at home, two evenings a week. Masterji scraped on the 'tien' with a finger and looked around for a red pen. He did not want his daughter speaking incorrect French for all of eternity.

A piercing voice – the Battleship's – made him turn to the window:

'We do not want your money, whether it is 200 per cent or 250 per cent. This is our home and no one can ask us to leave it.'

Silence from down below. The Battleship and both her children had risen to their feet.

'By our Lord Jesus Christ I will fight you. I know builders, and they are all liars and criminals. Better you leave now. Right now.'

It was one thing to oppose the deal, but why this personal attack? Did she know this Mr Shah to call him a liar? He closed the window.

He saw the Rubik's Cube lying on the teakwood table. It was stiff with age, and rotating the colours took effort, as if he were working the jaws of a small animal.

Half an hour later, when Mr Pinto walked in through the open door, he found Masterji asleep at the table, his daughter's sketchbook on the floor, its pages fluttering in the breeze from the window.

He shut the door, and went back down to 2A, where his wife lay in bed.

'Asleep, Shelley. In his chair. I fought so hard to keep his seat for him.'

'Mr Pinto. Don't be so petty. When we said no to the offer, he said no at once.'

He grumbled.

'Now go up and wake him. He hasn't had any dinner.'

Mr Pinto looked out of the window. The crowd below had gathered in two nuclei; some residents stood around Mrs Rego ('all builders are liars, and this one is no different') and another group, right below his window, were listening to Ajwani, the broker.

'Our place is 812 square feet. At 20,000 rupees a square foot, that is…'

Ajwani sketched the number of zeros in the air.

'And mine is bigger than yours, Ajwani,' Mrs Puri said. 'Twenty-two square feet bigger. That means I get…'

With a thick finger she superimposed her figure on Ajwani's figure. Now Ibrahim Kudwa added his on top of hers.

'But mine is slightly bigger than yours, Mrs Puri…'

Mr Pinto shook his head.

'Aren't they going to work tomorrow?' he whispered to his wife. 'Don't their children have to go to school? They've forgotten everything because of this money.'

'They're very excited, Mr Pinto. They're going to agree to the proposal and throw us out of the building.'

'What a thing to say, Shelley! This is a Registered Co-operative Society. Not a jungle. If even one person says no that means that the Society cannot be demolished. Let's have dinner now.'

His wife got up from the bed.

'Don't be angry. Please go upstairs and wake Masterji. We should all have some soup and bread.'

'All right,' Mr Pinto said, and put on his shoes.

The black Mercedes had been stuck in traffic near the Vakola highway for half an hour. 'Something's bothering you, Shanmugham.'

He turned from the front seat to face his employer.

'No, Mr Shah.'

'Don't lie. I watched you while I was talking to those people in Vishram. You kept rubbing your hands.'

'Nineteen thousand rupees a square foot, sir. Tower A was built in

1959 or 1960, sir. Ten thousand is a very good rate for a place like that.'

His employer chuckled.

'Shanmugham. Six years you've worked for me and still you are an idiot. I've *underpaid* by a thousand rupees a square foot.'

The traffic jam began to clear; Shah looked at his assistant's eyes in the driver's mirror.

'Those people would be thrilled at an offer of 10,000 a square foot. So 20,000 is unbelievable. Correct? And 19,000 is the same as 20,000 in a man's mind.' He hummed an old Hindi film song.

'Turn left,' Shanmugham told the driver, when they got on to the highway to Bandra. 'Quickly. Turn left. Down the service road, until I tell you to stop.'

'It's still 200 per cent of the market rate, sir. We'll have to sell the Shanghai at 25,000 a square foot – more – to make any profit. This is the east, sir. Who will pay that much money to live here?'

'You can't insult these people, Shanmugham. You can't offer them ten per cent or fifteen per cent above market value. You're asking them to give up their homes, the only homes some of them have ever had. You have to respect human greed.'

The driver now pulled on to the wasteland by the side of the highway.

'The Secretary said he'd join us here, sir. He'll give us a call when he reaches the highway.'

'Let's get out of the car, Shanmugham. I hate sitting still.'

A tall building stood at the end of the wasteland, bearing the letters 'YATT' in white, and a red arc below, like the finishing touch to a signature. Beyond it was the weak glow of Vakola. A few curious faces. Men crossing the wilderness to a row of huts in the distance.

'See where they've set up a few tents—' Shah pointed to a spot near the bushes. 'In five days that will become an entire slum. No property deeds, no titles, legal rights. What a hunger for land.' He rubbed his palms together, scraping his rings against one another. 'I've got it too. Your boss – as you know – is a villager. He has no college degree, Shanmugham: he chews *gutka*, like a villager. But hunger is an excellence. Look' – he pointed to the hotel – 'they've lost the "H". How careless posh people are. If it were my hotel I would have had the manager shot.'

Shah now pointed his finger northward, two or three times, to emphasize some place far, far away in that direction.

'In 1978, when I was still learning this business, a friend, a broker, offered me a whole floor in a new project in Cuffe Parade. Name of Maker Towers. Three fifty rupees a square foot was the rate. It would be a new kind of construction, a small city, built on reclaimed land. I went to see the building and the area. I phoned my friend, and said: "No." Why? That building was coming up where there had been sea just five years ago – and I thought, the land is the land and the water is the water. One day the water will swallow this land back. A square foot in Maker Towers would be worth today, what, 2,000 or 3,000 times my initial investment. That land is now worth more than land in London, more than land in New York. One day, ten years later, I came by Maker Towers, and I saw that building, how solid it looked, how many people had bought flats in it, and I thought: "I was beaten. Someone was dreaming bigger than me." And there and then, I promised Lord SiddhiVinayak: "I am never going to underestimate this city again." Mumbai's future is here in the east, Shanmugham. This is where the space is, and once the new roads and new metro lines come up, the east will grow. We'll get 25,000, maybe 30,000 a square foot for the Shanghai. Even more for the next thing we build. Vishram is an old Society. But it is the most famous building in the area. We'll take it and we'll break it – and everyone will know. Vakola is ours.'

He smiled at his assistant. 'For six years we've been together. You're like a son to me, Shanmugham. A son. Will you do this new job for me?'

For six years, at the start of each new project, Shah had asked him the same question, and for six years Shanmugham had answered this question in the same way. He extended his arm, showing a locked fist to his boss, and then opened it.

'I've got this Society in my palm, sir. I know these people inside out.'

A homeless man, one of those sleeping under the concrete bridge that went over the highway, had been watching the two of them from beneath the protection of a blanket. Seeing the tall one in the white shirt walking towards him, he ducked under it.

Shanmugham signalled to a slow-moving autorickshaw.

A few seconds later, Kothari, the Secretary, came back with him to where the builder waited.

'Sorry. Couldn't bring my scooter. Had to take an auto. And what traffic.'

Shah swept the apology away.

'If I were to leave every time a man got stuck in traffic, I would never meet anyone in this city. You didn't tell anyone you were coming here?'

'I was told not to tell anyone.' The Secretary looked at Shanmugham. 'Even my wife doesn't know. Even *I* don't know why I'm here.'

'Nothing secret going on. My son's birthday is next week, but we're having the celebration tonight. I just wanted you to join me for some food. Some drinks if you like.'

Kothari breathed out. 'Of course. How nice of you. Will we be waiting for Mr Ravi – the Secretary of Tower B?'

'No. He isn't invited.'

The car doors slammed, and then they were on their way into the city. Kothari sat slumped, hands between his knees.

'Have you been to Malabar Hill before?' the builder asked.

'To the Hanging Gardens once or twice. No other reason.'

'I've lived in Malabar Hill twelve years. And I've never been to the Hanging Gardens.'

Both of them laughed. The Secretary straightened his back and breathed out.

The barbecued mutton melted under his tongue like hot chocolate.

The Secretary opened his eyes, dried them with an index finger, and looked for the chicken kebabs. On a silver tray, floating about the far side of Mr Shah's terrace. All the other guests were there: in suits, silk shirts, saris and sherwanis, sitting at ebony tables lit by fat candles.

Kothari waved, so that the waiter would make an excursion to where he stood, alone, against the balcony. He felt the bald head beneath his comb-over becoming damp – *spicy*, that mutton. Rubbing his hands, he turned around to suck in cool air from the city: a panorama of glowing towers that stretched all the way to the distant dome of Haji Ali.

'Paneer, sir?'

A waiter brought a silver tray full of those paneer cubes that seemed to have little cucumber-bits inside. Clutching three cubes in his hand, Kothari said, 'Son, won't you call that mutton man back here?'

With each deposit of rich food in his stomach, Kothari became less conscious of his 70 per cent polyester 30 per cent cotton shirt, bought near Andheri train station for 210 rupees, and of his *banian*, bought for thirty-five rupees a pack of six, that glowed underneath like in an X-ray.

Oh, that gorgeous buffet table, which launched satellites of silver trays filled with kebabs.

In the centre of the table he saw a vision of a Johnnie Walker Black Label, five or six times the size of a normal bottle, suspended upside-down from a metal rack and ending in a little plastic tap on which a bow-tied attendant had a finger permanently placed.

'Mr Kothari! *There* you are!' The builder waved at him from the table.

Soon the Secretary found himself one of the charms auxiliary to the Johnnie Walker; Shah introduced him to each person who came up for a drink, saying, 'This is Mr Kothari.'

Each one of the guests appeared to run a construction company. One of them, after shaking his hand, asked: 'Which Group do you represent?'

'Vishram,' the Secretary replied.

The man nodded knowingly, as if recognizing the name. 'A good Group. Good work you fellows are doing.'

Now the Secretary found himself led to one of the tables, where he sat next to a chubby unhappy teenager in a golden jacket, whom he took for the birthday boy.

The host was speaking into a cordless mike.

'I want to thank all of you for coming here to attend my son's birthday. The community to which we belong, the builders' community, is known to be a close-knit one, and your presence here demonstrates

110

this continuing closeness.' (Scattered applause.) 'I will come to your tables to thank each of you personally. But first, as a surprise treat, I am honoured to present a man who brings back lots of memories for all of us: the original dream-merchant himself.'

Music blared on the loudspeakers. To the rhythm of the audience's clapping, a man in a grey suit got up from one of the tables, and came to the buffet table. A once-famous actor, now in his forties, a professional guest at birthday parties and weddings. With a forced smile, he turned a few steps with his right hand up in the air. A young girl in a red dress joined him in the dancing, and guests whistled. A mobile phone flashed its camera.

Back at the table, the star was out of breath, paunchy, and suddenly twenty years older. A guest asked for an autograph; the film star obliged on a napkin.

The napkin flew from the table. The builder had burst out coughing.

The film star was worth every rupee he charged to appear at such events: placing his hand on Shah's, he grinned, as if nothing had happened.

'They call me a dream-merchant, I am aware of this. But what am I, really? Just a small dream-merchant next to a big one.' He pointed at the builder, who was wiping his face with the sleeve of his shirt.

'When they come out of a film, people throw away the tickets, but the builder's name is always on the building. It becomes part of the family name. I am a Hiranandani Towers man. He is a Raheja Complex man.'

The builder swallowed his spit and turned to the Secretary.

'And what about you, Mr Kothari? Will you be a Raheja man or a Hiranandani man after 3 October? Or do you plan on spending all your money on expensive vices?'

The Secretary, who had been watching a platter of mutton kebabs, turned around. 'My vices are sandwiches and cricket. Ask my wife.'

People laughed. The film star clapped and said, 'Just like me.'

Which provoked much more laughter.

'What do you do, *exactly*?' Shah asked.

'Business,' Kothari said.

The builder coughed again.

Kothari handed him a napkin, and said, 'I was in timber. Now I keep myself happy with some bonds, some stocks. I don't have vices, but...' He took a breath and puffed his chest, as if the attention were expanding his personality, 'I do have a secret. I am moving, after 3 October, to Sewri.'

Shah, wiping his lips with the napkin, had to explain to the others.

'In most redevelopment projects, as you know, the residents are offered a share in the new building. In the case of the Shanghai, however, the new place will be super-luxury. A mix of Rajput and Gothic styles, with a modern touch. There will be a garden at the front, with a fountain. Art Deco style. Each place will cost two crores or upwards. The current residents certainly have the option of purchasing in the Shanghai, but they will be better served by moving elsewhere.'

Then he turned to the Secretary and asked: 'Sewri? Why not Bandra or Andheri? You'll have the money now.'

'The flamingoes, sir,' the Secretary said. 'You know about them, don't you?'

Of course, Shah *knew*. Sewri in winter was visited by a flock of migratory flamingoes, and bird lovers came to watch with binoculars. But he did not *understand*.

'Were you born here, Mr Shah?' the Secretary asked.

'I was born in Krishnapur in Gujarat. But I am a proud tax-paying resident of Mumbai.'

'I didn't mean it that way,' the Secretary said quickly. 'I have nothing against migrants, nothing. I meant, all of you at this table were born in India. Correct?'

'Of course.'

'Not me. Not me.'

The Secretary smiled. 'I was born in Africa.'

His father, lured from Jamnagar to Kenya by an African-born cousin, had set up a grocery shop in Nairobi in the 1950s; the shop had prospered; a son had been born there. Ashvin Kothari spoke now of things even his wife had never heard. Of an African servant lady wiping

112

a large porcelain dish and laying it on a table with a blue tablecloth; a market in Nairobi where his father was a big man; and then one more thing, a memory which blazed in his mind's eye like a pink flame.

Flamingoes. A whole flock of them.

When he was not yet five, he had been taken to a lake in the countryside full of the wild pink birds. His father had put his thumbs under his armpits and lifted him up so he could see to the horizon; the flamingoes rose all at once and he had screamed over his father's head.

Shah listened. The dream-merchant listened. Waiters gathered round the table.

Now the Secretary felt something he had felt only once in his life, when as a ten-year-old schoolboy he had recited the famous lines from the Ramayana:

> *Do as you will, evil king:*
> *I, for my part, know right from wrong*
> *And will never follow you,*
> *said the virtuous demon Maricha*
> *When the lord of Lanka*
> *Asked him to steal Rama's wife*

so perfectly at a poetry competition that everyone in the audience, even his father, had stood up to applaud. He sensed that same shimmer now around his bald head: his comb-over felt like a laurel wreath.

'And then?' Shah asked. 'What happened to your father?'

Kothari smiled.

'He found out that Africans did not like Indian men who did well.'

When he was eight years old, there was a threat to their business, and his father had sold it for a pittance to return to Jamnagar, to die there in a dingy shop full of green-gram and brinjal.

'That was how they treated us then,' the Bollywood actor remembered. 'Idi Amin saying to the Indians, get up and get out.'

The builder coughed. 'They look up to Indians in Africa now. We're drilling for oil in Sudan.'

A quarter of an hour later, with a valedictory flourish of dance steps, the dream-merchant bowed and vanished. Mr Shah looked at his guests and at once they knew it was time to leave. By the same power, Kothari was made to know he was not to leave. He sat at the table as hands came to shake the builder's; some of them shook his hand too.

'Do you know why I did not invite Mr Ravi of Tower B here tonight?' The guests had left. Shah watched the waiters clear the buffet.

Kothari sensed that Mr Shah, who had changed from a vivacious host into a sick man with a cough in the course of the evening, was now about to turn into yet another man. He shook his head. 'No, sir.'

'His building won't make any trouble: it's full of young people. Reasonable people. So you are the key man, Mr Kothari. Do you follow me?'

'Not exactly.'

The birthday boy joined the table, sitting between his father and the Secretary.

The builder moved his son out of his line of sight. He spoke softly.

'In my experience, some older people oppose a redevelopment project because they are frightened of any kind of change. Some just want more money. And then there is one kind of person, the most dangerous, who says no because he is full of negative will power: because he does not enjoy life and does not want others to enjoy life. When these people speak, you must speak louder and clearer than they do. I will not forget it; I repay kindness with kindness of my own.'

The waiters, having removed the food, were now taking away the totemic bottle of Johnnie Walker.

'My father used to say,' Kothari cleared his voice, 'my father... the one who was in Africa, he used to say, a man who lives for himself is no better than an animal. All my life I did nothing for anyone but myself. I even married late because I preferred to live alone. My wife is a good woman. She made me become the Secretary of Vishram: so I would do something for others. I am grateful for any... extra kindness you show me. But I cannot accept until I ask you this: what about everyone else in Vishram Society? Will you keep your word to them and pay each one his rightful share?'

Shah said nothing for a beat, then reached out and took the Secretary's hand.

'I am honoured, Mr Kothari, to be doing business with a man like you. Honoured. I understand why you are worried about me. Perfectly understand. In the old days, a builder in this city thought he could get rich only if he cheated his customers. He would cheat them as a matter of routine – on cement, on steel rods, on finishing. Every monsoon one of his buildings collapsed. Most of those you saw here today were old builders.' He dropped his voice to a whisper. 'They would strip you in a second if *they* were doing this redevelopment. But now there is a new builder in the city. We want to win, yes, but believe me, Mr Kothari: we also want our customers to win. The more winning there is, the better; because we think Mumbai will again be one of the world's great cities. Ask at *any* of my projects about Mr Shah's reputation. Find a single customer of mine who has a complaint. I am not one of the old builders of Mumbai.'

The Secretary sucked his lips and nodded. Satisfied.

Shah was still holding his hand; he felt the pressure grow.

'But I tell you one thing, Mr Kothari. Old builder or new, the basic nature of my business has not changed. Do you know what a builder is?'

'A man who builds houses,' Kothari said, hoping his hand would be released.

'No. Architects build houses. Engineers build roads.'

Kothari turned around for help. Shanmugham was looking at the night sky; the birthday boy was jerking his right arm back and forth behind his head for some reason.

Shah held up a gold-ringed index finger.

'The builder is the one man in Bombay who *never* loses a fight.'

With this he let go of Kothari's hand.

'Why were you gone so long?' Mrs Kothari asked, as her husband joined her in bed. 'People kept asking for you, but I didn't tell anyone you were at the builder's house.'

Saying the name of Lord Krishna three times, the Secretary switched off the bed lamp.

'Did his car drop you off? What is his home like? Gold fittings in the bathroom? Is there a jacuzzi?'

Her husband covered his face in the blanket and said nothing.

In the darkness he saw a flock of pink birds flying around him. He felt his father's fingers pressing on his – and then all the wasted decades in between fell away, and they were together once again at the lake in Kenya.

Ashvin Kothari fell asleep with tears on his cheeks.

Like an army that had been coming closer for months and was now storming a citadel, they went into the Fountainhead and the Excelsior with bricks on their heads.

It was the final surge of work before the monsoons. Those day-labourers who had wilted in the heat and fled to their villages were replaced by those offloaded from buses at ever-rising cost: the day rate for men was now 370 rupees. Heat or no heat, humidity or no humidity, all the civil work – walls, floors, columns – must be done before the rains.

Once again, as he had been every hot morning, Dharmen Shah was here, dipping his silk trousers in the slush and muck, pointing fingers at things and shouting at men. He stood by the roaring cement grinder, as women in bright saris and diamond nose-rings bent down and rose up with troughs of wet dark cement on their heads.

Shah put his foot on a pile of concrete tubes. 'Faster, son,' he told one of the workers. 'I'm paying you good money. I want to see you work.'

Shanmugham, running his fingers up and down the spine of a green financial prospectus, stood behind the boss.

Shah directed his assisant's attention to two teenagers breaking in half a long corrugated metal rod.

'Work. Hard work. A beautiful thing to see.'

The two muscled boys had rested the rod on a metal triangle; one of them raised a mallet. He brought it down. With each blow, the long rod trembled. Behind the boy swinging the mallet, a bag of cement rose into the upper floors of the Confidence Excelsior on a pulley.

'I've heard that Chacko never comes to his construction sites. He doesn't like the smell of cement and steel. What a third-rate builder he is.'

On the lift up to the fourth floor of the Excelsior, Shanmugham opened up his financial prospectus. Out of it he slid a small black book and opened its pages.

'I spoke to the Secretary, sir.' He read from the black book. 'As of now, four people in Vishram are saying no to the offer. Four in Tower A. Everyone in Tower B has said yes.'

'What is this black book?' Mr Shah took it from his assistant and turned it over.

'It has dates, and things we deal with, and wise sayings I hear from you. My wife encourages me to write things down, sir.'

Shah flipped through it.

'If only my son paid this much attention to what I say.' He returned the book to his assistant. 'You told me once there were teachers in Vishram Society. Are they among those who are saying no?'

They stepped off the lift.

'There is only one teacher, sir. And he *is* one of those saying no.'

'I knew it, Shanmugham. I don't like teachers. Write that down in your book.'

A worker's family was spending the nights on the unfinished fourth floor, which one day a technology executive or a businessman would occupy. Shah touched the workers' washing, which hung in the alcoves where Versace would soon hang; their little bars of soap and detergent did the work that expensive perfumes would soon do. And they probably did it better. Shah smiled; he wished Satish were here by his side, so he could show him little things like this. Folding a twenty-rupee note, he left it near a bar of soap as a surprise for the worker's wife.

An open-backed truck fought its way through the muck of the construction site loaded with marble tiles. At the edge of the floor, Shah squatted down and shouted:

'Don't unload the tiles!' He gestured at the workers. 'Don't touch them!'

On the way down, Shanmugham stood as far away as he could from his employer, who was on the mobile phone.

'"Beige". I wrote it down. In case you were too stupid to know what the word meant. You've sent "Off-white". You think I have time to waste like this? Everything has a schedule here. Everything is going to be delayed because of you. I want the correct shade of marble loaded and brought here by the end of the day!'

Reaching the ground Shah marched over to the truck and yelled at his workers, who had already begun to unload the marble. They blinked at him. He cursed them. They reloaded the marble. The diesel fumes of the departing truck spurted into Shah's face. He was still coughing a minute later.

Shanmugham accompanied him to the blasted tree that grew by the row of workers' huts. One of the workers' children was brushing his teeth by the water pump under the tree. Seeing the fat coughing man, he stepped back.

Shah sat by the water pump. Shanmugham saw, like first rain on the ground, red dots speckling the white scum of toothpaste on the ground.

'Sir, we should take you to the hospital...'

Shah shook his head. 'It has happened before, Shanmugham. It goes away in a few minutes.'

A cow sat nearby, whipping flies away with its tail. The worker's son stared at the two men; toothpaste dripped from his mouth.

'Come, sir. Let's go to Breach Candy Hospital. I'll call Doctor Nayak.'

'Nayak will frighten me again, and tell me to stop coming here. We have to finish the civil work before the rains come. That will happen only if I am here every single morning.'

Shanmugham knew it was true: the master's fat-bellied body was a human version of the cement mixers that churned and set the workers in motion.

'Mr J. J. Chacko,' Shah said. 'Right here. Under my nose.'

He looked over at the large plot of land, right opposite the Excelsior, with the big Ultimex sign on it.

'Do you know when he's starting work? Is there a date?'

'No date, sir. But he'll start building some time in October.'

'Let's go back.' Shah rose to his feet. 'I don't want the workers thinking something is wrong.'

He pointed a finger at his left-hand man's chest.

'I want each of those *Nos* to become a *Yes*, Shanmugham. At once.'

At the traffic lights before Malabar Hill, a headless cat lay on the road; from the neck up, it was just a smear of pink pulp imprinted with a tyre tread, an exclamation mark of blood. The builder's heart went out to it. In a world of trucks and heavy traffic, the little cat had not been given a fair chance. *But what about you, Dharmen*, the pulverized animal asked. *You're next, aren't you?*

Shah lowered the window and spat at the corpse.

BOOK THREE

Four or Five Seconds of
Feeling Like a Millionaire

4 JUNE

Vittal, the old librarian at St Catherine's School, was probably the only man in Vakola still unaware of the good news. Masterji was glad to be in his presence. Exercising his privilege as a retired teacher, he came to the school library every Monday to read the *Times of India* for free.

'We don't see the likes of you any more, Masterji,' Vittal said, as he bent low to arrange volumes of the *Encyclopaedia Britannica* on the bookshelf. 'Young people don't want to go into teaching. Computers or banking for them. Money, money, money.'

Masterji turned the pages of the newspaper. 'No sense of public service, is there?'

The librarian blew his nose into a handkerchief, moving his head from side to side.

'Remember when we were young. We had to walk to school every morning. Study by candlelight during exam-time. Now the computers do their work for them.'

Masterji laughed. 'I don't know anything about computers or the internet, Vittal. I don't even have a mobile phone.'

'Oh, that's extreme, Masterji,' the librarian said. He took a shiny red object from his pocket and smiled proudly.

'Nokia.'

Masterji turned the pages of his newspaper.

'Why does a physics teacher need these things, Vittal? The facts of life do not change: high tide is followed by low tide, and the equinox is still the equinox.'

He tapped a finger on his paper, and drew Vittal's attention to a proposal to restore Crawford Market to pristine glory.

'The sculptures outside the market were done by Kipling's father. Lockwood Kipling. Did you know that?'

Vittal stretched his back.

'Know nothing about Mumbai, Masterji. Not a genius like you. If you were a young man today, working at a foreign bank, playing with stocks, God knows how much money you would be making.'

'What would I spend it on?' Masterji folded the paper with a smile. He beckoned to the librarian.

'Vittal...' he whispered. 'Purnima's one-year death anniversary is around the corner. I want to call Trivedi about it.'

'Of course.'

It was a little conspiratorial luxury the old teacher enjoyed here; Vittal allowed him (provided no one was watching) to use the black payphone for free.

A student in white-and-navy-blue uniform sneaked in through the side-door as Masterji dialled. He gaped at the two old men as if he had discovered two palaeosauruses.

In the market, Masterji walked with his head to the ground, sniffing citrus and apple, raw shit (from the roosters in the chicken coops), raw carrot and cauliflower.

'Great man! Look up!'

Under the banyan tree in whose shade the business of the market was conducted, a vendor was waving at Masterji, from behind a stall full of onions.

Chubby, with a bulbous nose and knobby lumps on his dark fore-head, he looked like an anthropomorphic advertisement for his produce.

'I've seen you for a long long time.' The onion-seller found a small red stool and placed it before Masterji. 'But I never knew until now that you were a great one. There is something special about all of you in Vishram. The Confidence Group didn't pick you for no reason.'

Fruit- and vegetable-vendors drew towards the red stool, looking its occupant up and down with wonder, as if he had been struck by lightning and survived.

'My greatness – if there be any – is to do with my students,' Masterji explained.

He pointed to the discarded newspapers that the onion-seller had piled on his cart, to wrap his produce in: 'You'll find an article written by a man named Noronha in the *Times*. My student. Oh, I take no credit for Noronha. A smart boy, so hard-working – used to walk to school every day from Kalina. Boys were hard-working in the old days. I wonder where those days have gone…'

One of the vendors, a big swarthy man whose plump face was dotted with white stubble, turned to the onion-seller and asked loudly: 'Ram Niwas, there's a man here asking for "the old days". Are you selling them? Because I'm not. I'm selling only potatoes.'

And then he laughed at his own joke, before returning to his potatoes.

A horn sounded through the market. A man on a scooter was waving at Masterji.

'My wife told me you called – I came at once, came at once looking for you.'

Everyone in Vakola was familiar with the sight of Shankar Trivedi's shirtless, mesomorphic torso – a white shawl draped over the shoulders – dramatically entering or leaving a building on a red Honda scooter, like an angel of birth or death. He had been recruited by Purnima to conduct, each year, the memorial service for their daughter Sandhya; a service that Masterji, for his wife's sake, had always attended. When Purnima died, it was Trivedi who had performed the last rites, with coconuts and incense, at a temple in Bandra.

Drawing the old teacher away from the vendors, he pumped Masterji's hand in his. 'Congratulations, congratulations,' he said.

'Trivedi, Purnima's one-year death anniversary is coming up. October the 5th. It is five months away, but I wanted to make sure you mark it on your calendar. A very important day for me, Trivedi.'

The priest let go of Masterji's hand: he gaped.

'Masterji: when your daughter passed away, who performed the rites for her?'

'You did, Trivedi.'

'When your wife passed away, who performed the rites for her?'

'You did, Trivedi.'

'And when my son needed a science "top-up", who taught him?'

'I did, Trivedi.'

'So what's this talk of appointment and disappointment, Master-ji? It'll be an *honour* to perform your late wife's first-year Samskara. Don't worry.'

Trivedi offered to buy Masterji a little something for the heat – a coconut. Masterji knew the priest as a tight-fisted, even unscrupulous man – there was always some unpleasantness over the bill for his ceremonies – and he succumbed to the sheer novelty of the offer; with Trivedi walking his scooter, they went to the coconut-man who sat near the entrance to St Catherine's with a black knife and a large wicker basket that groaned with coconuts.

As the coconut-man began tapping on the green nuts to sound out the water in each, Masterji watched Trivedi's face. The priest, in between births, marriages, and deaths, gave lessons in the proper recitation of Sanskrit verse to paying pupils. The well-oiled moustache that sat on his lips was itself a fine line of poetry: supple and balanced, robustly black with a tinge of grey at the edges, punctuated in the middle by a perfect *caesura*. Trivedi was curling its ends and smiling, but the truth was leaking out of his eyes and nose.

He was almost on the verge of tears.

Burning with jealousy, Masterji thought. Indeed, it now seemed to him that a good portion of everyone's professed admiration for Vishram all these years had been a kind of condescension for an old, crumbling building. And now they had been startled into real respect for its inhabitants.

'I'll give you good news, Trivedi,' he said, taking pity on the man.

With a curved knife the coconut-man slashed open the mouth of one of the nuts.

The priest's eyes grew large.

'This Shah is going to make an offer for our place too?'

'No. The good news for you is that there is no good news for us. The Pintos have said no. Shelley won't be able to find her way around any other building.'

'Twenty thousand rupees per square foot! You could buy her

126

new eyes with so much money.' Trivedi grinned. 'You're teasing me, aren't you, Masterji?'

The market filled with noise: a funeral procession began to move, clamorously, towards the highway.

The coconut man handed each of them a sliced-open nut, brimming with fresh water and pierced by a pink straw.

Masterji knew he ought to refuse: the nut was meant for a man who would take Mr Shah's money.

'... of course you must be joking, Masterji... will you really say no? Once the deadline comes near, will you really really...'

He took the brimming coconut in his hands and felt its weight. *When you're rich, you don't have to give people things*, he thought. *They give you things*.

How wonderful.

Sucked through a straw, the cool sweet water was a bitter thrill: he understood, for four or five seconds, what it was to be a millionaire.

Bald, moist, chocolate-dark, the drummer's head glistened in the mid-morning light; behind him, a swaying man blew on a *nadaswaram*. Four teenagers carried the wooden bier; two followed them striking bronze cymbals. On the bier lay the body of an old woman draped in a bright green sari, her nostrils stopped with cotton balls. A boy at the head of the procession broke out, every few steps, into jubilant dance.

Standing in the Vakola market with folded arms, Ajwani, the broker in Vishram Society, watched Shanmugham, a few steps away, watching the funeral procession with folded arms.

The Confidence Group man wore his standard white-over-black uniform; under his arm he held what looked like a financial prospectus.

Shanmugham turned and noticed Ajwani noticing.

The broker approached him with a smile.

'I'm from Vishram Society. Name is Ajwani.'

Shanmugham returned the smile. 'I know. Ramesh. Tower A. You own the Toyota Qualis.'

Soon the two men were sitting together at a nearby restaurant.

Ajwani dispatched a mouse from under their table with a kick; he made a sign to the waiter.

He picked up the green prospectus that Shanmugham had laid on the table and flicked through its pages.

'Mutual Funds... I used to play the market in the nineties. Technology companies. I bought Infosys shares. Made no money. You won't, either.'

'I *have*,' Shanmugham said.

'Then you'll lose it all. Men like us don't become rich from shares.'

Ajwani slid the prospectus across the table; he looked his interlocutor in the eye.

'I want to ask you, Mr Shanmugham: what is your title in the Confidence Group?'

'Don't have one. I am helping out as a personal favour to Mr Shah.'

'No, you're not.' The broker clamped his hand down on the prospectus. 'Every builder has one special man in his company. This man has no business card to hand out, no title, he is not even on the company payroll. But he is the builder's left hand. He does what the builder's right hand does not want to know about. If there is trouble, he contacts the police or the mafia. If there is money to be paid to a politician, he carries the bag. If someone's knuckles have to be broken, he breaks them. *You* are Mr Shah's left hand.'

Shanmugham retrieved his prospectus from beneath the broker's hand.

'I've never heard of that term before. Left-hand man.'

The waiter put two cups of tea on their table.

'Bring me a bowl of sugar,' Ajwani said.

He courteously moved Shanmugham's tea a bit closer to him.

'Have you heard the saying, a broker is first cousin to a builder? I've seen redevelopments all my life. The builder always has a man on the inside. He gives you information about the other members of the Society. You give him a bribe. Unfortunately, you picked the wrong man this time.'

Shanmugham, who had begun blowing on his tea to cool it, stopped.

The broker continued: 'It's usually the Secretary who is picked. The Secretary of Tower B, Mr Ravi, is a good man. But *our* Secretary is a *nothing* man.'

'Nothing man?' Shanmugham asked his tea.

'Didn't have a son till he was nearly fifty years old. He can't do *this*.' Ajwani raised a finger. 'All he has done for days is say, *Africa, Africa, Africa.*'

'Then *who* can help us?'

Ajwani shrugged.

'Let me ask you this. How many people in Vishram Tower A are saying no to the offer?'

'Four.'

Ajwani tapped the table with his mobile phone.

'Wrong. Only one person really opposes it. The other three don't know what they want.'

'Which one?'

The waiter placed the sugar on the table; Ajwani tucked his mobile phone into his pocket. He smiled.

'The deadline is too tight, Mr Shanmugham. A project like this will take two years, minimum. Why is your boss pushing so hard?'

Shanmugham's eyes glistened. He drank his tea and moved the empty glass back to the centre of the table.

'Which one?'

Reaching for the sugar, Ajwani took a spoonful, and held it poised over his cup. 'You want information from me…' He vibrated the spoon. '… for nothing. That's greed. Give me a sweetener. Another thousand rupees a square foot.'

Shanmugham rose to his feet.

'I came to Vakola to deliver boxes of sweets to your Society. You will find one for you at the gate, Mr Ajwani. Other than that, I have nothing to give you.'

The broker stirred the sugar into his tea.

'You will never get Vishram Society to accept your offer without my help.'

*

Stopping at the gate of the building, Ajwani discovered that Shan-mugham had been telling the truth about the sweets.

Red boxes, each with an image of Lord SiddhiVinayak. Inside each one was 300 grams of dough-and-cashew sweets, cut into diamond-shaped slices. A handwritten letter strapped to every box. Signed. 'From my family to yours. Dharmen Shah. MD, Confidence Group.'

'I gave your box to your wife,' Ram Khare said.

Ajwani pointed to the stack by the guard's side. 'Why are there four boxes there?'

'Four people said they didn't want the sweets,' the guard said. 'Can you believe that?'

Ajwani peered at the boxes. 'Which four?'

A sunny smile from Ibrahim Kudwa's bearded face was a sure thing as one of his neighbours passed the jumble of wire, vegetation, brick, cheap roofing, and peeling paint that went by the title SPEED-TEK CYBER ZONE CYBER CAFÉ. The trunk of the banyan by the cyber-café had been painted white, in simulation of snow. Kudwa's long-time assistant, Arjun, had apparently converted to Christianity some years ago; last Christmas, he won the banyan tree over to his religion and placed a private crib with toy figures, arranged in a splendour of cotton-snow, at its foot. Other evidence of Christmas could be found in the large five-pronged star, surrounded by bunting, that Arjun had hung over the roof of the café; months later, it was still there, unexpected, colossal, the bunting fraying, and, with the light behind it in the morn-ing, looking like a symbol of the Apocalypse. As if drawn to the mystic star, a Hindu holy man sometimes sat outside the café. Mr Kudwa saw no objection to his doing so; indeed he had even encouraged the man with the occasional two-rupee coin.

Man of enterprise, Ibrahim Kudwa; lead singer in a rock-and-roll band at university, he had chosen, after graduation, not to remain in the Muslim-only building in Bandra East where his brothers and sisters still lived. Vishram was old, but he wanted his children to mix with Hindus and Christians. On the advice of a magazine article, he had decided that the future was in technology. Rejecting an offer from his brother to join the family hardware store in Kalanagar, he opened a cyber-café in the neighbourhood in 1998. Easy money. His rates rose from ten rupees per hour, to fifteen, to twenty, and then declined again to fifteen, and then to ten. A treacherous thing, technology. Within six months, an internet connection had become so cheap that only the rough, the rowdy and the tourists needed a cyber-café. Hardware held its price; his brother had recently bought a second two-bedroom flat as an investment property. Then the government decided that anyone using a cyber-café was a potential terrorist. User name, phone number, address, driving licence or passport number – the café owner was legally obliged to keep detailed records of every customer, and the police swooped on Kudwa's books for any excuse to extort a bribe.

Yet none of his neighbours would say that he was an unhappy man. He was a bear that could find honey at any level of a tree. He lavished his considerable free time on his two jolly children, ten-year-old Mohammad, who lost stout-heartedly to the little Ajwanis in tae kwon-do competitions, and two-year-old Mariam, who staggered elliptically about her father's cyber-café in a nightie, inviting herself on to the laps of customers to strike at the old keyboards with glee. Mumtaz, his wife, saved up discount coupons and credit card points, so they could take holidays to Mahabaleshwar each summer. In August the previous year they had even accomplished the miracle, subsidized by the credit card points, of a family holiday to Ladakh, where they had visited Tibetan monasteries and returned with holy beads and T-shirts for their Hindu neighbours.

'Why are you in the Opposition Party, Ibrahim?'

Ajwani had just lowered himself into the visitor's chair in the café.

'Opposition Party?' Kudwa asked. Little Mariam was on his lap, and he was stroking her hair.

'You are saying no to the offer. Why?'

Kudwa stared. '*Who* told you I had said no?'

He let Mariam crawl about the floor. 'Do you think I want to stay in this internet café business all my life? Do I want my children to grow up poor?'

'So you are going to support us, Ibrahim.' Ajwani grinned. 'Why didn't you take your sweet-box, then?'

'No, it's not that simple.' Kudwa gestured for patience by patting the air.

On the other hand, there was the thing Mrs Puri had called Masterji: 'An English gentleman'. Even though she wanted to accept the offer, she admired his gesture. How would his neighbours interpret *his* character if he rushed to take Mr Shah's money?

'I want to be well thought of. People in the Society think of me as a fair-minded man.'

Kudwa scratched his beard with both hands.

'Of course we do,' Ajwani said. 'By the way, that was a lovely joke the other day. What you wrote on that sign outside the Society. What was it, "Inconvenience is regretted, but work…"'

'Inconvenience in progress, work regretted.' Kudwa beamed. Mariam was venturing under one of the computers; he picked her up and brought her back to the chair.

'You are liked by everyone, Ibrahim. But will people still like you if you don't say yes – that I don't know.'

Kudwa winced.

'It upsets my stomach, Ramesh. Just thinking about this decision. My wife says I have a high ratio of nerves to flesh. A man with a bad stomach should *never* be asked to make decisions.'

Ajwani saw a strip of heart-shaped antacid tablets in Kudwa's shirt pocket, like multiple testimonials to his claim. He reached over and snapped his fingers against the strip of antacids.

'Come with me, Ibrahim. I'll solve your problem in a second.'

Picking little Mariam up from the floor – and shouting to Arjun, who was sweeping the courtyard behind the café, to mind things and make sure the customers did not surf on to 'dirty' sites while he was away – Kudwa followed his neighbour into Vishram Society.

As they passed their building, Kudwa glanced at the Secretary's office.

Kothari had told him his Africa story that morning, as he had told it to every other member of Vishram Society. It made sense to Kudwa at last – the Secretary's strange, secretive, and yet somehow sociable personality. All these years his African-returned father's shame – the shame of the expatriate who had returned empty-handed – had crushed his natural gregariousness. If not for his shame, Kothari would have been a different kind of man. All of them could have been different men.

'How strange that the Secretary should have a passion for flamingoes,' he said.

Ajwani turned. 'How strange that the Secretary should have a passion for *anything.*'

'Perhaps we will stay here, in the building, and know each other better. Maybe that is what this Shah's proposal is really meant to do.'

'No.' Ajwani minted invisible currency with his fingers. 'It's meant to make us rich.'

He cut across the compound in the direction of Tower B. In the parking area in front of the building, he pointed to a vehicle with a gold 'V' ribbon on its bonnet.

Fresh from the showroom, a Toyota Innova. It had been bought two days ago; the order, however, must have been placed weeks before Mr Shah's offer.

Ajwani, who hoarded information on all the middle-class residents of Vakola, had quickly discovered the name of the owner: Mr Ashish, a software engineer, one of the residents of Tower B.

'What do you see?' Ajwani asked.

'A car. A new car.'

'No. You see ten years of slogging, skimping, and sacrificing, before you can buy something like this. There is a new way to look at new things, Ibrahim. Touch it.'

'Touch it?'

Ajwani brushed a few spots of dandruff from Kudwa's shoulder, and gestured for Mariam.

'Don't worry about the owner. He *wants* you to touch it. You know what people in Tower B are like, don't you?'

Ibrahim Kudwa handed his daughter over to his neighbour. He ran his hands through his beard, then took a step towards the gold-ribboned car. His index finger reached for its shining metal skin: and at once the shell surrounding the Innova that said 'Ten years from now' broke and fell to pieces. He spread all his fingers on its skin, and could not repress a grin.

On the way back, Kudwa asked for his red sweet-box at the guard's booth.

Tapping his fingers behind his back, Ajwani went down to the fruit and vegetable market.

He did all his best thinking in the market. At least once a week he came here with his two boys to teach them how to bargain. An essential part of their education. If a man could not be cheated on his food, he could not be cheated on anything else.

Africa, Ajwani said to himself, as he went among carts full of ripe watermelons. He had never been to Africa. Nor America, Europe, Canada, Australia. Had never crossed the ocean.

Women had been his Africa. They come into a real-estate broker's office all the time – air hostesses, models, sales girls, single girls, divorced women – looking for rooms in a hurry, sometimes in a desperate hurry. A broker can seem a fatherly figure to them – benevolent, decisive. In his younger days, Ajwani, while never resorting to coercion or blackmail, had slept with plenty of his clients. Plenty. At first there was a hotel by the train station, the Wood-Lands, that rented rooms by the hour. Later he built an inner room in his office. A coconut to sip on, as they lay side by side in bed. The women were happy; he was happier than they were. That was how he liked his deals to be.

Money – money had been his India. He had not made a rupee on the stock market; even in real estate, his own field, his investments had flopped. Someone or other had always tricked him. He had bought the Toyota Qualis from a cousin so he could feel rich, but it was killing him. Drank too much diesel. Needed repairs month after month. Once again he had been cheated. In the movie of his own life, he had to admit, he was just a comedian.

But not this time.

Small dark apples sat in a pyramid on a blue cart like medieval munitions; pointy-tipped papayas, modern artillery shells, surrounded them on all sides. Ajwani picked up a papaya and smelled its base for ripeness. He would do the same with Masterji, the Pintos, and Mrs Rego; sniff and tap, sniff and tap, find their weak spots, break them open. Kudwa he had done for free, but Mr Shah would have to pay for the next three.

The talk in the market, as it was every year at this time, was that the rains would be late, and that the water shortage would soon become terrible.

Stale gossip to the left, mediocre produce to the right: Ramesh Ajwani knew that his eyes were the brightest things for sale in Vakola market.

BOOK FOUR

The Rains Begin

Intercepted raindrops fell from a coconut palm.

From their bedroom window Ramu and the Friendly Duck watched.

The metal trellis meant to guard the window from burglars came to life; the wrought-iron foliage dripped and became real leaves and real flowers.

'Oy, oy, oy, my prince. What deep thoughts are you thinking?'

Sitting next to her son, Mrs Puri pointed to the sky. The lines of diminishing rain were sparkling: the sun was coming out.

'Remember what Masterji says? When there is rain and sun together, there is a... You know the word, Ramu. Say it. It's a rai... a rain... a rainb...'

Shielding Ramu's wet head with her arm, Mrs Puri looked up. A drop of rainwater was hanging from the ceiling. Vishram's old walls glistened with bright seepage; moisture was snuggling into cracks in the paint, licking steel rods, and chewing on mortar.

Ramu, who could read his mother's thoughts, reached for her gold bangles and began to play with them.

'We don't have to worry, Ramu. We're moving into a brand-new home. Just three months from now. One that won't ever fall down.'

Ramu whispered.

'Yes, everyone, even Masterji and Secretary Uncle.'

The boy smiled; then plugged his ears and closed his eyes.

Mrs Puri turned and shouted, 'Mary! Don't make so much noise with the rubbish. I have a growing son here!'

*

Mary, as she did every day, was dragging a mildewed blue barrel from floor to floor of Vishram Society, emptying into it the contents of the rubbish bins placed outside each door, and cleaning up the mess made by the early-morning cat as it looked for food.

The people of Vishram Society did not praise servants lightly: but Mary they trusted. So honest that even a one-rupee coin dropped on the floor would be put back on the table. In seven years of service not one complaint of theft. True, there was always dirt on the banisters and on the stairs, but the building was an old one. It secreted decay. Why blame Mary?

Her life was a hard one. She had married a pair of muscled arms that drifted into and out of her life, leaving bruises and a child; her father sometimes turned up under the vegetable stalls in the market, dead-drunk.

Done with 5B, the last flat on the top floor, she rotated the blue bin down the steps, filling the stairwell with a noise like thunder. ('Mary! Didn't you hear me! Stop that noise at once! Mary!') With the branching veins on her forearms in high relief, as if the bin were tied to them, she rolled it out of the Society and out of the gate and down the road to an open rubbish pit.

The rains had turned the pit into a marsh: cellophane, eggshell, politician's face, stock quote, banana leaf, sliced-off chicken's feet and green crowns cut from pineapples. Ribbons of unspooled cassette-tape draped over everything like molten caramel.

Throwing plastic bags from her blue bin into the marsh, Mary, through the corner of her eye, saw a man walking towards her. She smelled Johnson's Baby Powder. She took a step closer to the rubbish pile, preferring its odours.

'Mary.'

She grunted to acknowledge Ajwani's presence. She disliked the way he looked at her; his eyes put a price on women.

'What was in Mrs Puri's rubbish bag this morning?'

'I don't know.'

'Will you find it for me?' he asked, with a smile.

She waded into the rubbish and picked out a plastic bag, which she threw at Ajwani's feet. He turned it over with his shoe.

'Do you remember, Mrs Puri said she was taking her Ramu to the temple yesterday? Sitla Devi in Mahim, she said, when I asked her. Now, when Hindus go to the temple they bring things back with them – flowers, coconut shells, kumkum powder – and you don't see any of them in her rubbish. What does that tell you?'

Mary, having emptied the blue bin, scraped its insides with her palm. Three dark hogs began snivelling in the muck; a fourth, its eyes closed, stood stationary in the slush, like a holy meditating thing.

'I don't know.'

'A man has no secrets from his rubbish bin, Mary. From now on, I want you to look through three rubbish bags every morning. Masterji's, Mr Pinto's, and Mrs Rego's.'

'That is not my work,' she said. 'It is the early-morning cat's work.'

'Then become the cat, Mary.'

With a smile Ajwani offered a ten-rupee note. She shook her head.

'Take it, take it,' he said.

'This is for you too.' Ajwani held out a red box with the image of Lord SiddhiVinayak on it. 'For your son.'

Mary looked at the red box: large spots of grease stained its cardboard sides.

Two scavenger-women had been waiting for Mary to toss out the contents of the blue bin; one was holding a car's windscreen-wiper. Now they went barefoot through the wet refuse, old jute bags on their shoulders, sifting through the rubbish with the wiper. They left Mrs Puri's bag alone. They were not looking for information: merely plastic and tin.

Back in Vishram, Mary hid the sweet-box in the servant's alcove, then swept the common areas, the stairwell, and the compound.

Half an hour later, with the sweet-box in one hand, she was buying vegetables at the market. Something fresh for her son. Beetroots. Good for children's brains, Mrs Puri said, who was always cooking them for her boy. *She should give me the beetroots*, Mary thought. What was the point of wasting them on that imbecile?

Balancing a *pav* of beetroots on top of the red sweet-box, she came to Hibiscus Society.

'Why are you looking for work here? Don't you have a job at Vishram?' the security guard asked.

'The builder has made them an offer. Everyone leaves on October 3.'

'Oh, a redevelopment.' The guard sucked his teeth. He was an old man; he had seen Societies. 'It will take years and years. Someone will go to court. You don't have to worry now.'

'Anyone living in the slum by the *nullah* – attention!'

A man came running through the market. He cupped his hands to his mouth: 'Slum clearance! The men are here!'

The guard at Hibiscus Society, scratching his head and contemplating Mary's proposal, said, 'All right. But what's my interest in this? Do I get a monthly cut? If I don't, then...'

But where the maid-servant had stood, a red box of sweets now lay on the ground, beetroots rolling around it.

Bumping into people, she ran. Pushing cycles and carts, she ran.

Past Vishram Society, past the Tamil temple, past the construction site where the two towers were coming up, and into the slums; passing narrow lane after narrow lane, dodging stray dogs and roosters to run into the open wasteland beyond. A plane soared above her. Finally she reached the *nullah*, a long canal of black water, on whose banks a row of blue tarpaulin tents had risen.

Her neighbours were chopping wood; a rooster strutted round the huts; children played on rubber tyres tied to the trees.

'No one is coming here, Mary,' her neighbour told her in Tamil. 'It was a false alarm.'

Slowing down, breathing deeply, Mary came to her tent, and looked inside its blue tarpaulin cover, held aloft by a wooden pole. Everything intact: cooking oil, cooking vessels, her son's school books, photo albums.

'They won't come till after the monsoons,' her neighbour shouted. 'We're safe till then.'

Mary sat down and wiped her face.

Among the patchwork of fully legal slums, semi-legal slums and pockets of huts in Vakola, this row of tents next to a polluted canal, the *nullah* that cut through the suburb, led the most precarious existence. Because they had come here after the last government amnesty for illegal slums, and because the canal could flood during a heavy monsoon, the squatters had not been granted the identification cards which 'regularized' a slum-dweller's existence and gave him the right to be relocated to a *pucca* building if the government bulldozed his hut. Municipal officials had repeatedly threatened the dwellers by the *nullah* with eviction, yet someone had always intervened to save them, usually a politician who needed their votes at the next municipal election. Last month, Mrs Rego had come down to explain to them that things had changed. It was now a season of will power in Bombay: the coalition of corruption, philanthropy, and inertia that had protected them for so long was disintegrating. A new official had been put in charge of clearing the city's illegal slums. He had smashed miles of huts in Thane and promised to do the same in Mumbai. Every day their slum survived should be considered a miracle.

The huts along the *nullah* were now glowing from inside. Mary had been given an old three-battery white fluoroscent lamp by Mrs Rego, which she had hung by a hook from the roof of her tent.

In a little while, someone had come by to check on her. It was the Battleship herself.

Wiping her hands on her sari, Mary came out to talk.

'Today was a false alarm, Mary, but sooner or later they will come to demolish this place. You should move while you can.'

'This is my home, madam. Would you leave yours?'

She asked the Battleship about Timothy, her son. 'Is he playing cricket by the temple?'

'Let him play, Mary. He's a child. There won't be time to play later on.'

'Those other boys don't go to school, madam. Some of them are nearly twenty years old. Do you let your son play with them?'

Mrs Rego, about to put Mary in her place, restrained herself.

143

'I'm the one who gives lectures here, Mary. I'm not used to hearing them from people who live by the *nullah*. But let's not fight. Both of us had good news today.'

She was on her way home from the office of a lawyer in Shivaji Park who specialized in Housing Societies and their disputes. Not true, he had told her, that every member of a Society has to say 'Yes' before it can be demolished. A three-quarters majority vote in favour may be enough, legally speaking. But the law spoke ambiguously on this matter. As on most matters, the lawyer added. The law in Mumbai was not blind: far from it, it had two faces and four working eyes and saw every case from both sides and could never make up its mind. But an ambiguous, ambivalent, and ambidextrous law was not without its advantages. The issue here – individual right *vis-à-vis* collective well-being – was so complicated that if a single resident of Vishram went to court, the demolition would be postponed for years while the judge scratched his head over the case and tried to find a pattern in half a century of conflicting legal precedents. Mr Shah would give up and go somewhere else.

Mary came out of her hut with an axe and started cutting firewood for her evening cooking.

Mrs Rego had wandered a few huts down the *nullah*.

'How many times have I told you,' she was shouting at a man who had a well-known drinking problem, 'not to even *think* of raising a hand at your wife?'

Mary was thinking of her Timothy. He should be in here, studying, not out there by the Tamil temple, playing cricket with those older, rougher creatures. He would soon start to look up to them.

She might hit him too hard for breaking her orders: better to take it out on the firewood. She swung and chopped.

'I used to take you and your mother to a street fair in Bandra when you were this high. I'm sure you remember.'

At the other end of town, Dharmen Shah walked with his son past coloured balloons and fluorescent plastic loops. They had had an awkward tea in the lobby of the Hilton Hotel, and emerged to find

Nariman Point closed to traffic for a street fair. Blobs of vanilla ice cream, in cones or in cups, materialized around them like snowballs; horses, drawing chariots plated with silver-foil and shaped like swans, clattered up and down the avenue.

'When am I getting my credit card back?'

'When I feel like giving it back. Have you been seeing those gang boys again?'

Satish stopped. 'Horse shit. Everywhere,' he said. The bottoms of his jeans dragged on the dirty road, but Shah assumed it was the reigning style and checked himself.

'I asked you a question about the gang, Satish. Do you still…'

The boy had put his fingers on his nose. 'I want to go home,' he said. His father asked only if he had money for a taxi.

Shah dialled for Shanmugham, who was at Malabar Hill, waiting to deliver the evening report to him.

'Come over to Nariman Point.'

He stood behind a row of children who had lined up to buy red crystalline ice candy in a cup. The children looked at him and giggled; he smiled. All around him he saw men with their wives and sons.

I'm losing my boy, he thought. He knew that Satish had probably not told his taxi to go to Malabar Hill – he was headed straight to the home of one of his friends.

A cluster of yellow balloons rose above the fair and floated into the darkness; Shah followed them.

Leaving light and noise behind him, he came to a car park . A metal fence stood behind the car park, and dark water beyond it. At the end of the water, he saw the lights of Navy Nagar: the southern tip of Mumbai.

Shah pressed his face on the cold metal ringlets of the fence. He gazed at the distant lights, and then rotated his face until he was looking at the earth.

This fence was supposed to mark the land's end, but a promontory of debris, broken chunks of old buildings, granite, plastic, and Pepsi Cola had sneaked past it – the enterprising garbage pushed several feet into water. Shah's fingers pulsed as he gazed at the amphibian earth of Nariman Point. Look: how this city never stops growing: rubble, shit, plants, mulch, left to themselves, start slurping up sea, edging towards the other end of the bay like a snake's tongue, hissing through salt water, *there is more land here, more land.*

A churning began in the promontory – plastic bags and pebbles started to ripple, as if mice were scurrying beneath them; then a sparrow shot out of the detritus. *It's coming to life*, Shah thought. *If only Satish were here to see it.* All of Bombay was created like this: through the desire of junk and landfill, on which the reclaimed city sits, to become something better. In this way, they all emerged: fish, birds, the leopards of Borivali, even the starlets and super-models of Bandra.

Now a homeless man began moving over the debris; he must have found a hole in the fence. He squatted and spat. His spit contributed to the reclaiming thunderhead, as would his shit, soon to follow. Shah closed his eyes and prayed to the debris, and to the man defecating in it: *Let me build, one more time.*

'Sir...' He felt a hand on his shoulder. 'It's not clean here.'

Shanmugham, in his white shirt and black trousers, was standing behind him.

They returned to light and noise.

'What is that Secretary doing?' Shah asked, as they walked back to the street fair. 'Why are three people still saying *No* at Vishram?'

'I don't know why they elected him Secretary,' Shanmugham said. 'Useless. Absolutely useless. But there is someone else... a broker... who might help us. He has asked for money. Should I agree? Sir?'

The builder had stopped and turned his head. A sugarcane juice stand had been brought to the side of the road as part of the fair. His eyes rose to the top of the stand, where the canes had been piled, six foot high, the tallest of them curling down at the ends, like the claws of a crab.

The cane-crushing machine was lit up by naked electric bulbs. In a square of raw light, a boy turned a red wheel, which turned smaller green wheels, which tinkled and crushed the cane, whose juice, dribbling down a gutter full of irregular chunks of ice, passed through a dirty strainer into a stainless-steel vessel that fogged up from the cold liquid. Poured into small conical glasses, and sold to customers for five rupees each, seven for a larger glass.

'I used to live on this juice when I came to Bombay, Shanmugham. Live on it.'

'Sir: they use dirty water to make the ice. Jaundice, diarrhoea, worms, God knows what else.'

'I know. I know.'

The bright, fast, musical wheels turned once again, crushing the cane – Shah imagined bricks rising, scaffolding erected, men hoisted miles into the air on such tinkling energy. If only he were new to Bombay again: if only he could drink that stuff again.

On the drive back, in his mind's eye he continued to see them, the sugarcane-crusher's wheels turning under the naked light bulbs, discs of speeding light punching holes into the night like spinning machines of fate, having completed their day shift, and now working overtime.

Late in the night, the first storm crashed into the city.

Low rentals, five minutes to Santa Cruz train station, ten minutes to Bandra by auto. There are many advantages to life in Vakola, yes, but Ajwani, an honest broker, advises first-timers that there is also one big negative.

Not the proximity of slums (they stay in their huts, you stay in your building, who bothers whom?). Not the Boeing 747s flying overhead (cotton in your ears, arm on your wife, off to sleep).

But-one-thing-you-must-know-before-you-move-here: Ajwani taps his mobile phone on his laminated table. *This is a low-lying area.* One day each monsoon, there is a storm, and on that day life in Vakola becomes impossible.

By morning floodwater had risen to waist height near the highway signal and in parts of Kalina. Vishram Society, on higher ground, was more secure, but the alley leading up to it was a foot below water; every now and then an autorickshaw arrived, scything storm water, discharging a client near the gate, and returning gondola-like. Abandoning the guard's booth, Ram Khare sought the protection of the Society. Not that this protection was absolute; a continuous spray came through the stars in the grille. Buckets kept under the leaky spots in the roof overflowed every fifteen minutes; tongues of fresh algae and moss grew under the stairwell. Shifting diagonals of rain lashed the rusty gate and the blue roof of the guard's booth; the water fell thick and glowing, and though the sun was hidden the rain-light was strong enough to read a newspaper in.

In the Renaissance Real-Estate Agency, Ajwani saw that it was futile to expect clients, told Mani 'This is the day that comes once a year', and staggered back to his Society under an umbrella.

At four o'clock, the sky was bright again. The thunderclouds, like a single dark bandage, had been stripped away, exposing a raw sun. People ventured out of their buildings into the water, the colour of Assam tea, on which floated rubbish and blazing light.

A man's past keeps growing, even when his future has come to a full stop.

His neighbours had not seen much of Masterji lately. Parliament no longer met because of the rains; and, in any case, all the talking now took place behind closed doors. A hush of covert business had fallen over a garrulous Society. While schemes and ambitions were germinating around him, Masterji sat looking at the rain and his daughter's drawings of Vakola, or playing with his Rubik's Cube, until there was a knock on the door and Mr Pinto shouted, 'Masterji, we are waiting, it's time for dinner.'

Though the men and women around him dreamed of bigger homes and cars, his joys were those of the expanding square footage of his inner life. The more he looked at his daughter's sketches, the more certain places within Vishram – the stairwell where she ran up, the garden that she walked around, the gate that she liked to swing on – became more beautiful and intimate. Sounds were richer. A scraping of feet somewhere in the building reminded him of his daughter wiping her tennis shoes on the coir mat before coming in. Sometimes he felt as if Sandhya and Purnima were watching the rain with him, and there was a sense of feminine fullness inside the dim flat.

When the sky cleared, he would notice it was evening, and walk along the garden wall. When the breeze scattered the dew from the begonia leaves on to his hand, she was at his side again, his little Sandhya, tickling his palm as in the old days. He superimposed her features on the women walking about the garden. Nearly thirty she would have been. Her mother was slim, she would have stayed slim.

At dinner the Pintos would say, 'Masterji, you've become so quiet these days', and he would only shrug.

They asked him once or twice if he had had his diabetes test done yet.

Though he was spending more time by himself, he would not say he had been bored; he was conscious, indeed, of a strange contentment. But now, when he wanted to talk to someone, he found himself all alone.

He opened the door and went into the stairwell. Instead of going down the steps, he walked up. He walked up to the fifth floor, and paused in front of a steep single-file staircase, which led to the rooftop terrace.

After the suicide of the Costello boy in 1999, the Society had discouraged the use of the terrace, and children were forbidden from going up there.

Masterji went up the staircase to the terrace. The small wooden door at the end of the stairs had not been opened in a long time, and he had to push with his shoulder.

And then, for the first time in over a decade, he was on the roof of Vishram Society.

Fifteen years ago, Sandhya had come up here in the evenings to play on a rocking-horse, which was still rotting in a corner. Planting a foot on it, he gave it a little kick. It creaked and rocked.

Years of uncleaned guano had calcified on the floor of the terrace, and rainwater had collected over it.

Masterji walked slowly through water to the wall of the terrace. From here, he could see Mary picking up leaves and twigs that littered the compound, and Ram Khare walking back into his booth.

Mrs Puri came out into the compound with Ramu; they went towards the black Cross with a bowl full of channa. As if she had a sixth sense, Mrs Puri looked up and saw her neighbour up on the terrace.

'Masterji, what are you doing up there?' she shouted. 'It's dangerous on the roof.'

Blushing with embarrassment, like a schoolboy who had been caught, Masterji came down the stairs at once.

To make up for his indiscreet walk around the terrace, he read from *The Soul's Passageway after Death* for a while; then tried playing with his Rubik's Cube. Eventually he yawned, shook himself awake, and walked down to the Secretary's office.

Ajwani was in a corner of the office, reading the front page of the *Times of India* through his half-moon glasses. Secretary Kothari had another section of the paper; he was examining the real-estate advertisements. The two men were about to sip tea from little plastic cups; Kothari found a third cup into which he poured Masterji some of his tea. Ajwani came to the table to do the same.

'Wonderful isn't it, the rain,' Kothari said, moving the little cup towards Masterji. 'The whole world has become green. Everything grows.'

'And buildings fall,' Masterji said. Taking the *Times of India* from Ajwani, he read aloud the big story on the front page: 'A three-storey building in Crawford Market fell during yesterday's storm, killing the watchman and two others. Since the building was home to over twenty people, the people say it is a miracle only three died.'

Masterji kept reading. The desire for self-improvement had been the cause of destruction. Against the advice of the municipal engineer, the residents had installed overhead water tanks, and these, too heavy for the old building, had bent the ancient roof, which broke in the storm. Death, because they had wanted a better life.

'There was also a collapse in Wadala. That's in the inside pages.'

Ajwani crumpled his teacup and aimed it at the wastebasket.

'Still, that makes it only six deaths this year. What was it last year? Twenty? Thirty? A light year, Masterji. A light year.'

A macabre competition that the men in Vishram had played for at least a decade. If it was a 'heavy' year for monsoon-related deaths, it accrued somehow to the advantage of one side (Masterji and Kudwa); a 'light' year was a point scored by the other (Mr Puri and the Secretary).

'A light year,' Masterji conceded. 'But I'm hopeful. There's a long way to go yet before this monsoon is over.'

'I don't like this competition,' Ajwani said. 'The roof that's collapsing could one day be our own.'

'Vishram? Never. This building would have lasted a thousand years.'

'*Will* last,' Masterji corrected the Secretary, with a smile.

'*Would* have lasted.'

Masterji looked at the ceiling with a stylish wave of his hand: sardonic forbearance, as a character in a play might express it.

'One point to your party,' he said.

'How is the girl in 3B? The journalist. Still troubling you?'

'Oh, not at all. We're friends now. She had tea with me the other day.'

'Import-Export gave her notice. She has to leave by 3 October.'

Masterji turned to his left to face the broker. 'Is Hiranandani finding a new tenant?'

'Yes,' Ajwani smiled. 'Mr Shah, of the Confidence Group.'

Masterji looked at the ceiling and raised his voice. 'Another point for that party. We're losing here, my fellow Opposition members.'

Removing his glasses, Ajwani smiled. 'I'll give you the point, Masterji. I'll give you one hundred debating points. But in return, will you do something for me? Both my boys are in your science top-up. Your two biggest fans in the world. Tell me *everything* you say. We must always make experiments before we believe things. Correct? Just for today, Masterji, let this Ajwani be a teacher to you. Make an experiment for him? Will you walk down the road, and take a look at what Mr Shah is building beyond the slums? And then will you honestly say that you are *not* impressed by this Mr Shah?'

Ramu, in T-shirt and jeans, had come down the stairs with his mother's NO NOISE sign in his hands.

'We're going to SiddhiVinayak temple – we'll pray for everyone,' Mrs Puri said, telling the boy to wave at his three uncles, who waved back.

Ajwani, drawing his chair up to the Secretary's table, summoned the other two with his fingers.

'She comes back every day with brochures for new buildings, which turn up in her rubbish next day. Yet she says she goes to the temple.'

Masterji whispered back: 'Your competition has just increased, Ajwani. God must have joined the real-estate business.'

Three men burst out laughing, and one of them thought: *Exactly like old times*. Nothing *has changed*.

When Masterji went outside, he found Ram Khare by the compound wall, examining a gleaming red object, a brand-new Bajaj Pulsar motorbike.

'It's Ibrahim Kudwa's,' Ram Khare said. 'Bought it yesterday.'

'He shouldn't be spending money he doesn't have.'

The guard smiled. 'The mouth waters before it has food. It's the human way, Masterji.'

The Pulsar's metal skin gleamed like red chocolate. The segments of its body were taut, swollen, crab-like; the owner's black helmet was impaled on the rear-view mirror. Masterji remembered the scooter he had once owned, and his hand reached out.

A rooster, one of those that wandered about Vakola and sometimes slipped into the compound of a Housing Society, flew on to the driver's seat and clucked like a warning spirit.

This is what a woman wants. Not gold, not big cars, not easy cash. *This*.

Rich dark fine-grained wood, with a fresh coat of varnish and golden handles.

Mrs Puri moved her hands over the face of the built-in cupboard, pulled the doors open, and inhaled the fresh-wood smell.

'Madam can open the drawers too, if she wants.'

But Madam was already doing that.

The family Puri were in a sample flat on the sixth floor of the Rathore Towers – beige, brand-new, double-bedroomed, approximately 1,200-square-foot built-up area. Mr Puri stood by the window with Ramu, showing his son the common swimming pool, the gym with weight-loss guarantee, and the common table-tennis room down below.

The guide, who was holding a brochure in her hands, turned on a light.

'And here is the second bedroom. If Madam would come this way?'

Madam was too busy opening the drawers. She was imagining the

154

sunlight glowing on this beautiful piece of dark wood every morning for the rest of her life. Stocked chock-a-block with Ramu's fragrant clothes. His towels in this drawer. His T-shirts here. T-shirts *and* shorts here. Polo shirts here. Fluffy trousers here.

'Come this way, sir. And the child. And you too, madam. I'm sorry, I have another appointment after this.'

'He's not a child. He's eighteen years old.'

'Yes, of course,' their guide said. 'Observe the fittings and finishings. The Rathore Group is all about fittings and finishings…'

'Why are there no curtain rods in the rooms?'

'Madam is correct. But the Rathore Group would be happy to add curtain rods for someone like Madam.'

Red curtains would be perfect here. The place would look like a lighthouse at night. Neighbours would notice; people on the road would look up and say, 'Who lives there?'

Mrs Puri pressed the soft hand that was in hers. *Who else?*

What an enormous, high-ceilinged, light-welcoming apartment. And look at the floor: a mosaic of black and white squares. A precise, geometrical delineation of space, not the colourless borderless floors on which she had fought and eaten and slept all her married life.

In the lift, she asked her husband: 'You didn't tell anyone you were coming here, did you?'

He shook his head.

The Evil Eye had blighted Mrs Puri's life once. Back when she was pregnant, she had bragged to her friends that it was going to be a boy for sure. The Evil Eye heard her and punished her son. She was not going to make that mistake again.

She had kept up the same charade for weeks now, announcing to Ram Khare that she and the boy were off 'to the temple' – before catching an autorickshaw to the latest building she was inspecting. Her husband arrived directly. Everything was hush-hush. The Evil Eye would not hear of her good fortune this time.

Mr Puri placed his hand on his son's head, tapping along the close-cropped hair to the whorl at the centre.

'How many times have I told you not to do that?' Mrs Puri pulled

Ramu away from his father. 'His skull is sensitive. It's still growing.'

When the door opened, Ritika, her friend from Tower B, and her husband, the doctor, were waiting outside.

They stared at each other, and then burst out laughing.

'What a surprise, if we ended up neighbours again,' Mrs Puri said, half an hour later. 'A lovely surprise, of course.'

The two families were at a South Indian restaurant just below the Rathore Towers, in an air-conditioned room with framed photographs of furry foreign dogs and milkmaids.

'Yes,' Ritika smiled. 'Wouldn't it be?'

Mrs Puri and Ritika had been at the same school in Matunga, then together at KC College in Churchgate. Mrs Puri had had her nose ahead. Debating. Studies. Prize competitions. Even when they were looking at boys to marry. Her groom had been taller. Two inches.

Now Ritika's two children by her short husband were short, ugly, and normal.

'How much are you getting for your place?' Ritika asked. 'We have 820 square feet.'

'Ours is 834 square feet. They were going to put common toilets in Tower A, then added that little bit of floor space to the C flat. There are advantages to being in an old building.'

'So that means you're getting...' Ritika looked around for pen and paper, before sketching into the air.

'1.67 crores,' Mrs Puri said. 'And you?'

Ritika withdrew her finger from the air, smiled with dignity, and asked: 'Did you see one of those three-bedroom places on the top floor? That's what we were thinking of buying.'

'We can't spend more than sixty-five lakhs.' Mrs Puri mouthed the next sentence: 'The rest is for Ramu's future. Only problem is, this gentleman...' She leaned her head towards her husband. '... wants to leave the city.'

Fighting, like love-making, should be hidden from the child: the eighteen-year rule in the Puri household. But *this* was open provocation.

'Why would anyone want to live in Mumbai today?' Mr Puri

snapped at his wife. 'Let's go to a civilized place like Pune. Some place where ten thousand beggars don't come every morning by train. I'm sick of this city, I'm sick of its rat race.'

'The thing to do in a rat race is to win it. Not run away.'

'A civilized place. Pune is civilized. So is Nagpur.'

Mrs Puri tied a knot into her sari to remind herself. This would be settled *after* Ramu went to sleep with his Friendly Duck.

'We have checked this Confidence man,' Ritika's short husband said in a low voice. 'I know someone who knows someone in the construction business. He delays with the money: *always* delays. But he does pay. We may have to fight him in court to get the money, but we will get it. I don't worry about him. Not about him.'

'Then who?'

'Sangeeta...' Ritika smiled. '... we have heard that some people in Tower A are opposing the deal?'

'Absolutely no one in our Society opposes it. One person is saying "Maybe". She's a Communist. We'll make her change her mind.'

'But she's not the only one, Sangeeta. That old teacher in your Society too.'

'Masterji?' Mrs Puri laughed. 'He's just a big jackfruit. Prickly outside, soft and sweet inside. He's a born quarreller, not a born fighter. Always complaining about this, about that. But the moment the Pintos say yes, he'll say yes. I know my Masterji.'

The waiter approached with plates of crispy dosas.

'Just you wait and see, Ritika, we'll beat you to it. Tower A will have our special general meeting and hand in our forms first.'

When the waiter put down their dosas, everyone noticed that the biggest one had been placed in front of Mrs Puri.

They sat on a bench in the small open square outside the restaurant, in the shade of a small Ashoka tree. Mrs Puri had not forgotten the knot in her sari, but it had to be established that there was no fighting between Mummy and Daddy, so they sat close to each other. Ramu, swinging his legs in between them, played alternately with her fingers and his.

157

A couple came up to them. The woman asked: 'We're looking for Rathore Towers.'

'Right behind us.' Mrs Puri pointed.

The woman wore a svelte black salwar kameez. Her man was in a nice business shirt. Smart young couple.

Mrs Puri put her arm around Ramu and told the young woman: 'This is my son. His name is Ramesh. We may be your neighbours.'

Mr Puri raised his eyebrows: a thing like this had never been done before. Introducing Ramu to a stranger.

All these years his wife had lived a leper's length away from people. Her normal response when strangers came by was to tuck Ramu behind her body; that may have been why she let it grow so fat after his birth. He was still thinking about her extraordinary behaviour, when:

'This Sunday we are all going to the Taj. Did you hear me?'

'The Taj?' Mr Puri asked. 'Have you gone mad now, Sangeeta?'

Of course not. Since she was a child, she had seen its pale conical lampshades behind the dark windows: the Sea Lounge at the Taj Hotel. This Sunday they would walk in, hand in hand, and ask the waiter: 'A table in Sea Lounge, please.' ('*The* Sea Lounge,' Mr Puri corrected her.) Then they would sit down and say: 'We want coffee, please.' Good behaviour would be observed by all, especially by Ramu, who would not rub his gums, drool, or kick legs about. Maybe a film star would come in. After settling the bill (hundreds and hundreds of rupees), they would keep it as a memento.

Mr Puri, who was going to protest, kept quiet. *Why not?* he thought. Other human beings did it.

Two sharp fingers scraped his leg: a beggar child. Feeling guilty for his Taj fantasy, he gave the child a two-rupee coin.

'Don't criticize me for doing that,' he said, expecting the worst from his wife.

'Why would I?'

'For twenty-five years I've always wanted to give to beggars. Even one rupee, and you became angry.'

This was a slander on her; but she let it stand – if it made Mr Puri happy, let him say it. He too had suffered enough in life.

It began to rain. They scampered for a rickshaw; Mr Puri got in first with the boy, and his wife, after undoing the knot in her sari, joined them.

The end of the earth. As the sun dies out, it cools and turns into a red giant, and then expands and expands, until it has consumed all the inner planets, including the earth.

At this point, the ceiling lights go off – to add drama. Shadows are cast on the wall in the glow of the lamp light.

The preparations for the day's 'top-up' were all in place. With two hours to kill, Masterji picked up *The Soul's Passageway after Death* and made another attempt to finish it.

He followed the *atma*'s flight of enlightenment over the seventh and final ocean of the afterlife, beyond which glittered the peaks of snowy mountains. Another 10,000 years of purgation awaited it here.

He closed his eyes. At the age of sixteen, when other boys his age in Suratkal were playing cricket in the maidan or chasing college girls, Masterji had gone through a 'spiritual' phase, spending his afternoons reading Dr Radhakrishnan on Hindu and Buddhist philosophy, performing exercises from a second-hand copy of B. K. S. Iyengar's *Light on Yoga*, and teaching himself Sanskrit. This 'spiritual' phase ended the night he watched his father's corpse burning in the cemetery and thought: *That's all there is to life. Nothing more.* After his father's death, when he went to Mumbai to live with an uncle, he left Dr Radhakrishnan and B. K. S. Iyengar behind him. Bombay was a new world, and he had come here to become a new man. Now it seemed to him that, oddly enough, he had spent his forty-four years in Bombay exactly in the manner prescribed by the Hindu philosophers: *like a lotus in a dirty pond, be in the world but not of it.* Nothing had made him cry for years. Not even his wife's death. Was he really sorry that she had died? He did not know. He did not know.

He heard something strike the floor, and realized it was his book. 'I'm falling asleep. During the day.'

Not once in his adult life, not even when sick, had he allowed himself this luxury; he had scolded his wife and daughter if he caught them napping in the afternoon, and punished, by a stroke of a steel foot-ruler applied to the knuckles, his son. With a concentrated exertion of will he broke through the settling surface of sleep and got up.

He turned the tap in the living-room sink to wash his face in cold water, but the customary trickle had dried up completely.

How, in the midst of the monsoons, could he have no water in his living room? He struck the tap with his fist.

From the stairwell, as if to taunt him, came the words:

'By the rivers of Bab-y-lon

Where we sat dowwwwwn.'

The song was in English and the voice was deep: Ibrahim Kudwa, going up to his flat.

An hour later, the children were in the room, and Masterji was casting shadows on the wall to show how a healthy star changes into a red giant.

He was still talking and casting shadows, when the red giant flickered on the wall and vanished. Flashes of light and great explosions from near at hand overwhelmed the stars and black holes of Masterji's distant galaxies.

The residents of Tower B were setting off firecrackers.

The physics students watched from Masterji's window, craning their necks to get the best view.

'What is going on?' Masterji asked. 'Is it a festival today?'

'No,' Mohammad Kudwa said.

'Is someone getting married, then?'

The lights came on in the room: Mrs Puri had walked in through the open door.

'Have you read the notice, Masterji?' she asked, her fat fingers still

161

at the light switch. 'They beat us to it. Tower B. They have accepted the offer.'

'You are interrupting the physics top-up, Mrs Puri.'

'Oy, oy, oy...' She flicked the light switch on and off. 'Masterji. This cannot go on any longer. Speak to the Pintos. Must we all lose the light because of Shelley's blindness? Here...' She held out a paper. '... read this. And let the boys go. What kind of class can you have with all that noise outside?'

'All right,' Masterji shouted to the boys at the window. 'Go down and play with those fellows. That's what you want, isn't it? No one cares about physics. Go. And you too, Mrs Puri.'

She stood at the door with the notice in her hands.

'I'll go, Masterji. But will you do what Ajwani asked? Will you go down and see Mr Shah's new buildings?'

He closed the door behind all of them.

How did she know what Ajwani asked me to do? he wondered. *Are they talking about me behind my back?*

He read what Mrs Puri had left for him:

NOTICE

Vishram Co-operative Hsg Society Ltd, Tower B, Vakola, Santa Cruz (E), Mumbai – 40055

Minutes of the extraordinary general meeting held on 24 june

Theme: Dissolution of Society (Approved)

As the quorum was sufficient, the meeting commenced on time, at 12.30 p.m.

Mr V. A. Ravi, Secretary, suggested that the members should dispense with formalities and deal with the main issue, which was to consider the generous offer of redevelopment presented by...

He opened the window and tried to get a good view of Tower B. Standing in front of their building, men and women were lighting sparklers, rockets, dizzying *sudarshan*-chakras, and things in bottles with no purpose but to emit raw noise and light.

The doorbell rang.

'Masterji... *Please*... just go down and *look* at Mr Shah's...'

Mrs Puri had brought Ramu with her this time. The boy smiled; he too was pleading with his Masterji.

A tower of Babel of the languages of construction.

Bricks, concrete, twisted steel wires, planks, and bamboo poles held up the interiors. Long metal spokes stuck out from the floors with green netting, which sagged between the spokes like webbing, as if a fly had been squashed into the blueprint of the building. Holes in the concrete as big as a giant's eyes, and massive slabs that appeared to be aligned incorrectly, overlapping and jutting over each other. Everything was an affront to a man's sense of scale and order, even the sign that identified the thing, large as a political advertisement, and lit from beneath:

THE CONFIDENCE EXCELSIOR

Masterji stood before the two half-built concrete towers.

One day they would be glassed and sheathed, but now their true nature was exposed. This was the truth of 20,000 rupees a square foot. The area already had a water shortage, how would it support so many new homes... and what would happen to the roads?

Lights came on at the top of the second tower: somehow a crane had been lifted up there, and it began to move. In the glare of the lights Masterji saw men sitting on the dark floors like an advance army concealed in the entrails of the building.

He lifted his foot just in time: a dead rat lay before him imprinted with a tyre-track.

He walked past the huts and the Tamil temple, to return to the gate of his Society. The celebrations continued outside Tower B.

He was halfway up the stairs, when a red missile hurtled down in the opposite direction.

'Sorry, Masterji.'

It was Ms Meenakshi, his next-door neighbour: wearing a red blouse that did not quite reach her jeans.

'Don't worry, Ms Meenakshi. How are things?'

She smiled and kept going down the stairs.

'How is your boyfriend?' he shouted.

From somewhere near the ground floor, she laughed. 'My boyfriend is scared of you, Masterji. He won't come here any more.'

He listened to her charge out of the building. Exactly the way Sandhya, when her friends called her for a game of volleyball, dropped her sketchbook and rocketed downstairs.

He placed his hand on the warm building. Just as when a drop of formaldehyde falls on a dead leaf in a science class, revealing a secret life of veins, Vishram throbbed with occult networks. It was pregnant with his past.

Back in his flat, he turned the tap at the washbasin sink. He slapped it. Water spurted out brown and then red and then stopped. He slapped it again, and now the tap spat out a stone. A final red spurt, and finally the water flowed clear and strong.

Who says it is falling down? he thought, washing his face in the cold water. *It will last for ever, if we take care of it.*

Friday mornings in 1B, Vishram Society Tower A. Kellogg's, warm milk, lots of sugar. Marmalade on toast. Wedges of Amul cheese.

The dishes had been cleared from the dining table and immersed in a kitchen sink brimming with frothy soap-water.

Sitting on their mother's bed, Sunil and Sarah watched as Mrs Rego, at her reading table, slit open the latest letter from her younger sister, Catherine, who lived in Bandra.

Hair brushed, double-windsor-knotted, wearing his navy-blue-and-white school uniform, fourteen-year-old Sunil, Mummy's 'senior adviser', closed his eyes to concentrate. Next to him in her pretty uniform (pink and white), Sarah, eleven, the 'junior adviser', kicked her legs and watched a dragonfly.

A black-and-white photograph of Arundhati Roy hung from the bedroom wall next to a framed poster for a Vijay Tendulkar play performed at the Prithvi Theatre.

Putting on her glasses, Mummy read Aunty Catherine's letter out loud, until she reached the sentence that began: 'Even though you have not written for a week, as it is your *wont* to do...'

Reading it aloud a second time, Mrs Rego put a hand to her heart. Gasp. 'Wont' was a *most* stylish word, she explained to her children. Which meant that the three of them had been well and truly 'trumped'.

The aim of this Friday-morning epistolary jousting was for each sister, in an apparently banal letter to the other, to slip in a 'stylish' word or phrase, which would catch the other off guard, and force her to concede that she had been 'trumped'. Even though they were just minutes apart from each other (depending on the traffic in the east–west passage), Mrs Rego each Friday sealed a blue prepaid letter, addressed it with formal pomp ('Mrs Catherine D'Mello-Myer of Bandra West') and walked over to the postal workers' colony near the Vakola mosque to drop it into the red box there.

A week later, the postman would deliver the riposte from Bandra. Now Mrs Rego had to 'trump' Aunty Catherine back.

Taking out her best Parker fountain-pen, using her most florid hand, she wrote on the blue prepaid letter:

Dearest Darling Catherine…

… while preparing for an important executive meeting at the Institute, I found, quite serendipitously, your lovely little letter…'

'"Serendipitously" is a *very* stylish way of saying "by chance",' Mrs Rego explained to the children. The three shared wicked giggles. The moment she got to the line, Catherine would have to swivel about in her chair, saying, 'Oh, but I've been *trumped*.'

Sunil took Mummy's Parker and underlined the phrase three times, just to stick it to his Aunty Catherine.

'Time for school, children.' She rose from the bed. 'I'll get a plastic bag.'

Mrs Rego went into the kitchen to check on Ramaabai, the maid. Standing at the sink, the old woman removed one wet utensil after the other from the foamy water and wiped each one clean with a pink Brillo pad.

'Ramaabai, if you break any of the glasses today I'll deduct the cost from your month's salary,' Mrs Rego said. 'And be on time in the evening.'

The maid kept cleaning the dishes.

Mrs Rego and her children went from floor to floor in Vishram Society, inspecting the doors. Another shipment of sweets had arrived from the builder last night, to celebrate Tower B's (unanimous) acceptance of his plan, and Mrs Rego knew from the last time what would happen. The golden Ganeshas from the red sweet-boxes, cut out by those who did not wish to discard a god's image, had turned up alongside the overlapping Shivas and Jesuses on the doors.

Mrs Puri, naturally, had put up a Confidence Group Ganesha on her door. Two of them, in fact. Mrs Rego's nails scraped at the god's pot belly until it bulged out. She did the same to the second Ganesha. Sunil held up the black bag; his mother flicked the gods into it.

Saying goodbye to her two advisers at the gate – they would catch their school bus from the market – Mrs Rego went the other way. Her fingers touched her black handbag, her elbow thrust out at a sharp angle; her lips were sucked in and her eyes were narrowed. Not a square inch of vulnerable surface.

She pitched the black bag into the open rubbish pit, where, to her delight, a stray hog took an interest in it. She wished she had rubbed some honey over the Confidence Group Ganeshas she had removed from the doors.

'Liar,' Mrs Rego said, as if goading the animal to attack. 'Liar, liar, liar': she clapped three times.

Leaving the hog to enjoy Mr Shah's gifts to Vishram, she walked towards her institute.

A life like Mrs Rego's provided an excellent schooling in the ways of liars.

Georgina Rego, the 'Battleship', was one of two daughters of a famous Bandra doctor who would have been rich if he had not trusted every man he met on the street. Catherine, the younger sister with whom she played her game of 'trump', still lived in Bandra, in a flat in the Reclamation. Disobeying their father, Catherine had married an American exchange student, a half-Jew – a scandal in the community in those days; now the foreign husband, a quiet, goateed man, wrote articles on village life in India that were published in foreign magazines and in the copies of the *Economic and Political Weekly* that came to Mrs Rego's desk at the Institute.

Her own husband, Salvador, had been picked by her father. A Bombay Bandra Catholic who liked worsted wool suits and dark shirts embroidered with his initials: 'S.R.' After two years in Manila working for a British merchant bank he confessed one evening by long-distance that he had found another, a local, younger. Naturally, a Catholic. They were all good Catholics in the Philippines. 'You were never going to be enough for a man like me, Georgina.'

He cleaned her out.

Her entire dowry. Sixteen George V half-sovereigns, her father's share certificates in the Colgate-Palmolive company, two heavy silverware sets – all smuggled in her husband's luggage to Manila. Her father was dead and she could not live off Catherine's handouts, so she had left Bandra, a single mother with two children, and moved to the eastern side of the city, to a neighbourhood without roads and reputation, but with Christians. Va-kho-la. (Or was it Vaa-k'-la? She still wasn't entirely sure.)

From Catherine she heard about big changes in Bandra. One by one, the old mansions on Waterfield Road were melted down like ingots – even her own Uncle Coelho's. It was always the same builder, Karim Ali, who broke down the houses. When he wanted to snatch Uncle Coelho's house on Waterfield Road to put up his apartment block for Bollywood stars, he too had come with sweets and smiles – it was all 'Uncle and Aunty' at first. Later on, the threatening graffiti on the walls and the late-night phone calls, and finally the day when four teenagers burst in when Uncle Coelho was having dinner, put a cheque on one side of the table, a knife on the other, and said: 'Either the knife or the cheque. Decide before dinner is over.' This Confidence Shah was the same kind of man as that Karim Ali – how could anyone believe those oily smiles, those greasy sweets? Behind the smiles were lies and knives.

'Hey!' Mrs Rego shouted. 'Turn your phone off while driving!'

A motorcyclist was wobbling down the road, his head propped to one side as he talked on his phone. He grinned as he passed her, and kept talking.

Breaking the law in broad daylight. Did the police care? Did *anyone* care? You would never get away with talking on your phone while driving in Bandra – that much had to be said for the western side of the railway lines. Raise property prices in Vakola by 20 per cent, and fellows like this – she snapped her fingers – evaporate.

The Institute for Social Action lay halfway between Vishram Society and the slums that lay further down the road. An old tiled building, the door left open at all times.

Saritha was standing outside the door, waiting for Mrs Rego.

Along with Julia and Kamini, Saritha was one of the three socially committed girls from good families (employment at the Institute was strictly restricted to good families) who answered to Mrs Rego. Saritha's role was to conduct research into public interest litigation on slum redevelopment, and kill the lizards that overran the walls. For if there was much compassion at the Institute for the poor, there was none for reptiles or arachnids; Mrs Rego hated and feared anything that crawled on walls.

'What is it?' she shouted at Saritha. 'Is there a lizard in the office?'

Saritha tilted her head.

Now Mrs Rego saw it: there was a black Mercedes parked right by the Institute. Shanmugham stood by the car. He smiled, and made a sort of salute, as if he worked for her.

'Mrs Rego, my boss wants to have a word with you. He sent the car for you.'

'How dare you,' she said. 'How dare you! Get out of here, or I'll call the police.'

'He just wants to have lunch with you, Mrs Rego. Please… just for ten minutes.'

She went into her office and closed the door. She took up the papers on her desk and read. A reply from a German government-run social welfare body; yes, there was funding available for those doing work for the poor in Mumbai. The deadline, unfortunately, had… A request from a social worker studying for her Ph.D. at the University of Calicut. She was collecting data on child sponsorship; did the Institute have any information on children…

Mrs Rego looked at the clock.

'Is that man still outside?' she shouted.

Saritha came into the office and nodded.

From her office window, she saw Mr Shah's half-built towers in the distance: blue tarpaulin covered them against the rains, and work went on inside the covers.

A gust of wet wind blew through the window; Mrs Rego rubbed her goosebumpy forearms.

'That's a shark, sir. Freshwater. A small one. But authentic.'

The smell of beer, prawn, curry, butter, oil thickened the recycled air-conditioned air inside the restaurant. An aquarium had been set into the near wall. The thing that had been called a shark gaped with a stupid open mouth in one corner, while smaller fish glided around, scoffing at its sharkish pretensions.

Mr Shetty, the manager, stood with his hands folded in front of his crotch.

'A recent addition to the aquarium,' he said. 'I hope you approve of it.'

In the restaurant in Juhu – Mangalorean seafood, his favourite cuisine – Dharmen Shah sat in silence at a table with a view of the door. The ceiling of the restaurant was vaulted, an allusion to the caves of Ajanta; the wall opposite the aquarium was covered with a bas-relief, in plaster of Paris, of the great civic monuments of the city – VT, the Rajabai Tower, the columned façade of the Asiatic Society library.

The manager waited for Mr Shah to say something.

A waiter brought a whole lobster on a plate and placed a bowl of butter by the side. More food came: crab, fish curry, a prawn biryani. Wrapped in aluminium foil, a stack of glistening naans arrived in a wicker basket. Four flavoured cream spreads were placed next to it: pudina, garlic, lemon, and tomato.

Maybe she isn't going to come, Shah thought, as he tore apart the bread with his fingers.

She had quoted God's name, after all. 'By the Lord Jesus Christ I will…'

He wondered which of the four cream spreads to dip his bread in.

Remember, Dharmen: he told himself. A person who quotes Jesus is not, in real-estate terms, a Christian. No. A person who quotes Jesus is looking for a higher price to sell.

Humming a Kishore Kumar tune, he dipped the bread into the pudina cream.

Next he went for the buttered crab. With a long thin spoon, Shah scooped the baked flesh from the salted and peppered exoskeleton of the crab; when all the easy meat had been carved from the chest and eaten, he tore the limbs apart, and chewed on them, one at a time, biting into the shell and chewing till it cracked open, before sucking at the warm white flesh. The waiters were prepared to carve out the flesh and bring it on a small plate, but Dharmen Shah did not want it that way. He wanted to feel he was eating a thing that had been breathing just an hour ago: wanted to feel, once again, the extraordinary good fortune of being one of those still alive.

Maybe she was not going to come? No. A social worker needs a builder. We make each other: she can be so pure only if I am so evil. She will come to me.

He spat out shell and cartilage on to the porcelain plate. With a finger he checked the colour of the mucus that covered the shell.

The restaurant door opened: Shanmugham stepped in from blinding light, like a figure in a revelation.

He's come alone. Mr Shah could not breathe.

The restaurant door opened again: silhouetted against the painful white light, Shah saw a middle-aged woman.

He wiped his lips and stood up.

'Ah, Mrs Rego, Mrs Rego. How nice of you to come. I assume the traffic kept you so long?' he asked, looking at Shanmugham.

Who made a quick negative movement of his head.

Mrs Rego did not sit down.

'Why have you brought me here, Mr Builder? What is the business?'

Shah spread his arms over the dishes on the table.

'*This* is the business. We Gujaratis don't like to eat alone. Would you like some fresh-lime soda, Mrs Rego? – and you must sit down, please.'

'I'm not hungry. I may go back now.'

'No one is stopping you at any time, Mrs Rego. There are autorickshaws right outside. You will be back in Vakola in ten minutes.'

Mrs Rego looked around the restaurant; she looked at the vaulted ceiling, at the bas-relief, and stared at the fish. 'But why *have* you brought me here?'

Shah shared the joke with his food.

'She is frightened I will do something to her. With that shark near by: I must look like some James Bond villain. Shanmugham, please call the manager of the restaurant here.'

Who came, with folded hands, leaning forward, eager to please.

'Mr Shetty: this is Mrs Rego. You have seen her with me at… what time is it? 1.20 p.m. I want you to write it down in your register. Mrs Rego, resident of 1B, Vishram Society Tower A, Vakola, seen in the presence of Mr Shah. I want that down, word for word – do you have that?'

'Yes, sir.'

'And please send a waiter for our order.'

The builder looked at his nervous guest.

'Now: if anything happens to you, I will go to jail. You are a social worker: the press and the television people will show me no mercy. I took the liberty of ordering some dishes of seafood and crab before you got here. Shanmugham, you too sit down, and eat.'

Mrs Rego did not move. She stood staring at Mr Shah's plate, on which gristle, bone, flesh, had piled up around bread, rice, and red curry.

'You're my guest, Mrs Rego. You may not like my offer, but you must eat the food at my table. A lady like you, who grew up in Bandra, must know not to snub her host. If it's too much you can take it back for your boy. You have two boys, don't you? A son and daughter, sorry. Well, you'll take it back for both of them.'

Pulling out a chair, Mrs Rego sat.

A waiter cleared the napkin from her plate. Mr Shah himself served a portion of curried lobster, and offered Mrs Rego a naan, which she declined.

She never had carbohydrates in the afternoon.

*

Sunil Rego, coming home dirty from his cricket, found his mother sitting on the bed, with Sarah on her lap. The bedside lamp had been turned on.

'There's food for you in the fridge, Sunil. It's wrapped in silver foil.'

Mrs Rego looked at her daughter. 'Very good, isn't it?'

Sarah nodded.

'Why did you buy it, Mother?' Sunil sat next to them.

'I didn't buy it. You know we don't have money to spend on restaurant food.'

Mrs Rego whispered: 'The builder sent it. Mr Shah. He has made us an offer.'

'Yes, Mummy. I know.'

'No, Sunil. He has made us a separate offer. This afternoon.'

Sunil listened to everything – how Shah had ordered food, listened to her life story, sympathized with her life story, then pushed a folder and a blank envelope over to her.

Not a bribe; a first instalment of the money to come – that was all. Don't want it, she had said – thinking it was a trap. It will be deducted, will be deducted from the final payment. Take it, Mrs Rego. Think of your two sons. Your son and daughter, sorry.

'What did you do, Mummy?'

'I said no, of course. He said we could think about it and let him know.'

Sunil covered his mouth with his palm. Sarah did the same as her brother did.

'What do we do now? Should we call your father in the Philippines and ask him?'

'No, Mother,' Sunil said sternly. 'How could you even think of that? After all that he's done to us?'

'You're right. You're absolutely right.'

'Are you calling Daddy?' Sarah kicked her legs about. 'Daddy in the Philippines?'

Sunil put his finger on his lips and glared at his sister.

'Let's take a walk, Mummy.'

Mrs Rego understood. The walls of Vishram were thin.

Mother and children, hand in hand, went to the main road, where she told them again, in slightly different words, all that had happened; and soon they were at the Dhobi-ghat, the part of Vakola where clothes were washed in the open air, in small cubicles seething with soap-suds and foam. Mother and children stood outside a laundry cubicle and talked. Behind them a long white petticoat rose and fell like a sail in a storm, as it was slapped on a granite slab. On the other side of the road, a bhelpuri-vendor sliced a boiled potato into cubes while his lentil broth simmered.

Mrs Rego turned around: the washerman had stopped his work to watch them.

Hailing an autorickshaw, Mrs Rego and Sunil said, almost in one voice: 'Bandra.'

The dividing wall between the west and the east of Mumbai is punctured at Santa Cruz at just three places – indeed, the difficulty of passage is the harshest kind of tax imposed on the residents of the poorer east (for it is usually they who have to make this passage). Two of these passages are called 'subways', tunnels under the railway tracks, and both of these, Milan and Khar, are equally congested at rush hour. The third option, the Highway, is the most humane – but, being the longest, is also the most expensive by autorickshaw.

For reasons of economy, Mrs Rego asked that their driver take the Khar subway; turning left just before the station, their rickshaw joined the queue of vehicles hoping to make it through the tunnel to the west.

South Mumbai has the Victoria Terminus and the Municipal Building, but the suburbs, built later, have their own Gothic style: for every evening, by six, pillars of hydro-benzene and sulphur dioxide rise high up from the roads, flying buttresses of nitrous dioxide join each other, swirls of unburnt kerosene, mixed illegally into the diesel, cackle like gargoyles, and a great roof of carbon monoxide closes over the structure. And this Cathedral of particulate matter rises over every red light, every bridge and every tunnel during rush hour.

In a narrow passageway like the Khar subway, the pollution chokes, burns, ravages human tissue. When their rickshaw finally came, after twenty minutes of honking and crawling, to the mouth of the tunnel, Mrs Rego covered Sarah's nose with her kerchief, and instructed the boy to cover his face too. The line of autos moved into the choked tunnel, passing under a giant advertisement offering cures for kidney stones by the latest ultrasonic methods to make, in this primitive fashion, the passage to the west.

Ahead in the distance, where the tunnel ended, the three Regos could see light, clean air, freedom.

In the shade of a group of king palms, a woman in a burqa lifted up her face-mask and whispered to a young man. Watching them, Mrs Rego thought: *I am almost old. I am forty-eight years old.*

Hand in hand, she and her children walked down the Bandra bandstand.

They spilled over, as if from the ocean: girls with golden straplets on their handbags, boys with buff shaved chests showing through their white shirts, on every brow and lip the moisture placed there by the warm night, and sucked away by the ocean breezes.

Mrs Rego waited for darkness to fall.

An old woman's night is so small: a young woman's night is the whole sky.

When the street lamps came to life, they took another rickshaw so she could see her Bandra again – the Bandra of her college days, where even the façade of a Catholic church had the quality and excitement of sin.

Getting off at National College, the three walked towards the old neighbourhood.

Girls were shopping for handbags and sandals in the lit stalls of the Linking Road. Just as she had done, all those years ago. If her younger self, searching for a handbag, were to bump into her, would she believe that this was her destiny in life – to end up as a left-wing radical in Santa Cruz (East)?

On Waterfield Road, she stopped by a café and looked into the glass window: what were all these young people, in their black T-shirts and turtleshell-rimmed glasses, talking about? How fat and glossy they looked, like glazed chicken breasts turning on a rotisserie spit.

The touch of cold glass on the tip of Mrs Rego's nose was like a guard's rebuke.

Not yet. Not till you sign that document.

'Are we moving to Bandra, Mummy?'

'Quiet. Mummy's watching the people on the other side of the glass.'

'Mummy—'

'Anyway, we *can't* move to Bandra, so don't disturb her.'

'Why not, Sunil?'

'Because the builder is an evil man. Just like Karim Ali who robbed Grand-Uncle Coelho.'

'Mummy, let's move to Bandra. I like it here.'

Mrs Rego looked at her son, and then at her daughter, and nodded at both of them.

BOOK FIVE

The End of an Opposition Party

BOOK FIVE

The End of an Opposition Party

Ajwani took the slice of lemon and pressed it with dark fingers: seeds and juice oozed out.

'That's what she feels like. Pretends to be special, a social worker helping the poor, but every day the deadline comes nearer, this is what is happening to her brain.'

Mrs Puri glared at him; she bent and picked up the lemon seeds from the carpet of her living room. 'Don't do that. Ramu might slip on them.'

Ramu lay under his blue aeroplane quilt, the door to his bedroom ajar; as he sipped lemon tea on the living-room sofa, Ajwani waved to the boy.

'I know Shah has seen Mrs Rego,' he whispered. A teenager in the slum, one of his connections down there, had seen a Mercedes driving down to the Institute. The next morning wrappers from a very expensive seafood restaurant at Juhu had been discovered in her rubbish.

'How do you know what is in her rubbish?' Mrs Puri asked.

Ajwani grinned; the gill-like lines on his cheeks deepened.

'Do you want to fight over small things, Mrs Puri? I know I am the black sheep of this Society. I do things you good people will not do. But now you must listen to the black sheep, or all of us will lose the money.' He whispered, 'Mrs Rego was offered a small sweetener. By Mr Shah. That is my guess.'

'A small sweetener?' Mrs Puri turned the words upside-down as if they were a pair of suspect jeans. 'You mean *extra* money? Why only her? Are *you* getting one, Ajwani?'

179

The broker threw up his hands in frustration.

'I won't even *ask* for one. If everyone wants a small sweetener, no one will get the cake. On my own personal initiative, I am convincing the Opposition Party, one by one. *Why?* Because I take responsibility.'

Mrs Puri closed Ramu's bedroom door. She whispered, indicating to Ajwani the appropriate decibel level for a home with a growing child. '*You* took responsibility for Mrs Rego? Then why hasn't she agreed?'

Ajwani winced.

'A man can't put pressure on a woman beyond a certain point. A *man* can't.'

'So that's why you came here,' Mrs Puri said. '*I* am not going to speak to that Communist woman.'

'Mrs Puri...' The broker joined his hands in prayer. '... this old fighting, this old pettiness – they have to end. This is why we have never gone anywhere in this country.'

Telling Ajwani to watch over Ramu while he slept – the Friendly Duck nearby, in case he woke up – Mrs Puri limped down the stairs, breathing stertorously as she transferred her weight from foot to foot. No one answered the bell at 1B. She pressed a second time.

'It's open,' a voice said from within.

She found the Battleship at the dining table, staring at the wall.

'What is wrong, Mrs Rego?'

'It's on the wall. Do you see it?'

It was the first time Mrs Puri had been inside the Battleship's home.

She saw framed posters in Hindi and English, and three large black-and-white photographs, one of which she recognized as that of President Nelson Mandela.

'Ramaabai usually handles them when they come inside the house. I can't do anything until someone kills them for me.' Mrs Rego pointed a finger.

Now Mrs Puri saw it. Above President Mandela.

Thick and curvy as something squeezed out of a tube, pistachio in colour, the lizard was moving towards the fluorescent tube-light, where the flies had gathered.

A fellow like this one Mrs Puri had never seen: a monarch of his species. Seizing a dragonfly hovering near the tube-light he tossed back his head; the translucent wings glowed golden against the tube-light and then disappeared into crunching jaws. His engorged body went inside the tube-light, a grey form making precise black marks where the feet pressed on the illuminated cylinder.

'*This* is the problem?' she asked.

Mrs Rego nodded.

Mrs Puri went into the kitchen, removed the gold bangles from her forearms, and put them on a newspaper on the table. She looked for a chair that would help her reach the tube-light.

She saw, above the fridge, a poster of a human being formed entirely by hands and feet clasping each other, with the slogan:

None of Us is as Strong as All of Us
Vote in every election
It is your right and duty

Mrs Puri shook her head. Even the kitchen was Communist.

Searching for a weapon, she settled on the Yellow Pages lying on the microwave oven. She climbed on to a chair by the dining table. Tapping a corner of the Yellow Pages against the tube-light, she drew the monster out, tap by tap.

Mrs Rego had withdrawn into the kitchen for safety.

'Are you killing it?' she shouted from there.

'No, I'm throwing it out.'

'Its tail will fall off! You must kill it!'

The tail had indeed fallen off. Mrs Puri caught the body of the wriggling lizard, went outside, and dropped it down the wall of the Society. She came back for the tail.

'Over,' she said, walking into the kitchen to wash her hands.

She held out her arm with the fingers bunched together. Mrs Rego picked up the bangles from the newspaper and slid them one by one over her neighbour's wrist, until the forearm was again sheathed in gold.

'Why are you so scared of them? My husband draws them to amuse Ramu. Spiders, too.'

'You know he stole all my gold coins,' Mrs Rego said, as she slid the final bangle on to Mrs Puri's forearm.

'Who? The lizard?'

'Sovereigns. George V sovereigns. Half-sovereigns. This fat. All gone.' Mrs Rego smiled. 'The man from whom I take my last name.'

'I never met him, Mrs Rego.'

'He is a thief. He made me a poor woman. Did I ever tell you that my father was one of the richest men in Bandra?'

'Many times.' Mrs Puri gave the bangles a shake to settle them down her arm.

'It's true. We had the best of everything. Catherine and me. Yet we fought over everything. For dinner our father would serve us biryani. Mutton. We fought so much, you're getting more, I'm getting less, he decided to weigh each portion of biryani on a scale before he served us. That way neither would "trump" the other. Catherine was light-skinned; each time we stood in front of a mirror she trumped me. When she married that Jewish man, and I married a *pucca* Catholic, I thought I had trumped her for good. But now... she still lives in Bandra. Her husband is well known. And she has a Sony PlayStation in her flat. I have to take my children there so they can play with it.'

Mrs Puri gave her left hand another shake. 'You have your work.'

'Who am I, Arundhati Roy? Just a woman in Vakola sending letters to foreigners asking for money. Once in a blue moon I help someone in the slums. Mostly I just sit and watch as this city is ruined by developers.'

A new Heinz ketchup bottle stood on the Regos' table, but the empty one, which it superseded, had not yet been thrown out. Mrs Puri placed the new bottle adjacent to the empty one. 'This is what we want in life,' she said, pointing to the new bottle. 'And this is what we get.' Mrs Rego laughed.

'I've admired your way with words all these years, Mrs Puri. Even when we fought.'

'In college you should have seen my short stories, my poems.' Mrs Puri swiped her hand over her head, to indicate past glories. 'I could've been a writer, anything I wanted. We have all had to accept other lives.'

'The Confidence builder gave me a bribe, Mrs Puri. To accept the offer.'

Mrs Puri nodded. 'I know. Ajwani told me.'

'How does Ajwani know?'

'He knows all kinds of things. He's like one of these lizards, going up every wall.' Mrs Puri came closer to Mrs Rego to say: 'He is a *dirty* man.'

'Dirty?'

'He goes to unclean women. In the city. I know it for a fact. My husband once saw him near Falkland Road.'

Mrs Rego, about to ask what Mr Puri had been doing near Falkland Road, suppressed her question.

'Money is nothing to me,' Mrs Puri said. 'When I'm hungry I butter a loaf of bread and eat. But Ramu I have to think of. And Sunil and Sarah you have to think of. Even the poor live better than we do. When you drive on a high road over the slums, you see satellite TV dishes like lotus leaves on a pond. You've thought about the poor for years. Now think about your children. I know what I want to do with my money. Take care of Ramu. Buy a home in Goregaon. Do you know what I want to do with the rest? A clinic for injured dogs. This city is full of disfigured animals.'

'How Christian of you, Mrs Puri.'

'I know you don't like builders. Don't do it for Mr Shah. Do it for your children. When small people like us compromise, it is the same as when big people refuse to compromise. The world becomes a better place.'

Mrs Puri needed another half an hour. Then the two women embraced; Mrs Puri saw, through a veil of sincere tears, a shining wooden cupboard full of Ramu's fresh, fragrant clothes. She closed her eyes in happiness. The harder she cried, the bigger the cupboard grew.

If anyone's getting a small sweetener, she thought, eyes closed, patting her friend's back, *it's me and Ramu*.

*

In 2A, Vishram Society, Mrs Pinto and her husband held hands across their dining table.

Masterji cracked his knuckles. He was on the sofa.

'So what if Mrs Rego has changed her mind? There are three of us, and that is enough. In Rome they had this triumvirate. Caesar, Crassus, Pompey. We'll be like that. The Vakola Triumvirate.'

'Do *you* want the money, Masterji?' Mr Pinto asked. 'If you want it, Shelley and I will agree. We don't want to hold you back.'

'What a thing for you to ask, Mr Pinto. What a thing for you to…'

'Like a lemon being squeezed. That is how they feel with every passing day,' Mr Pinto said, thinking of what Ajwani had told him in parliament the previous evening. 'Yesterday Mrs Saldanha smiled at me when I walked out of the gate. But she didn't smile when I came back. In those five minutes she must have heard the ticking of the deadline clock.'

'I haven't noticed anything changing,' Masterji said. 'Our neighbours are solid people.'

'We'll give in to Mr Shah for *your* sake, Masterji. Won't we, Shelley?'

Masterji felt things shifting beneath his feet, as if he were standing by the waves at Juhu beach. *But I'm doing it for* their *sake*, he thought.

He looked at Mr Pinto's old face staring into Shelley's old face; he saw their osteoarthritic fingers knitted together on the table. *They don't want to be thought of as the people who are holding everyone else up.*

His gaze moved to the dining table with the red-and-white cloth, where he had eaten his meals since his wife's death.

'I do not want to take Mr Shah's offer,' he said. 'I have lived in Vishram Society with my friends and I wish to die here with them. As there is nothing more to say, I will see you at dinner.'

In the crepuscular light of the stairwell he examined the old walls of his Society: the yellow paint, nicks, blotches, and rain-stains.

Now it seemed to him that Mr Pinto was right. They *had* been changing for some time. His neighbours. When Ajwani met him in the street, he would turn away and pretend to be on his mobile phone. Masterji touched a fresh white indentation in the wall. The Secretary. Here the change was more subtle: the laugh-lines around the snowy eyebrows spread wider with each smile.

Purnima's function in life had been to restrain him; and now this dim stairwell forced him into self-reflection, as if her spirit had been reincarnated here. *You're doing it again*, she said. *Imagining the worst in humans*. He stood in the stairwell, scooping out dirt from the wet octagonal stars of the grille.

Half an hour later, the pink orthopaedic bandage fastened around his knee to ease the tension in it, he was on his bed turning the Rubik's Cube when two sets of knuckles knocked on his door: one rhythm insistent, the other unctuous.

'I'm coming, Sangeeta. And don't knock so loudly, Ajwani.'

When he opened the door, Mrs Puri smiled.

'Masterji, I just went down to the Pintos' house. And asked them again if they would sign.'

Ajwani stayed a few feet behind Mrs Puri, looking at his feet. Masterji felt that there had been some tension between the two of them, and that he was the source of this tension.

'Don't speak to the Pintos. Speak to me. My answer is still no.'

'Masterji, I am not a brilliant human being as you are. I just have one question for you. Why do you want to stay in a building that is about to fall down?'

He knew, from the absolute nature of the silence, the ceasing of all ambient noise, that the Pintos were listening in.

'I have memories here, Mrs Puri. My late daughter, my late wife. Shall I show you Sandhya's sketchbook? It is full of drawings of the garden. Every tree and plant and spider's web and stone and...'

She nodded.

'I remember her. A beautiful girl. But you are not the only one with memories in this building. I have them, too. I have one of this very spot. Do you remember, Masterji, that day eighteen years ago, when I came here and told you what the doctors had told me about Ramu? Purnima was at the door and you put your book down on your teakwood table. And you remember what you did, what your eyes did, when you heard the news about Ramu?'

The old man blinked with emphasis. He remembered.

'Masterji, I love the Pintos as much as you do. For years they have looked after my Ramu as he played in the compound. But will they pay for his hospital and his nurse when he grows old and needs medical attention? Ask them.'

He listened: not a cough, not a scratch on a table, from downstairs. The Pintos did not object to the logic.

'Thirty years,' Mrs Puri said, 'I've come to you for advice. Now I ask you to listen to a foolish, fat woman just this once. Speak to Gaurav. Ask him what he thinks, as a father should ask his son. Will you do that for me, for your Mrs Puri?'

She glared at the small dark man next to her.

The markings on Ajwani's cheeks rose ingratiatingly: he forced out a grin.

'Masterji, my two sons are your biggest fans. R and R. I am your third-biggest fan in the world.'

When the rain had ended, Masterji walked down the stairs to the compound. Mrs Saldanha's door opened.

'Masterji, I have avoided meetings all my life, as you may have noticed. But I have something to tell you.'

'Yes, Mrs Saldanha.'

She stood in a shapeless green gown; worry-lines cut into her brow and strands of untidy silver coiled out of her hair. He remembered her twenty years ago: the most beautiful woman in the building.

'Masterji, my Radhika wants to study Journalism. At Syracuse University.'

He avoided her eyes.

'There was a Syracuse in the Roman empire. A place of learning.'

'This one is in America. New York State. And they won't give scholarships to Indians, so we have to pay for everything...'

He passed through his neighbours sitting out in the parliament and walked around the compound. Mrs Kudwa, bringing along little Mohammad, in his white tae kwon-do outfit, came to see him next.

The boy hid his face behind his mother; he had skipped Friday's science tutorial.

When she was gone, others followed: Mrs Ganguly from the fifth floor, Mrs Vij from the second floor. In addition, Masterji received petitions from an invisible party. He was sure he heard his wife whispering to him as he crunched the gravel of the compound. These people were her neighbours too. She urged the cause of the living.

Before going into the building, he stopped by Mrs Puri's chair in parliament, and told her that he would go see his son tomorrow. Not in the morning, though. The rush on the trains would be too great then.

'It's over. Even Masterji has agreed,' Mary said.

Standing outside Silver Trophy Society, she explained her situation to the security guard: 'When this Shanghai comes up, they'll have maids who wear uniforms and speak English. They won't want me. I have a son in school; I can't miss a month's pay.'

The guard was a lean light-skinned man; he assured Mary he would keep an eye out, but then asked about her 'family' with a gleam in his eye that could only signify lechery.

The guard at a building near the Dhobi-ghat had told her to check with him after noon; a doctor's family had just moved in from Delhi.

Rain clouds were regrouping in the evening sky. Mary crossed the road, and walked past the rows of fish-sellers with their glistening fresh catch, to be told:

'Those people from Delhi found a servant girl just ten minutes ago. Not even ten.'

Thanking the guard, she sat on a stone wall near the fish-sellers, and breathed into a fold of her sari. She had been out since seven in the morning. On either side of her, in baskets, or spread on blue tarpaulin sheets on the ground, she saw dried anchovies, fresh crabs, prawns in plastic buckets, and small slimy things that were still wriggling. An old fisherwoman scraped the scales off a two-foot yellow-finned tuna with a curved knife.

As if the departed souls of the fish were rising in a great host, a boom filled the air.

Mary looked up. A Boeing, climbing up from the Santa Cruz airport, cut through the darkening sky.

A blind man sat selling jasmine in the compound of the Tamil temple. The gate of the altar was open, and a small oil lamp glowed in front of a black Ganesha, resinous from decades of holy oil.

The side wall of the temple with the painted demon's mouth was once again doing duty as a wicket.

Kumar, who worked as a cleaner in the kitchen of a nearby hotel, stood near the side wall, slapping his thighs in anticipation.

Dharmendar, the cycle mechanic's boy, was running up to bowl with the red rubber ball in his hand.

Timothy, who had 'bunked' school to be here, had been given the honour of batting first, and took guard in front of the demon's mouth.

Instead of releasing the red ball, Dharmendar dropped it and grinned.

'It's your lucky day, Timothy. Your mother is coming.'

'Shit.'

The boy dropped his bat, grabbed his school satchel, and ran. Screaming his name – as the cricketers whistled with glee – Mary chased after him with her right hand raised and her fingers flexed.

Lightning forked over their heads, and large drops of rain fell on mother and son as they ran towards the *nullah*.

An old man leaned out of the open door, relishing the wind in his hair like a fourteen-year-old on his first unaccompanied ride. He stared at a train going in the opposite direction.

What *power*. The passing locomotive was a vector of raw momentum, rushing from another dimension at an angle through this one. A fragment of a dream slicing into the waking world.

It was two o'clock in the afternoon.

The first-class compartment was almost empty. But on an impulse Masterji had got up from his seat and done something he had not for decades – come to the open door of the compartment.

Insanity.

He, above all other men, should know the danger of standing here: he who had warned his students so many times against doing so: he, who had suffered so much from the tracks.

Another express sped past, and this time, the warm wind rushing between the trains felt like a spell. The faces of the commuters opposite him looked potent, magical, even demonic – as if they were creatures from another world: or perhaps always present in his world, well-hidden, exposed now by the jarring energy released by the passing of the engines.

A touch on his shoulder.

'Radium, sir? It works. Real radium.'

Masterji turned round. It took him a second to recover from the illusion of the passing demon-faces.

A man in a dirty shirt was offering him a packet of glow-in-the-dark stars: 'Radium for Children.' Ten rupees. Suitable for bedroom walls.

Sparks the intellect, sends them to university.

Masterji looked at the packet; he had forgotten to bring a gift for Ronak.

Paunchy, with his breasts pressing against a patterned silk shirt, Gaurav Murthy walked down the aisle of the grocery store. He pointed at peanut *chikkis* and golden ladoos, at fried banana chips and spicy *farsan* packets; the storekeeper swept them all into a plastic bag.

Ten rupee packets of peanuts, natural and masala batter-coated, one packet of Frito-Lay's masala *kurkure*. One more packet of peanuts? Why not.

'My father is coming home again, you see.'

'A happy occasion,' the store owner said. 'Buying sweets for him. You're a good son.'

'Why not give me some banana chips, just in case? A small packet will do.'

With a half-kilo of snacks in a bag, Gaurav Murthy walked home. A quarter to five. His father had said he would come at five. Which meant he was already there.

He shouldn't have strayed this far from his Society, but the snacks in Dhobi Talao, just around the corner, were cheaper. Stopping outside his building to catch his breath, he noticed a star from last Deepavali on the terrace; he was sure his father had noticed it too. ('Why is it still up there? Don't you pay the maid to...') Reaching into his shopping bag, he ripped open a packet of *chikki*. He chewed the peanuts. His father would mock him for having put on weight; he chewed faster.

'His father's tail.' That was what his mother had called him in the earliest days, when with a dumb, animal joy he had jumped up when the doorbell rang in the evening and had followed his father around the house, even into the bathroom, which he had to be pushed out of. The disenchantment began when he was fourteen, and his mother came back from Suratkal robbed by his uncles: he discovered that his father, who struck him on the knuckles with a steel foot-ruler for minor infractions, could not stand up to two provincial thieves. Contempt was born in Gaurav, the contempt of a son who has been hit by a weak father. As his shoulders grew, the contempt grew with them. His father wanted him to become a scientist or a lawyer, a man who worked with his mind; he decided to study commerce. In the university library he looked up from his textbooks of finance and thought of something his father had done or said the previous day: like a common stock on the Bombay Sensex, the value of Yogesh Murthy's reputation was re-calculated daily in his son's mind, and daily it fell.

A man has no choice in his father; but if he keeps his distance from an unlikeable one, Society always blames *him*. It seemed wildly unfair to Gaurav.

As he pressed the doorbell, he could hear screams from the compound of his Society; he identified the particular shrillness that was his son's. *Why hasn't the boy come up right away?*

The maid opened the door. His father stood in the living room, admiring Sonal's latest acquisition: a large bronze ornamental plate, filled to the brim with water, on which floated red gulmohar petals.

'Look, Gaurav: Father-in-law has brought a nice gift for Ronak,' his wife said, showing him the packet of Radium stars. 'How sweet of him to spend the money.'

Saying it was time to feed her father, she retreated into an inner room, leaving the two men to the business of the day.

'Life is difficult, Father. Sonal's life is very difficult.'

'I thought you had a good job, son.'

When Gaurav spoke, Masterji had the impression he was addressing someone on his right shoulder. He moved his head to intercept his son's gaze; the boy shifted his eyes further to the right.

'Job is good, Father. Other things in life are not good. Stress. All the time. I see a Guru now for my stress. Sangeeta Aunty told me about him. He gives me mantras to chant.'

His father was a rationalist, of course. Something stinging would be on its way soon. Gaurav bit into the *chikki*.

'When are you signing the acceptance form, Father, and taking the money?'

Sonal, from the other room, supplied the lines he had forgotten:

'Father-in-law, there are questions of... income tax, estate tax. Life insurance. We have to plan. Sooner you say "yes", the better for all of us.'

Masterji glared at the *chikki* as he spoke.

'Son, there are the things we know about Vishram. Physically it has fallen behind but the memories of my late wife...'

'You mean my mother.'

'Yes, your mother, and your sister. It is not such an easy thing, to pack up and leave.'

As his father watched, Gaurav ripped open another packet of *chikki*; his wife spoke for him.

'Have you seen the new buildings in Parel, Father-in-law?'

Leaning back, so that he could see her with her feeding spoon, dripping with yoghurt, Sonal smiled.

'They're duplexes. Not yet built and each is sold already. NRIs from England. You know how much they cost?' She fed her father yogurt. 'Twenty-seven crores each. All sold.'

Twenty-seven crores each. Trying to make sense of how much money that was, Masterji thought of the ocean.

'Twenty-seven crores,' Gaurav said. 'Twenty-seven.'

Look at the boy, bleating his wife's words. Masterji glared once again at the *chikki* in his son's hand.

The maid brought in a piece of *barfi* and six or seven fried banana chips and put them on the table in front of him. The portions were small. This was always the case when he came here; food merely tip-toed across his plate.

'We have your mother's one-year anniversary coming up in October, son. I spoke to Trivedi, he's eager to perform the ceremony. The three of us will go to Bandra like last time. I hope you'll join us this year, Sonal. And bring Ronak too.'

He ate the banana chips one by one.

Gaurav picked up the Radium packet and sniffed. 'Father, this is a cheap thing, not good for the boy.' He let it fall.

Masterji got up and went to the balcony. Spotting Ronak playing down in the compound, he clapped. Without turning to his son, he said: 'Not one of my gifts for Ronak is liked in this household. I give him a book, a wonderful blue book. *The Illustrated History of Science.* It was returned to me by his mother.'

He clapped again.

Sonal leaned back from the inner room to look at her husband. *Answer, answer*, his eyes urged her.

Moving towards her father with another spoonful of yoghurt, she disappeared from sight.

'Father, you always expected me to read books, even when I was a boy. You made me learn French. I am no good at these things. Mother told you this: I am not intellectual like you.' Gaurav opened a new bar of peanut-*chikki*. 'And, Father, the practice among Sindhis is to give gold when a child is born. Sonal once told you this, thinking that a south Indian like you might not know it. But you never gave Ronak any gold. One of Mother's necklaces is still in the old place. A Vummidi necklace. In her *almirah*. It doesn't matter. It doesn't matter.'

After clapping once more – 'Ronak, it's me, come up!' – Masterji returned to the room. He sat down in front of his son.

'You're too lazy to read, but it doesn't mean you shouldn't encourage Ronak. It is life's greatest joy and power: the ability to learn. Remember what I used to tell you. Lord Elphinstone refused the governor-generalship so he could write his history of India.'

Gaurav ate more *chikki*.

Sonal, Sonal, please come out – he licked his thumbnail, thumb, index finger nail, index finger, and the webbing in between thumb and index finger. *Come out before I get up and shout at the old man.*

But then the smell of sweat and sun entered the room; a wooden cricket bat dropped to the ground; and a boy was hoisted up into the air in his grandfather's arms.

In the kitchen Sonal did mathematics. 'It's 810 square feet, you say, Father-in-law? That would be… 1.62 crores. Let me double-check. 810 times 20,000. Yes, I think that's right… 1,62,00,000.'

She came out with a glass of pineapple juice on a tray.

'Not for me, Sonal, too much sugar.'

He offered the glass to Ronak, who sat next to him on the sofa, but the well-mannered child refused.

'This Mr Shah had better pay on time, Father-in-law. If not, Gaurav has a connection at work who knows a good property lawyer. Once you sign the agreement, you can move in here,' Sonal said. 'Both our fathers will be with us.'

'It might be a good idea,' Masterji said. 'To be close to Ronak.'

His son reached for the bar of *chikki*, broke off a chunk, and began chewing again.

Sonal smiled at her husband. 'Of course, if Father-in-law doesn't want to stay with us, he can always buy a one-bedroom flat in Vakola.' She said it out loud: 'One-six-two-zero-zero-zero-zero-zero!'

Masterji, stroking his grandson's wet hair, heard a gurgling noise from the inside room – as if even that brain-dead old man was excited. *Senility for a banker*, Masterji thought, *must consist of lots of zeroes going round and round in his head.*

'Are you sure you won't drink that pineapple juice before you leave?' Sonal said. 'Just a sip? Share it with your grandson?'

The lift was broken, so he walked down the stairs.

When he raised his leg, the stair dissolved, and he put it down into soft, wet black air. He held on to the solid banister to stop himself sliding. His arthritic left knee throbbed. O, Purnima, he prayed, Purnima. His blood sugar was sputtering like the engine of an old autorickshaw. O, Purnima.

Explosions of glucose – comets and supernovae – lit up his private darkness.

Holding on to the banister he lowered himself down on to the steps. He could hear Purnima yelling at him from the oceans of the other world. Why hadn't he taken that diabetes test yet?

Is it possible, he wondered, *that Sonal gave me that pineapple juice* precisely *to make this happen? She kept insisting.*

Down below on the landing, a man in rags, one of the servants of Gaurav's Society, slept with his arm over his face.

Masterji touched the wall of his son's Society. It did not remember Purnima or Sandhya. Soon he would be living within four walls like this.

Striding over the sleeping servant, he walked on down, still wondering about Sonal and the pineapple juice.

'Why is it taking him so long to come back?' Mrs Puri asked.

Half a dozen residents had gathered in the Secretary's room to celebrate Masterji's return. The moment he would walk in with a smile and say, 'Yes.' A microphone had been placed near the black Cross; the plan was to hold an impromptu general meeting and have the whole thing done with in ten minutes.

The Secretary patted his comb-over into place. 'He is stuck in the train, maybe.'

Ajwani had been standing in a corner of the office looking at his mobile phone: now he turned the phone around and tapped it against a filing cabinet.

'I'm getting worried. Look here...' He smiled at the Secretary. '...why don't you type out our Acceptance form now? Just type a form saying, *All Members of Tower A have agreed and signed.* As soon as he comes, get him to sign it. He may change his mind any minute. A man like that, he's unpredictable. Remember what he did to the modern girl's boyfriend?'

Ajwani gave the air a push.

Kothari put two fingers over the keys of the Remington, and then retracted them one by one.

'I think it's against the rules to type a form like that until everyone has actually said yes.'

The broker shook his head, punched on his mobile phone and murmured something.

'What did you call me?' The Secretary got up. 'I know that you've been calling me that behind my back, Ajwani. Nothing man.'

The broker looked up from his mobile phone. 'I speak my mind, Kothari. Don't hide things.'

'What does that mean? What have I been hiding all these years?'

Ibrahim Kudwa was waiting in the office; Mumtaz was by his side, with baby Mariam on her lap. He was going to intervene in the quarrel when Mrs Puri walked in and said: 'Ibby.'

He smiled. 'Sangeeta-ji,' he said.

'Ibby, the internet connection at home is a bit slow today. I don't know if it's a loose cable or...' She smiled at Mumtaz. 'Your husband is so good with computers and wires.'

Mumtaz watched her husband follow Mrs Puri up the stairs. He would come down speaking like her. Saying 'Oy oy oy' in every other sentence. In the way that the body of an unfaithful husband took on other fragrances, Ibrahim's voice took on the accents of the women he was trying to impress.

If asked to decide who made the most incompatible couple in their building, the residents of Vishram would have had a hard time choosing between the Puris and the Kudwas. Before Mohammad's birth Mumtaz Kudwa had worked at a dental clinic in Khar (West); now she left home once a day, to bring Mohammad back from school, and the other residents rarely spoke to her except on festivals like Republic Day. Ibrahim made his nest in other people's homes. Always pressing the bell to chat, to offer a ride on his scooter, the free use of his internet café, and you felt he would have been happier watching TV on your sofa than on his own.

It had been an arranged marriage; even in the earliest, happiest days, Mumtaz had noticed odd things about her husband. If Ibrahim was treated like an adult, he acted like a child. Grateful to be included in a group, he would do anything others wanted of him, even if it demeaned or endangered him. In his own home, with his own father and mother, he was so thrilled when he got attention at the dinner table. One day she felt bold enough to ask: 'Why do you worry so much about what they think about you?' He was angry for days; and then, without consulting her, he announced that they would now live away from his family. They moved to an old building full of Hindus and Christians, and Ibrahim's behaviour became worse. Mrs Puri pestered him for little favours – a free tube of potassium nitrate toothpaste for Ramu's sensitive teeth, for instance – and Ibrahim, incapable of saying no, had forced her to smuggle six tubes out of the dentist's clinic ('it's not stealing, it's for a neighbour').

She thought it would be worth leaving Vishram just to take her husband away from that woman.

With her child on her lap she looked at the door, only dimly aware that voices were rising around her as Ajwani and the Secretary argued.

Feeling too weak for the evening train, Masterji had hailed a taxi outside Gaurav's building. Why not? A rich man could travel like a rich man. He put his hand out of the window and tapped at the side of the black Fiat. The trip by road took at least half an hour longer than the train would have; by the time he passed the Mayor's mansion near Shivaji Park, Masterji felt stronger. Alighting near the Bandra mosque, he crossed the busy road and waited for an autorickshaw to economize on the last leg of his trip home.

He had barely unlatched the gate of Vishram Society when a dark body ran out of the bright building and put its arms around his neck.

'Thank you, Uncle! Thank you so much.'

Radhika Saldanha – he realized, after some confusion, as she turned and bolted back into her home.

Mrs Saldanha, watching through the tear in her window, smiled at him as he entered the building.

He stopped, from habit, at the noticeboard: a new typewritten sign had been hammered with a nail into the central panel.

NOTICE

**Vishram Co-operative Hsg Society Ltd,
Vakola, Santa Cruz (E), Mumbai – 400055**

**Minutes of the extraordinary general meeting
of 'A' Building, held on 6 July**

Theme: dissolution of Society

All members were present by the time, 5.30 P.M.
Ramesh Ajwani (2C) took the chair and presided over the meeting.

```
ITEM NO. 1 OF THE AGENDA:

All members have agreed, unanimously, to accept
the offer made by the Confidence Group. The
residents of the Society have agreed
unanimously to the dissolution of the Society,
and to the demolition of its physical
structure.

No other items were discussed in the meeting.

For the Vishram 'A' Tower Executive Committee,

Signed,
Ashvin Kothari,
Secretary, Vishram Tower (A)

Copy (1) To Members of 'A' Building, Vishram
Co-op Hsg Society Ltd

Copy (2) To the Secretary, Vishram Co-op Hsg
Society Ltd

Note: Signatures of all members of the Society
are listed below, next to their respective unit
numbers (with square footage in brackets)
```

The Secretary emerged from his office with a smile.

'What is this?' Masterji asked, his index finger on the noticeboard. 'I just got back to Vishram. I haven't signed anything yet.'

Kothari came to the noticeboard and squinted; the lynx-like laugh-lines spread from his eyes. 'Well, I was just saving time, Masterji. Since you've agreed, I thought I'd type up the notice.'

Masterji's index finger had not moved.

'Did I agree? When did I agree? I said I was going to speak to my son. That was all.'

The Secretary stopped smiling. 'It was not my idea, actually. Ajwani's idea. He forced me to put it up before you came back... he...'

Dislodging Masterji's hand from the glass, the Secretary lifted it open. He tore off the notice, one half of which fell to the floor.

'There, Masterji, are you happy?'

He was not.

'Who gave you the right to say I have agreed? Why do you say I've signed something?'

'Thank you, Masterji.' Mrs Puri was coming down the stairs. 'Thank you for thinking of all of us.'

Masterji's index finger was again on the empty noticeboard.

'Sangeeta, did you know the Secretary thinks he can forge my signature?'

'Masterji!' The Secretary raised his voice. 'This is too much drama. It is just a simple thing – a simple mistake that we made! And I keep telling you, it was not my idea. It was Ajwani!'

Masterji took the crumpled form from the floor and straightened it out. He read it again.

'It is a signature,' he whispered. '*My* signature.'

'Mrs Puri…' The Secretary looked up. 'You are his champion in the building. Talk to him, won't you?'

'Masterji. We waited for hours for you. I didn't collect water for Ramu's evening bath. You *did* tell us you would sign it.'

A voice boomed: 'Don't blame us, Masterji. We just put that notice up half an hour ago. Why did you take so long to come back?'

Ajwani's small black face looked down from the second-floor banister.

'It's true, Masterji,' the Secretary said. 'If you had come back *just* half an hour ago…'

'I couldn't come sooner, because… I wasn't feeling well…'

People looked down from various places along the stairwell: Mr Ganguly, Ajwani, Mr Puri, Ibrahim Kudwa, Mr Vij.

He wanted to breathe in the camphor-scented air from his wife's cupboard. Mrs Puri stepped aside to let him go. The sick dog lay on the first landing, trembling from its joints. Masterji stopped in front of it and looked up at his neighbours. It was like being at the train compartment's edge again, with the warm wind blowing into his eyes and the other train rushing past: he saw the demonic faces crowding around him.

He spoke so all would hear:

'… have not said yes, have not said no.'

BOOK SIX

Fear

'… you said it was *over*, Shanmugham. A week ago.'

Driving through Juhu in the morning, sunk into the black leather cushions of his Mercedes, chewing *gutka* from his blue tin, Mr Shah watched the only thing there was to watch.

All night long rain had pounded Mumbai; now the ocean retorted.

Storm-swollen, its foam hissing thick like acid reflux, dissolving gravity and rock and charging up the ramps that separated beach from road, breaking at the land's edge in burst after burst of droplets that made the spectactors, huddled under black umbrellas, scream.

Shah told his driver to take slow circles around Juhu; as the car made a U-turn, he moved to the other window, so he could keep watching the ocean. 'I don't care about that old teacher and his mood swings. Now you tell that Secretary, he won't see one rupee of his sweetener – what did we promise him, an extra one lakh? – unless he earns it. Didn't I tell you from the start, that teacher was going to make trouble? And you, Shanmugham, don't ever again tell me something is done, until it is done, until the signature is there, until—'

Mr Shah threw the mobile phone into a corner of the car.

He had hoped there would be no fighting this time. With an offer this generous. But there would *always* be a fight. The nature of this stupid, stupid city. What he wouldn't have built by now if he were in Shanghai – hospitals, airports, thirteen-storey shopping malls! And here, all this trouble, just to get started on a simple luxury housing…

The mucus in his chest thickened; his breathing sounded like a feral dog's growling. Shah coughed and spat into his handkerchief. He checked the colour of the spit with a finger.

Bending down to pick up the mobile phone, he dialled Shanmugham's number again.

Parvez, the driver, turned on the windscreen-wipers. The rain had started again.

'Wait,' Shah said. 'Stop here.'

The boys inside the bus stand to their left were cheering.

Across the road, in the sheeting rain, one man in rags was bearing another on his back towards the bus stand. The fellow on top was covered in a cape of blue tarpaulin which billowed around them both. The man doing the carrying was pushed sideways by the wind and the weight on his shoulders; vehicles flashed their headlights at him through the rain; yet he came closer and closer to the cheering spectators, who, as if by will power alone, were pulling him to safety.

'Sir?' Shanmugham was on the line. 'Do you want me to start taking action in Vishram? Should I do what I did last year in that project in Sion?'

Shah looked at the men in the rain. Adding his will to that of the spectators, he urged the two of them on until they staggered into the bus stand.

The builder smiled; he struck the window with a golden ring, making Parvez turn around.

Fine wrinkles radiated from Ram Khare's eyes as he read from his holy digest, like minute illustrations of the net that Fate had cast over him.

When he was in his teens he had had hopes of playing cricket for Bombay in the Ranji Trophy; when he was in his twenties he dreamed of buying a home of his own; when he was in his thirties of taking his old parents on a pilgrimage to the city of Benaras.

At the age of fifty-six, he found that his life had contracted to three things: his daughter Lalitha, an alumna of St Catherine's School, now studying computer engineering in Pune; his rum; and his religion.

Mornings were for religion. Standing inside his guard's booth with a string of black *rudraksha* beads in his left hand, he kept a finger on page 23:

'What are the marks by which a soul may be known? Listen to the words of our Lord Krishna. The soul is not born and it does not...'

Footsteps came towards Vishram Society. He turned to the gate and said: 'One minute, Masterji. One minute.'

Opening the tin door of the watchman's booth, Khare stepped to one side, inviting Masterji to enter. The old teacher, who was return-ing with a bundle of fresh coriander for the Pintos, held it up: a gesture of protest.

Khare said: '*One* minute.'

Disarmed by the servant's insistence, Masterji gave up, and so, for the first time in thirty-two years, entered the guard's booth at Vishram Society.

'Now if you wait just a second, sir, I'll show you my life's work.'

There was a large spider's web growing in a corner of the guard's booth; Khare seemed to have no objection to its existence. Objects from the ground – twigs, chalks, pen-tops, snippets of metal wire – had been conveyed into this web, several feet off the ground: the whole thing looking like a project in mild black magic that Khare carried on in his spare time.

'This is my life's work, sir. My life's work.'

Ram Khare's fingers rested on another magical object: the long, stiff-spined Visitors' Log Book.

He ran his clean fingernail down the columns.

Guest Name
Occupation
Address
Mobile Number
Purpose of Visit
Person to See
Time Entry
Time Exit
Remarks (if any)/Observations (if any)
Signature of Guest
Signature of Guard

'Every single guest is noted, and his mobile number registered. For sixteen years it has been this way—' he pointed to the old registers stuffed into plastic trays. 'Ask me who came into the building on the morning of 1 January 1994, I'll tell you. What time they left, I'll tell you. Sixteen years, seven months and twenty-one days.'

Khare closed the log book and sniffed.

'Before that I was the guard at the Raj Kiran Housing Society in Kali-na. A good Society. There too they had an offer of redevelopment from a builder. One man refused to sign the offer – a healthy young fellow, not like you – and one morning he tripped down the stairs and broke his knees. He signed in his hospital bed.'

Masterji closed his eyes for a beat.

'Are you threatening me, Ram Khare?'

'No, sir. I am informing you that there is a snake in my mind. It is long and black.'

The guard spread his arms wide.

'And I wanted you to see this black snake too. Every day Mrs Puri or Mrs Saldanha or someone else comes to your door and knocks, and asks: "Have you made up your mind? Will you sign?" And everyday you say: "I'm thinking about it." How long can this go on, Masterji? Now it makes no difference to me whether you say yes or no. If this building stands, I have this job. If it falls, I have a job somewhere else. But...'

Ram Khare opened the door for his guest: '... there is the question of my duty to you. And whatever happens now, I've discharged it. The Lord Krishna has taken note of that.'

And with that, he went back to his holy digest: '... it does not die. It cannot hurt and cannot be hurt. It is invincible, immortal, and...'

What cheek, Masterji thought, walking to the entranceway of his Society. *Talking of a 'black snake' in Vishram.*

He should complain to the Secretary. Mrs Rego was right; Ram Khare was drinking too much. He had smelled molasses in that booth.

Mrs Puri was at her window, watching him from behind her grille.

'Mrs Puri,' he shouted, 'will you listen to what Ram Khare just said? He said I should be worried about what you and my other neighbours will do to me.'

As he watched, she shut the window and pulled down the blind. *Must not have seen me*, he thought. He did it all the time himself, ignored people right in front of him. Can't be helped after a certain age.

He walked into the building with the coriander.

Retreating to the mirror in her bedroom, Mrs Puri brushed her long black hair to soothe herself.

Her husband had yelled at her in the morning as he left. The first time he had yelled at her in Ramu's presence. *He* had never trusted that old man. She was the one who described Masterji as 'an English gentleman'. *She* was the one who had called him a 'big jackfruit'.

Ramu, sensing his mother was upset, sat by her side, and imitated her with a phantom brush. She saw this, and in gratitude, sobbed a little.

Wiping her mobile phone clean on her forearm, she re-dialled a number.

'Gaurav, it's me again,' she said. 'Why don't you come here, Gaurav. Speak to him. Bring Ronak. He will change his mind: he is your father. Don't be obstinate like him, Gaurav. You must come to see him. Do it for your Sangeeta Aunty, won't you?'

Wiping the mobile phone on her forearm, she put it down on the table and turned to her son.

'Can you believe it, Ramu? All those mangoes, all those years. I cut them into long thin slices and put them in his fridge. You remember, don't you?'

She could hear Masterji opening the fridge to pour himself a glass of cold water.

'What a selfish, greedy old man he has become, Ramu. He wants to take our wooden cupboards away from us. The Evil Eye must have found out about my good luck. This time too.'

Ramu had put his fingers in his ears. His face began to shake; his teeth chattered. Mrs Puri knew what was coming, but he beat her to it, ran into the toilet, and slammed the door. No: he wouldn't open the door for Mummy.

'Ramu, I won't say anything bad about Masterji again. I promise.'

The door opened at last, but Ramu wouldn't get up from the toilet bowl. Breathing as normally as she could, to show that she was not angry with him, that he had *not* made a stinky mess in the toilet, Mummy washed his behind clean with a mug of water, changed his trousers, and put him into bed with Spiderman and the Friendly Duck.

She struggled down to her knees and scrubbed the toilet floor clean. When he was frightened, he missed the bowl.

When she opened the door of his bedroom, Ramu was sitting up, angling the book in which his father had drawn lizards and spiders so that the Friendly Duck could see the pictures too.

Just outside the bedroom, a bird began to trill, its notes long and sharp like a needled thread, as if it were darning some torn corner of the world. Mother and son listened together.

When Mrs Puri came down the stairs, she found three women on the first landing, talking in whispers.

'He plays with his Rubik's Cube all day long. But does *he* have a solution?' Mrs Kothari, the Secretary's wife, asked. 'He's just a block of darkness.'

'Won't even do it for his son. Or his grandson,' Mrs Ganguly said.

'It's that girl next door. She made him crazy,' Mrs Nagpal, of the first floor, said.

They went silent as Mrs Puri passed. She knew they suspected her of sympathy with Masterji.

She took a left at the gate and walked past the slums. Soon she was at the site of the two new Confidence buildings. Under the blue tarpaulin covers, the work of laying slabs of granite and marble continued despite the rains. A drizzle began. She waited under an umbrella and hoped Ramu had not woken up.

A tall man came running up to her from one of the buildings. He got under her umbrella; she spoke to him and he listened.

'Mrs Puri,' Shanmugham smiled. 'You are a person of initiative. Just last year, in a redevelopment project in Sion, we encountered a problem like this Masterji of yours. There are many things we can do, and we will try them one by one. But you *must* trust me and Mr Shah.'

The lift at Vishram Society moved like a coffin on wheels. When a button was pressed, a loud click followed: ropes, levers, and chains went into action. Through the lattice of the metal shutter guarding the open elevator shaft, you could see a wooden rectangle – a counterweight – sliding down the wall, and a circular light on the top of the lift rising, as the large box scraped past to the floor above, carrying with it a sign: 'ITS YOUR SOCIETY. KEEP IT CLEAN'.

Masterji saw the lift pass him before slamming its dark mass into the fourth floor. A latch clicked and the door opened, but he heard no one come out.

It was one of those phantom trips that the Otis sometimes took on its own – compensating for weeks of inertia with these spectral bursts of activity.

No children yet. He went back to his room, leaving the front door open.

It was seven o'clock on a Monday. Time for the first science top-up of the week. The ceiling lights were turned off in anticipation, and the lamp light projected on to the far wall.

Ten minutes later, Masterji ran down the stairs and found the boys playing cricket in the compound. Mohammad Kudwa was bowling; Anand Ganguly held a bat high. Sunil Rego was fielding at cover point.

'Masterji, don't stand there,' Mohammad called out, 'the ball might hit you.'

'It's time for class, Mohammad.'

The boy turned and grinned.

'*Boycott*, Masterji.'

He released the ball towards Anand Ganguly, who leaned back and smacked it high and hard; it bounced off a grille at a fourth-floor window and returned to the ground.

'Boycott?' Masterji asked, stepping back to avoid the bouncing ball. 'Is this a new excuse not to come to the top-up?'

He walked towards parliament, where he found Mrs Saldanha talking to Mrs Kudwa, who was tickling Mariam on her lap.

'Your son is refusing to attend the top-up class, Mrs Kudwa. Are you aware of this?'

The two women at once got up from their chairs, went into the building, and stood by the noticeboard. There they continued to talk.

'They are not speaking to us either,' Mr Pinto said.

Masterji went up the stairs to 3C. Mrs Puri opened the door with her left hand, the fingers of her right bunched together and stained with the curd and rice she had been feeding Ramu. He was seated at the table in his apron; he gave his Masterji a big smile.

'Sangeeta, what is going on?'

'Ramu...' She turned to her son and said (forcing a big smile on her face so he would not suspect the content of her words), '... tell your Masterji that the boycott is going on.'

'Boycott?' Masterji said. 'What does that mean?'

'Ramu...' Mrs Puri smiled again. '... Masterji, being a famous teacher, must know all about Gandhi and Nehru and what they did to the British. So tell him not to ask us what a boycott is.'

'Gandhi and Nehru and... Mrs Puri, this is madness.'

'*Madness?*' Mrs Puri chuckled. Ramu, at the table, joined in the fun.

'And refusing an offer of 250 per cent the market value of his flat is not madness, Ramu? Some people should not speak of madness, Ramu.'

'I haven't said no. I'm still thinking about Mr Shah's proposal.'

Mrs Puri looked at her neighbour.

'*Still* thinking? You've always been happy to share your deep thoughts with us, haven't you, Masterji? Have we ever asked you to be Secretary of this Society? What does that tell you about how we felt about your deep thinking?'

'I *haven't* said no. But I won't be forced into—'

Mrs Puri shut the door in his face. Returning to his flat, Masterji sat by the teakwood table and tapped the arms of his chair, as if he did not really believe that the boys would not come.

Masterji opened the door. His rubbish bin had been overturned.

Pieces of rubbish – the banana peel, for example – had been flung far from his doorstep, as if someone had kicked them there.

He got down on one knee and began gathering in the errant garbage.

A young woman's foot scraped the banana peel towards him.

'Leave it alone, Ms Meenakshi, I'll clean it.'

'I'm only trying to help.'

His neighbour's sleek black jeans exposed inches of skin above the ankles, and she wore no socks; bunched together within the silver criss-crossing of her sandals, her plump white toes, incarnadined with lacquer, looked like *bonsai* cleavage. Once she got rid of the braces and bought better glasses, Masterji decided, she would make a very good marriage.

He put pressure on the wrong leg as he stood up: a sharp angular pain cut into his left knee like an accent over a French 'e'.

Accent aigu. He sketched it in the air: pleased that he could civilize his arthritis by connecting it to a beautiful language.

Ms Meenakshi leaned on her doorway, grinning and exposing her braces.

'That woman must hate you even more than she hates me.' She leaned her head towards Mrs Puri's door. 'She just *looks* through my rubbish.'

'This is the early-morning cat, Ms Meenakshi,' Masterji said, massaging his knee-cap. 'Mrs Puri has not done this.'

His neighbour adjusted her hexagonal glasses before closing her door. 'Then why is your rubbish bin the only one that has been overturned?'

At one o'clock that day, Ibrahim Kudwa, uninvited, came and joined the Pintos' table for lunch.

Perhaps because Kudwa, the only Muslim in the building, was considered a fair-minded man by the others – or perhaps because, being the owner of a not-so-busy internet café, he could leave his business in the afternoon – he had been designated a 'neutral' in the dispute, and sent, in this capacity, by the rest of the Society. Halfway through lunch, when Nina, the maid-servant, was serving steaming *appams*, he said: 'Masterji, I don't approve of this thing. This boycott.'

'Thank you, Ibrahim.'

'But Masterji… understand *why* people are doing this. There is so much anguish in the building over your strange actions. You say you'll sign, then you go to see your son, and say you won't sign.'

'I never said *yes*, Ibrahim.' Masterji wagged his finger. 'I said *maybe*.'

'Let me teach you something today, Masterji: there is no *maybe* in this matter. We think you should go and meet Mr Shah in his house. Have a talk with him. He holds teachers in high regard.'

Ibrahim Kudwa washed his mouth and wiped his lips and beard on the Pintos' hand-towel. He put the towel back on its rack and stared at it.

'Masterji, when the builder's offer was made, I suffered, because I did not know what to do with the money – I took an Antacid to sleep. Now that there is the possibility of the money I never had being taken away from me – I need two Antacids to sleep.'

He wiped his hands again and left, apparently abandoning whatever remained of his neutrality on the wet hand-towel.

'Boycott – it's just a word,' Masterji told Mr Pinto. 'Remember the time Sangeeta's Aquaguard machine leaked water into Ajwani's kitchen, and from there into Abichandani's kitchen? Remember how they stopped talking to her until she paid for the repairs? She never agreed to it. After two weeks they were talking to her again.'

After an hour, he went down the stairs, kicked aside the stray dog, and sat on the 'prime' chair in front of Mrs Saldanha's window. The small TV was on in her kitchen, a ghostly quadrilateral behind the green curtain; a slice of the newsreader's face showed through the almond-shaped tear like a kernel of truth. As he watched, Mrs Saldanha came to the window and closed its wooden shutters.

Masterji surveyed the compound of his Society as if nothing had happened.

On his way up the stairs, he saw the sick dog lying once again on the landing. At least it looked at him the same way as it had before. He let it lie there.

He was looking so intently at the dog that he almost missed the hand-written sign that had been stuck with Scotch tape to the wall above it.

Some facts about 'a certain person' who has received respect from us for thirty years. But why? Now we find out the truth.

1. Because he was a retired teacher, he got respect from all of us. He offered to help children with exams, true. But what kind of help? He would talk about the parts of the sun, like the corona, and the dense core of hydrogen and helium, and so on, far beyond the strict requirements of the syllabus, which meant that when the exam papers appeared, the children found nothing of use in his tutorials. So to go to him for tuition, or private lessons, was the 'kiss of death'.

2. For DEEPAVALI, CHRISTMAS, OR EID, he has never given one rupee in baksheesh to Ram Khare. He is always saying, I have no money, I am retired, but is this true? Do we not know otherwise?

3. Even though he liked to boast loudly 'he had no TV', every evening he would sit in front of Mrs Saldanha's kitchen in the exact position

where he would block everyone else's view and
then he would watch TV.

4. NEVER GIVES TIPS, for large waste material
left outside the door, to the Khachada-wali.

SO WHY HAVE WE RESPECTED HIM BLINDLY?

He read it twice before he could understand it. Tear it down? He withdrew his hand. A man is not what his neighbours say he is. Laugh and let it go.

When he bent to his sink a few minutes later to wash his face, the water burned his eyes and nose.

But a man *is* what his neighbours say he is.

In old buildings truth is a communal thing, a consensus of opinion. Vishram Society had retained mementoes, over forty-eight years, of all those who had lived in it; each resident had left a physical record of himself here, like the kerosene handprint made by Rajeev Ajwani on the front wall on the day of his great tae kwon-do victory. If you knew how to read Vishram's walls, you would find them covered with handprints. These prints were permanent, but they could move; a person's record was alterable. Now Masterji felt the opinion of him that was engraved into the building – in its peeling paint and 48-year-old brickwork – shift. As it moved, so did something within his body.

He could not say, looking at his wet face and dripping moustache, how much of what was written in the poster was untrue.

He went down and read it again. Nothing about the Pintos in it: they were hoping to drive a wedge between them. He ripped it down.

But that evening another appeared glued to the lift door, different in handwriting, similar in its complaints ('never taught English to students even though he knew Shakespeare and other big writers who were part of the examinations') – and then there was one on Ram Khare's guard-booth ('Put your own poster up,' he said, when Masterji protested). Though he tore each one down, he knew another would go up: the black handprints were multiplying.

216

In the old days, you had caste, and you had religion: they taught you how to eat, marry, live, and die. But in Bombay caste and religion had faded away, and what had replaced them, as far as he could tell, was the idea of being respectable and living among similar people. All his adult life Masterji had done so; but now, in the space of just a few days, he had shattered the husk of a respectable life and tasted its bitter kernel.

It was nearly 8 a.m. He was still in bed, listening to savages screaming below him.

Down in 2C, Rajeev and Raghav Ajwani practised tae kwon-do under their father's supervision.

He imagined he could hear similar noises from all the rooms of his Society: all of them were jabbing fists and lancing kicks to gouge him out of Vishram.

Now he heard the Secretary's footsteps from above. He was sure they were louder than they had been for the past twenty-five years.

He did not want to get up; did not want to walk down the stairs and read the new notices they had posted about him.

If, in the early days of the 'boycott', there was an apologetic smile on the Secretary's lips when he evaded Masterji's attempts to make small talk, now there were neither smiles nor apologies.

They treat me like they would treat an untouchable in the old days, he thought: even at the thought of his shadow falling on them, his neighbours cringed and withdrew.

Degree by degree, they were turning their faces from him, until, as he passed the parliament, he confronted a row of turned backs.

If, in defiance, he sat among them, they got up and left. The moment

217

he went up the stairs, they would regather. Then the taunts began. Always directed at him, never at the Pintos.

'... if only Purnima were alive, wouldn't she be ashamed of him?'

'... his own son. A man who does not care for his own son, what do you...'

So this is what they mean by the word: *boycott*. Even in his bed he felt it, their contempt, like the heat radiating from a brick wall on a summer night.

He went down to the bottom of the stairwell. Through the octagonal stars of the grille, he saw Ajwani, pacing about the compound, talking on his mobile phone – to a client, no doubt.

I could never do that, Masterji thought: *negotiate. Use the 'personal touch'*. He had none of the small-bored implements of personality that other men did; no good at charm and fake smile, he never bartered or traded in the normal human way. Which is why he had only two real friends. And for the sake of those two friends he was rejecting a windfall. Not so long ago they had called him an English gentleman for doing this. These very people.

He struck the grille with his fist.

It was a 'top-up' day; he looked at the round water stains on the ceiling of his living room and saw asteroids and white dwarves. In the cursive mildew he read $E = mc^2$.

He straightened out the books in his cabinet (where had all the Agatha Christies vanished?), dusted the teakwood table, tried to limit his use of the Rubik's Cube by hiding it on a shelf of his wife's cupboard, and drew the blinds and lay in bed.

He closed his eyes.

He did not see her until too late. The old fish-seller had a leathery face, cunning with wrinkles, and she walked with a basket on her head. Closer and closer she came towards him, grinning all the time: and just as she passed him he saw that a large wet tail was poking out of her basket.

He awoke to find his face and arms smelling like fish. He swatted the pillows off his bed and got up.

I've slept during the day, he thought. Around him the living room trembled, like a cage from which light had just sprung out. It was thirty-five minutes past four.

To expunge the sin of afternoon indolence, his first lapse since childhood, he washed his face in cold water three times, slapped his cheeks, and decided to walk all the way to the train station and back.

Tinku Kothari, the Secretary's son, dressed in a crumpled school uniform, stood outside his door. Masterji paused with the key in his hand.

'They're calling you.'

'Who?'

The fat boy went down the stairs. Still holding the key in his palm, Masterji followed the boy through the gates of Vishram; every now and then, Tinku would turn around, like a dark finger that was summoning him. Masterji thought he smelled more and more strongly of fish's tail. He followed the boy to Ibrahim Kudwa's cyber-café.

Tinku ran in and shouted: 'Uncle! He's here!'

Arjun, the Christianized assistant, had climbed up to the glass lunette above the doorway of the café to fix a loose rivet with a screwdriver. From up there he looked down, monkey-like, on the fat boy who had run into the café. *How all creatures*, Masterji thought, watching Arjun, *have their niche in this world. Just two weeks ago I was like him. I had somewhere to perch among the windows and grilles of Vishram.*

A Mercedes was parked not far from the doorway of the internet café.

Kudwa came to the doorway. Ajwani stood by his side; he knew the two had just been talking about him. Now, Ajwani and Kudwa seemed to say with their eyes, they could – if he entered the café, if he accepted the logic of the boycott – give him back his place in the hierarchy of Vishram Society. Ajwani, a natural-born middle-man, could broker the deal: at a rate of so much rage forsaken, of so much pride swallowed, he would be readmitted into the common life of his Society.

'Mr Shah has sent his car for you; he is waiting in his Malabar Hill home. You have *nothing* to fear. He admires teachers.'

Masterji could barely ask: 'What is all this about?'

'I've been asked to bring you to Mr Shah's house. We will drop you back to Vishram, Masterji. The driver is right here.'

Tinku Kothari, standing on the threshold of the café, watched Masterji.

'Is there a bathroom in there?' he asked – he could still smell the dream-fish on his moustache and fingertips.

'Arjun has a toilet in the back,' Kudwa said. 'It's not very clean, but...' Monkey-like Arjun, from the lunette, indicated with his screw-driver the way.

He was standing before the toilet bowl when the engine of the Mercedes came to life, and once that noise started, he simply could not urinate.

Everything in the moving car was sumptuous – the air-conditioned air, the soft cushions, the floral fragrance – and all of it added to Masterji's discomfort.

He sat in the back, his arms between his knees.

Ajwani, seated by the driver, turned every few minutes, and smiled.

'Is everything okay back there?'

'Why would it not be?'

He was sure he reeked of fish, all the way from his moustache-tips to his fingertips, and this shamed and weakened him. He closed his eyes and settled back for the long ride into the city.

'Why is there no traffic today?' he heard Ajwani asking. 'Is it a holiday?'

'No, sir. We're almost alone on the roads.'

'I know that: but why?'

Some time passed, and then he heard Ajwani say: 'There *really* is no traffic. I don't understand.'

Masterji opened his eyes: as if by magic, they were already at the foot of Malabar Hill.

Resplendent in his circle of fire, his foot pressing down on the demon of ignorance, the bronze Nataraja stood on the table in the living room. The plaster-of-Paris model of the Shanghai sat at the god's feet, in ambiguous relationship, of either deference or challenge, to his power.

In a corner of the room, far from the gaze of the bronze Nataraja statue, Shanmugham opened the glass panels of his employer's drinks cabinet. Three rows of clean crystal glasses filled the wooden shelves above the cabinet.

All the pots and pans in the kitchen shook in a bout of metallic nervousness: Giri was hacking at something with a cleaver.

Shanmugham closed the cabinet door.

His phone rang. It was Ajwani: they had reached the building.

'But Mr Shah has just left,' Shanmugham said. 'He's gone to his boy's school for a meeting. You're not supposed to be here for another hour.'

'There was no traffic. I've never seen a thing like it. Should we go up and down Malabar Hill? Stop at Hanging Gardens?'

'No. Come in, and wait here for Mr Shah. I'll text him that you're early.'

He waited for them in the doorway under the golden Ganesha medallion. When the old teacher stepped out of the lift, Shanmugham noticed that he had a slight limp. Arthritic in one leg. A weakness. He namasted the old man with great warmth and ushered him into the living room.

'Can I get you something to drink, Masterji? We have Coca-Cola, Pepsi-Cola...'

Ajwani came in behind them.

'Black Label for me,' he said.

'Only Mr Shah can open his drinks cabinet. You'll have to wait.' Shanmugham turned to his other guest. 'Are you sure, nothing for you? Not even a Pepsi?'

Masterji sat hunched over on the beige sofa, looking at the floor.

'I have to go to the toilet,' he said, getting up.

'The guest-room toilet is out of order. But if you have no objection' – Shanmugham paused, and added with a significant smile, 'you can use Mr Shah's. That's his bedroom there.'

Entering a dark room with a double-bed, Masterji located the toilet and closed the door behind him.

Here, at last, he could urinate.

If someone could see me now, he thought, *wouldn't they say, this is exactly what Masterji had planned from the start. To carry on a show so convincing even his son, his neighbours, would be taken in by it: and then allow himself to be driven here, in a chauffeured car, to the builder's home, drink his water, piss in his piss-pot, and be "persuaded" by him, for a few extra lakhs?*

He splashed water on his face. His eyebrows were damp and matted. He changed his pose to see his face from another angle.

Closing the toilet door behind him, he walked on tiptoe. The two of them were whispering on the sofa like old friends.

'... I'm telling you, no traffic of any kind. What can I...'

'And did you *have* to talk of drinks in the old man's presence?'

'He drinks. He's quite modern. I know him, he's my neighbour.'

'Why is he taking so long, by the way?'

'He pissed just before we headed out. He has that disease, which is called D-something. It weakens the lower organs.'

'Diarrhoea?'

'No, sir. Another D-word.'

'Dementia?'

'Not that.' Ajwani tapped his forehead. 'Listen, pour me something, won't you? I am the man doing all the work here, remember that. And tell your boss' – he dropped his voice – 'one lakh is not enough as a sweetener. I want *two*. In cash.'

The two stopped talking. On a table in the corner of the room Masterji saw a sheaf of papers lying under a golden paperknife. What was the story about Mrs Rego's Uncle Coelho and the builder who stole his property... didn't it involve a knife?

'May I recommend the view from the terrace, Masterji? It is the best view of the city you have ever seen, I guarantee it.'

'Of course Masterji will appreciate the view,' Ajwani giggled. 'Such a *sweetened* view it is of Bombay.'

Masterji followed the men through glass doors on to a rectangular balustraded terrace, where the sea breeze blew into his hair. An agglomeration of skyscrapers, billboards, and glowing blocks spread before the old teacher's wondering eyes. He had never seen Bombay like this.

A cloud of electric light enveloped the buildings like incense. Noise: a high keening pitch that was not traffic and not people talking but something else, something Masterji could not identify. A huge sign – 'LG' – stood behind the main bulk of towers; beyond it, he recognized the white glow from the Haji Ali shrine. To his left was dark ocean.

'Breach Candy,' Masterji reached for it with his finger. 'This used to be the dividing line between Malabar Hill and Worli island. During high tide the water came in through there. The British called it the Great Breach of Bombay. I've seen it in old maps.'

'Masterji knows everything. About the sun and moon, the history of Bombay, so much useful information.'

Ajwani turned and whispered to Shanmugham, who leaned down towards the short broker and listened.

His hands on the balustrade of the terrace, Masterji looked at the towers under construction in the dark. He thought of the shining knife on the desk. Each building seemed to be illuminated by its price in rupees per square foot, glowing like a halo around it. By its brightness he located the richest building in the vista.

'Why have you come before us?' the towers asked. Each glowing thing in the vista before him seemed like the secret of someone's heart: one of them out there represented his own. An honest man? He had fooled his Society, the Pintos, even himself, but here on the open terrace he was stripped of all his lies. He had come here, frightened by the boycott, not oblivious to the possibilities of money, ready to betray the Pintos. Ready to betray the memories of his dead wife and dead daughter that were in the walls and paint and nails of Vishram Society.

'Construction,' Shanmugham said, coming close to Masterji. 'Do you know how many cranes there are below us right now? The work continues all night. Dozens of buildings are coming up around us. And when all the work is finished… my God. This part of the city is going to be like New York. You must have been there, sir, to New York?'

He shook his head.

'You can now,' Ajwani smiled. 'A holiday.'

'No.' Masterji leaned forward. 'Oh, no, I won't go. I won't go anywhere. I won't leave Vishram Society ever again.'

He saw Shanmugham turning to Ajwani, who rolled his eyes.

'Masterji…' the builder's assistant came close. 'Masterji. May I talk to you, man to man?'

Masterji smelled something bad from the man's mouth, and thought of the green-covered cage at the zoo.

'There's a term we use in the business. A sweetener. Another thousand rupees per square foot? We don't reward teachers enough in this country.'

He understood now. It was the smell of his own cowardice, blown back at him from this creature's mouth.

'And what was that redevelopment project you were telling me about, Ajwani… where the old couple refused to take the offer, and then one day… did they fall down the stairs? Or were they pushed, or… old people should take care. It's a dangerous world. Terrorism. Mafia. Criminals in charge.'

'Oh, yes. That old couple in Sion you were talking about, they were pushed. For sure.'

In the light of the towers Shanmugham's thoughts seemed to crystallize into giant letters in front of Masterji: 'This is how I will flatter the old man, and very subtly, bully him. I will show him the kingdoms of the earth and give him a hint of the instruments of torture.' So they had shown him all the kingdoms of Bombay and told him: 'Take your pick.' And he knew now what he wanted.

Nothing.

Masterji could see black water crashing into the ocean wall that was meant to keep it out, rolling back and crashing again.

Once before, when Purnima had been threatened by her brothers, he had been weak. Not wanting trouble at his Society, he had again been weak.

'And Masterji – the Pintos want you to agree. For their sake you must say yes.'

'Don't *you* speak about the Pintos.'

'Your friend Mr Pinto is not the man you think he is, Masterji. Until two weeks ago he used to drink Royal Stag whisky. The other morning, a used Blenders Pride quarter-bottle carton turns up in his rubbish. He has started paying fifteen rupees more for a bottle of whisky. Why? Because he loves money more than he loves his wife's blindness.'

So he is examining our rubbish, Masterji thought. *But a man's rubbish is not the truth about him, is it?*

'You don't know a thing about Mr Pin... Mr Pint... Mr Pint...'

Masterji felt the floor slipping beneath his feet: 'It's starting again.' He heard his blood sugar chuckling. His left knee swelled up in pain; his eyes dimmed.

'Masterji,' Ajwani reached for him. 'Masterji, what's the matter?'

'Nothing,' he shook off Ajwani's hand. 'Nothing.'

'Just stay calm, Masterji. And breathe deeply. It will...'

Look down, a voice said. *Look at me.* Masterji turned to his left and saw the swirls in the ocean, the foam that was hitting the wall along the shore of Bombay. The foam thickened. The ocean rammed into the wall of Breach Candy like a bull. *Look at me, Masterji.* The bull came in again and rammed into the wall of the city and back he went to gather his strength. *Look at me.*

The oceans were full of glucose.

'What are you saying, Masterji?' Ajwani asked. He looked at Shanmugham with a grin.

Shanmugham remembered the sign on the mansion that he saw every morning on his drive up Malabar Hill. 'This place is dilapidated, dangerous, and unfit for human beings to be around.' The Municipality should hang the same sign on old men like this. He tried to touch Masterji, who took a step back and glared at him: 'Did you bring me here to *coerce* me?'

Said in English, the force of that word, *coerce*, weakened both Ajwani and Shanmugham.

The aroma of batter-fried food blew on to the terrace. Giri was walking towards the men with a silver tray full of just-fried pakoras sitting on paper stained with fresh grease.

'Hot, hot, hot, hot.'

'Please offer the pakoras to Mr Murthy from Vishram Society,' Shanmugham said. 'He's a teacher.'

'Hot, hot, hot, hot…' Giri brought the tray over to the distinguished visitor.

The old man's left hand slapped at the tray; it slipped in and out of Giri's hands, then crashed to the floor. Shanmugham and Ajwani moved their feet to dodge the rolling pakoras. Giri stared with an open mouth. When the three of them looked up, they realized they were alone on the terrace.

In the morning, at the dining table with the red-and-white cloth, the Pintos heard what had happened at Malabar Hill, while in the kitchen, Nina, their maid-servant, obscured by steam, took idlis out of the pressure cooker.

'So you just left?'

'They were threatening me,' Masterji said. 'Of course I left.'

'Ten thousand appointments are missed in this city because of too much traffic, and you missed Mr Shah because of too little traffic. Fate, Masterji,' Mr Pinto said, as the maid tipped three idlis on to his plate. 'The very definition.'

'You sound bitter, Mr Pinto.' Masterji leaned back and waited for his idlis. Three for him too.

'And what do we do now?' Shelley asked. As usual, she received only two idlis.

'We will wait till October 3. The deadline will expire and that Shah fellow will go away. He said so, don't you remember?'

'And until then the boycott will get worse.'

'There's something bigger than us involved here, Mr Pinto. Yesterday, when I was at the builder's terrace I saw something in the ocean. Things are changing too fast in this city. Everyone knows this, but no one wants to take responsibility. To say: "Slow down. Stop. Let's think about what's happening." Do you understand me?'

But that was not it, either. There was something more in the foaming white waters: a sense of power. Breaking an implicit rule – never to touch another man's body while they were eating – he reached over and gripped his friend's shoulder. Mr Pinto almost spat out his idli.

After dinner the maid poured tea into small porcelain cups.

'This boycott,' Mr Pinto said. 'It is already so difficult to bear. Shelley cries every night in bed. How can they do it to us, after all these years of living together?'

'We mustn't think badly of our neighbours.' Masterji sipped his tea. 'Purnima would not like it. Remember what she used to tell us about man being like a goat tied to a pole? There is a radius of freedom, but the circumference of our actions is set. People should be judged lightly.'

Mr Pinto, who had never been sure how well Purnima's image squared with Catholic teaching, grunted.

Masterji was cheerful. Breaking a rule not to impose on the Pintos' generosity, he asked Nina for a second cup of tea.

The defecators have left the water's edge at the slummy end of Versova beach; while, in an equal exchange, the posh end of the beach has rid itself of the joggers, callisthentic stretchers, and t'ai-chi practitioners. It is a quarter past ten. Down a concrete path comes a saddled white horse. This path cuts between boulders to lead to the beach; drawing the horse by its stirrups, a boy stops to whisper into its ear. *No one here, Raja. In the evening they will come, children to be taken for a ride over the sand. For now we are alone, Raja.*

The ambient murmur of the waves makes their privacy more exclusive; on a high rock the boy sits to bring his mouth level with Raja's large ear.

The boy stops talking. There is someone else on the beach. A fat man is standing at the water's edge, looking out at the blue-grey mess of towers on the distant Bandra shoreline. The boy strokes his horse's ear, and watches the fat man.

Shah had been staring at the turrets of the hotel at Land's End in Bandra. Somewhere beyond it, where the planes were landing, was Santa Cruz. Somewhere in there was Vishram Society Tower A. He saw the building in front of him, dirty, pink, rain-stained. Six floors. He held out his palm and closed his fingers.

Footsteps behind him. Shah turned.

Descending from the rocks behind him, the tall chastened figure of Shanmugham walked on to the beach with a small blue tin in his hands.

'This is for you, sir,' he said, handing it over to Shah.

Rosie, who had seen her Uncle alone down by the beach, had summoned Shanmugham and handed over the blue tin of *gutka*.

Shah scooped out some *gutka*, and chewed.

Shanmugham could see the thinking part of his employer, his jaw, struggling to make sense of things.

'I still don't understand. You and that broker – all you had to do was keep that teacher there till I got back.'

'He became violent, sir. Ask Giri. He hit the tray and then he ran out.'

'I don't like blaming another man when it's my fault,' Shah said, chewing fast. 'Going to see that headmaster – a total waste of time. What does the man do? Namastes me, says, what an honour to meet you, Developer sir, and then asks for advice on a one-bedroom he is buying in Seven Bungalows. Would the Four Bungalows area be a better investment? Will Andheri East show superior appreciation once the Metro comes up? I should have stayed home and finished off this Vishram Society teacher. My fault. *My* fault.' He bit his lower lip.

'Sorry, sir.'

'Don't say sorry, Shanmugham. It is a worthless word. Listen to me: every midget in Mumbai with a mobile phone and a scooter fancies himself a builder. But not one in a hundred is going to make it. Because in this world, there is a line: on one side are the men who cannot get things done, and on the other side are the men who can. And not one in a hundred will cross that line. Will you?'

'Yes, sir.'

Shah spat on the beach.

'We have been reasonable in every way with this old teacher. We asked him what he wanted from us, and promised to give it to him.'

'Yes, sir.'

'Now let him find out what it means to want nothing in Mumbai.'

Shanmugham held out his fist to his employer and opened it. 'Yes, sir.'

On the way back, the builder stopped to stroke the horse. Ignoring him, the boy whispered into the large pink ear.

'Fellow,' Shah said. 'Take this.'

'What's this for?' The boy did not touch the banknote the stranger offered.

'Because I feel like it.'

The boy shook his head.

'Then take it for keeping your horse in good shape. I like looking at beautiful things.'

Now the boy took the hundred-rupee note.

'Where are you from, son?'

'Madhya Pradesh.'

'How long in Mumbai?'

'Two months. Three months.'

'You shouldn't spend all your time talking to the horse. You should look around you, at people. Rich people. Successful people. You should always be thinking, what does he have that I don't have? That way you go up in life. You understand me?'

Stroking the side of the horse, Shah left.

The horse-keeper was still examining his windfall when Shanmugham swooped down on him.

'Give that to me,' he said. The boy shook his head and pressed his face into his horse's neck.

'The Sahib meant to give you a ten-rupee note. He gives money and then he changes his mind; he'll send someone down to take you to the police.'

The boy considered this, found it believable, and surrendered the gift. Shanmugham exchanged it for a ten-rupee note; then he leapt up the rocks with the spring of a man who has just become ninety rupees richer.

What do you want?

In the continuous market that runs right through southern Mumbai, under banyan trees, on pavements, beneath the arcades of the Gothic buildings, in which food, pirated books, perfumes, wristwatches, meditation beads and software are sold, one question is repeated, to tourists and locals, in Hindi or in English: *What do you want?* As you walk down the blue-tarpaulin-covered *souk* of the Colaba Causeway, pass the pirateers at the feet of the magical beasts which form the pillars of the Zoroastrian temple in Fort, someone will demand, at every turn: *What do you want?* Anything can be obtained; whether it is Indian or foreign; object or human; if you have no money, perhaps you will have something else with which to trade.

Only a man must want *something*; for everyone who lives here knows that the islands will shake, and the mortar of the city will dissolve, and Bombay will turn again into seven small stones glistening in the Arabian Sea, if it ever forgets to ask the question: *What do you want?*

Lunch at the Pintos' was served, as usual, at fifteen minutes past one o'clock. Nina went around the dining table, ladling out steaming prawn curry over plates of white rice. As Masterji settled into his chair, Mr Pinto asked: 'Is anything wrong with your phone?'

Masterji, about to stab a prawn with his fork, looked up.

'Why do you ask?'

'No reason,' Mr Pinto said, as he mixed curry into his rice.

Sometime before two o'clock, Masterji said goodbye to the Pintos. The moment he opened the door of his flat, the phone rang.

'Yes?'

A few minutes later, it rang again.

'Who is it?'

As soon as he put his phone down, he heard the phone ringing in the Pintos' living room. Then his rang again, and the moment he picked it up it went dead and the Pintos' was ringing again.

The door of the Pintos' flat was open. They were sitting side by side on the sofa, and Nina, their maid, stood next to them, protectively.

'It's just the children,' Masterji said, standing by the door with his arms folded. 'It must be Tinku or Mohammad. At school there was a boy who stuck notes on the backs of teachers. Tall boy. Rashid. *Kick Me. I Love Girls.* I caught him, and he got two weeks' suspension. The maximum penalty, short of expulsion.'

'I wonder why God made old age at all,' Mrs Pinto said. 'Your eyes are cloudy, your body is weak. The world becomes a ball of fear.'

'We're the Vakola triumvirate, Mrs Pinto. Caesar, Pompey, and Crassus. No one can make us budge.' Masterji refused a glass of cold water that Nina offered. 'I'll go down and speak to Kothari.'

'Someone rings and hangs up the phone,' he explained to the Secretary, who sat in his office, reading the real-estate pages of the *Times of India*. 'I think it's someone inside the building.'

The Secretary turned the page.

'Why?'

'Because the moment I enter my room, they start calling. And when I leave, they stop calling. So they know where I am.'

The Secretary folded his newspaper. He patted his comb-over into place and leaned back in his chair, exhaling a breath of curried potatoes and onions.

'Masterji' – he burped – 'do you know, another person died in a building collapse on Tuesday?'

Kothari grinned; the lynx-whiskers spread around his slitted eyes.

'I forget the name of the place now. Someone in that slum near the ocean... that wall near their slum collapsed when the rains... it was in the papers...'

'Are *you* the one making the phone calls, Kothari?' Masterji asked. 'Are you the one threatening us?'

'See?' Kothari said, gesturing helplessly to a phantom audience in his office. 'See? For 2,000 years we've played this game, this man and I, and now he asks if this is a threat. And then he hears phone calls. And soon he'll see men with knives and hockey sticks coming after him.'

Back in the Pintos' flat, they talked it over.

'Maybe it is just in our minds,' Mr Pinto said. 'Maybe Kothari is right.'

'When in doubt, make an experiment,' Masterji said. 'Let's put the phone back on the hook.'

When no one had called for an hour, Masterji walked up to his room. As he turned the key in his door, the phone rang. The moment he picked it up, it went dead.

*

At midnight, he went down the stairs and knocked on the Pintos' door. Mr Pinto opened it, went to the sofa, and held his wife's hands.

'I heard it,' Masterji said.

The Pintos' children in America did sometimes miscalculate the time difference and call late at night; but the phone had rung four times without being picked up. Now it began to ring again.

'Don't touch it,' Mr Pinto warned. 'They are speaking to us now.'

Masterji picked up the receiver.

'Old man, is that you?' It was a high-pitched, taunting voice.

'Who is this calling?'

'I have a lesson for you, old man: if you don't leave the flat, there will be trouble for you.'

'Who is this? Who told you to call? Are you Mr Shah's man?'

'There will be trouble for you and for your friends. So leave. Take the money and sign the paper.'

'I won't leave, so don't call.'

'If you don't leave – we'll play with your wife.'

'What?'

'We'll take her down to the bushes behind the building and play with her.'

Masterji let out a laugh.

'You'll play with a handful of ashes?'

Silence.

'It's the *other* one who has a—' A voice in the background.

The phone went dead. Within a minute it rang again.

'Don't pick it up, please,' Shelley said.

He picked it up.

'Old man: old man.'

This time it was another voice: lower, gruffer. Masterji was sure he had heard this voice somewhere.

'Act your age, old man. Grow up. Take the money and leave before something bad happens.'

'Who is this? I know your voice. You tell your Mr Shah...'

'If anything bad happens, you alone are responsible. You alone.'

Masterji slammed down the phone. He walked up the stairs to Mrs

Puri's door and knocked; when there was no response, he banged. She opened the door, with bleary eyes, as if she had been sleeping.

'What is this about, Masterji?'

'The phone calls. They just called us again. They're threatening us now.'

Mrs Puri swallowed a yawn.

'Masterji, you have been talking and talking about these phone calls but no one else can hear them.'

'Either someone in the building is calling, or someone in here is giving a signal to the callers. Their timing is too good. I'm sure I recognized one of the voices.'

She laughed.

'Mine? Is that what you're saying?'

'No... I don't think so.'

'I am not making the phone calls. Shall I ask Ramu if he is making the calls?'

She began to close the door: but Masterji pushed it back towards her.

'What about your sense of shame, Sangeeta? I am your neighbour. Your neighbour of thirty years.'

'*Our* sense of shame? Masterji, you say *our*...? After the way you behaved at Mr Shah's house? After the way you lied to your own son about accepting the offer?'

When she closed the door on him, Masterji struck it with his fist.

'You borrowed money from my wife, and never repaid it. Do you think I didn't know?'

He walked down into the compound. In the darkness, distances were obscured; masses dissolved; lit window called out to lit window; he saw rhymes in light. One lamp went out in a nearby Society; another came on in Tower B.

Were *they* doing it?

An autorickshaw drove past the gate, heading towards the slums.

Woken up in his room at the back of the Society, Ram Khare, when the situation was explained to him, pouted his lower lip.

'Speak to the Secretary. Phones are not the guard's responsibility.'

He turned on his bedside lamp. His khaki shirt hung on a nail from the wall; old black-and-white photographs in which a bare-chested yoga teacher demonstrated the four stages of the *Dhanush-asana* were taped above his bed.

'What does that mean, Ram Khare? We're being threatened. It's night-time: you're the guard.'

A half-bottle of Old Monk rum stood on the only other piece of furniture in the room, a wicker table. Exhaling boozy breath, Ram Khare crossed his arms and scratched his back with long fingernails.

'I warned you, sir. I warned you.'

He turned in bed, and, showing his visitor his back, bumpy with mosquito-bites, went back to sleep.

'Why don't you call Gaurav,' Mr Pinto asked, when Masterji was back in their flat, the door safely locked behind him.

'Ask him to come over and spend the night with us. In the morning we'll go to the police.'

Masterji thought about it, and said: 'We don't need anyone's help. We're the triumvirate.'

He yanked the Pintos' telephone cord out of the wall and threw it on the floor.

'All three of us will sleep right here. First thing in the morning we'll go to the police.'

Mr Pinto made up the sofa for him; Shelley came from the bedroom with a spare pillow in her blind arms.

Masterji went up to his living room and returned with a smile and a large blue book.

'What's that for?' Mr Pinto asked.

'It's my *Illustrated History of Science*.' Masterji made a motion of hitting someone on the head with the book. 'Just in case.'

The produce stalls were now covered with gunny sacks, and the vendors were sleeping beside them. Mani, the assistant, sat outside the glass door of the Renaissance Real-Estate Agency, yawning.

The office was dark, and the broker's laminated desk was deserted. Yet Mani knew that business was still going on; his boss might need him.

All the children at Vishram Society knew that below the Daisy Duck clock on the wall of Uncle Ajwani's real-estate office was the door that led into an inner room. None of them had been in there, and it was variously speculated that the broker used the room to sell black-market pharmaceuticals, pornographic magazines, or national secrets.

Shanmugham had just been led through the office into the inner room; the broker shut the door behind him.

The inner room had a cot with no cover, and two wicker baskets, one full of coconuts, and the other full of coconut shells. Sawdust, masking tape, nails, a hammer lay on the floor. Avoiding the nails, Shanmugham sat down on the bare cot.

'What do you use this room for?'

Ajwani pointed to the treasure hoard in the wicker basket. The coconuts were large and green; a curved black knife lay on top of them. 'I buy them wholesale. Six rupees each. Much better than your Coke or Pepsi. Fresh and tasty.'

'A room just for coconuts?' Shanmugham frowned.

The broker slapped the cot. 'Not just coconuts.' He winked. 'Do you want one now, by the way? Full of vitamins. Best thing for the health.'

'The news, Ajwani. What did you call me here for? Have the old men agreed?'

Ajwani stirred the coconuts with his foot.

'No, things have become worse. Tinku Kothari, the Secretary's son – hungry eyes – saw them at the school today. He spoke to the old librarian and got the facts. They were looking up the numbers of Masterji's old students and calling them from the library phone.'

'Is this a problem?'

'No. People respect a man like Masterji. No one loves him. No one will help him.'

'So why did you call me here, Ajwani?'

'Because that wasn't the only thing the librarian told Tinku. He said: they are going to see a lawyer. Tomorrow.'

'Where?'

'That I don't know. They may bring something back with them. Business card, brochure. It will end up in their rubbish.'

'Let's call them right now. *You* call them. You're so good at it.'

Ajwani chuckled. He picked up an imaginary phone receiver and lowered his voice an octave. 'Old man, sign the paper. Or we'll break your head. We'll play with your wife. They were more frightened when I spoke to them.' Ajwani beamed. 'Admit it.'

Shanmugham picked up a coconut and tapped it with his finger. 'You're a natural at this, Ajwani. You should be working for us full-time. You and your wife.'

'Wife? She just text-messages me when Masterji enters or leaves his room. I'm the one making the calls. It's good that you're giving me a sweetener, but I'd do it anyway. I *like* this work.'

The broker's face broadened with pleasure. Even though they were alone in the room, he moved closer to the Tamilian, and lowered his voice.

'Tell me what you've done. A few things you've done.'

With his fingers poised above the coconut, Shanmugham looked up.

'What do you mean, done?'

Ajwani winked. 'You know. For Mr Shah. Things like this. Phone calls, threats, *action*. Tell me a few stories.'

'You don't do these things yourself,' Shanmugham said. 'Usually get someone else. Some eager fellow from the slums. No shortage.'

'Tell me. I won't tell anyone. I promise.'

A corner of Shanmugham's lip rose; his tongue cleaned his angular tooth. 'We're partners now. Why not?' He rotated the coconut in his hands.

Three years ago. A tough redevelopment project in Chembur. One old man had refused to sell his flat. Mr Shah said: 'Get him out of there, Shanmugham.' He had hired two boys to smash chairs to pieces outside his window. No implements. The old man stared out of his window and watched them break wood with their bare hands and feet all day long. When he looked out, they grinned and showed him their teeth. He sold out after a couple of days.

'That's clever,' Ajwani said. 'Very clever. The police can't do a thing to you.'

Shanmugham dropped the coconut on to the pile; then he gave the basket a kick. 'Always use your brains, the boss says.'

The nuts trembled together.

'There was once a Muslim man in a chawl, a Khan. This fellow fancied himself tough. Boss made him an offer to leave. Generous offer. "I have no pity for a greedy man," Boss said. I paid a boy to sit on the steps of a building opposite and watch this Khan. That was all. Just watch him. This Khan who would not have left if threatened by a gang of goondas signed and left the building within a week.'

Ajwani rubbed his hands together.

'You're a genius at this, Mr Shanmugham.'

'It can't always be brains, though. Sometimes, you just have to...'

Picking up the curved black knife that lay on the coconuts, Shanmugham stuck it into a green nut. Ajwani shivered.

'Tell me. Please. What have you done? Broken a leg?' He dropped his voice. '*Killed* a man?'

Shanmugham looked at the black knife.

'Just a year ago. A project in Sion. One old man kept saying no, no. We kept offering money, and it was always no, no. Boss was getting angry.'

'So?' Ajwani came as close as he could.

So, in a bolt of rage and calculation, six-foot-two-inch-tall Shanmugham ran up the stairs of the building, kicked open a door, grabbed something that was playing backgammon with its grandson, shoved its head out of a window, saying: *Sign, mother-fucker.*

'You really did that?' Ajwani stared at the black knife.

Shanmugham nodded. He took the knife out of the coconut. 'The old man signed on the spot. I was scared, I tell you that. I thought I might go to jail. But... the truth is, even if they say no, *deep down*' – he pointed the knife at Ajwani – 'they want money. Once you make them sign, they're grateful to you. Never go to the police. So all I'm doing is making them aware of their own inner intentions.'

He threw the knife back into the pile of coconuts.

Ajwani gazed in admiration at Shanmugham's hands. 'What else have you done for Mr Shah?'

'Anything he wants. The call can come any time, day or night. You have to be ready.'

He told Ajwani of the time a famous politician had phoned the Confidence office, and quoted a figure, in cash, that would have to be transported that evening to his election headquarters. Shah and Shanmugham had driven to a warehouse in Parel where five-hundred-rupee notes were counted by machines, tied into bricks and loaded into an SUV – the cash, filling the vehicle's front and back seats, was covered with a white bedsheet. Shanmugham, with no more than a hundred and seventy-five rupees for food and drink, drove the SUV across the state border, to the politician's henchmen. Safely delivered. The politician won the election.

'I could have been like you. An *action* man.' Ajwani gouged out his lower lip and shook his head. 'If I had met a man like Mr Shah in time. Instead, I'm…

'But tell me.' He tapped the Tamilian's forearm. 'There must be girls in your business. Pretty girls. Dance bar girls?'

'I'm a married man,' Shanmugham said. 'My wife would cut my throat.'

Which made them both laugh.

The broker got up from the cot. 'Let's finish this phone call business now.'

'Not from your phone—' Shanmugham produced a small red mobile phone. 'This one has a SIM card that they can't trace.'

He threw it to the broker.

'Old man,' Ajwani said into the phone. 'Old man, are you there? Pick up the phone, old man…' He shook his head and gave the mobile back.

Shanmugham got up from the cot, smacking dust off his trousers.

'That's it for phone calls.'

'What happens next?' the broker asked, as they left the office through a back door. 'Are you going to send boys to break wood outside the Society?'

239

Shanmugham tied the straps of his helmet. 'Some things,' he said, 'you don't tell even your first cousins.'

Kicking the Hero Honda to life, he drove off into the night.

2 AUGUST

The banging noise on the door woke Masterji. Seizing the *Illustrated History of Science*, he got up from the sofa, and checked the safety catch. He stood by the door with the book raised in both hands.

The Pintos waited at the threshold of their dark bedroom.

'Not here,' Mrs Pinto whispered. 'Upstairs. They're banging on *your* door.'

Mr Pinto reached for the light switch.

'Wait,' Masterji said.

Now they heard footsteps coming down the stairs.

'Let's call the police. Someone please call the…'

'Yes,' Masterji said from the door. 'Call them.'

'But Masterji pulled the phone cord out of the wall. You have to put it back in, Mr Pinto.'

The footsteps grew louder. Mr Pinto got down on his knees and slapped at the wall. 'I can't find the plug…'

'Quickly, Mr Pinto, quickly.'

'Keep quiet, Shelley.'

'Don't fight!' – Masterji from the door. 'And both of you keep quiet.'

The banging started on the Pintos' door.

'Stop that at once, or I'll call the police!' Masterji shouted.

There was a jangling of bangles from outside, and then:

'Ramu, tell your Masterji who it is.'

'Oh, God. Sangeeta.' Masterji lowered the *Illustrated History of Science*. He turned on the light. 'Why are you here at *this* hour?'

'Ramu, tell your Masterji we are all walking to SiddhiVinayak temple. We'll pray for his heart to soften. Now come, Ramu,' she said, 'and no noise: we don't want to wake up the good people.'

The Puris were taking that boy on foot to SiddhiVinayak? How would Ramu walk such a distance?

He almost opened the door to plead with Mrs Puri not to do this to Ramu.

It was three in the morning. Another three and a half hours before it was light and they could go to the police station. With the *Illustrated History of Science* lying on his ribs, he closed his eyes and stretched out on the sofa.

Six and a half hours later, he was walking with Mr Pinto down the main road.

'I know we're late. Don't blame me. If you still had your scooter we could have gone to the station in five minutes.'

Masterji said nothing. Walking was good on a day like this. With each step he took, the threat of violence receded. He had lived in Vakola for thirty years, his bones had become arthritic on these very pavements. Who could threaten him here?

'It's the fortunate men of Vishram!'

Bare-chested Trivedi, the Gold Coin priest, came towards them with embracing arms. He had just performed a little cleansing ritual at the police station, he explained. Someone had died in the station years ago, and they called him in once a year to purge the ghost.

'Let me buy you a coffee or tea. A coconut?'

'Tea,' Mr Pinto said.

'We have to go,' Masterji whispered. 'We're late already.'

'Just a few minutes,' Mr Pinto said.

He followed the priest to a roadside tea shop, beside which a burly man in a *banian* stood pressing clothes with a coal-fired iron. A metal trough full of spent coals rested by the side of his ironing board.

With a glass of chai in his hand, Pinto motioned for Masterji to join him and Trivedi at the tea shop.

It had been a morning full of delays, Mr Pinto at every stage misplacing something – his glasses, umbrella. Now, watching the trembling tea glass in his old friend's hand, Masterji understood.

'I'll go into the station and file the complaint. You can go home alone, Mr Pinto. It's perfectly safe in daylight.'

The police station of Vakola stands right at the traffic signal leading in from the highway, giving the impression you are coming into a suburb where the law is securely in charge.

From the chastening aromas of coal and laundry outside the station, Masterji walked into an atmosphere of burning incense and marigold flowers.

It was his first visit to the station in nearly a decade; in the mid-1990s Purnima's handbag had been snatched just outside the school on a Saturday afternoon – such an unusual event that it had led to neighbourhood talk of a 'crime wave'; he and Purnima had come here, and spoken to sympathetic officers; a First Information Report (FIR) with the details of the crime had been filled out by a policeman over carbon paper, and that appeared to have been the bulk of the investigative work done. The bag was never recovered; nor did the crime wave materialize.

He saw a drunk, half asleep; a foreign tourist who had clearly not slept in a long time; two vendors from the market who had probably been behind on their payments to the station; and then the men with vague, varied, and never-ending business who populate any police station.

'Masterji,' a pot-bellied constable saluted him. 'Did your wife lose her handbag again?'

He remembered that he had taught this constable's son. (Ashok? Ashwin?)

He sat down and explained his situation. The constable heard his story and made sure that the senior inspector at the station, a man named Nagarkar, heard it too.

'These calls are hard to trace,' the inspector said, 'but I will send a man over – that's usually all it takes, to frighten these builders and their goondas. This isn't a neighbourhood where a teacher can be threatened.'

'Thank you, sir.' Masterji put his hand on his heart. 'An old teacher is grateful.'

The inspector smiled. 'We'll help you, we'll help you. But, Masterji. Really.'

Masterji stared.

'Really what, sir?'

'You're holding out to the very end, aren't you?'

Now he understood: the policemen thought this was about money. They were not the police force of the Indian Penal Code, but of the iron law of Necessity: of the notion that every man has his price – a generous figure, to be sure, but one he *must* accept. Say – *I have no figure* – a cell door swings open, and you find yourself in with the drunks and thugs. Above the head man's desk, he saw a glass-framed portrait of Lord SiddhiVinayak, blood-red and pot-bellied, like the living incarnation of Necessity.

The inspector grinned. 'Your Society's famous man is here, by the way.'

Masterji turned in his chair; at the entrance to the station stood Ajwani.

The entire station warmed at his appearance. Any person looking to rent in a good building had to furnish, by law, a Clearance Certificate from the local police station to his prospective Society. In a less-than-*pucca* neighbourhood like Vakola, people were always turning up at Ajwani's office without authentic drivers' licences, voter ID cards, or PAN cards; men with flashy mobile phones and silk shirts who could afford any rent demanded of them yet could not prove (as the Clearance Certificate required) that they were employed by a respectable company.

The broker came here to procure the necessary certificates for these men, in exchange for the necessary sums of money. With a smile and a hundred-rupee note, he invented legitimate occupations and respectable business offices for his clients; conjured wives for unmarried men, and husbands and children for single women. The real-estate broker was a master of fiction.

This is the real business of this station, Masterji thought. *I should get out of here at once.*

It was too late. Ajwani had spotted him; he saw the broker's eye ripening with knowledge.

*

Mr Pinto's white hair was loose in the wind, and he kept patting it back into place. He was still sitting on the bench at the roadside stall.

The burly man who had been pressing clothes near the tea stall had finished his work, which was piled on to his ironing board; kneeling down, he opened the jaws of his enormous pressing iron. The black coals that filled it began to fume; Masterji watched an exposed part of the machinery of heat and smoke that ran his world.

Mr Pinto got up.

'How did it go, Masterji? I was going to come, but I thought you might not want...'

Masterji held back the words of reproach. Who could blame Mr Pinto for being frightened? He was just an old man who knew he was an old man.

'I told you not to worry, Mr Pinto.'

A group of schoolgirls wearing white Muslim headscarves over their navy-blue uniforms stood by the side of the road, waving little Indian flags, tittering and gossiping. They appeared to be rehearsing for Independence Day; their teachers, dressed in green salwar kameez, tried to impose order on them.

They *still believe in Independence Day*, Masterji thought, looking at the excited little schoolchildren.

'We live in a Republic, Mr Pinto.' He placed his hand on his friend's shoulder. 'A man has his resources here. Now watch my hand.'

Mr Pinto watched his friend's fingers as they emerged one by one from his fists:

Police.

Media.

Law and order.

Social workers.

Family.

Students and old boys.

Masterji was doing what he did best: teaching. What is there in the world of which a man can say: 'This is on my side?' All of these. Mr Pinto's resources, as a citizen of the Republic of India, were more than adequate to any and all threats at hand. The sun and the moon were in their right orbits.

They would start with the law. The police had been friendly, true, but you could not just say to them: 'Fight evil'; the law was a code, a kind of white magic. A lawyer would bring his magic lamp, and only then would the Genie of the Law do their bidding.

Over lunch, Mr Pinto said that he knew of a lawyer. A connection had used him in a property dispute.

'Not a rupee is charged unless there is a settlement in the matter. This is guaranteed. His address is somewhere here.'

Nina served them a speciality from her native South Canara, jack-fruit seeds boiled to succulence and served in a red curry with coriander. Masterji wanted to praise Nina, but repressed the impulse lest she ask for a pay rise from the Pintos.

Raised to good spirits by the jackfruit seeds, Masterji sat down at Mr Pinto's writing table, and took out his Sheaffer pen, a gift from his daughter-in-law two years ago.

Mr Pinto prepared the envelopes; Masterji wrote three letters to English-language newspapers and two to Hindi newspapers.

Dear Editor,

It being said that we live in a Republic, the question arises whether a man in his own home can be threatened, and that too on the eve of Independence Day…

Nina made them ginger tea; Mr Pinto stuck stamps on the envelopes and sealed them, and Masterji, after drinking the tea, began another letter, this one to his most famous ex-pupil.

My dear Avinash Noronha,

Remembering well your fine character in your schooling days, I know you cannot have forgotten your alma mater, St Catherine's High School in Vakola, nor your old teacher of physics, Yogesh A. Murthy. It is with such pride that I read your weekly columns in the Times of India, *and your timely*

warnings against the spread of corruption and apathy.
Little will it surprise you, hence, to know that this tide of
decay has now reached your old neighbourhood and
threatens your old…

'Nina will post them on her way home,' Mr Pinto said.

'And this is just the start,' Masterji added. They had not been able to find any of his ex-students at home when they had telephoned, but he planned to write letters of appeal to all those old boys who had signed the photograph of his farewell party.

Mr Pinto approved of this plan; he would go to the school library and get their mailing addresses from old Vittal. But he wanted Masterji to go and see the lawyer first.

'What do we have to lose? It's a free consultation. And his office is right here, near Bandra train station.'

Masterji agreed. 'You stay with Shelley,' he said. 'I'll go on my own.'

'Don't take the train to Bandra, take an auto,' Mr Pinto said.

He put a hundred-rupee note into Masterji's shirt pocket.

'Okay,' Masterji said, patting his pocket, 'we'll enter it in the No-Argument when I get back. Fifty rupees: what I owe you.'

'No.' Mr Pinto looked at the thing in his friend's pocket. 'We won't enter that in the book. You owe me nothing.'

Masterji understood: this must be Mr Pinto's way of apologizing.

As his rickshaw fought its way to Bandra through the Khar subway, Masterji thought: *I wonder how Ramu is doing, poor boy*.

For maximum chance of winning favour from the red elephant-god, the temple of SiddhiVinayak must be visited, the devout believe, on foot: the farther from the temple you live, the longer your journey, the greater the accumulation of virtue.

The Puris had so often talked about walking to SiddhiVinayak in the past eighteen years that some of their neighbours believed they had done so, and Mr Ganguly had even asked Mrs Puri for advice on how to make the trip.

These things catch up with you, for the gods are not blind.

Mrs Puri calculated the trip from Vakola to Prabhadevi would take them about four hours. Everything depended on Ramu. If things became really bad they would have to make him pee or shit on the road, like some street urchin. But he had to come along: that was the sacrifice she was going to make to Lord Ganesha. Not enough that she and her husband should ache from the walk. God would see that she was even prepared to make her son suffer: the thing she had fought for eighteen years to prevent.

They walked down the highway into the city. The sky brightened. Streaks of red ran through an orange dawn, as if the skin had been peeled from heaven. A man inside a tea stall struck a match; a blue flame ignited above his portable gas cylinder.

Every few minutes, Ramu whispered into his mother's ear.

'Be brave, my boy. The temple is just around the corner.'

If he stopped, she pinched him. If he stopped again, she let him rest a minute or two, and – 'Oy, oy, oy!' – they were off.

Two hours later, somewhere beyond Mahim, they sat down at a roadside tea stall. Mrs Puri poured tea into a saucer for the boy. Ramu, high on caffeine, lost in his delirium of fatigue and pain, began to rave until his mother patted his head and soothed him with her voice.

Two municipal workers began sweeping the pavement behind the Puris. Their faces filled with dust; they were too tired to sneeze.

Mrs Puri closed her eyes. She thought of the Lord Ganesha at the temple in SiddhiVinayak and prayed: *We said we were going to temples but we went to see new homes. We were afraid of the Evil Eye but we forgot about you. And you punished us by placing a stone in everyone's path. Now move the stone, which only you, God, with your elephant's strength, can do.*

'Ramu, Ramu,' she said, shaking her son awake. 'It's only another hour from here. Get up.'

When the clock struck five, Shelley Pinto was in bed, her purblind eyes staring at the ceiling.

She heard her husband at the dinner table, scribbling away with paper and pencil, as he used to when he was an accountant.

'Is something worrying you, Mr Pinto?' she asked.

'After I said goodbye to Masterji, I saw a fight in the market, Shelley. Mary's father was drunk, and he had said something. One of the vendors hit him, Shelley. In the face. You could hear the sound of bone crushing into bone.'

'Poor Mary.'

'It's a horrible thing to be hit, isn't it, Shelley. A horrible thing.' He spoke to himself in a low voice, until his wife said:

'What are you whispering there, Mr Pinto?'

He said: 'How many square feet is our place, Shelley? Have you ever calculated?'

'Mr Pinto. *Why* do you ask?'

'I have to calculate, Shelley. I was an accountant. It gets into the blood.'

'I'll be blind in another building, Mr Pinto. I have eyes all around Vishram Society.'

'I know, Shelley. I know. I'm just calculating. Is that a sin? I just want to turn into US dollars. Just to see how much it would be.'

'But Mr Shah is paying us in rupees. We can't send it in dollars.'

When they had gone to America in 1989, Mr Pinto had acquired, on the black market, a small stash of US dollars from a man in Nariman Point. The government in those days did not allow Indians to convert rupees into dollars without its permission, so Mr Pinto had made her swear not to tell anyone. The dollars proved to be redundant, for the children took care of them in Michigan and Buffalo. On the return stopover in Dubai, they exchanged their original dollar stash, plus the gifts of American money Deepa and Tony had forced on them, for two 24-carat gold biscuits, one of which Mr Pinto smuggled into India in his coat pocket while a trembling Shelley Pinto carried the other in her purse past a customs officer.

That was her abiding memory of the word 'dollar'. Something that turned into gold.

'Oh, all that's changed, Shelley. All that has changed.'

Mr Pinto sat by her bedside and explained. It was all there on the Reserve Bank of India's website. He had been to Ibrahim Kudwa's cyber-café a few days ago and had navigated the site with Ibrahim's kind help.

'If it is a gift, we can only send out 10,000 dollars per annum. But if it is investment, we can send 100,000 dollars. And soon they may increase the limit to 200,000 dollars each year. It's *perfectly* legal.'

The darkness that enveloped Mrs Pinto grew larger. They, from India, would now have to send the children, in America, money?

'Will Tony have to come back?'

'He has a Green Card. Don't be stupid, Shelley. Their children are citizens.'

'But he has no money?'

'Things are difficult over there. Deepa may lose her job. I didn't want to frighten you.'

'Everything is so expensive in the States. Don't you remember how much the sandwiches cost? Why did they leave Bombay?'

'Just tell me how many square feet this place is, woman. Let me worry about things.'

'812 square feet,' she said. 'We had it measured once.'

Mr Pinto sat at the dinner table again and rubbed his pale hands together: 'I feel young again, Shelley.' She wondered if he was asking for a resumption in their relations, which had ceased some twenty-seven years ago, but no, of course not, all he meant was this: he was being an accountant again.

'It would be so simple, Shelley. Two-thirds of the money we send in dollars to the children, and with the rest we buy a small flat right here in Vakola. Nina could come and cook there too.'

'How can you talk like this, Mr Pinto?' she said. 'If Masterji says no, we must say no.'

'I'm just cal-cu-la-*ting*, Shelley. He is my friend. Of thirty-two years. I will never betray him for US dollars.'

Mr Pinto walked around the living room, and said: 'Let us go for our evening walk, Shelley. Exercise is good for the lower organs.'

'Masterji warned us not to leave the building while he was gone.'

'I am here to protect you. Don't you trust your own husband? Masterji is not God. We are going down.'

With her husband behind her, Mrs Pinto descended the steps. Just before she reached the ground floor, something bumped into her side – she knew, from the smell of Johnson's Baby Powder, who it was.

'Rajeev!' Mr Pinto called after Ajwani's son. 'This is not a zoo, run slowly.'

'Don't fight with anyone today, Mr Pinto,' she said. 'Let's be quiet and stay out of trouble.'

Holding on to each other, they walked out of the darkened entranceway into the sunlight. Mrs Kudwa, seated on the prime chair in parliament, talking to Mrs Saldanha at her kitchen window, was silent as they passed.

The guard was in his booth, keeping a watch on the compound.

Mr Pinto coughed. Smoke billowed in from over the compound wall; gathering the stray leaves from the Society, Mary had set fire to them in the gutter outside. Suspended in a dark cloud, the hibiscus flowers had turned a more passionate red.

'Are you all right?'

'Fine, Shelley. Just a cough.'

Mr Pinto heard singing in the distance: children rehearsing patriotic songs for Independence Day:

'*Saarey jahan se accha*
Yeh Hindustan hamara
Hum bulbule hain iski
Yeh gulistan hamara.'

'Better than all the world
Is this India of ours;
We are its nightingales,
It is our garden.'

A few steps down, he turned to his wife and said: 'Wait.'

They were in the 'blood stretch', and he held his breath. Leaning over the wall, he saw a pack of stray black dogs, down in the gutter, running after a small white-and-brown puppy. It squealed as if this were no game. The four dogs chased it down the length of the gutter. Then all of them vanished.

'What is happening there, Mr Pinto?'

'They're going to kill that little thing, Shelley.' He paused. 'It looks like Sylvester.'

The Pintos had once had a dog, Sylvester, for the sake of their son Tony. When Sylvester died, the Society had allowed them to bury him in the backyard so they could be near him as they walked around Vishram.

The squealing noise broke out again from inside the gutter.

The old accountant put his hand on his wife's back. 'You walk on along the wall, Shelley; you know the way, don't you? I have to see what they are doing to that puppy.'

'But Masterji said not to leave the building till he came back with a lawyer.'

'I'm going right outside, Shelley. We have to save that little fellow.'

Shelley waited by the wall, holding her breath against the stench from the beef-shop. The squealing from the gutter grew louder, and then died out. She heard footsteps from the other side of the wall. She recognized them as Mr Pinto's. She heard him lower himself into the gutter.

'Don't walk in the gutter, Mr Pinto. Do you hear me?'

Now she heard a second set of footsteps. Younger, faster footsteps.

'Mr Pinto,' she called. 'Who is that coming close to you?'

She waited.

'Mr Pinto… where are you? And who is that who has come in to the gutter? Say something.'

She put her hand on the wall; from a bruise in the brick, she knew that the guard's booth was to her left, about thirty-four small steps away.

She walked with her hand on the wall.

The guard's booth was still twenty-nine steps away when Shelley Pinto heard her husband cry out.

Masterji, on his way to the lawyer's office, stopped and sniffed. Balls of batter-coated starch were sizzling inside a snack store.

Quick dark arms emerged from a white *banian* to grate potatoes into a vat of boiling oil. Another pair of arms waited with a scoop; now and then the scoop dipped into the vat to come up with sizzling wafers.

Big bins full of snacks surrounded the two men: fried potatoes (red and spicy, or yellow and unspiced), fried plantains (cut into round slices, or sliced longitudinally into strips, or coated in spices, or dusted in brown sugar), and batter-fried greens. Next door, in a rival establishment, a rival vat of raucous oil hissed with potatoes. Between them, the two shops produced the continuous competitive buzzing of boiling oil that is as much a dialect of the Bombay street as Hindi, Marathi, or Bhojpuri.

The competition of painted signs came next.

FERROUS NONFERROUS METALS
IQBAL ROZA PROPRIETOR

D'SOUZA BRAND WEDDING CARDS
BULK SALES

The old buildings began to ooze out fresh juice; ensconced in arched niches in the rotting façades, vendors sat before pyramids of oranges and lemons, operating electric mixers that rumbled apoplectically.

The sound of metallic snipping warned Masterji to slow down.

FAMOUS HAIR CUTTING PALACE

– this was the landmark mentioned in the advertisement. The next doorway must lead into the Loyola Trust Building.

The pigeons landing on the metal grilles of the windows made a constant cooing as he walked in; a sapling had cracked the cornice above the doorway. No reception area, no signboard in the lobby. A metal cage went up the airshaft, as if protecting the lift, which seemed, in any case, to be broken. Masterji knew at once the story of this building. The landlord could not – because of tenant protection laws – force his tenants out; they were probably paying the same rent they were in 1950, and he was retaliating by refusing to provide even the basics – light, safety, hygiene. You could almost hear him praying every night to God: make my tenants fall down the stairs, break their bones, burn in fire.

It grew darker as Masterji climbed the steps. A plaque of dense black wires criss-crossed the wall like a living encrustation growing over old plaster and brick. He could even smell the acridity of cockroach on the wall. He heard talking from above him:

'There are three great dangers in this city.'

'Three?'

'Three: children, goats, and a third thing I forget.'

'Children – a danger?'

'The greatest. Responsible for half the traffic accidents in this city. *Half.*'

He climbed more steps to see a pale pot-bellied idol of Ganesha in a niche, like a soft white rat living on the staircase. There appeared to be no electricity up here, and uniformed men sat beneath a paraffin light. He walked unchallenged past the men, just as one cried: 'I remember the third danger now. I remember it. Shall I tell you?'

Along a dim corridor, a bright metal sign on an open door announced:

PAREKH AND SONS
ADVOCATE
'LEGAL HAWK WITH SOUL & CONSCIENCE'

A small man in a grey uniform sat on a wooden stool between the metal sign and a glass door. A red pencil behind his ear.

'You are here to see…' he asked, taking out the pencil.

'I am a man in need of legal help. A connection of mine told me about Mr Parekh.'

The man wrote in the air with the pencil. 'What is the *name* of your connection?'

'Actually, it was a connection of a connection. He had used Mr Parekh's services.'

'So you want to see…'

'Mr Parekh.'

'*Which* Parekh?'

'Legal hawk with a conscience. How many of them are here?'

The peon held up four fingers.

With the red pencil behind his ear, he went into the office; Masterji sat on his chair, raising his feet as an old servant woman mopped the floor with a wet rag.

Having apparently figured out which Parekh he was after, the peon opened the glass door and beckoned with the red pencil.

Masterji stepped into fluorescent light and air-conditioning breeze.

With its low dark wooden ceiling, the office had the look of a ship's cabin; a man wearing thick glasses sat beneath a giant framed photograph of Angkor Wat with the legend: 'World's Biggest Hindu Temple'.

The air smelled of disinfectant.

Mr Parekh (so Masterji assumed) was drinking tea. He stopped to blow his nose into a handkerchief and turned to use a spittoon before returning to his tea; he was like some non-stop hydrostatic system able to function only while accepting and discharging liquids. As with liquids, so with information; he was simultaneously talking on a mobile phone propped on his shoulder, and signing documents that an assistant held out for him, while somehow finding himself able to whisper to Masterji: 'Tea? Any tea for you, sir? Sit. Sit.'

Putting down his mobile phone, he sipped the last of his tea, turned to one side to spit, and said: 'State the problem in your own words.'

The lawyer had a bald, baby-pink scalp, but three immortal silver strands went from his forehead to the base of his neck. An ailment, possibly related to the pinkness of scalp, had eaten away his eyebrows, so that his eyes looked at Masterji with startling directness. A neck-chain with a gold medallion dangled over his white shirt. The size of the gold medallion, contrasting with the palsied state of eyebrows and scalp, suggested that though Mr Parekh had endured much in life, he had survived and prospered.

Sipping tea, he listened to Masterji's story with fast-blinking eyes (Masterji wondered if the lack of eyebrows affected the beating of the eyelashes), and then turned to a younger man, who was quietly sitting in a corner chair.

'I know of Vishram Society. It is a famous building in Vakola.'

The younger man said: 'It used to be a jungle there. Now it's an up-and-coming area.'

'These builders – *all* criminals. Engaged in nothing but *number two* activities. Who is this Confidence Shah? Must be some slum rat.'

The younger man said: 'I think I've heard of him. Did redevelopment work in Mira Road. Or maybe Chembur.'

Old Parekh ran his hand over his three long silver hairs.

'A *slum rat*.' He smiled at Masterji. 'You've come to the right place, sir. You're looking at a man who deals with a baker's dozen of slum rats every single day. But first, we must know, what is your position in the eyes of the law. And the law has very specific eyes: Are you the sovereign of the place, or a representative of the said sovereign?'

'I've lived there for over thirty years. Since I came to Vakola to teach at the school.'

'A teacher?' Mr Parekh's jaw dropped. He blew into his handkerchief. 'It is against Hindu Dharma to threaten a teacher. I have studied Western law and Indian Dharma alike, sir. I have even been to see the world's biggest temple—' He tapped the glass-faced photograph behind him. 'Name of Angkor Wat. Let us see your share certificate in the Society,' he said, with inquiring fingers. 'At once, at once.' Masterji felt as if he were being asked to undress at the doctor's office. He had brought the document in a manila folder, and produced it now.

'It is in your wife's name.'

'In her will I am named as the inheritor.'

'It should have been transferred to your name. We can manage. As long as you have her will in your secure possession.'

He gave the document to the younger man, who almost ran from the office.

Masterji's entire legal claim to 3A, Vishram Society, was now out of his hands; he followed its progress – via footfalls, and then creaking in the wooden planks of the ceiling – into the body of a machine; a photocopier, presumably; levers moved and cameras clicked. His certificate – his claim to a piece of Vishram Society – was being multiplied. His case felt strengthened already. The thumps and footfalls repeated in reverse – the young man re-entered the office with the original certificate and three photocopies. He pulled his chair up next to Parekh's; almost cheek to cheek, the two men looked over the certificate together. Father and son, Masterji decided.

'There is also another petitioner in the matter,' he said. 'Mr Pinto. My neighbour.'

The senior Parekh spoke first.

'Excellent. That doubles the sovereignty in the matter. Now, as per Mofa Act—'

A whisper from the young man: 'He may not know...'

'Do you know of Mofa?'

Masterji smiled meekly.

'Maharashtra Ownership of Flats Act 1963. Mofa.'

'Mofa,' Masterji agreed. 'Mofa Act.'

'As per Mofa Act, 1963...' The old lawyer paused; breathed. '... and also the MCSA Act 1960, which is to say, Maharashtra Co-operative Societies Act 1960, you are the sole sovereign authority of said flat. Now the Society cannot force you to sell said flat, even by majority vote. This is confirmed by Bombay High Court decision 1988, in Bombay Cases Reporter 1988, Volume 1, page 443.'

'443?' said the other man. 'Not 443, Mr Parekh. 444.'

(*Mr Parekh? Not his son, then*, Masterji thought.)

The old man closed his eyes.

'444. Correction acknowledged. Bombay Cases Reporter 1988, Volume 1, page 444. Dinoo F. Bandookwala versus Dolly Q. C. Mehta. The Honourable Judge has frankly stated as per the authentic interpretation of the Mofa Act and the MCSA Act, neither BMC nor MHADA nor the Building Society is the sovereign and supreme trustee of the flat but the said owner. In this case, your good self, acting as the legal inheritor of your deceased spouse. So there is every reasonable confidence and expectation of victory. As per authentic interpretation of Mofa Act 1963 and MCSA Act 1960.'

Masterji nodded. 'I cannot pay you. It is a case you must take in the public interest. The security of senior citizens in this city is at stake.'

'I understand, I understand,' Parekh said. He swiped his hand through the air, like an experienced slayer of slum rats.

'You can settle your bill when there is a settlement,' his younger partner explained with a smile.

'My share certificate, please' – Masterji gestured. The lawyer did nothing, so he reached over and almost pulled it out of his hands. Now he felt strong enough to say: 'There will be no settlement in this matter.'

'*Eventually* there will be a settlement,' Parekh corrected him. 'How long do you and your Mr Pinto plan on resisting this slum rat?'

'For ever.'

For a moment everything in the office seemed to come to a stop: the fluids in Parekh's head ceased to circulate, the rats in the wall and the termites in the old wooden ceiling stopped burrowing; even the particles of disinfectant spreading through the air stopped their dispersion.

Parekh smiled. 'As you wish. We'll fight him...' He turned towards the spittoon: '... for ever.'

With a papaya wrapped in newspaper under his arm, Masterji returned to Vishram Society. Waiting for him at the gate were Ajwani, the Secretary, Mr Ganguly from the fifth floor, Ibrahim Kudwa, and the guard.

They did not make way for him. Ajwani's hand was clamped down on the latch.

'Gentleman,' he said. '*English* gentleman.'

Thinking they had heard about his visit to the lawyer, Masterji said: 'It is my right: it is my right as a citizen to see a lawyer.'

'He doesn't know yet,' Ram Khare shouted. 'Let him go in and see. Please. It is a difficult hour for the Society.'

Ajwani removed his hand from the latch. As Masterji walked in, the guard said: 'I told you, Masterji, that this would happen. God has seen that I have done my duty.'

He saw people standing around the plastic chairs: the two Pintos were the only ones sitting down. Mr Pinto's foot was bandaged, and it was propped up on a cushion. Mrs Puri was dabbing Mrs Pinto's forehead with a wet end of her sari.

When she saw Masterji, she let out a sharp cry: 'Here comes the madman!'

Ajwani and the Secretary, along with Ibrahim Kudwa, walked behind Masterji.

'What happened to you, Mr Pinto?'

'Look at him, asking!' Mrs Puri said. 'Does this thing and pretends not to know about it. Tell him, Mr Pinto. Tell.'

On her command, the old man spoke: 'He said he was going to hurt... my wife – at her age – old enough to be his grandmother. He... said he was going to come with a knife next time... he... and then I got frightened and fell into the gutter.'

'*Who* told you this?' Masterji knelt to be at eye level with his oldest friend. 'When did this happen?'

'Just outside the gate... Shelley and I were walking... it must have been four o'clock, and then I heard this puppy whimpering, and I went outside, and got down into the gutter to save the puppy. Then this boy, he had a gold chain on his neck, eighteen-nineteen years old, and a hockey stick with him, he stood over me and said, are you the man from Vishram who wants nothing? And I said, who are you? And then... he put the stick on top of my head and he said, next time, it will be a knife...' Mr Pinto swallowed. '... And then he said, "Do you understand now, what it means, to want nothing?" And then I turned and tried to run but I fell into the gutter and my foot...'

'We had to take him to Doctor Gerard D'Souza's clinic on the main road,' Mrs Puri said. 'Thank God, it's just a sprain. Doctor D'Souza said at his age he could have broken his foot. Or something else.'

Mrs Pinto, unable to hear more, sank her face into Mrs Puri's blouse. Masterji stood up.

'Don't worry, Mr Pinto. I'll go to the police at once. I'll tell them to arrest Mr Shah. I taught the sons of some of the constables. You don't worry.'

'No,' said Mr Pinto. 'Don't go again.'

'No?'

The old accountant shook his head. 'It's all over, Masterji.'

'What is all over?'

'We can't go on like this. Today my foot is hurt, tomorrow...'

Leaving the papaya on the ground, Masterji stood up.

'You must be brave, Mr Pinto. This Shah cannot threaten us in daylight.'

Mrs Pinto pleaded with her face and fingers. 'Please, Masterji, let's forget about this. Let's just sign Mr Shah's document and leave this building. I began all this by saying I didn't want to go. Now I tell you, it's over. Let's go. You come and have dinner with us this evening. We'll eat together.'

'I won't eat with cowards.'

Masterji kicked the papaya; shedding its newspaper wrapping, it scudded along and smacked the wall of Mrs Saldanha's kitchen.

'I'm going to the police station, with or without you,' he said. 'This builder thinks he can frighten *me*? In my own home?'

Mrs Puri got up.

'The police? You want to make things even worse?' She put a finger on Masterji's chest and pressed. 'Why don't we take *you* to the police?'

From another side, another finger poked him: Ajwani.

'You have turned this Society into a house of violence. In forty-eight years nothing like this has happened in Vishram.'

Mrs Puri said: 'A man who fights with his own son – and such a *lovely* son at that – what kind of a man is he?'

Ibrahim Kudwa stood behind her: 'Sign Mr Shah's agreement now, Masterji. Sign it *now*.'

'I will not be made to change my mind like this,' Masterji said. 'So shut up, Ibrahim.' Kudwa tried to respond, then sagged, and stepped back.

Moving him aside, Ajwani stepped forward. The Secretary came from the other direction. Shouts – people poked Masterji – someone pushed. 'Sign it now!'

Ajwani turned and cursed. Mrs Saldanha's waste water pipe was discharging right on to his foot. 'Turn the tap off, Sal-dan-ha!' he shouted.

'Have!' she shouted back, but the water still flowed, like a statement on the violence in parliament. The dirty water separated the crowd; from the stairwell, there came a barking – the old stray dog rushed out – the Secretary had to move, and Masterji ran up the stairs.

As he bolted the door behind him, he could hear Mrs Pinto's voice: 'No, please don't go up. Please, be civilized!'

*

He barricaded the door with the teakwood table. When he went to the window, he saw them all gathered below, looking up at him. He stepped back at once.

So I'm the last man in the building now, he thought.

He sniffed the air, grateful for the tannic smell that lingered from the brewing of ginger tea.

Pouring out what was left in the porcelain pot, he drank bitter cold tea.

He called the number on the business card he had brought with him.

'Just lock yourself in,' Mr Parekh said. 'Tomorrow, come see me again: if I am not here, my son will see you.'

'Thank you. I am all alone here.'

'You are *not* alone. Parekh is with you. All four Parekhs are with you. If they threaten you I will send a legal notice: they'll know they're dealing with an armed man. Remember Dolly Q. C. Mehta versus Bandookwala. The Mofa Act is with you.'

'How can they threaten good people in daylight? When did things change so much in this city, Mr Parekh?'

'They have not changed, Masterji. It is still a good city. Say to yourself, *Mofa*, *Mofa*, and close your eyes. You sleep with the law by your side.'

But Ram Khare's black snake was in his room now. Right in his bed, moving up his thigh. The snake's tongue of violence flickered before him. *You're next, Masterji*. A young man with a gold necklace and thick, veined arms comes to him one evening and says: *I just want to have a word with you, old man. Just a quick…*

He had been too scared to protect Purnima from her brothers: he would not be scared this time.

'Go away,' he said.

Slithering down his legs, the black snake left.

As the lawyer's card rose and fell on his chest, Masterji looked at the sagging, scaly skin that covered his hands. *Mofa*, he recited as instructed. *Mofa*, *Mofa*. He gave his fingers a shake, and old age flew away: he saw young strong hands now.

3 AUGUST

To,
All Whom It May Concern
Within my Society and outside it

From,
Yogesh A. Murthy
3A, Vishram Society
Vakola, Mumbai 55

This is to state that intimidation in a free country will not be
tolerated. I have been to the police station and received every
assurance from the Senior Inspector that this is not a
neighbourhood where a teacher can be threatened. I am
not alone. The famous legal team of Bandra, Parekh and
Sons, with whom I am in constant touch, will initiate action
against any person or persons threatening me via phone or
mail. In addition, I have students in high places such as
the Times of India *office. Vishram Society Tower A is my*
home, and it

Will not be sold
Will not be leased or rented
Will not be redeveloped

Signed (And this is the real signature of the man)
Yogesh Murthy.

*

262

The inspector at the Vakola police station meant what he said about his neighbourhood being safe for senior citizens.

A fat constable named Karlekar came to Vishram Society within half an hour of Masterji's phone call in the morning.

After taking a statement from Masterji (who, it turned out, had not actually seen a thing, as he had been away in Bandra consulting a famous lawyer) Karlekar sat down at the Pintos' dining table, wiping his sweaty forehead and looking at Mr Pinto's bandaged right foot.

Mr Pinto said: 'No one threatened me. I slipped outside the compound and twisted my foot. Serves me right, walking so fast at my age, doesn't it, Shelley?'

Mrs Pinto, being all but blind, had nothing to say on the matter.

The constable jotted things in his notepad. The Secretary came up to the Pintos' flat to say that the so-called 'disturbance' was, essentially, an exaggeration.

'We are an argumentative people, no doubt about it,' the constable agreed, with a smile. 'The station receives imaginary complaints all the time. Burglars, fires, arson. Pakistani terrorists.'

'A melodramatic people,' the Secretary said. 'It is all the films we watch. Thank you for not making a *sensation* of this matter.'

Constable Karlekar's mouth had opened. 'Look at that... oh, no... no...' He pointed at a moth circling about the rotating ceiling fan in the Pintos' living room; sucked in by the whirlpool of air, it drew closer and closer to the blades until two dark wings fluttered down to the floor. The constable picked up each wing.

'I don't like it when a moth is hurt in my neighbourhood,' he said, handing over the severed wings to the Secretary. 'Imagine what I feel like when an old man is threatened.'

The wings slipped through the Secretary's fingers.

An hour later, the constable had dropped by Vishram Society again. He lit a cigarette by the gate and chatted to Ram Khare. The Secretary saw him getting down on his knees and peering at the dedicatory marble block outside Vishram, as if examining the 48-year-old certificate of good character issued to the building.

*

'People will soon be talking all over Vakola. A policeman came to Vishram Society? The famous, respectable, honourable Vishram?'

'Quiet, Shelley.'

Mr Pinto was at the window. A Burmese mahogany walking stick, a family heirloom, leaned on the wall next to him.

He and his wife were now in a new relationship to their Society. Neither of one camp nor of the other. Masterji no longer came to their table for food, nor did they go down to parliament, in which there was usually only one topic of discussion: the character of the resident of 3A.

This evening, the parliamentarians had begun by talking about Masterji and ended up fighting.

'You got a secret deal. A *small sweetener*' – Mrs Puri to Ajwani.

'Don't talk about things you don't understand, Mrs Puri.'

'A-ha!' she shouted. 'You confess. You did get one.'

'Of course not.'

'I've heard things,' Mrs Puri said. 'One thing I tell all of you here – even you, Mrs Saldanha in your kitchen: even you listen. No one is getting a secret deal unless my Ramu and I get one too.'

'No secret deal has been given to anyone,' the Secretary protested.

'You must have been offered the very first one, Kothari.'

'What an accusation. Didn't you vote for me at the Annual General Meeting? I kept maintenance fees fixed at 1.55 rupees per square foot per unit, payable in two instalments. Don't accuse me now of dishonesty.'

'Why was the building never repaired all these years, Kothari? Is that how you kept the costs flat?'

'I have often wondered the same thing.'

'You're every bit as bad as Masterji, Mrs Puri. And you too, Ajwani. No wonder Masterji turned evil, living among people like you.'

Using the Burmese walking stick, Mr Pinto limped to the bedroom, and lay down next to his wife.

'Did Masterji have breakfast, Mr Pinto? He must be hungry.'

'A man won't die if he eats less for a few days, Shelley. When he gets hungry he'll come back.'

'I don't think so. He is such a proud man.'

'Whether *I'll* let him back here is another thing, Shelley. Don't you remember he called me a coward? He borrowed one hundred rupees from me to take an auto to Bandra West to see that lawyer. I've entered that in the No-Argument book. He'll have to apologize, and pay my hundred rupees back, before he can eat at my dinner table again.'

'Oh, Mr Pinto, really... not you, too. They abuse him so much in parliament these days.'

'Quiet, Shelley. Listen,' Mr Pinto whispered. 'He's walking to the window. He always does that when they start up about him, Shelley. Why? Have you thought about it?'

'No. And I don't want to.'

'He wants to listen when they say bad things about him. That's the only explanation.'

'That can't be right. Why would any man want to listen when such things are said about him? The other day Sangeeta said he used to beat Purnima. What a lie.'

Mr Pinto did not understand why the man did it, but each time parliament met down there to gossip about him, Masterji stood by the window, and sent down aerial roots to suck up slander and abuse. *That must be his new diet*, Mr Pinto thought. *He is chewing their thorns for lunch and nails for supper. From mockery he is making his protein.*

As he looked at the chandelier, it seemed to be mutating into something stranger and brighter.

6 AUGUST

In the wild, rain-wet grass outside the Speed-Tek Cyber Café, a white cat, rearing up, slashed at a russet butterfly just beyond its reach.

There was only one customer inside the café: hunched over terminal number six, emitting chuckles. Ibrahim Kudwa, sitting with little Mariam at the proprietor's desk, wondered if it was time to make a surprise inspection of the chuckling customer's terminal.

'Ibby. Pay attention.'

Ajwani and Mrs Puri had been in the café for several minutes now.

Mrs Puri put her forearms on the table and pushed the piece of paper towards him.

'All the others have agreed, except for you.'

To free Ibrahim's arms, she asked for Mariam, who was wearing her usual striped green nightie.

'My wife says I have a high ratio of nerves to flesh,' Kudwa said, as he handed Mariam over to Mrs Puri. 'I should never be asked to make decisions.'

'A simple thing, this is,' Ajwani said. 'In extreme cases, a Housing Society may expel a member and purchase his share certificate in the Society. It's perfectly legal.'

Ibrahim Kudwa's arms were free: yet he would not touch the piece of paper lying before him.

'How do you know? Are you a lawyer?'

Ajwani moved his neck from side to side and then he said: 'Shanmugham told me.'

With Mariam in her hands, Mrs Puri glared at Ajwani. But it was too late.

'And *he's* an expert?' Kudwa's upper lip twitched. 'I don't like that man, I don't like his face. I wish we had never been picked by that builder. We are not good enough to say no to his money, and not bad enough to say yes to what he wants us to do for it.'

'Money is not the issue here, Ibby. It is the *principle*. We cannot let one man bully us.'

'True, Sangeeta-ji, true,' Kudwa said, looking at the ventilator of the cyber-café. 'I teach both my children that. Hold your head up high in life.'

Putting a finger to his lips, he got up from his chair, and tiptoed over to his customer at terminal six.

Pulling the customer from his seat, Kudwa dragged him to the door of the café, and shoved him out; the white cat meowed.

'I don't want your money, fine. Get out!' he shouted. 'This is not a dirty shop.'

'Typical.' He wiped his forehead and sat down. 'Leave them alone for five minutes, and there's no saying *what* they download. And if the police come here, who will they arrest for pornography? Not *him*.'

'Listen, Ibrahim,' the broker said. 'I have always fought oppression. In 1965, when Prime Minister Shastri asked us to sacrifice a meal a day to defeat the Pakistanis – I did so. I was eight years old and gave up my food for my country.'

Kudwa said: 'I was only *seven* years old. I gave up dinner when my father asked. All of us sacrificed that meal in 1965, Ramesh, not just you.' He ran his fingers through his beard while shaking his head: 'You want to throw an old man out of his home.'

Ajwani took Mariam from Mrs Puri; he gave the girl a good shake.

'Ibrahim.'

'Yes?'

'You have seen how a cow turns its eyes to the side when it shits, and pretends not to know what it's doing? Masterji knows exactly what he's doing to us, and he's *enjoying* it. Repressed, depressed, and dangerous: that's your beloved Masterji in a nutshell.'

Mrs Puri slid the paper across the table, closer to Kudwa.

'Ibby. Please listen to me. Masterji knows the builder can't touch him now. The police are watching Vishram. This is the only way out.'

Kudwa put on his reading glasses. He picked up the paper and read:

... as per the Maharashtra Co-operative Societies Act, 1960,
Section 35, Expulsion of Members, and also points 51 through
56 of the Model Bye-laws, a member may be expelled from his
Society if he:

1. *Has persistently failed in payment of his dues to the Society*
2. *Has wilfully deceived his Society by giving false information*
3. *Has used his flat for immoral purposes or misused it for*
   illegal purposes habitually
4. *Has been in habit of committing breaches of any of the*
   provisions of the bye-laws of his Society, which in the
   opinion of the fellow members of his Society are serious
   breaches

Kudwa removed his glasses. 'He hasn't done any of these things.'

Mrs Puri, her mouth open, turned to Ajwani.

'Hasn't? Didn't he say he would sign the form and change his mind? Isn't that deceiving his Society? Hasn't he invited the police into our gates? And the things that Mary has seen in his rubbish, tell him, Ajwani, tell him...'

The broker tickled little Mariam's belly rather than describe those things.

Kudwa took his daughter back.

'I want to please you by saying yes to this. This is my weakness. I wanted to please my friends in college, so I joined the rock-and-roll band. I send my boy to tae kwon-do because you wanted someone your boys could practise with. I want to please my neighbours who think of me as a fair-minded man, so I pretend to be one.'

Ibrahim Kudwa closed his eyes. He held Mariam close to him.

He wanted to tell her how different his early life had been from what hers would be.

His father had set up and closed hardware shops in city after city, in the north and south of India alike, before settling in Mumbai when his son was fourteen. The boy had never been anywhere long enough to make friends. From his mother he learned something better than having friends – how to sit in a darkened room and consume the hours. When she closed the door to her bedroom she slipped into another world; he did the same in his. Then the doorbell would ring, and they came out running into the real world together. Visitors, relatives, neighbours: he saw his mother bribe these people with smiles and sweet words, so they would let her return, for a few hours each day, into her private kingdom.

Only when he grew up did he understand what his upbringing had done to him. Instead of a man's soul, he had developed a cockroach's antennae inside him. What did this man think of the way he dressed? What did that man think of his politics? The way he pronounced English? Wherever he went, the opinions of the five or six people living near him became a picket fence around Ibrahim Kudwa. One day when he was fifteen or sixteen years old, playing cricket with his neighbours, he had chased the ball until it fell into a gutter. Black, fibrous, stinking, that swampy gutter was the worst thing he had ever seen in his life. But he knew his neighbours wanted him to get that ball; pressed down by their expectations, he had dipped his hands into the muck, up to the elbow, to find the ball. When it came out, his arm was green and black and smelled like rotten eggs. Ibrahim showed the dirty ball to the other boys, then turned around and tossed it back into the gutter; he never played cricket with them again.

Each time he detected the ingratiating impulse within him, he became rude, and from this he earned a reputation in his university years for being woman-like in his mood swings. When he married Mumtaz, he thought: *I have found my centre, this girl will make me strong*. But the shy dentist's assistant had not been that kind of wife: she cried by herself when she was unhappy. She refused to steady his hand. Sometimes Ibrahim Kudwa wanted to abandon everything – even Mariam – and run away to Ladakh and live with those Tibetan monks he had seen on his recent holiday.

He looked at the document that Mrs Puri and Ajwani had brought for him, but he would not touch it.

'Just three, four months ago you were calling him an English gentleman. Yes, you, Sangeeta-ji. And now...'

'Ibrahim, do you know what the *Kala Paani* is?' Ajwani asked. 'That's what they called the ocean in the old days. Black water. Hindus weren't allowed to sail on the *Kala Paani*. That is what kept us backward. Fear. All of us are now at the *Kala Paani*. We have to cross it, or we'll be stuck in Vishram Society for the rest of our lives.'

'Theft,' Kudwa whispered. 'You're asking me to approve of theft.'

'It is not theft. I'm telling you, Ibrahim, because I know what it is to steal. I am not a good man like you are. I tell you: this is *not* theft.'

Kudwa slapped the table, startling Mariam, who began crying.

His visitors got up; Kudwa consoled his child. When they had reached the door, he thought he heard Ajwani whisper: '... so typical of his community.'

He could hear Mrs Puri whisper back: '... do you mean?'

He saw Ajwani at the door, playing with the white cat, and speaking to Mrs Puri, who was hidden behind the banyan tree.

'Do they join the army? The police? Zero national spirit. Zero.'

Kudwa could barely breathe.

'Why bring in religion, Ajwani?' Mrs Puri asked from behind the tree. 'He has been in Vishram for ten years... well, nine...'

The broker pressed the white cat with his shoe; it curled itself helplessly around his foot.

'It is time to say it, Mrs Puri. If he were a Christian, a Parsi, a Sikh, even a *Jain* – he would have agreed to this.'

And then the two voices faded away.

Kudwa closed his eyes; he patted his daughter.

Did Ajwani think he could not see through his plan? Mrs Puri was in it, too. They had probably rehearsed that speech before coming into his café. Next they would be teasing him for his dandruff. But it would not work. Would *not*. With his left hand he brushed at his shoulders.

He tried to break into his neighbours' minds. Did Ajwani not see that expulsion would boomerang on them? This new tactic would only harden Masterji.

But maybe Ajwani *wanted* things to go wrong.

Kudwa had heard the rumour that the broker had been promised a 'sweetener' by Mr Shah. Maybe the worse things became at Vishram, the higher Ajwani's price would climb. The web was so complex now. Kudwa saw intentions buried in intentions within Vishram Society, and was so absorbed in his thoughts that he did not notice when the white cat came into the office, climbed up on his table, and almost scratched Mariam's face.

A man in danger must follow a routine.

Masterji now went out only twice a day. Morning for milk, evening for bread. In public he kept close to the crowd; every ten steps or so he turned around and checked behind him.

He gave in to an afternoon nap. In the evenings, in the dark, he could summon the memory of Purnima if he stood in front of the *almirah* breathing in the camphor and her old sari. But the afternoons were bright and difficult; the world outside beckoned to him. A regular nap helped him pass the time.

This afternoon, however, he had had a nightmare. He had been dreaming of Purnima's brothers.

Waking in the dim evening, he limped to the basin in the living room. He struck the tap with the heel of his palm.

He stared at the dry tap, and felt there was nothing strong inside him at that moment.

Closing his eyes he thought of a full moon he had seen many years ago, during a week-long holiday in Simla, up in the Himalayas, just a few months before his marriage. He had stayed in a cheap hotel; one night the moonlight was so powerful it had woken him up. When he went outside, the cold sky above the mountains was filled with a bigger and brighter moon than he had ever seen before. A voice had whispered, as if from the heavens: 'Your future will be an important one.'

He drew a circle in the dry basin.

He walked to the threshold of the toilet and stopped: black ants were crawling over the tiled floor. Placing his hands on the doorframe, he leaned in. At the base of the toilet bowl, the black things had lined up like animals at a trough.

Could there be any question now? They had come for the sugar in his urine. He could hear Purnima's voice pleading with him: 'You have to get yourself checked. Tomorrow.'

He went to the kitchen, and counted off on her calendar. Forty-seven days to go. With his finger on the circled date, he said, aloud, so it would reach her clearly: 'If I go for a check-up and they say I have diabetes, it will weaken me, Purnima. I won't go until 3 October.'

He went back to the toilet to flush the ants away. But no water flowed from the tap here, either.

He flicked the light switch: the lamp above the toilet basin did not respond.

Opening his door, he found that the doorbell to 3B rang clearly; below him, he could hear Nina, the Pintos' maid, running water from their taps.

The mystery was solved when he went down the stairs to the notice-board.

NOTICE

Vishram Co-operative Hsg Society Ltd, 'A' Building
Minutes of the general body meeting
of 'a' building held on 16 august

Theme: Expulsion of a member from Society

As the quorum was sufficient, the meeting commenced as per schedule at approximately 7.30 p.m.

Mr Ramesh Ajwani (2C) took the chair and brought the members' concerns to the fore.

ITEM NO. 1 OF THE AGENDA:

As noted in Section 35 Expulsion of Members, Maharashtra Co-operative Societies Act, 1960, and in conjunction with Byelaws 51 through 56 of the Model Bye-laws, it being noted that a society may, by resolution passed by a majority of not less than three-fourths of the members entitled to vote...

... or has used his flat for immoral purposes or misused it for illegal purposes habitually.

On these grounds, it was proposed by Mr Ajwani that Yogesh Murthy, of 3A (formerly known as 'Masterji') be expelled from the Society; as he has not paid his dues with regularity, and has engaged on questionable, and immoral, activities within his premises.

Ibrahim Kudwa (4C) seconded the proposal.

Despite repeated requests – and his door being knocked on, several times – Mr Murthy did not agree to defend himself in front of the Society.

It was unanimously agreed to approve of the resolution, expelling Mr Murthy from the Society, and asking him to vacate his premises within thirty days...

... the meeting concluded at about 8.30 p.m. with a vote of thanks to the chair.

The full list of members' signatures is attached. Fourteen of the sixteen shareholders in the Society have signed the form.

Copy (1) To Members of 'A' Building, Vishram Co-op Hsg Society Ltd

Copy (2) To Mr Ashvin Kothari, the Secretary, Vishram Co-op Hsg Society Ltd

Copy (3) To the Registrar of Housing Societies, Mumbai

*

He lay in the dark; feeling the weight of two floors of people above and three below who had expelled him from his home of thirty-two years; who do not even consider him a human any longer – one that needs light and water.

He had called Parekh at once.

'This is utterly *number two*,' the lawyer said. 'Point one. Expulsion from a Society is a grave matter – the taking away of a fundamental right to housing – and enforceable only on criminals and pornographers. The Registrar of Housing will not permit it in the case of a distinguished teacher. Point two.' The lawyer cleared his throat. 'Point two. Under Essential Commodities Act 1955, cutting off water or electricity without court order is a criminal offence. The Secretary of your building can be sent to jail. I will dictate a note, which you should give to the said Secretary.'

'Let me find a pen, Mr Parekh.'

'Give me this *number two* Secretary's number,' the lawyer said, 'and I will call him myself. I deal with a baker's dozen of corrupt Secretaries every day.'

At the start of summer, there had been talk of power cuts in Mumbai, and in anticipation, he had bought candles. One of them sat burning on the teakwood table. The wax dripped; the blackened wick was exposed. He thought of Purnima's body blackening on her funeral pyre. He thought of Galileo's framed picture over his mirror.

He held up his fist; in the weak light of the candle it cast a shadow on the wall. The earth, in infinite space. A point on it was the city of Mumbai. A point on that was Vishram Society. And that point was *his*.

His arm began to tremble, but he did not unclench his fist.

Suddenly the lights came back on. The water was running in the basin. He flushed the toilet clean of the black ants and washed his hands, saying, as he did so, the magic mantra, *Mofa*, *Mofa*.

Mr Parekh had done it again.

BOOK SEVEN

Last Man in Tower

Shanmugham loved, more than any other part of the city he lived in, this drive over the Bandra bridge. At night, with the water in the Mahim creek glossy black, the glowing signs of the Lilavati Hospital ahead, the square lights of the slums puncturing the darkness below him, it was like gliding over a film set.

Now, in the late afternoon, he saw the hazy blue piers of the half-built Worli SeaLink, standing in the distant water like a bridge from this world to the next. Sweat dripped from his helmet into his eyes and burned them.

He dreamed of orange juice served on crushed ice with lots of sugar and a sprinkling of red masala powder on top. He hoped he would find a fresh-juice stand close to the lawyer's office.

Parking his bike near the train station, he removed his helmet and gave his hair a good shake, scattering sweatdrops around him like a dog that has taken a bath.

Among the ramshackle buildings by the train station he searched for the lawyer's office. The glint of an open razor in a barber's shop caught his eye. Famous Hair Cutting Palace. This was the landmark near the office.

He waited on the other side of the road.

Next to him, a man stood in a wooden booth surrounded by tomatoes, cucumbers, and boiled potatoes in buckets of water. With stacks of white bread and a bowl of butter on his table, he sliced the vegetables fine. A series of cardboard signs in English hung by thread from the ceiling of the little booth:

DO NOT ASK FOR CREDIT
DO NOT DISCUSS OUR COMPETITORS RATE
DO NOT ASK FOR FREE PLASTIC BAG
DO NOT ASK FOR EXTRA TOMATO SAUCE
DO NOT STAY FOR LONG TIME AFTER EATING

Shanmugham looked with envy at all those interdictions. The sandwich-maker might be a poor man, but he could lay down his own law.

But me, I have to do what the boss says. He throws the stick, I have to catch.

He wondered if he should get a quick toast sandwich.

An old man with an umbrella and a slight limp in his left leg went past the Famous Hair Cutting Palace, and turned into the building next door. Shanmugham stopped thinking about food.

A milky lunette let grey light into the stairwell of the Loyola Trust Building; a pigeon was thrashing its wings on the other side.

Masterji stopped on his way up to his lawyer's office to kick the pain out of his left leg. He looked at the restless silhouette of the bird. He thought: *Where did the rains go?*

Taking out his handkerchief, he patted his moustache, which was soaking wet, and put the damp cloth back in his pocket.

The anaemic Ganesha sat in its dim niche on the landing. The small votive oil lamp added burnt fuel to the smell of meat curry. The four khaki-clad security guards were once again playing cards beneath the idol of the Ganesha. Their chappals, shoes, and socks napped together in a heap by the wall.

Within the Milky Way of the city, you can sometimes recognize an autonomous solar system: like these men playing their card games in near silence on this landing, breaking only to eat lunch or replace the wick of the oil lamp. Rich they would never be, but they had this eternal card-and-companionship afternoon. Masterji wondered, as he walked around the guards' hands and feet, which looked like another set of cards placed on the ground, if they maintained a No-Argument book here.

PAREKH AND SONS
ADVOCATE
'LEGAL HAWK WITH SOUL & CONSCIENCE'

The courtesy in the lawyer's office was much improved this time. The peon with the red pencil behind his ear smiled and said: 'I'll *on* the air-conditioner, sir, you're sweating. The worst time of the year, isn't it? The rains stop and it's the middle of summer again.' He took Masterji's black umbrella, gave it a shake, and placed it in a green plastic bucket with umbrellas of other colours.

A glass of water arrived on a brown tray; the peon bowed before Masterji.

'I've brought you the coldest glass of water in Mumbai city, sir. Cold-est.'

Is he expecting a tip for this? Other petty workers, going about the office with their files, smiled at Masterji. He remembered the feeling – which he had had once at the Vakola market – of being mistaken for a millionaire. Sipping the ice-cold water, he considered the mystery of his situation, when the peon said: 'You can go in to see Mr Parekh, sir.'

Head down, Parekh was on his mobile phone, the three silver strands over his bald head shining in the light. The gold medallion was tucked into his shirt, and bulged between the second and third button.

Parekh looked up, and stared through his thick glasses at Masterji, who had decided to sit down.

'You phoned me, Mr Parekh. You said there was good news and I should come to see you before noon.'

Nodding, as if he remembered now, the lawyer summoned his mucus and discharged it into the spittoon.

'You are not my only client, Masterji. I am at any given moment fighting a baker's dozen of slum rats.'

Masterji, appropriately chastened, nodded. A peon came in with tea for the lawyer. Some minutes passed like this, with Parekh reading a typewritten letter and squinting at his mobile phone each time a text message arrived with a loud chime. Feet thumped on the low ceiling. The cracks in the wooden planks expanded.

The door to the office opened, and an assistant – or was it his son? – approached the lawyer. Parekh took a document from him, squinted, and threw it back at him.

'This is not the right good news. Not relevant to Masterji's case.'

The assistant left; Masterji waited; feet moved across the ceiling.

'One thing has to be confessed, Masterji,' Parekh said. 'I had doubts: that night when they cut off the power, for instance. Or when your co-petitioner, that Mr Pinto, was threatened. But you have stayed true. You have proved yourself sovereign of your plot of earth.'

Masterji nodded. 'Men of our generation, we have seen much trouble. Wars, emergencies, elections. We can survive.'

'True,' Parekh said. 'Men of a certain generation, you and I are.'

The assistant reappeared in a few minutes with another document; and this time, the old teacher knew it was relevant to his case. Parekh looked at Masterji; his browless eyes sparkled.

'The good news is a sizeable one.'

Masterji smiled. 'What is the good news?'

Still flipping through the pages of the document, Parekh said: 'A settlement. It will be a famous settlement. Shah versus Murthy.'

'But who has given me this settlement?'

Mr Parekh turned to his assistant or son, as if in appreciation of this joke.

'Oh, Masterji,' he said. 'The builder, of course. And in fact – between us, Masterji – we have fooled Mr Shah.' He wiped his lips. 'Because you had a weak case to begin with. We can say it openly now.'

'A weak case?'

'Of course.'

Masterji turned from Parekh to the other, and back to Parekh.

'How can *you* make a settlement without speaking to me? I have the share certificate: I own my flat.'

Parekh smiled sadly. 'No, sir. You don't. Fundamentally speaking, sir, neither you nor any member of any registered co-operative housing society anywhere in this state is the proprietor, strictly speaking, of his or her flat. Your Society is the sovereign of your flat. You own a share certificate in that Society. If the Society decides to sell your flat, you have no right to dissent. Regarding which...' He turned to clear his throat. The son or assistant recited: 'Dhiraj T. Kantaria and others versus Municipal Corporation and Co., 2001 (3) Bom. C.R. 664; 2002 (5) Mh. L.J. 779; 2004 (6) LJSOFT 42.'

The lawyer wiped his lips and said: 'Exactly.'

'But Mofa...' Masterji mumbled. 'Mofa, Mofa?'

The lawyer ran his hand over his three silver strands. 'The name of Mofa Act is not to be taken lightly.' He shook his head. 'For thirty years you have taught your students in accordance with Dharma. Now let us be two teachers to you, Masterji. Even some lawyers who have been twenty, thirty years in this honourable profession don't understand what Mofa Act is, frankly speaking. Common man cannot understand subtleties of Mofa Act. Because you have to think of how Mofa behaves with MMRDA and BMC.'

'MHADA,' the other reminded him. 'MHADA.'

'Very true. In this city, MHADA is always there. Somewhere in background. Sometimes in foreground. We must not forget that the government is about to repeal ULCRA any day. Urban Land Ceiling Regulation Act? All this we have to think before we bring up the name of Mofa Act. Understand? Don't worry. We understand on your behalf.'

Masterji saw before him not just two bullying lawyers, but the primal presence of authority. *Is this how my students saw me all those years?* Beneath that low ceiling, an old teacher sat crushed under understanding.

This lawyer with the hidden gold medallion, and this young man, son or assistant, were crooks changing coins in the temple of the law. That was why Parekh had asked for the phone number of the Secretary; all this time the two of them had been in contact.

Masterji looked at the photograph of Angkor Wat, and asked: 'You spoke to Mr Shah? Behind my back?'

'Mr Shah contacted *me*. His man came here – nice Tamilian fellow, what was his name? Shatpati? Shodaraja?' The lawyer tapped a tooth.

'No business card, but he gave his number. I can renegotiate. Squeeze an even better settlement for you.'

'I don't want a better settlement.'

'We'll get you the *best* settlement.'

'I want *no* settlement. I will find another lawyer.'

'Now, Masterji.' Mr Parekh leaned in to him. 'The others will ask for a retainer and waste your time and tell you the same. Frankly, sir: I don't understand what it is you want.'

'I keep telling you: *nothing.*'

At once the A/C seemed to stop working: Mr Parekh wiped the back of his neck with a handkerchief.

'Sir: these real-estate men pick on us senior citizens. Politicians and police are in their pay, you must know that. They shot an elected member of the city corporation dead the other day. In broad daylight. Didn't you see it in the papers? Old men must stick together in this new world.'

'*You* are threatening me now?' Masterji asked. 'My own lawyer?'

Mr Parekh sneezed into a handkerchief, and then said,

'I am threatening you, sir, with the facts of human nature.'

Instead of an Angkor Wat behind the lawyer's head, Masterji now saw an image of the High Court of Bombay: a Gothic structure with a soaring roof, ancient and massive, sitting like a paperweight on the city, and symbolizing, for its residents, the authority of law. Now this High Court and its high roof shuddered and its solid Gothic arches became shredded paper fluttering down on Masterji's shoulders. Mofa. MHADA. ULCRA. MSCA. ULFA. Mohamaulfacramrdama-ma-ma-abracadabra, soft, soft, it fell on him, the futile law of India.

Just then he heard Mr Parekh's young colleague say, 'You didn't even charge him for your basic expenses, Father. All the photocopying we had to do. You have a conscience, that is why. All senior citizens are your family.'

So he is the son, Masterji thought. The possession of this fact – trivial, and irrelevant to his troubles – mysteriously filled him with strength. He put his hands on the arms of his chair and stood up.

'Now wait here,' the younger Parekh said, realizing that the bird was about to fly. 'If you're going to leave like this, what about our dues? What about all the photocopying we did for you?'

From behind him, Masterji heard the young man's voice protesting: 'Let's stop him, Father – at once. Father, let's run after him.'

The green bucket fell over as Masterji pulled his umbrella from it, and splattered his ankles with water.

Past the guards and their blind deity he walked, down the old stairs – past the pigeon, thrashing behind the blind lunette.

Purnima, he prayed, *swoop down and lift me from the land of the living.*

His wife answered him, as he ran out of the Loyola Trust Building, in an aroma of freshly fried potatoes.

He stopped at a fried-snacks shop.

In seconds a ball of batter-fried *vada pav*, bought for four rupees, was dissolving in Masterji's gut. Oil, potato, cholesterol, trans-fats slowed the whirlpool in his stomach.

Wiping away the humiliating slick of grease on his lips, he found a grocery store where he could make calls from a yellow payphone wrapped in plastic. Gaurav would be at work now. The one place where that boy might be free of his wife's influence. Umbrella under his arm, he called Vittal, in the school library, and asked for the phone number of Gaurav's bank, the Canara Cooperative Society. With a second rupee, he called the bank and asked for Mr G. Murthy, junior branch manager.

'It's me. Your father. I'm calling from Bandra. Something very bad has just happened.'

There was silence.

'What is it, Father? I'm at work.'

'Can you speak now? It's urgent, Gaurav. No, it's a payphone. *I'll* call back from this same number. Ten minutes.'

Telling the grocery store owner to keep the phone free for him, he ran over to the fried-snacks store, and bought another *vada pav*.

Munching on the batter-fried potatoes, he walked back to Parekh's office: at the barber's shop, he saw a familiar dark face reflected in one of the mirrors.

He turned and found a man in a crisp white shirt standing right outside the Loyola Trust Building.

He stared at Mr Shah's left-hand man. The metal grilles of the building groaned as pigeons landed on them.

'Mr Masterji...' Shanmugham held out his hand. 'Don't do this to yourself. This is the last chance.'

Masterji shivered at the sight of that hand. Without a word he walked away from his ex-lawyer's office.

'Hire another lawyer,' Gaurav said, when his father, calling him from the pay telephone, had explained everything. 'There are thousands in the city.'

Masterji found his son's voice changed, ready to listen.

'No,' he told Gaurav. 'It won't work. The law won't work.'

He could hear the builder's tongue vibrating within Parekh's mucus. Just like the tuning fork he had used in class for an acoustics experiment. Corruption had become Physics; its precise frequency had been discovered by Mr Shah. If he engaged another lawyer, that thick tongue would fine tune him too.

'My last hope is Noronha. At the *Times*. I've written letter after letter, and he won't write back. If there's some way to reach him, son...'

More silence. Then Gaurav said: 'I have a connection at the *Times*. I'll see if we can reach Noronha. In the meantime you go home and lock the door, Father. When my connection gets back to me, I'll phone you.'

'Gaurav,' he said, his voice thickening with gratitude. 'I'll do that, Gaurav. I'll go home and wait for your call.'

A cow had been tied up by the side of the fried-snacks store, a healthy animal with a black comet mark on its forehead. It had just been milked, and a bare-chested man in a dhoti was taking away a mildewed bucket inside which fresh milk looked like radioactive liquid. Squatting by the cow a woman in a saffron sari was squeezing gruel into balls. Next to her two children were being bathed by another woman. Half a village crammed into a crack in the pavement. The cow chewed on grass and jackfruit rinds. Round-bellied and big-eyed, aglow with health: it sucked in diesel and exhaust fumes, particulate matter and sulphur dioxide, and churned them in its four stomachs, creaming good milk out of bad air and bacterial water. Drawn by the magnetism of so much ruddy health, the old man put his finger to its shit-caked belly. The living organs of the animal vibrated into him, saying: all this power in me is power in you too.

I have done good to others. I was a teacher for thirty-four years.

The cow lifted her tail. Shit piled on the road. When they saw Masterji talking to the cow and telling her his woes, those who had been born in the city perhaps thought that he was a mad old man, but those who had come from the villages knew better: recognizing the piety in his act, the woman in the saffron sari got up. The two children followed her. Soon the cow's forehead was covered with human palms.

Giri laid out dinner on the table. White rice, spinach curry, curried beans, and *pappad*, around a *hilsa* fish, grilled and chopped, mixed with salt and pepper, and served in a porcelain bowl. The fish's head sat on top, its lips open, as if pleading for breath among its own body parts.

The *hilsa* made Shah's mouth water. He walked around the dinner table in his Malabar Hill home with a piece of silk in his hand – a handkerchief that Rosie had bought him, one of those tiny portions of his own money that she returned to him, perfumed and gift-wrapped in damask. He rubbed it between his fingers.

He had been walking about the flat ever since Shanmugham had come back from the lawyer's office, sweating with bad news.

Fresh breeze: he went up to the window. Down below, in the gutter outside his building, a man in rags scavenged for empty bottles.

Even down there, Shah saw wanting. That beggar with the gunny sack, if the story so far were told to him, would be appalled by this old teacher. A man who does not want: who has no secret spaces in his heart into which a little more cash can be stuffed, what kind of man is that?

'I have seen every kind of negotiation tactic, Giri. I can classify them. Saying you're ill. Blind. You miss your beloved dead dog Timmy or

Tommy that lived in that flat. But I have never seen this tactic of simply saying "No", permanently.'

'Yes, Boss.' Giri said. 'Will you eat now?'

'We are dealing with the most dangerous thing on earth, Giri. A weak man. A weak man who has found a place where he feels strong. He won't leave Vishram. I understand now.'

Giri touched his master.

'Sit. Or the *hilsa* will get cold, and what did Giri go to all this trouble for?'

Shah looked at the fish: and he had a vision of the old teacher, sliced and chopped the same way, salted and peppered, sitting on the dinner table. He shivered, and rubbed the silk again.

All Shanmugham had done so far was to send a boy with a hockey stick to speak to that old man – Mr Pinto. Nothing criminal in that. He had just been sending Vishram Society a gift from reality. He had assumed that would be enough, for a building full of older people. Social animals.

Now Shanmugham was waiting in the basement for instructions. He could see him standing by a car's rear-view mirror or in the lift, practising his threats: 'Old man, we have given you every chance, and now we are left with no…'

The silk grew warm in Shah's fingers.

A dirty business, construction, and he had come up through its dirtiest part. Redevelopment. If you enjoy fish, you have to swallow a few bones. He made no apology for what he had had to do to get here. But this was not how the Shanghai was meant to happen: not after he had offered 19,000 rupees a square foot for an old, old building.

The hot silk handkerchief fell to the floor.

Hanging above the writing desk in his study was Rosie's gift, the framed three-part black-and-white poster of the Eiffel Tower being raised into place. With all his fingers on the polished mahogany table Shah saw, as if through a periscope, the rabbit-warren of cash networks that ran beneath it: he spied into the deepest, most secret paths through which the Confidence Group moved its money and followed the flipping serial numbers of accounts in the Channel Islands and in the Maldives. He was master of things seen and things unseen. Buildings rising above the earth and concourses of money running below it.

And why had he built these things above and below the earth?

Now everyone believed India was going to be a rich country. He had known it ten years ago. Had planned for the future. Skip out of slum redevelopment. Start building glossy skyscrapers, shopping malls, maybe one day an entire suburb, like the Hiranandanis in Powai. Leave something behind, a new name, the Confidence Group, founder Dharmen Vrijesh Shah, a first-wife's son from Krishnapur.

And some stupid old teacher was going to get in the way? One of the neighbours had told Shanmugham that Masterji's son had contacted her. He had told her that his father planned on going to the *Times of India* the next day. To say that the Confidence Group was threatening him.

The builder slapped both palms against his skull. Of all the good housing societies in Vakola, of all the societies *dying* to receive such an offer, why had he picked this one?

Fate, chance, destiny, luck, horoscopes. A man had his will power, but there were dark powers operating all around him. So he sought protection in astrology. His mother had died when he was a boy. Wasn't he marked out for bad luck from the start? The first wife's son. Krishnapur, he smelled its cow shit in his nostrils. He had rebelled against it, but it was still there, the village mud, village fatalism.

He could not leave Vishram now. He would lose face in Vakola. J. J. Chacko would take out advertisements up and down the highway mocking him.

And that meant there was only one thing to do with this old man. Only one thing could make the Shanghai happen.

Shah thought of the chopped *hilsa*.

In the old days, if a builder had a problem, that problem would end up in pieces in the wet concrete: it became part of the building it had tried to obstruct. A bit of calcium was good for the foundations. But those days were gone: the lawless days of the 1980s and '90s. Vishram was a middle-class building. The man was a teacher. If he died suddenly, there would be an immediate suspect. The police would come to Malabar Hill and press his doorbell the next morning.

On the other hand, the palms of the policemen had been well greased. He might get away with it if the job were done well: scientifically, no fingerprints left behind. His reputation in Vakola would certainly improve: deep down, everyone admires violence. It was a risk, a big risk, but he might get away with it. He bent down and picked up the silk cloth.

As it became warm again between his fingers, he heard snoring.

The door to his son's room was ajar. Satish's thick legs were curled together on the bed. Shah closed the door behind him and sat down by his son's side.

Seeing his son like this, a breathing thing amidst dishevelled sheets, Shah thought of the woman with whom he had made this new life.

Rukmini. He had never seen her before the wedding day; she had been sent by bus from Krishnapur after he refused to return for the marriage. They had been wed right here in the city. He admired her courage: she had adapted to the big city in a matter of hours. The evening of the wedding, she was fighting with the grocery store man over the price of white sugar. After all these years, Shah smiled at the memory. For thirteen years she had kept his house, raised his son, and supervised his kitchen while he shouted at his colleagues and left-hand men in the living room or on the phone. She seemed to have no more of an opinion about construction than he did about cooking. Then one evening – he could not remember what she had overheard – she came to the bedroom, turned off his Kishore Kumar music, and said: 'If you keep threatening other people and their children, one day something might happen to your own child.' Then she turned the music on and left the room. The only time she had ever commented on his work.

Shah touched the dark body on the dishevelled bed. He felt the boy's future like a fever. Drugs, alcohol. Jail time. A spiral of trouble. All because of *his* karma.

He felt he had tripped over something ancestral and half buried, like a pot of gold in the backyard: a sense of shame.

'Master' – it was Giri, silhouetted in the blinding light through the open door. 'The *hilsa*.'

'Throw it out. And close the door, Giri, Satish is sleeping.'

'Master. Shanmugham… has come upstairs. He asks if you have anything to say to him.'

His wife's *almirah* was open, the fragrance of her wedding sari and the old balls of camphor filled the bedroom air.

Masterji sat like a yogi on the floor.

Mrs Puri was shouting at her husband next door; the Secretary was pounding his heavy feet above his head. Then he heard feet from all around the building heading for the door below him. They were speaking to the Pintos. He heard voices rising, and then Mr Pinto saying, 'All right. All right. But leave us alone then.'

A few minutes later, the doorbell rang.

When he opened the door, a small thin woman stood outside with a red notebook. A blue rubber band had been tied twice around it.

'Mr Pinto gave this to his maid to give you, Masterji.'

'So why are you giving it to me, Mary?'

Mary looked at her feet. 'Because she didn't want to give it to you herself.'

Masterji took the red book and removed the rubber band. The No-Argument book had been returned to him, with a yellow Post-it note on its cover, *All debts settled and accounts closed.*

'Don't be angry with Mr Pinto,' Mary whispered. 'They forced him to do it. Mrs Puri and the others.'

Masterji nodded. 'I don't blame him. He is frightened.'

He did not know whether to look at Mary. In all these years, he had not exchanged, except on matters directly related to her work, even a dozen words with the cleaning woman of his Society.

She smiled. 'But you don't worry, Masterji. God will protect us. They're trying to throw me out of my home too. I live by the *nullah*.'

Masterji looked at Mary's hands, which were covered in welts. He remembered a boy in school whose mother was a scavenger. Her hands were scored with rat-bites and long scratches.

How could they throw a poor woman like this out of her hut? How many were being forced out of their homes – what was being done to this city in the name of progress?

Closing the door behind Mary, he leaned forward and pressed his forehead against the cool wood: 'Must not get angry. Purnima would not want it.'

The phone began ringing. Though he was waiting for Gaurav's call, he approached the phone as he had recently learned to, with trepidation.

He picked up the receiver and brought it to his ear. He breathed out in relief.

Gaurav.

'Good news, Father. I got through to Noronha. My connection put me through. I explained the situation: the threats, the phone calls, the attack on Mr Pinto—'

Masterji was so excited he passed the receiver from one ear to the other.

'And today's deceit by the lawyer? You didn't leave that out?'

'—that too, Father. Noronha is going to meet us.'

'Wonderful, wonderful.'

'Five o'clock tomorrow. At the *Times of India* lobby.'

At Mr Shah's Malabar Hill home, Giri had wiped the kitchen clean, turned off the gas, opened the day's mail, and sorted the letters. The last thing he had to do before leaving was to forge his employer's signature.

Taking out his bifocals – a gift from his master on his fiftieth birthday – Giri sat at the table with the poster of the Eiffel Tower-under-construction behind him. He turned on the desk lamp, and opened the second drawer, which stored the chequebooks. Giri's hand, which reproduced his master's 1978 signature with exactness, was considerably more authentic than Shah's, which had shifted in character over the years. For this reason Shah had long entrusted the signing of monthly bills to him. Giri took them out of a blue manila folder one by one. The electricity bill. The monthly maintenance charge from the Society. A 5,000-rupee voluntary request for the installation of 'water-harvesting' tanks in the building.

'Voluntary.' Giri sniffed. That meant in English you give money if you want. He crushed the paper and threw it into the waste basket.

Next he studied his master's credit card bill before signing a cheque for it. He went through another credit card bill and signed a second cheque for the 'Versova person' – whom he refused to dignify with a more precise title.

He turned off the desk lamp.

Nearly nine o'clock. He would have to take an hour-long train to Borivali, where he lived in a one-bedroom with his mother. In the kitchen Giri changed out of his blue lungi into a pair of brown polyester trousers, and put on a white shirt over his *banian*.

Satish had left his bedroom. Giri straightened the sheets.

Mr Shah was in bed, his arm around that plaster-of-Paris building which had been near the dancing Nataraja statue all these weeks. Giri tried to prise the model out of his master's arms, and gave up.

He turned off the lights inside the flat, and opened the door to find Shanmugham, with his arms folded.

'When is the boss going to give me an answer?' the left-hand man asked. 'If we're going to break that old teacher's arms and legs, we have to do it now.'

3 SEPTEMBER

It was not yet four o'clock.

Masterji stopped at Flora Fountain to wipe his face with a handkerchief; cool water trickled down the old stained marble, down its goddesses and trees and porpoise.

He passed the bronze statue of Dadabhai Naoroji and went through the shade of arcaded buildings towards the *Times of India* office. Half expecting to find Shanmugham behind him, he kept glancing over his shoulder, and for this reason missed it until it was right in front of him.

Victoria Terminus.

It had been years since he had seen the great train station, the city's grandest Gothic structure. Demons, domes, gables and gargoyles grew all over the crazy mass of coloured stone. Stone mastiffs flew out from the central dome; rams, wolves, peacocks, other nameless hysterical beasts, all thrusting out of the station, screamed silently above the traffic and clutter. Multiplying the madness, a cordon of palm-trees fanned the building – frolicking, sensual, pagan trees, taunting, almost tickling, the gargoyles.

The heart of Bombay – if there is one – it is me, it is me!

The *Times of India* building was just around the corner; he still had an hour. He crossed the road. In the cool portico of the station, he saw stone wolves perched on the capitals of columns, as if about to spring down on the people below. Taped to one of the pillars of the station, he saw a poster for a boy gone missing in the city: like a real victim of the imaginary wolves of the architecture. The print, in Hindi, was smudged, and he read it with difficulty, thinking of the lonely parents looking for this boy, begging the indifferent police for information, until they went back on a train to Bhopal or Ranchi, worn out and defeated.

He had once been a migrant like these ones pouring through the door of the station into the city, men and women from Bihar and Uttar Pradesh carrying everything they owned in bundles of cloth. They stepped out of the shade of the stone wolves and blinked in the harsh light of Mumbai. But their bundles did not contain what his did, an education. How many of them would end up like the boy in the poster – beaten, kidnapped or murdered? His heart filled with pity for their lesser struggles.

'Point! Point! Point!'

The taxi-drivers who were waiting by the station demanded to take him to Nariman Point. He shook his head: yet the yelling went on and on. He could feel their will power as something physical, a battering ram, trying to crush his own.

Entering the lobby of the *Times of India* building, he looked at a black-and-white photograph of Jawaharlal Nehru and Indira Gandhi scanning a copy of the *Times*. He sat down and waited. Half an hour to go. People streamed in and streamed out of the lobby. *How many*, he wondered, *have come to see Noronha?* He felt the familiar pride at seeing a student prosper, which is like the rush of growth hormone that straightens out a sapling, and makes an old teacher eager for another round of living.

He found a chair. He began to snooze. When he opened his eyes he saw Gaurav, in a blue business shirt, pleated trousers and tie, shaking him by the shoulder.

'Sorry, son. I was tired.' Masterji got up from his chair. 'Shall we go in now to see Noronha?'

The words were sitting there on Gaurav's tongue – *I. Didn't. Call. Noronha. I. Didn't. Call. Him* – but when they came out, they had become: 'Yes. But I want to eat something first, Father.'

'What about our appointment?'

'We have time, Father. Plenty. I'm hungry now.'

Father and son went to the McDonald's across from Victoria Terminus station. Masterji sat at an outdoor table and waited for Gaurav to come out with his food. He wished he had his Rubik's Cube with him. Someone had left an advertising pamphlet on the table:

IMPATIENCE IS NOW A VIRTUE
HIGH-SPEED BROADBAND INTERNET
512 KBPS @ 390 RUPEES A MONTH ONWARDS

Turning it over, he doodled on the back with a blue ballpoint pen, and superimposed words on the doodles:

> *Police*
> *Media*
> *Law and order*
> *Social workers*
> *Family*
> *Students and old boys*

Then he struck out 'law and order', and 'social workers', and 'police'.

Gaurav came out of the restaurant carrying a chocolate-covered sundae. He gobbled it down with a plastic spoon.

At his son's house, Masterji spoke in Hindi so Sonal would understand; now he mixed English with Kannada, their ancestral language: 'What time did Noronha say he would meet us, son?'

Gaurav swallowed his ice cream in an almost simultaneous contraction of tongue and oesophagus.

'He's not seeing us, Father. Your Noronha.'

'What do you mean?'

Closing an eye, Gaurav dug into the chocolate mud that sat at the bottom of the disappearing vanilla.

'It's not a story for his newspaper.'

'Why not? One retired man fights a big builder. "Last Man in Tower Fights Builder." That sounds like a story to me.'

Gaurav shrugged; he ate his ice cream.

Masterji stared at his son, his mouth open. 'Did your connection really speak to Noronha? Do you *have* a connection at the *Times*?'

Gaurav's spoon scraped the last of the chocolate mud from the bottom of the cup.

'I was waiting for you to call me, Father. For so many days. I said to Sonal, there is trouble at Vishram. Sangeeta Aunty keeps phoning me. My own father does not phone. But when you do call, what do you say?'

Gaurav crushed his cup.

'Contact Noronha for me. Set up an appointment. I do have a connection at the *Times*, Father. I wouldn't lie to you. I got Noronha's number, and I picked up the phone to call him, and I thought, my father is treating me like a servant. Not like his only living child.'

A small red moth flitted about Masterji's hand, like a particle of air trying to warn him about something.

'Gaurav, I called you because I have nowhere else... You are the last place.'

'Father, what is it you want from the Confidence Group?'

Masterji had never seen Gaurav sound and look so decisive. He felt the strength draining from him.

'Nothing.'

The boy raised his upper lip in a sneer. Purnima used to do that.

'You're lying, Father.'

'Lying?'

'Don't you see what's behind this nothing? *You*. You think you are a great man because you're fighting this Shah. Another Galileo or Gandhi. You're not thinking of your own grandson.'

'I *am* thinking of Ronak. This man Mr Shah threatened the Pintos. In daylight. Would you want Ronak to grow up in a city where he can be bullied or threatened in daylight? Gaurav: listen. Dhirubhai Ambani said he would *salaam* anyone to become the richest man in India. I've never *salaamed* anyone. This has been a city where a free man could keep his dignity.'

Gaurav glared. His sharp features and oval face, except for the fat that had accumulated on them, resembled his father's: but when he frowned, a dark slant furrow cut into his brow, like a bookmark left there by his mother.

'Maybe you *should* have saluted more people, Father.'

For months now he had imagined himself speaking to Purnima,

and hearing soft distant replies: but now it was as if his wife were talking from right in front of him.

'Maybe Sandhya would not have had to take the train if you had made more money. Maybe she would have been in a taxi, safe, that day she was pushed out. She was my sister, I think of her too.'

'Son. Son.' Masterji pressed down on the piece of paper he had been writing on. 'Son.'

'Every other parent in Vishram Society has thought of their children. But not you. It's always been this way. When I was in your physics class in school you punished me more than the others.'

'I had to show the other boys there was no favouritism.'

'All my life I've been frightened of you. You and that steel foot-ruler with which you hit my knuckles. *For sleeping in the afternoon.* Is that a crime? You made my mother's life a living hell. Fighting with her over every five rupees she spent. Don't you remember what she said, on her deathbed, when I asked if she had had a good life? She said, I had a happy childhood, Gaurav. *A happy childhood*, Father – and nothing after that.'

'Don't bring your mother's name into this.'

'Your students always came first for you. Always. Not that they had any love for you.' He grinned. 'They used to give you nicknames in class. Dirty nicknames.'

'That's enough.' Masterji got up. 'I'm going to see Noronha myself.'

'Go. Go. You think your darling *Noronha* will see you? Has he responded to your letters or phone calls? He was the one who gave you all those nicknames in class. Go. But before you go, let me give you some advice. Just once let me be a teacher to you, Father.'

(*Why does* everyone *say that?* Masterji wondered.)

'It's people like you who are holding this country back, Father. Saying no to everything. The deadline is just a few days away.' Gaurav stood up. 'Keep saying no and we'll find you one morning in the gutter. I have to go back to work now.'

Masterji read the words he had written on the piece of paper:

Media

~~*Law and order*~~

~~*Social workers*~~

The paper flew into the busy road.

Walking out of the McDonald's, he stood in front of Victoria Terminus.

High up on the building a gargoyle was watching him. Sticking its tongue out it said: *I have students in high places.* He turned his eyes away. Another gargoyle grinned: *I claim no credit for Noronha.* And a third smirked: *A teacher is not without his connections.*

Then all the stony mass of the Terminus was blown away: a horn had sounded just inches from Masterji's ears. Members of an off-duty band were coming down the pavement; a man with the tuba was giving an occasional short blast to warn people to give way. They wore red shirts with golden epaulettes and white trousers with a black stripe down them, tucked into bedraggled black boots. Suddenly they were all around Masterji, with their silvery instruments; drawn by the blasts of the tuba, he followed. The musicians' shirts were sweat-stained and their bodies slumped. He walked behind the man with the tuba; staring into its wide mouth, he began counting the nicks and dents on its skin.

Perhaps observing his presence in their midst, the musicians got rid of him as they came close to Crawford Market by taking a sudden right turn together. Masterji kept on walking in a straight line, like an animal dragged by its collar. His body was in the possession of inertia, but he had full control of his neck and eyes as he observed that the clock on the Crawford Market tower was broken. The pavement became dim. Now he was on Mohammad Ali Road. The dark canyon of concrete and old stone amplified the noise of the traffic. On either side, thick buildings blocked the light, while the JJ flyover, raised on columns, its grooved body winding and twisting like an alligator on the hunt, secreted its shadow on to the road below.

Something touched him from his left.

Three goats had come out from an alley, and one of them rubbed against his left leg.

Day-labourers slept on the pavement, oblivious to the moving feet around them. The wooden carts that they had been pulling all day long lay beside them; from beneath one, a dog's claws jutted out, as if the cart were relaxing its animal digits in the cool of the evening. An old man sat beside stacks of newspapers held down by rocks: each rock looking like a crystallization of some hard truth in the newsprint. Masterji stopped to watch the newspapers.

They shot an elected member of the city corporation dead. It was in the papers.

He remembered that Bhendi bazaar, one of the recruiting grounds of the mafia, was just around the corner. Any of these unshaven men by the side of the road, with nothing to do but suck tea, would do it for Mr Shah. A knife would be stuck into his neck. Worse: his knees would be smashed. He might be turned into a cripple. Blinded.

Beads of sweat fell from his neck all the way down to the tip of his spine.

Wasn't Gaurav right – wasn't it just pride that kept him from running to Mr Shah and saying: 'I accept your offer. Now leave me alone!'

Smoke blew at him from the charcoal kebab grills outside the continuous cheap restaurants that line Mohammad Ali Road. Masterji turned into one restaurant, which was so filthy he knew he had broken his one-rat rule even before going in. A small figure crouching by the door folded its legs to let him in.

He sat down on one of the communal benches, where labourers waited for tea and bread and biscuits on wet dirty plates.

'What?' the waiter asked, swatting a dirty red rag on the table, in simulation of an act of cleaning.

'Tea. And – put all the sugar in the world in it. Understand?'

'All the sugar in the world,' the waiter said. He grinned.

He came back with a glass of tea and a packet of milk biscuits. Standing at the end of table he ripped open the packet, letting the biscuits spill *tunktunktunk* into a stainless-steel plate.

The other customer at the table – Masterji noticed him now – a gaunt, middle-aged man in a dirty blue shirt, looked Muslim because of his beard. Masterji guessed he was one of those who had been pulling carts on the road – he thought he could even identify the man's wooden cart resting against the door of the café. The labourer picked a biscuit from the stainless-steel plate and chewed. Done with it, he breathed, picked a second biscuit, and chewed. Each movement of his bony jaws spoke of fatigue; the permanent fatigue of men who have no one to care about them when they work and no one to care about them after they work. The thin body broadcast a raw animal silence. Middle-aged? No. His hair was greying at the edges, but youth had only recently been exorcised from his face. Twenty-seven or twenty-eight at the most. Masterji watched this young man with sunken, shocked eyes and barely enough strength to lift one milk biscuit at a time. *This is his daily life. Pulling that cart and coming here for these biscuits*, he thought.

The tired Muslim man returned Masterji's gaze. Their eyes met, and the labourer, without moving his lips, spoke at last.

Fight. Fight for your piece of the earth.

Leaving the restaurant, Masterji held out a five-rupee note to the waiter, and pointed to the plate of biscuits, still being consumed, one at a time.

Outside, a car with a huge plastic Red Bull on top of it was cruising down the road. The bull glowed in neon, and its snout blared a popular Hindi song, as the car stopped to hand out free cans of Red Bull to onlookers. The beat of the song tuned Masterji's blood. In the dark dirty valley under the concrete overpass half-naked labourers pushed and slogged, with such little hope that things might improve for them. Yet they pushed: they fought. As Mary was fighting to keep her hut by the *nullah*. And maid-servants like her across Vakola were fighting to keep their huts.

Strips of incandescence from behind the buildings fell on the road, and people crowded into them as if they were the only points of fording the traffic. Illuminated in these strips, the straining coolies looked like symbols: hieroglyphs of a future, a future that was colossal. Masterji gazed at the light behind the dirty buildings. It looked like another Bombay waiting to be born.

He heard the tuba again: the marching band, as if it had lost its way, had doubled back on its steps, and was heading again towards Victoria Terminus, greeting the hordes of new migrants with its blasts.

Masterji walked behind the marching band towards VT, and felt – for the first time since his wife had died – that he was not alone in the world.

4 SEPTEMBER

Oval Maidan at sunset.

Dust everywhere, and the sun doing wonderful things to the dust: electrolysing it into a golden cloud in which the stone of the Gothic towers, the singed green of the palm fronds, and the living brown of humans were blended into one.

Driving past the maidan, the bars of the fence broke the cricket matches into large rectangular panels, like frames from a film put up on a wall for analysis.

'Feeling better, Uncle?'

'You're a good girl, Rosie. A good girl to come to the hospital.'

Resting his head on Rosie, Shah watched as the driver, who had collected the two of them from Breach Candy Hospital (Rosie, in the waiting room, had flicked through a copy of *Filmfare* magazine while they took his X-rays), now drove in slow circles around the heart of the city.

'I know what you're thinking about, Mr Confidence.'

'What?'

'Money. The only thing on your mind.'

Her fingers moved into his pocket.

'Your phone is ringing, Uncle.'

'Let it.'

'There are fifteen missed calls.'

'Let there be a sixteenth. I don't care about my work. I don't care about anything.'

'Why are you talking like this, Mr Confidence?' She smiled at him.

My Shanghai, Shah thought. *Gone. Because of one old teacher.*

He felt as if a hand had entered his abdomen and surgically removed the breath.

In the driver's mirror he saw his blackened teeth and thought: *Not nearly enough.* Neither the damaged teeth, nor the disease in his chest, nor the blood he spat out, were nearly enough punishment. For the sin of being a mediocrity. The only real sin on this earth. He should have stayed in Krishnapur and cleared cow shit from the family shed.

Fingers ran through his hair; he felt a breath on his face.

'*To-re-a-dor. To-re-a-dor.*'

'Leave me alone, Rosie.'

Prising the blue X-ray folder away from him, she slid out the grinning phosphorescent skull.

'So this is who you really are, Uncle.'

He took it back from her and held it up against the light. Taking out a pen he began to sketch over the skull.

'Don't!'

He slapped Rosie's fingers away. He drew more lines up and down the glowing skull and showed her.

'That's my Shanghai, Rosie. Gothic style, Rajput touch, Art Deco fountain. My life's story in one building. Why does that old teacher keep saying no to it? In China, you know what they would have done to a man like him by now?'

She snatched at the X-ray; he raised his hand high to dodge her.

'Teachers are the worst kind of people, Rosie. All that time they spend beating children, it makes them cruel. Twisted on the inside.'

'Unlike builders, of course.'

And though he wished she wouldn't make jokes like this, he had to chuckle.

She laughed at her own joke as she slid his X-ray back into its manila folder. A husky cackle: it made Shah shiver. One of the things he loved about Rosie – her voice always had its knickers down.

'Come here,' he said, though the girl was already beside him. 'Come *here*.' He kissed her on the neck.

It was first time he had done something like this in the car; Parvez, his driver, pretended not to notice.

Shah did what he had not done for days. He forgot about the Shanghai.

At the next traffic signal, they stopped by a bus painted with advertisements for a new Bollywood film – *Dance, Dance.*

'What's the inside scoop, Rosie?' Shah asked, tapping the glass with his fingers. 'Why is that Punjabi man wasting so much money on this flop?'

It was a film that had excited much speculation in the papers. The case was an unusual one: the film was a 'comeback' vehicle for the 1980s film star Praveena Kumari. Ms Kumari, at the height of her fame, had quit Bollywood to settle in America; now, visibly ageing and heavy, she had been cast in a big-budget film – a certain flop. The film's producer was a walnut-headed Punjabi, noted for cunning and parsimony. That he would waste such money (for the production was lavish, and the marketing too) was *the* subject for discussion in Bombay that month, trumping such other questions as a possible change in the government in Delhi, the deteriorating situation in Afghanistan, or new national figures on child malnutrition.

Oh, yes. Rosie had the inside 'scoop'. Leaning forward, she whispered into the builder's ear: 'Her blowjobs sing across the decades.'

Shah grinned. It made sense. Old walnut-head, who had cast Kumari in her first film, had never forgotten her, and the moment she phoned him long-distance – 'I want to be big in films again, Uncle' – he had laid a project worth millions at her thick feet.

He laughed so much he had to cough.

'Here's your Shanghai,' Rosie said, handing him the folder with the X-ray.

She had just entertained him; he was vulnerable.

'I want to be taken into your home,' she said. 'I want to see where you eat and sleep.'

At once Parvez turned the car towards Malabar Hill.

A quarter of an hour later, a blue cleaning-rag on his shoulder, Giri stood at the dining table, his hand on the breadknife, and watched the girl in the short skirt.

Shah was out on the open terrace; Rosie, in the living room, was looking over the model of the Shanghai that was sitting near the dancing Nataraja.

Next she peeked into the bedrooms. Giri followed, making sure she did not steal anything. He knew about the theft at the Oshiwara gym. When she went into the kitchen, he stood in the doorway and folded his arms.

To-re-a-dor – emitting little contralto bursts the girl opened the wooden cupboards in the kitchen wall. *To-re-a-dor*. Giri watched with his mouth open.

He made way; the boss had come into the kitchen. From the look on his face Giri knew he had been talking to Shanmugham about the mess in Vakola.

Shah exhaled, and said: 'All right, Rosie. You've seen the house. Now let's go.'

She turned around with twinkling eyes.

'Why? What's the hurry?'

'My son will be home soon. Isn't it time for Satish, Giri?'

'So why should I leave? I want to meet him. Heard so much about him.'

'We're going to the Versova flat, Rosie. Right away.'

'Oh, you want to fuck me, but you don't want your son to meet me, is that it?'

She opened and shut another kitchen cupboard.

He pulled her hands back from the shelves; they wriggled out of his and opened another panel.

'Enough of this, Rosie. I've just been to the hospital and I'm tired.'

To-re-a-dor – she put her hands inside, and tapped on the pots and pans. *To-re-a-dor!*

Shah watched her sniffing inside his wife's cabinets, playing with his wife's utensils and vessels.

Louder and louder she sang in the foreign language, until Shah reached over her head with his thick arms and – as if he were closing a trap on an animal – slammed the panel doors shut on her nose.

She was too surprised even to cry; bending over, she began sobbing and spitting. A drop of blood fell from her nose.

'Spit into the sink,' Shah said. 'The car is leaving for Versova in five minutes.'

As she washed her nose, Giri handed her the blue rag from his shoulder: 'Take this, Miss. Take it. And don't cry, please. It makes Giri want to cry too.'

Rosie winced; Shah had taken her white arm in his right hand. With his other, he dialled Shanmugham's number.

'I've made up my mind,' he said when the phone was answered.

His fingers pressed up and down Rosie's arm; he heard his left-hand man's voice quiver with excitement.

'I've got the man from Andheri, Boss. He's the one who helped me deliver the Sion project for you. The boy we used to scare that other old man – Mr Pinto – won't be good for anything more than threatening words. But this Andheri fellow will be perfect. No police record.'

'Shanmugham: shut up and listen to me.'

And then, still holding on to Rosie's arm, he told his left-hand man what he wanted done at Vishram Society.

A pause. Then the voice on the phone said: 'Boss: are you *sure*? We're paying them? *Why?*'

'Shanmugham,' Shah said, 'I found you in a slum in Chembur. Correct?'

'Yes, Boss.'

'And if you ask one more question like that, I'll send you back there.'

He hung up and turned to Rosie. A pink plaster sat on her nose: Giri had brought out the Band-Aids kept for Satish's football wounds. She was looking at the kitchen floor.

'See what you made me do to your pretty face, Rosie? Come, let's go to Versova. I'm hungry. Come.'

She turned: her eyes were livid, and the fingers of her right hand trembled. Shah braced himself. Was it coming – the slap? But a need greater than retribution – the promised hair salon, her future independence – relaxed her fingers.

'All right,' she said. 'Let's go.'

307

Shah grinned. Texting his driver to get the car ready, he led Rosie out of the flat: towards toast, beach, and bed.

Giri stayed in the kitchen and wiped away the stains of water and blood.

BOOK EIGHT

Deadline

BOOK EIGHT

Deadline

Humming a favourite film song (... *geet amar kar do*) and walking up to his flat with a packet of fresh milk, Masterji found Ms Meenakshi waiting at his door. The girl showed him a set of keys.

'I'm leaving today.'

Masterji nodded. 'In that case you must come in, Ms Meenakshi. Tea? Biscuits?'

She wore a white T-shirt, and a denim skirt that left most of her knees uncovered; she sat on the sofa while he put milk on the gas stove and chopped a piece of ginger in the kitchen.

'Masterji, your life could be in danger and you're talking about tea and biscuits?'

He ignited the burner of the stove with a match.

'What will that man Shah do, Ms Meenakshi? We have gone through things in our generation that I can't explain to you. Do you know about PL 480? During the 1965 war the Americans stopped our food supply to help Pakistan. PL 480 was their wheat programme, and they cut it off. Prime Minister Lal Bahadur Shastri asked each Indian to give up a meal to help the nation win the war. This trouble is *nothing*.'

The living room filled with the smell of burned milk. Masterji came out of the kitchen with two cups of steaming ginger tea.

Ms Meenakshi sipped her tea. 'You're all alone here, Masterji. Do you really understand this? A man with a gun could come to your door and shoot you. It's been done before.'

Masterji put his cup down on the teakwood table.

'No. I am not alone, Ms Meenakshi.'

He wanted to throw shadows on the wall to explain to her.

'There are more parties involved in this dispute than just Mr Shah, my neighbours, and me. Millions are involved. Even after you leave Vishram, you will still be involved.'

She waited for him to explain. He smiled and stirred the sediment in the teacup.

Wiping her hands on her skirt, the girl said: 'You asked what Public Relations is, Masterji. Go to the papers. Tell them your story.'

'I wrote to a student of mine at the *Times*... and it came to nothing.'

'Not the *pucca* papers. A tabloid. My boyfriend works for the *Sun*, Masterji – the one you...' She smiled. 'I told him what is happening here, and he said at once: "It's a story!" He'll interview you. The paper will run your photo. You'll become famous. People will follow you on FaceBook.'

Masterji got up.

Everyone wants something from me, he thought. *Shah wants to steal my home, and she wants to take my story.*

He went to the window and opened it. A potted creeper from the Secretary's flat had grown down to his window; its lush green tendrils were blocking a part of his view. He began to snap its tendrils.

Ms Meenakshi realized that this was a sign for her to leave.

'I ask you once again, Masterji,' she said from the door. 'Will you tell your story? Every day, the danger to your life grows.'

He stood at the window until she closed the door behind him. So now she was gone: soon she would be moving out of the building, this girl who had once disturbed him so much. He could not locate within himself the man who – just a few feet from where he now stood – had shoved Ms Meenakshi's boyfriend with more-than-human strength. Maybe that was why she had been sent to this building: to discompose him at the time Shah made his offer.

An autorickshaw entered the compound. He saw the girl get into it with her suitcases and bags.

She was right. The deadline was coming close: and Mr Shah was going to send someone round soon.

With a smile, he continued to break the creeper, which now smelled of raw, invigorating sap.

Despite the runny noses, high temperatures, and inflamed conjunctiva that accompanied the change in the weather, Ram Khare still conceded that it was the ideal time of the year to enjoy life.

October was almost here. The sun was now bothering other people in other cities. Evenings were becoming pleasant. So he did what he did once a year, and invited security guards from around the neighbourhood for a round of chai.

They gathered around his booth in grey or khaki uniforms, smoking beedis or twirling keychains; Khare, perhaps more conscientious as a host than as a guard, made sure each one had a full glass of tea, before he took one for himself from the tray that the chai-wallah had left.

'Well, Ram Khare, what is happening at Vishram Society these days? Has it been hockey sticks or knives recently?'

The other guards had heard the news about old Mr Pinto and the boy with the hockey stick. Looking around, Ram Khare confronted an impromptu tribunal of his colleagues. He put down his tea glass and stood before them.

'Look: was Mr Pinto threatened inside the wall – or *outside* the wall?'

'Fair enough,' one of the guards said. 'He can't watch over every bit of the earth, can he?'

'But is this Masterji of yours a good man or a bad one?' another guard asked. 'Does he give good baksheesh?'

Khare snorted. 'In sixteen years, eight months, and twenty-nine days of knowing him, not a single tip.'

313

General outrage. Let him be thrown from his window, kicked sense-less, shot to death – anything!

Since the holy digest was sitting right in the window of his booth, Ram Khare had to point out, in fairness: 'But he did include my Lalitha in his lessons. The residents were not happy that a guard's daughter was being taught with their children, but he said, nothing doing. She is a student like everyone else.'

A piercing whistle came from the gate in front of Tower B: the guards turned.

A truck began to move in reverse gear into the compound, direct-ed by the whistle-blowing guard of that tower.

'My friends, things have been bad in Vishram Society,' Ram Khare said, raising his tea in a toast, 'but from today, they become *worse*.'

Mrs Puri and Ibrahim Kudwa watched from her window.

Wooden beds and Godrej cupboards, carried down the stairwell of Tower B, were loaded on to the back of the truck. Then came writing tables covered in old newspaper and personal luggage wrapped in plastic.

Having received their second instalment of money from the Confidence Group (paid by Mr Shah, in a surprise move, *ahead* of schedule), the families of Tower B were leaving for their new homes, one by one.

Mrs Puri had heard the news from Ritika, her friend in Tower B, a couple of weeks ago.

'One morning the money just comes into our Punjab National Bank account,' Ritika had said. 'More than a month early. The first instal-ment he paid as soon as we signed the vacating forms. We've got two-thirds of the money now – all those zeroes in our bank statements, Sangeeta. Everyone has run out and put down a deposit on a brand-new place. No one wants to stay in Vishram Society one day longer than they have to.'

The schedule of departures had been posted for the residents of Tower A to see on Ram Khare's booth. The last family would leave Tower B by 5 p.m. on Gandhi Jayanti, 2 October.

'Isn't the builder supposed to give eight weeks' rent while they search for a new home?' Kudwa asked.

'That's in the bank too. Some of them are moving into a rental home first. I wouldn't do *that*. Why rent when you can move into your own home right away?' Mrs Puri smiled sadly. 'You see, Ibby, I always told you Shah would pay. All the new builders are like this, they say. Honest men.'

Ibrahim Kudwa put both hands in his beard and scratched.

'It is very strange, Mrs Puri. Paying people ahead of schedule. There is some kind of plan here.'

'*Plan*, Ibby? What kind of plan can the builder have?'

'I don't know exactly...' Ibrahim Kudwa scratched his beard faster. '... but something is going on here.' He picked up an *India Today* magazine that was lying on the floor and brushed it clean; then he picked up a *Femina* magazine and did the same.

Telling Ibby to let the magazines stay on the floor, Mrs Puri offered him a glass of milk with rose-syrup stirred into it; as he drank she checked on Ramu, who was sleeping under his blue aeroplane quilt.

In the evening, she went down to see Ritika, who was leaving. The two women stood by the gate of Tower B, watching over the workmen who were loading the bags on to the truck. Ritika held a big red box of sweets, which the Secretary of Tower B was handing out to each departing family as a farewell gift from the builder. Mrs Puri saw that this red box was twice the size of the earlier ones.

'Do you want an *almirah* for free, Sangeeta?' Ritika asked. 'We can't take that old one with us.'

'Can't take it to Goregaon? Why not?'

'We're not going to Goregaon,' Ritika said. She tapped on her red box. 'We're first going to Bandra, to stay with my in-laws. Next year, we'll be moving to Kolkata. What is one and a half crores in this city, Sangeeta? Nothing. Ramesh asked for a transfer. We can have a nice big place near Minto Park for the same money. He grew up in Bengal, you know.'

Mrs Puri felt better at once: how lucky could anyone be, if they were going to live in Calcutta?

'What do *we* need an *almirah* for, Ritika? We too will be moving soon.'

'Oh, I *do* hope so, Sangeeta. I *do* hope so.'

The two old college friends embraced; and then Ritika left Vishram Society for good.

On her way back into the building, Ram Khare came up to Mrs Puri and said: 'That man wants to speak to you. The one from Confidence.'

Shanmugham, on his red bike, was right outside the gate.

She wished she had had time to put her make-up on. At least a bit of blusher.

She sat on the back of his Hero Honda; they drove down towards the highway, where they stopped at the red light.

At last. Her one-on-one with Mr Shah.

Mrs Rego had been to some restaurant in Juhu; Masterji had been asked to his palace in Malabar Hill; she thought the minimum for her would be a five-star. Probably the Hyatt, right here in Vakola. Over Italian coffee and cakes, Mr Shah would offer her a little sweetener. For the work she had done with Mrs Rego. And a little more, if she could persuade Masterji.

Of course, Masterji and Mrs Rego had been brought to see him in the Mercedes. Not like this. She would have to mention this to the builder. Her *disappointment*.

To her surprise, Shanmugham did not turn either left or right at the signal, but went straight down to the train station.

The bike stopped in front of Vihar. She knew the place: a dingy south Indian restaurant where she had tea when she took the train home from the city. She brushed her hair as she got off the bike.

Ceremonial strings of fresh *moosambi* and oranges, tied high up, welcomed visitors to the outdoor eating area. Mr Shah sat at one table, talking to the man in khaki whom she recognized as the constable, Karlekar, who had come once to Vishram.

The constable smiled at her, and left with a red box in his hand.

Shah sat next to a plastic bag full of sweet-boxes; he was sipping tea from a glass. He glanced at her as she sat down.

'The deadline is almost over, Mrs Puri.'

'Don't I know it, Mr Shah? I've been telling people from day one to sign your agreement. Maybe if we could have another day or two added to the deadline. I will do my best to help...'

Shah finished his tea. She assumed that a waiter had been told to bring her something.

The builder put his glass down; he licked his teeth and spat into the glass.

'The same thing that is wrong in this city is wrong in your Society: no will power. One after the other, you have come to me and offered your help. First the Secretary. Then your Mr Ajwani. Now you offer. And one after the other you have let me down. That teacher has still not signed. I don't want to see you people suffer, Mrs Puri. Good, solid, hard-working people. I began in life like you. When I came to Mumbai I had not even the shoes on my feet. I was a beggar like you. No, I don't wish hardship on you or your neighbours. But principles are principles. I gave you my word when I came to your Society that I would not extend the deadline by one minute. I own Tower B. I will put a wall down the middle of your compound and build my Shanghai on that side. Half a Shanghai, but it will come up. And then I'll build another, bigger tower somewhere else in Vakola.'

Shanmugham, sitting down next to them, had taken out his black book, as if he planned to record the conversation. Shah snatched the book and turned one of the pages, with its neat small handwriting, towards Mrs Puri.

He knocked on the page. 'This is Vishram, Towers A and B.'

He folded it, ripped the page down the middle, and held up one half.

'This is Tower A.'

He shoved the piece of paper into the dregs of his tea-glass. Sangeeta Puri's mouth opened; tears came into her eyes. Shah smiled at her.

'Why are you sobbing? Is it the thought of staying on in Vishram for ever? Is that old building like hell for you?'

Mrs Puri nodded.

'Yes. I have to clean my son's bottom every day. That is what the future means for me without your money.'

'Good,' Shah said. 'Good. That old teacher makes you clean your son's bottom. *I* know this. Does *he* know it? Have you made him understand what it is, to clean a child's bottom day in and day out for the rest of your life?'

She shook her head.

'Another thing. He has a son in Marine Lines who is fighting with him. I am told you are close to this boy.'

'He is like a child to me,' she said.

'Then use him. Don't you know how much a son can hurt his father?'

On the way back, Mrs Puri declined Shanmugham's offer of a 'drop-off'. She caught an auto to Vishram. Making sure Ramu was asleep, she went up to Ibrahim Kudwa's door and rang the bell.

'Gaurav,' Mrs Puri fought her sobs. 'I want to speak to Gaurav. This is his Sangeeta Aunty from Vishram Society calling. Thank you, Sonal.'

She was using her mobile phone in Ibrahim Kudwa's living room. She could not call from her own home; it might upset her Ramu.

The table lamp had been turned on, and excavated half of Ibrahim Kudwa's face from the evening gloom. Sitting on the sofa with his feet crossed, he watched Mrs Puri. Mumtaz was in the bedroom, with the door closed, feeding Mariam.

'Wait,' Kudwa said. 'Don't speak to Gaurav, Sangeeta-ji. Don't do it.'

'Why not, Ibby?' she asked, holding the phone an inch away from her ear. 'I told you what Mr Shah said, didn't I? The deadline is almost over. We have to do this.'

'Mr Shah is tricking us. Don't you see? It's obvious.'

Kudwa got off the sofa and came up to Mrs Puri. He could hear the ringing from her phone: Gaurav's number had already been dialled. With a glance in the direction of the closed bedroom door, he dropped his voice to a whisper.

'You know what his reputation is, Sangeeta-ji.'

Mrs Puri saw flakes of dandruff on her neighbour's shoulders, and smelled cologne. She nodded.

'We've discussed it in parliament,' Kudwa said. 'He pays, but he always delays his payments as long as possible. So why is he paying Tower B on time? Why is he paying them *ahead* of time? I was thinking about this all of today in my cyber-café. Now I see it. It's so obvious. But some traps work like that: you have to see them to fall into them. When those people who are left behind see their neighbours getting the money, it will turn them mad with envy. I'm talking about *us*. He is turning good people into bad people. Changing our nature. Because he wants us to do it to Masterji ourselves,' Kudwa said. 'What other builders do to men like him in situations like this.'

Mrs Puri frowned, as if she were going to think about this. But it was too late.

There was a clicking noise from her phone, and then a voice said: 'Yes? Sangeeta Aunty, is this you calling?'

'Gaurav,' she said, 'the builder just spoke to me. Yes, that Mr Shah. We are about to lose everything.' As she looked at Ibrahim Kudwa, her eyes began to fill with tears.

'I've been like a mother to you, haven't I, Gaurav? For so many years. Now you must help me, Gaurav, you are my other son, you are my only help in this building where no one loves me and no one cares…'

Standing by her side, Ibrahim Kudwa shook his head and sucked his teeth, before murmuring: 'Oy, oy, oy.'

1 OCTOBER

When Masterji came down the stairs in the morning, he saw the Secretary hammering something into the central panel of the noticeboard. Without a word to Masterji, Kothari closed the glass door, tapped it shut, and went into his office with his hammer.

Masterji stood before the noticeboard. He read the new notice, and then closed his eyes and read it, his lips moving, a second time:

```
To: the Residents of Vishram Society Tower A

I, GAURAV MURTHY, SON OF Y. A. MURTHY, AM
PUTTING THIS NOTICE UP TO SAY I HAVE NO FATHER.
I am shamed by the actions of the present
occupant of flat 3A, Vishram. After promising my
wife and me that he would sign the proposal, he
has not signed. This is not the first time he
has lied to us. Many jewels in my mother's
possession, and also bank certificates in her
name meant for me and my son Ronak, have never
been transferred to us. My son Ronak, my wife
and I will perform the one-year Samskara rites
of my mother on our own. We request all of you
not to associate us with the actions of the
present occupant of 3A, Vishram Society.

Signed,
Gaurav Murthy
Joydeep Society 5A, Marine Lines
Mumbai
```

He sat down below the noticeboard. Through the open door of the

Secretary's office, he saw Kothari at his desk, behind his Remington, eating a sandwich. Up on the landing, he could smell the stray dog; he could hear its laboured breathing.

I am no longer fighting Mr Shah, he thought. *I am fighting my own neighbours.*

Through his tears Masterji saw a mosquito alight on his forearm. He had been weak and distracted; it had seen opportunity. He watched its speckled stomach, its tingling legs, as the proboscis pierced his skin. Not a second wasted in a calculating world. Not his neighbours – he was fighting *this*.

He slapped his forearm: the mosquito became a blotch of someone else's blood on his skin.

He went up the stairs to his flat and lay in bed, covering his face with his forearm. He tried to think of all the insults that bearded labourer in Crawford Market must have had to put up with.

It was evening before he came out of his room.

He walked down the stairs, trying not to think about the noticeboard. He went out of the gate and into the market: and there he received his second shock of the day.

His story was in the newspaper.

Ramesh Ajwani had his back angled to the ocean breeze to shield his copy of the *Mumbai Sun*. He was reading an article on page four.

OLD MAN IN TOWER SAYS NO TO BUILDER

Residents of Vishram Society, Vakola, have become trapped in a peculiar 'situation' that has pitted one retired teacher against all the other members of his Society, and also against the might...

He closed the newspaper and folded it on his knees. *Such* bad news. But it was a pleasant evening, and Ramesh Ajwani was in the heart of the city of Bombay. He took a deep breath and exhaled Masterji out of his body; then he looked around.

Marine Drive. The commonwealth of Mumbai had come to sit by

the water's edge. Ajwani saw representatives of every race of the city around him: *burqa*-clad Sunni Muslims with their protective men; Bohra women in their Mother Hubbard bonnets chaperoning each other; petite, sari-clad Marathi women, jasmine garlands in their braided hair, nuggets of vertebrae in their fatless backs glistening at each twist of their excited bodies; two thick-shouldered sadhus, saffron robes streaming, chanting Sanskrit to the waves; shrieking clumps of college students from Elphinstone; the baseball-cap-wearing sellers of small fried things and chilled water.

Ajwani smiled.

Sunbaked and sweating, looking like a big pink baby, a foreign man in a singlet and blue shorts was jogging down the pavement, slowly enough for his Indian minder to follow him on foot.

Ajwani saw four young men in polyester shirts gaping at the foreigner. They had been chatting and cackling a moment ago, commenting on every passing car and young girl. Now they watched in silence.

He understood.

Having dreamed all their lives of better food and better clothes, the young men were looking at this rich foreigner's appalling sweat, his appalling nudity. Is this the end point, they were wondering: a lifetime of hard work, undertaken involuntarily, to end in this – another lifetime of hard work, undertaken voluntarily?

The city of wealth was playing its usual cat-and-mouse games with migrants: gives them a sniff of success and money in one breath, and makes them wonder about the value of success and the point of money in the next.

The broker turned his neck from side to side to relieve a strain.

A man wearing black and white came through the crowd and sat on the ocean wall next to the broker.

'Nice to see you here,' Ajwani said. 'First time we've met in the city.'

'I was in Malabar Hill when your call came. What are you doing here?' Shanmugham asked, looking at the newspaper on Ajwani's lap.

The broker grinned. 'I come to the city every now and then.

Business, you know.' He winked. 'On Falkland Road. Fun business. *Girls.*'

Shanmugham pointed at the newspaper. 'You saw the story?'

The broker turned the pages. 'I opened the paper on the train, and I closed it at once from shame. A man wants to read about other people's Societies in the *Sun*, not his own.'

He glanced through the article again, and closed the newspaper.

'The Confidence Group is being mocked in public. If *I* were in your position...' Ajwani cracked his knuckles. '... I kept hoping something would have happened by now to Masterji. Not a thing. Even the phone calls have stopped. What is wrong with your boss?'

Shanmugham twisted round to look at the ocean. Marine Drive is buffered from the waves of the Indian ocean by a row of dark tetrapodal rocks, which look like petrified starfish and run for miles along the shore. A man in rags was hopping from tetrapod to tetrapod, like an egret on a hippo's teeth. From between them he pulled out discarded bottles of water, which he tossed into a sack.

He spoke as if addressing the scavenger.

'I asked the boss, the deadline is here, what should the people in Vishram do? And he said, they must help themselves. The way I helped myself. Do you know his life's story?'

Ajwani did not. So Shanmugham, as the breeze blew in from the ocean, told the story of how Mr Shah came to Bombay on bare feet.

Ajwani closed one eye and looked towards Malabar Hill.

'So that's how men become rich. It's a good story. Have *you* paid attention to it, Shanmugham?'

The Tamilian turned to face the broker. 'What does that mean?'

Ajwani drew near. 'I know that in many redevelopment projects, the left-hand man is smarter than his boss. He skims ten, fifteen per cent off each project. And he gives some of the money to those within the redevelopment project who have been his friends.' Ajwani placed his hand, covered with iron and plastic rings, on top of Shanmugham's.

'Why don't *you* get rid of the problem in Vishram? Show some initiative, do it on your own – do it *tonight*. I can help you in return: I can show you how to skim a bit off the Shanghai. Men like you and me are not going to become rich off mutual funds or fixed deposits in the bank, my friend.'

Shanmugham shook the broker's hand off his. He stood up; he brushed the dust from his trouser bottoms. 'Whatever has to happen now to your Masterji, you have to do yourself. Before midnight on 3 October. Don't call me after this.'

Ajwani cursed. Crushing the newspaper, he threw it at the tetrapods; the startled scavenger looked up.

Masterji realized he had become one of those things, like good cabbage, ripe chikoos, or rosy apples from the United States, that people came to the market looking for.

As he went about his rounds for milk and bread, strangers followed him and waved; three young men introduced themselves. They said they were his old students. Da Costa, Ranade, Savarkar.

'Yes, of course, I remember you. Good boys, all three of you.'

'We saw you in the newspapers, Masterji. There was a big article on you this morning.'

'I have not yet read the article, boys. He didn't speak to me, that reporter. I don't know what he's written. I gather it's a small article, just three or four inches.'

Yet those three or four inches of newsprint, like a bugle call, had instantly summoned these students whom he had failed to locate for all these months.

'We are proud you're not letting that builder push you around, sir. He must give you good money if he wants you to leave.'

'But I don't *want* the money, boys. I'll explain again. India is a republic. If a man wants to stay in his home, then it is his freedom to do so. If he wants to go, then...'

The three listened; at the end, one of them said: 'You used to quote Romans in class, sir. The one who knew about the sun.'

'Anaxagoras. A Greek.'

'You're as tough as any Roman, sir. You're like that fellow in the movie... Maximus the Gladiator.'

'Which movie is this?'

That made them laugh.

'Maximus Masterji!' said one, and all three left in a good mood.

Masterji saw his story – the interpretation of his recent actions, which had until now been held securely in his conscience – slipping away from him. He had become part of the market: his story, in newsprint, was used by the vendors to cover their produce. The okra was wrapped in him; fresh bread lent him its aroma.

'Masterji!' It was Mary. She had a copy of the *Sun*.

'You're in the English papers.' She grinned and showed him her big front teeth. 'We're all so proud of you. We passed it around the *nullah*. When my son comes back from school, I'll have him read it to us.'

'I haven't read it, Mary,' he said.

'You haven't?' Mary, scandalized, insisted that he take the paper. She turned to the article with the photograph of Vishram Society.

OLD MAN IN TOWER SAYS NO TO BUILDER

Masterji skimmed:

> … only one man, Yogesh Murthy, retired teacher at the nearby school, has resisted the generous offer of the reputable… 'it is a question of an an individual's freedom to say Yes, No, or Go to Hell'…
>
> By describing himself thus as the small man in this situation, Murthy may hope to win the sympathy of some, but how honest is this picture he paints? One of the residents of the Society, not wishing to be identified, said, 'He is the most selfish man in the world. His own son does not speak to him now…'
>
> …was borne out by many others to whom this reporter spoke. According to one of Mr Murthy's former students, who did not wish to be named, 'He had no patience and he was always ready to punish. We used to call him names behind his back. To say that we remember him fondly would be the biggest…'

Mary bent down to pick up the paper; it had fallen from Masterji's hands.

Looking down, Masterji saw a bird, smaller than the centre of a man's palm, thrashing about on the ground like a vitalized chunk of brown sugar. *This only makes things worse*, he thought, as he followed the bird's dizzying movements. *My neighbours will blame me for it.*

A little boy with a black string amulet around his neck began circling Masterji in off-balance, chick-like loops, hands flapping by his side. The onion-seller came running behind him: 'Bad boy!' He caught the little fellow and pinched him; the chastised boy cried with operatic emotion: 'Pa-pa-jee!'

Seconds later, he had escaped his father again, had been caught again, and was now bawling: 'Ma-maa-jee!'

To make the boy stop crying, Masterji offered him a piece of bread. 'Would you like this?'

A big nod of the little head; the boy nibbled.

Masterji insisted that Mary take the rest of his fresh bread for her son.

For over thirty years he had handed out sweet, soft things to the children of Vishram Society on Gandhi Jayanti.

He stopped at the whitewashed banyan outside Ibrahim Kudwa's cyber-café. Arjun, Kudwa's assistant, had placed a photograph of the Mahatma in a niche in the banyan, and he and the Hindu holy man who sometimes stopped there, clapping their hands in unison, were chanting Gandhi's favourite hymn:

'*Ishwar Allah Tero Naam*
Sabko Sanmati de Bhagavan.'
'Ishwar and Allah are both your names
Give everyone this wisdom, Lord.'

The national tricolour had been hoisted above the Speed-Tek Cyber Café; Masterji saw it reflected in the tinted window of a moving car, streaming in reverse like a dark meteor over Vakola.

In the middle of the night, Ashvin Kothari woke up sniffing the air.

'What is that smell?'

He turned on his bedside lamp. His wife was staring at the ceiling.

'Go back to sleep.'

'What is it?'

'Go back to—'

'It's something you women are doing, isn't it?'

The Secretary followed the smell down the stairs to the third floor.

Something brown, freshly applied by hand, the fingermarks still visible in it, covered Masterji's door. A fly buzzed about it.

The Secretary closed his eyes. He raced up the stairs to his flat.

His wife was on the sofa, waiting for him.

'Don't blame Mrs Puri,' she said. 'She asked me and I agreed.'

The Secretary sat down with his eyes closed. 'O Krishna, Krishna...'

'Let him smell what we think of him, Mr Kothari. That's what we women decided.'

'... Krishna...'

'It's Ramu's shit – that's all. Don't become melodramatic. Masterji talked to the *Mumbai Sun*, didn't he? Famous man. He wants Mrs Puri to clean it herself for the rest of her life, doesn't he? So let him clean Ramu's shit one morning, and see how much he likes it. Let him use that same *Sun* to clean it.'

With his fingers in his ears, her husband chanted, as his father had taught him to do, years ago in Nairobi, the name of Lord Krishna.

Their noses covered with handkerchiefs, saris, and shirtsleeves, they filled the stairs to see what had been done to the door of 3A. Hunched over, Masterji was scrubbing his door with a wet Brillo pad. He had a bucket of water next to him, and every few minutes squeezed the Brillo pad into it.

Brought back down the stairs by his sense of responsibility, the Secretary dispersed the onlookers. 'Please go back to bed,' he whispered. 'Or the whole neighbourhood will find out and talk about us.'

The door to 3C opened.

Had Masterji shouted, Mrs Puri would have shouted back. Had he rushed to hit her, she would have pushed him down the stairs. But he was on his knees, scraping the grooves and ridges into which Ramu's excrement was hardening; he glanced at her and went back to his work, as if it did not concern her.

A man pushed from behind Mrs Puri and stepped into the corridor.

Sanjiv Puri saw what was on Masterji's door; he understood.

'What have you done, Sangeeta?' He looked at his wife. 'What have you done to my name, to my reputation? You have betrayed your own son.'

'Mr and Mrs Puri,' the Secretary whispered. 'Please. People will hear.'

Sangeeta Puri took a step towards her husband.

'It's all *your* fault.'

'My fault?'

'You kept saying we couldn't have children till you had a manager's job. So I had to wait till I was thirty-four. That's why Ramu is delayed. The older a woman is, the greater the danger. And now I have to clean his shit for the rest of my life.'

'Sangeeta, this is a lie. A lie.'

'I wanted to have Ramu ten years earlier. *You* talked of the rat race. *You* complained that migrants were taking the jobs, but *you* never fought back. *You* never became manager in time for me to have a healthy child. It was not the Evil Eye: it was *you*.'

Masterji stopped scrubbing.

'If you shout, Sangeeta, you will wake Ramu. No one did this thing. Sometimes plaster falls from the ceiling, because it is an old building. I say the same thing has happened here. Now all of you go to sleep.'

The Secretary got down on his knees and offered to help with the scrubbing, but Masterji said: 'I'll do it.'

He closed his eyes and remembered the light from behind the buildings at Crawford Market. Those labourers pulling carts under the JJ flyover did work that was worse than this every day.

2 OCTOBER

The compound wall was dark from Mary's morning round with the green garden hose. Water drops shivered off the hibiscus plant; Ramu was prodding its stem with a stick.

Walking up from the black Cross, where she had been standing for a while, his mother called to him. The hibiscus plant shook.

She came near and saw what he was doing.

'... what is the meaning of...?'

The boy would not turn around. He had sucked in his lips; he kept poking the thing at the root of the plant. Mrs Puri pulled him back and looked at him with disbelieving eyes.

'Don't hurt the poor worm, Ramu. Is it hurting you?'

Shaking his mother's hands off him, he thrust his wooden stick back into the coiled-up earthworm, which squirmed under the pressure, but did not uncoil. Mrs Puri felt as if someone had poked a rod into her side.

'Oy, oy, oy, my Ramu, it is Mahatma Gandhi's birthday. What would he say if he saw you?'

He must have overheard someone talking in the stairwell or in the garden. He knew what had happened last night.

'If Masterji doesn't say yes, we won't ever get our new home. Remember, Ramu, the wooden cupboard in that nice new building in Goregaon... the fresh smell, the sunlight on the wood?'

He did not turn around. She saw that he had cut the earthworm into two writhing pieces.

'I promise: not *one* thing to upset Masterji after this. I promise. Don't hurt the worm.'

But he would not turn.

'Ramu. Are you fighting with your mother?'

Masterji, who had walked in through the gate, came towards the hibiscus plant. 'Happy Gandhi Jayanti,' he said to the woman who had applied excrement to his door only a few hours ago.

She said nothing.

The boy dropped his stick and came to him; the old teacher put his arms around his neighbour's son and whispered: 'Mustn't fight with Mummy, Ramu. The deadline will end soon. After that your Mummy and I will be friends again.'

He left the two of them alone and went up to his flat.

Standing at the window of the living room, he was hoping to see some celebrations for Gandhi Jayanti. It was traditionally a big day at the Society. An old picture of Mahatma Gandhi kept inside the Secretary's desk for such occasions would be placed over the guard's booth. A black Sony three-in-one would play old film songs from Ibrahim Kudwa's window.

His phone rang. It was Ms Meenakshi, his ex-neighbour. She was calling from her new home in Bandra.

The response to the story about him – the one her boyfriend had written – had been 'fantastic!' Would Masterji consider a follow-up? Would he keep a blog? Not a blong, a *blog*.

'Thank you for your help, Ms Meenakshi, and give my regards to your boyfriend. But my answer remains no.'

He put the phone down. He went back to the window.

Another truck had stopped in front of Tower B; beds and tables had been brought down from the building and were being loaded on to it. The last residents were leaving. The remaining children of Tower B were playing cricket by the truck with the children of Tower A.

He closed his eyes: he imagined the living room full of his neighbours' children again. Dirty cricket bats and bright young faces again.

'Today we shall see how sound travels at different speeds in solids and in liquids' – he stretched his legs – 'right here in this room. And you, Mohammad Kudwa, make sure you don't talk while the experiment is going on. No, I haven't forgotten what you did last time...'

When he woke from his nap, the truck was gone.

The security grilles, removed from what used to be Vishram Tower B, had left rusty ghost-shadows around the windows and balconies, like eyebrows plucked in a painful ceremony. Pigeons flew in and out of the rooms, now no one's rooms, just the spent cartridges of old dreams. Yellow tape criss-crossed the base of the building:

THE CONFIDENCE GROUP (HEADQUARTERS: PAREL)
HAS TAKEN PHYSICAL POSSESSION OF THIS BUILDING
MARKED FOR DEMOLITION

*

Holding the latest letter from Deepa in her fingers, re-creating her daughter's face and voice from the texture of the paper, Mrs Pinto lay in bed. The stereophonic buzz of evening serials from TV sets on nearly every floor of the building penetrated her thoughts, as if they were long-wave messages from her daughter in America.

The door to the flat scraped open; she heard her husband's slow footsteps.

'Where were you gone so long?' she shouted. 'Leaving me alone here.'

Her husband sat down at the dining table, breathing noisily and pouring himself a glass from a jug of filtered water.

'The deadline has almost passed, Shelley. I really thought he would say yes in the end, Shelley. I really did.'

She spoke softly.

'What will that Confidence Man do to him now, Mr Pinto?'

'Anything could happen. These are not Christian men. These builders.'

'Then you must save Masterji, Mr Pinto. You owe it to him.'

'What do you mean?'

'The number of times you cheated him, Mr Pinto. You owe him.'

'Shelley Pinto.' Her husband sat up on his side of the bed. 'Shelley Pinto.'

'In the No-Argument book. When you were an accountant at the

Britannia Biscuit Company you cheated people at work. I think you cheated Masterji too.'

'This is a lie, Shelley. How dare you speak to your husband like this?'

'I have been your wife for thirty-six years. That one time you and Masterji went to Lucky Biryani in Bandra. You came back very happy that night and I thought: *He must have cheated Masterji again*. Didn't you change numbers in the No-Argument the way you changed numbers at the Britannia Biscuit Company?'

She heard a creaking of springs; she was alone in the bedroom. Mr Pinto had turned on the television set.

She went to the sofa and sat by him.

'We don't have to save him, Mr Pinto. The others will do it. We just have to keep quiet.'

'*What* are they going to do?'

She motioned for him to increase the volume of the television.

'Sangeeta and Renuka Kothari came today and said, if all of us agree to do something – a simple thing – would you and Mr Pinto agree?'

'What is this simple thing, Shelley?'

'I don't know, Mr Pinto. I told them not to tell us.'

'But when is it happening?'

'I told them not to tell me *anything*. Now turn the television down a bit.'

'What did you say?'

'Turn the TV down.'

'I like it loud,' Mr Pinto said. 'You go into the garden.'

Treading on 'the Diamond', Mrs Pinto went down the stairs.

She thought of 1.4 crore rupees of Mr Shah's money: the figure was part of the dark world around her. She went down two more steps. Now she thought of 100,000 dollars, sent to Tony, and another 100,000 dollars, sent to Deepa: her eyes filled with light, and the wall glowed like a plane of beaten gold.

When she had descended another flight of steps, her foot struck something warm and living. It did not smell like a dog.

'Stop prodding me with your foot.'

'Why are you sitting on the steps, Kothari?' she asked.

'My wife won't let me watch television, Mrs Pinto. Renuka has cut the cable connection. My wife of thirty-one years. Without TV, what is a home?'

She sat a step above him.

'What a strange situation. But you can watch in our house.'

'My wife of thirty-one years. Yet she does this. See what is happening to our Society.'

'If I may ask, Mr Kothari... *why* has she cut your cable connection?'

'Because I won't do the simple thing. The one she and the others want to do to Masterji. Do you know what the simple thing is?'

'They did not tell me what it was. I thought it was your idea.'

'Mine? Oh, no. It was Ajwani's.'

The Secretary tried to remember: was it Ajwani's idea? It didn't matter: like one of those wasps' nests that sometimes grew on the walls of the Society, the idea of the "simple thing" had materialized out of nowhere, swelling in size in hours, until every household in Vishram seemed to have become one of its cells. All of them wanted it done now. Even his own wife.

'This simple thing... will it hurt Masterji?'

'I don't know, Mrs Pinto, what the "simple thing" is any more than you do. It's Ajwani's idea. He has connections in the slums. They just want me to give him the duplicate key to Masterji's flat. I can't do that, Mrs Pinto. It's against the rules.'

Mrs Pinto sucked in the dark air of the stairwell.

'Will Mr Shah really not extend the deadline?'

The Secretary exhaled.

'Every time I hear a car or an autorickshaw, the tea spills from my teacup. It could be that Shanmugham fellow, coming to say, *Sorry, it's over.*'

'Then we won't see the dollars.'

'Dollars?'

'Rupees.'

'Why doesn't Masterji see it the way we do?'

'He doesn't even come down to have dinner. Thinks he's too good for Mr Pinto and me. After poor Mr Pinto broke his leg for Masterji's

333

sake. Thinks he's a great man because he's fighting this Shah. Went and spoke to the papers about his own Society.'

'After all the times he came down to your house and ate your food. Ingratitude is the worst of sins, my father always said.' He paused. 'My father was the greatest man I ever knew. If he had stayed in Africa, he would have become a millionaire. A prince. But the foreigners didn't want him to succeed. Isn't that always the story of our people?'

Mrs Pinto placed her cold hand on his. 'Is someone walking up the stairs?' she whispered.

The Secretary peered down the stairwell. 'Just the dog.'

With his palm he wiped the sweat from his forehead.

'Why don't *you* make a duplicate of Masterji's key?' Mrs Pinto put her hand on the Secretary's shoulder. 'That won't be against the rules. The key will always be in your possession. Just give the duplicate to Ajwani.'

'I could do that.' Kothari nodded. 'It would be within the rules.'

'My husband will come with you, if you want.'

'No, Mrs Pinto. It's my responsibility. I'll go to Mahim, so no one will recognize me.'

'Bandra is far enough.'

'You're right.' He smiled. 'In all these years we've never talked like this, Mrs Pinto.'

'In parliament we have. But not like this. I have always admired you. I never thought you stole money from the Society. *I* never did.'

'Thank you, Mrs Pinto.'

She got up, with her hand to the wall.

'It's for his own sake, remember. This Confidence Shah is not a Christian man.'

Kothari prodded the stray dog to get it out of Mrs Pinto's way and she went on down the stairs.

In the lowest drawer of his desk, the Secretary of Vishram Society keeps a box of the spare keys to all the units in the building. To be loaned to the rightful owner in case of emergency: no key to leave the box for more than twenty-four hours.

A pair of fingers disturbed the keys. One key was removed. Then the man who had stolen the key closed the door of the Secretary's office behind him.

Something growled at him from the black Cross: the stray dog was looking up from its bowl of channa.

Kothari bought a twice-buttered sandwich at the market; he ate it in the autorickshaw that took him to the train station, and licked his fingers as he stepped out.

Full, he dozed on the Churchgate-bound local, until the smell of the great black sewer outside Bandra woke him.

Straightening his comb-over to make sure it covered his baldness, Kothari descended on to the platform. A pink palm shot out at him from a dark blazer: 'Ticketticket.'

He handed over his three-month first-class rail pass to the ticket inspector; as the man in the blazer checked the validity of the pass, he recited:

'Do as you will, evil king:
I, for my part, know right from wrong
And will never follow you,
said the virtuous demon Maricha
When the lord of...'

Except for that one time he thought he was going to jail because he forgot to pay his advance tax, the Secretary had never felt like this.

The evening rays of the sun, intercepted by trees and shop fronts around the station, fell near his feet like claw marks on bark. He was heading down one of the alleys by the side of the Bandra train station. On every side of him, he saw bananas, cauliflower, apples, burnished and expanded by the golden light. Like another strange kind of fruit, giant cardboard keys, yellow and white, dangled from the branches of the next banyan tree; each bore the legend:

RAJU KEY-MAKER.
MOBILE PHONE: 9811799289

Beneath them, the key-maker sat on a grey cloth, his tools and keys spread before him. He worked with a knife, cutting a piece of iron into a new key, closing an eye to compare it with another key that he brought out from his shirt pocket.

'Can you make a duplicate for me?' the Secretary asked. 'It's for my mother-in-law's house – in Goregaon.'

The key-maker indicated that he should move so his shadow fell to the side.

Kothari felt the key grow hot in his hand.

'Had some free time on Gandhi Jayanti, thought, let's get it done… Go to my mother-in-law's house in Goregaon and check for yourself. The building is right there. Near the Topi-wala cinema hall.'

'Look here,' the key-maker said. 'I've got six orders ahead of yours.'

Nearly two hours later, Ajwani opened his door to find the Secretary standing with something wrapped in a handkerchief in his hand.

He smiled and reached for the handkerchief; but the Secretary hid it behind his back.

'Look here, Ajwani, if you're getting anything extra for this from Shah – and I know you are – I want half of it. I did all the work today.' Coming close to Ajwani's ear, he whispered: 'I want a large glass panel in my living room in Sewri. For a full view of the flamingoes. A large glass panel.'

Ajwani grinned. 'You're becoming a man, Kothari. All right, fifty fifty.'

He reached behind the Secretary's back and took the thing wrapped in a handkerchief; in return he handed the Secretary a large soft packet.

'Cotton wool,' he said. 'Distribute it to everyone in the Society. Before 9 p.m. I'm going right now to see the boys.'

The Secretary turned his face to the right and held the cotton bale up to his ear. '*Don't* tell me what is going to happen.'

Outside Vishram Society, the street lamps were flickering to life. Mrs Puri was out in the market, shopping for fresh, vitamin-rich spinach with which she would stimulate her son's slow neurons.

A jarring noise of brakes tore through the market. The Tata Indigo, which had swerved from the main road, slowed down, but not fast enough: there was a mad squealing, and a thrashing of living limbs under its wheels.

'You've killed it!' someone shouted at the driver. 'And on Gandhi Jayanti!'

Two men came out of a grocery store; one of them, who wore a blue lungi, tied it up around his knees. 'Pull him out of his car and give him a thrashing!' he yelled.

The Indigo sped away; the grocery-store men went back to their work.

The stray yellow dog, an uninvited and unexpelled guest at Vishram Society for so many months, lay in a puddle of dark sticky blood near the market. A crow hopped by the side of the animal. It picked at its entrails.

Mrs Puri shielded Ramu's face with her palm. He whimpered. Hugging him into her side, she led him back to Vishram, and left him there with Mrs Saldanha.

She shook Ram Khare out from his guard's booth.

Ram Khare brought water in the channa bowl Ramu had left near the black Cross. The dog was too weak to drink it. They lowered the animal into the gutter, so that it might pass away in dignity, if not in comfort.

'Ask the municipality men to take it with them when they come here in the morning, Ram Khare. We can't leave its body out here.'

She went back and explained to Ramu: that wasn't their friendly stray dog. No, it was another dog that looked a bit like theirs. Ramu brightened. His mother promised that they would see their yellow dog in the morning, eating channa from the bowl. Promise.

She was tucking him into bed with the Friendly Duck when the Secretary knocked on the door.

'Double lock your door tonight, Mrs Puri,' he said.

She came to the door and whispered: 'Is it really going to happen? The *simple thing*?'

Kothari said nothing; he handed her a small plastic bag full of cotton wool, and went down the stairs. Mrs Puri stood in the stairwell, listening as he knocked on the Pintos' door.

'Double-lock your door tonight, Mr Pinto.'

'We lock them every night.'

'Lock it extra tight tonight. Wear cotton in your ears if you have any. You don't? Then take some of this. It's in the bag. Wear it at night. Do you understand?'

'No.'

'Try. It is a simple thing, Mr Pinto.'

She heard Kothari's footsteps go down another flight of stairs, and then his voice saying: 'Double-lock your door tonight, Mrs Rego.'

Just as he was turning from Mrs Saldanha's door, the Secretary saw Mary, standing near his office. She was staring at him.

'What do you want?' he asked.

'I clean your office every evening at this time,' she said. 'I was going to get the broom.' And then she added: 'I didn't hear anything.'

'Clean the office tomorrow, Mary. You may take the rest of the day off.'

She stood there.

'Mary' – the Secretary lowered his voice – 'when the Shanghai comes up, they'll hire you. I'll make sure that they do. They'll give you a uniform. Good pay. I'll make sure. Do you understand?'

She nodded.

'Now go home,' Kothari said. 'Enjoy the evening with your son.'

He watched until she went out of the gate and turned left towards the slums.

There was now a night-time silence in Vishram such as they had not heard in decades; the deserted Tower B with the yellow *Marked for Demolition* tape around it seemed to secrete stillness. The Pintos, as they lay in bed, could hear once again the roar of the planes going over Vakola.

'There,' Mr Pinto whispered.

'Yes,' Mrs Pinto whispered. 'I heard it too.'

Masterji was back in his room. He was washing his face in the basin.

'Maybe nothing will happen tonight,' Mrs Pinto whispered.

'Go to sleep, Shelley.'

'He has stopped walking. He's gone to bed,' she said. She strained her ears.

'But someone's walking above him.'

A little after midnight, the Secretary woke up.

He had dreamed that he was standing before a panel of four judges. They wore the expected black robes and white wigs of the judiciary, but each had the face of a flamingo. The senior judge, who was larger than the others, wore a shawl of golden fur. The face of this flamingo-judge was so terrible that the Secretary could not look at it; hoping for sympathy, he turned to the lesser judges. All three were reading aloud, but all he could hear was one word, repeated endlessly, *Bye-law*, *Bye-law*. The senior judge, adjusting his wig, said: 'Human beings are only human individually: when they get together they turn...' His three junior colleagues were already tittering. '... *birdy*.' The three laughed together in high-pitched cackles. Then the senior flamingo adjusted his golden shawl, for he was a vain judge, and spoke in a deep voice, which the Secretary recognized as his father's:

'Now for the verdict on Ashvin Kothari, Secretary, Vishram Society Tower A, incorporated in the city of Mumbai, who made a duplicate of a key entrusted to his care to facilitate a break-in into his own Society, and that too on the holy day of Gandhi Jayanti. In accordance with the law of the land, and to avoid giving offence, the verdict of this panel shall be read in English, Marathi, Hindi, Urdu, Punjabi, Gujarati...'

Kothari opened his eyes. He turned on his lamp so he could see the clock. His wife, lying next to him, began to grumble.

In the dark Kothari walked over the carpet in his living room. Holding his comb-over in place, he lowered himself on to the sofa.

No one should point a finger at *him*. Ajwani had arranged for the 'simple thing'.

Yet he wanted to scream for help, or run to the police station near the highway and tell the fat constable Karlekar everything, before something terrible happened in the night, and they woke to find Masterji with his legs broken, or worse, much worse...

His wife snored from the bed. Getting down on his knees, Kothari put his ear to the carpet and listened. All he could hear was the sound of his own voice, whispering:

'Do as you will, evil king:

I, for my part, know right from wrong…'

A little after two o'clock, the Pintos heard Masterji's door open again.

It was like the way you hear someone making love in another home, their bed creaking and their sighing, and you're trying hard to shut it out of your ears. They wanted not to hear.

Something was walking upstairs. *Two* somethings.

'The boys are here.'

'Yes.'

The two old bodies moved in bed, following the footsteps; a flurry of steps, and then a little cry of pain: bone had hit table.

'The teakwood table.'

'Yes. Oh, no.'

This was followed by more shuffling; the table fell over; a scream.

'Thieves!'

No one stirred. No one moved. The two Pintos joined hands. Everyone in the building, prostrate in the same way, must have heard the cry. The Pintos could feel the warming of hearts in every listening bedroom – the same 'At last.'

Then there was a muffled wrestling – and then there was the sound of swatting, as if someone was hitting at a rat running around the room. Then – piercing the night – not a human cry, but the howling of an animal.

The Rubik's Cube saved him.

One of the boys stepped on it, slipped, and hit his knee against the teakwood table, which toppled over.

Masterji awoke.

He had grabbed the blue *Illustrated History of Science* at once – had some secret part of him been waiting for this, rehearsing this moment? – and rushed out of his bedroom; before they had even seen

340

him he had hit the first one on the head with the book. Screaming –
Thieves! – and with a strength that he would not be able to reproduce
in daylight, he had shoved one of the boys – who, staggering back, had
hit the other one, who fell by the phone. The *Illustrated History of Science*
went up high and then came down on the skull of the boy, who
howled. It was by now a rout, and the two hooligans rushed out through
the open door, where one tripped and tumbled down the stairs; by
which time they were in a frenzy just to survive, realizing they had been
sent to bully and threaten not a helpless old man, as they had been
told, but a live ogre. They ran into the compound and leapt over the
gate.

Masterji pushed the sofa against the door, to barricade it against a
second attack. Purnima, he chanted, Purnima. He moved the chair
against the sofa.

Then it seemed to him that this was the wrong thing to have done.
He had to be able to run in and out if there was another attack, and
the door should be open. He moved the sofa and the chair back to their
places.

He let the water run into a pot; he turned on the gas, and brought
water to a boil. He would pour it on their heads when they came back.
On his knees, he examined the gas cylinder. Perhaps he could explode
it in their faces?

Purnima, he thought, *Purnima*. He tried to summon his wife's face
but no image came into his mind: he could not remember what she
looked like. Gaurav, he called, Gaurav, but he could not remember
his face, either... he saw only darkness, and then, emerging from that
darkness, people, men of various races, standing in white shirts,
close together. He recognized them: they were the commuters on the
suburban train.

Now a ray of sun entered the compartment and their varied faces
glowed like a single human light refracted into colours. He searched
for the face of the day-labourer from Crawford Market; he could not
find him, but there were others like him. The vibrating green cushions
and the green-painted walls of the carriage were luminous around
them. 'Calm down, Masterji,' the radiant men in the white shirts said,

'for we are all with you.' He understood now that he had not struck the two boys down: *they* had done it for him. Beyond the grille, the faces in the yellow second-class compartment turned to him, and said: 'We are with you too.' Around him they stood thick and close; he felt hands come into his hand; and every murmur, every whisper, every jarring of the train said: *You were never born and you will never die: you cannot hurt and cannot be hurt: you are invincible, immortal, indestructible.*

Masterji unbolted the latch, left his door open, and slept.

'Sir.' Nina, the Pintos' maid, turned to her employer. 'You should see for yourself who it is.'

Mr Pinto, rising from a breakfast of a masala three-egg omelette, served with buttered toast and tomato ketchup, came to the door dragging his brown leather sandals along the floor.

He saw who was at the door and turned around: 'Nina,' he cried. 'Come back here.'

Masterji was standing outside.

'I was sure in the night it was Mr Shah who had done it,' Masterji said. 'And I felt safe until the morning. But when I woke up, I thought, those boys did not break down the door. They had a spare key. Who gave them this spare key?'

Mr Pinto turned and gestured to the table.

'Come have breakfast with us. It's the three-egg omelette. Your favourite. Nina – one more omelette, at once. Come, Masterji, sit at the table.'

'Did you know what was going to happen last night?' Masterji asked. 'Did the Secretary tell everyone to keep quiet when I screamed? That was something else I didn't think about until this morning. No one came to help me.'

Mr Pinto gestured helplessly. 'For our part, honestly, we heard nothing. We were asleep. Ask Shelley.'

Mrs Pinto, rising from the breakfast table, stood next to her husband, and took his hand in hers.

'We wanted to save you, Masterji,' she said in her rasping voice. 'They told us if we kept quiet we would save you.'

343

'Shelley, shut up. Go back to the table. We didn't know anything, Masterji. We thank God that you are safe. Come in and eat now—'

'You're lying, Mr Pinto.'

Masterji pulled the front door from Mr Pinto's grasp and closed it on himself. He pressed his forehead against the door. Rajeev and Raghav Ajwani, in their school uniforms, tried to tiptoe past him.

Hearing voices from below, Masterji went down the stairs.

Three women sat in the white plastic chairs.

Mrs Puri was speaking to the Secretary's wife; Mrs Ganguly, bedecked in gold and silk, apparently on her way to a wedding ceremony, was listening.

'So what if the Sisters at the Special School want Ramu to play David Slayer of Goliath in the pageant? What is it to me that David was a Christian and we are Hindus? Jesus and Krishna: two skin colours, same God. All my life I have gone in and out of churches like a happy bird.'

'You're right, Sangeeta,' the Secretary's wife responded. 'What difference is there, deep down?'

Masterji went from Mrs Puri to Mrs Kothari to Mrs Ganguly, trying to find a face that revealed guilt when he stared at it. None paid the slightest attention to him. *Am I looking at good people or bad?* he thought.

Mrs Puri brushed a housefly from Mrs Kothari's shoulder and continued.

'Didn't I pray at St Antony's and then at St Andrew's and then at Mount Mary that the doctors should be wrong about Ramu? Just as I prayed in SiddhiVinayak temple, Mrs Kothari.'

'You are a liberal person, Sangeeta. A person of the future.'

'Did all of you know what was going to happen last night?' Masterji asked. 'Am I the only human being in this building?'

Mrs Puri continued to talk to the Secretary's wife.

'I make no distinction between Hindu and Muslim and Christian in this country.'

'So true, Sangeeta. Let the heart be good, that's what I say.'

'I agree with you one hundred per cent,' Mrs Ganguly joined in. 'I never vote for the Shiv Sena.'

Now Masterji saw Tinku Kothari, the Secretary's son. Squished into a plastic chair with his miniature carom board, the fat boy was playing by himself, alternately striking black and beige pieces. With his fingers tensed to hit the blue striker, he paused, turning his eyes sideways to Masterji.

He was chuckling. His jelly-like flesh rippled beneath his tight green T-shirt with its golden caption, *Come to Ladakh, land of monasteries*. The grins of Tibetan monks on the boy's T-shirt widened.

The blue striker scattered the carom pieces. One black piece ricocheted over the board's edge, and rolled through parliament, until it touched Masterji's foot: he shivered.

He went up the stairs to his living room and waited for his old friend. If only Shelley would persuade that stubborn old accountant to knock on the door and say one word. 'Sorry.'

Just one word.

He waited for half an hour. Then he got up and reached for the No-Argument book, still wrapped in a blue rubber band, lying on top of *The Soul's Passageway after Death* in the bookshelf.

He undid the rubber band. He tore the pages out of the No-Argument book one by one, then tore each page into four pieces, and then tore each piece into smaller pieces.

Down in 2A, Mr Pinto, sitting at his dining table, turned to the window to watch the snowfall of paper pieces: all that was left of a 32-year-old friendship.

A scraping noise began in the compound. Mary was sweeping the confetti into a plastic bag. Masterji watched. He was waiting for her to look up at him, he was waiting for one friendly face within his Society. But she did not look.

He understood: she was ashamed. She too had known of what was going to happen.

A shadow fell over Mary's bent back: a hawk went gliding over her into one of the open windows of Tower B.

'Come to *this* tower!' Masterji called out.

From his window he watched as the hawk, as if at his command, came out of Tower B and flew back.

And not just you.

Pigeon, crow, hummingbird; spider, scorpion, silverfish, termite and red ant; bats, bees, stinging wasps, clouds of anopheles mosquitoes.

Come, all of you: and protect me from human beings.

The cricket game at the Tamil temple had ended. A good game for Timothy; his mother had not caught him playing, and he had scored the most runs this afternoon.

Kumar, tallest of the boys who played with Timothy, had not had a good game. His shift as a cleaner at the Konkan Kinara, a cheap restaurant near the Santa Cruz train station, would start soon, and he was walking through the wasteland around Vakola to his home in one of the slums behind the Bandra-Kurla Complex. He was limping this evening; with the cricket bat in his hand, he slashed at the tall grass to either side of the mud path. A few paces ahead of him, Dharmendar, the cycle mechanic's assistant, walked with his hands in his pockets, staring at the ground.

From the tall grass, a small dark creature in a blue safari suit leapt out at them.

'Ajwani Uncle,' Kumar said.

The broker slapped Dharmendar on the head. 'The simplest of jobs.' A second slap. 'All you had to do was scare an old man. A 61-year-old man.'

Ajwani's forehead bulged and his scalp retracted. The tendons in his neck became taut. His spit came out in a spray; he swore.

Kumar put down his cricket bat, and stood by Dharmendar's side, to indicate his share of the responsibility. He bowed his head: Ajwani disdained to slap it. He wiped his palms on his safari suit, as if he had soiled them by touching one so unworthy.

'You had the key, you had to go in and put a hand over his mouth and give him a message. And you couldn't do that.'

'He was... very fierce, Ajwani Uncle.'

The broker scowled. 'And now you're playing *cricket*.'

'Forgive us, Uncle,' Kumar said. 'We're no good for work like this.'

A plane with the red-and-white Air India colours rose into the sky.

Below its roar, Ajwani cursed and spat into the grass.

'How many boys wait for a call like this? A chance to make some easy money. The beginning of a career in real estate. And I had to pick the two of you. Kumar: didn't I find your family a place in the slums? Was there any other way you could have got a roof over your heads for 2,500 rupees a month?'

'No, Uncle.'

'And you, Dharmendar: didn't I help your mother find a job as a maid in Silver Trophy Society? Didn't I go there and speak to the Secretary personally?'

'Yes, Uncle.'

'And you boys let me down like this. Running from a 61-year-old…' He shook his head. 'And now the police will be here. After me.'

'Forgive us, Uncle.'

'What happened to the key I gave you?' Ajwani gestured for it with his fingers.

'We lost the key,' Kumar said.

'When we were running out of the building, Uncle.'

'Lost the key!' Ajwani shouted. 'When the police come to arrest me, I should give them your names and say it was your idea.'

'We'll go to jail for you, Uncle. You are like a father to—'

'Oh, shut up,' Ajwani said. 'Shut up.'

Almost choking with disgust, he walked back to the market and crossed the road to his office.

When Mani returned to the Renaissance Real-Estate office, he found his boss lying on the cot in the inner room, with one foot stretched out and playing with the coconuts in the wicker basket.

'Why, Mani? Why did I give the job to those boys? I know so many people along the highway. I should have gone to a real goonda. Someone with experience.'

'Yes, sir.' Mani sat in a corner and watched the boss.

'I have failed in everything I've put my hand to, Mani. I bought Infosys shares in 2000. Four days later the Nasdaq crashed. Even in real estate I keep buying at the wrong time. I am just a comedian in my own movie.' His eyes filled with tears; his voice broke. 'Get out of here, Mani.'

'Yes, sir.'

'And take care of my children when the police come to question me, Mani.'

'Yes, sir.'

Picking up the black curved knife, the broker sliced open a coconut, drank its water, then got down on the floor and did twenty-five push-ups in an attempt to improve his morale.

At three o'clock, when Mani came back to the inner room, he was still lying on the cot, looking at the ceiling.

'The way he dealt with those two useless boys, Mani. There's guts in a 61-year-old doing that. Even in an enemy I admire courage.'

Now that he had done this terrible thing to Masterji, Ajwani felt closer than ever before to the stern sanctimonious old teacher, whom he had neither liked nor trusted all these years.

To wake up every morning white and hot and angry. To become a young man again at the age of sixty-one. What must it feel like? Ajwani clenched his fist.

At four o'clock, he called the Secretary's office.

Kothari's voice was relaxed. 'You have nothing to worry about. He hasn't gone to the police.'

'He isn't going to file a complaint against us?'

'No.'

'I don't understand...'

'I've been thinking about it all morning,' the Secretary said. 'Like you, I sat here shaking in my office. But the police never came. Why didn't Masterji call them?'

'That's what I asked you, Kothari.'

'Because,' the voice on the phone dropped to a whisper, 'he knows *he's* the guilty one. Not going to the police, what does it mean? Full confession. He accepts responsibility for everything that has gone wrong in this Society. And to think we once respected the man. Now listen, Ajwani. The deadline ended yesterday. At midnight. Correct?'

'Yes.'

'But no one has come from the builder's office. To tell us that it is over, and Tower A is no longer wanted by the Confidence Group.'

'What does it mean?' Ajwani whispered back. 'Is Shah giving us more time? He said he would never do that.'

'I don't know what it means,' the Secretary said. 'But look – all of us have signed and dated our agreement forms before October 3. Correct? If Shanmugham comes tomorrow and says, it is over, we can always say, but we *did* sign the forms. *You* did not come yesterday.'

Ajwani exhaled. Yes, it could still work. Nothing had been lost just yet.

'But this means...'

'This means,' the Secretary continued for him, 'we have to try something even more simple with Masterji. *Tonight.*'

'Not tonight,' Ajwani said. 'I need a day. I have to plan things.'

The voice on the other end of the phone paused.

'And you call *me* a nothing man, Ajwani?'

'Why do I have to do everything? Do it yourself this time!' the broker shouted. He slammed the phone down.

You stink. You people.

He could smell them from his room too well. He burned the candle, he burned an incense stick, he sprayed a perfume about the rooms, but he could still smell them.

I'll go up as high as possible, Masterji thought.

So he climbed the stairs and went out on to the terrace again. Standing at the edge, he looked down on the black Cross, which was being garlanded by Mrs Saldanha.

She must be praying I should die, he thought.

He circled about the terrace. After a while, he saw small faces down in the compound, staring up: Ajwani, Mrs Puri, and the Secretary were watching him.

Those who had tried to attack him in his room the previous night now gaped at him from down there, as if *he* were a thing to fear. How monstrous a child's face with a torch-light must seem to a poisonous spider. He smiled.

The smile faded.

They were pointing at him and whispering into each other's ears.

'Go down at once,' he told himself. 'By staying up here you are only giving them an excuse to do something worse to you.'

Half an hour later he was still up there: with his hands clasped behind his back, walking in circles around the terrace, as helpless to stop moving as those down below were to stop watching.

BOOK NINE

The Simplest of Things

BOOK FOUR

The Simplest of Thing

They stood, white and pink, on a metal tray in front of the glass-encased figure of the Virgin; their individual flames merged into a thick fire and swayed, alternately answering the sea breeze and the chanting of the kneeling penitents. Thick, blackened wicks emerged from the melting candles like bone from a wound.

White and pink wax dripped like noisy, molten fat on to the metal under-plate, then hardened into white flakes that were blown around like snow.

'How long is Mummy going to pray today?'

The Virgin stood on a terrace with the sea of Bandra behind her and the stony grey Gothic façade of the church of Mount Mary in front of her.

Sunil and Sarah Rego waited at the wall of the terrace; Mrs Puri stood beside them, ruffling Ramu's hair and goading him to say the words (which he once knew so well): 'Holy Roman Catholic.'

It had been Mrs Puri's idea that they should come here: the black Cross in the compound had failed them. Eaten prayer after prayer and flower garland after flower garland and done nothing to change Masterji's mind.

So she made them all climb into two autorickshaws, brave the fumes of the Khar subway, and come here, to the most famous church in the city.

Mrs Rego was on her knees before the Virgin, her hands folded, her eyes closed, her lips working.

Sunil had prayed for a respectable time; now he leaned over the edge of the terrace, reading aloud the holy words painted along its steps.

'That word is "Rosary". And the next word is "Sacrifice". And that word is "Re-pa-ra-tion". It's a big word. Mummy can use it to trump Aunty Catherine.'

Mummy had not moved for half an hour. The person praying by Mrs Rego's side got up; an old woman in a purple sari moved in to fill the gap, touching her forehead three times to the ground.

'Is someone ill? Is it Daddy in the Philippines?'

'Keep quiet, Sarah,' Sunil whispered.

'Why else is Mummy praying so long?'

Half an hour later, all five of them walked down the hill to the Bandra bandstand. They bought four plates of bhelpuri from a roadside vendor and sat in the shade of the pavilion; Sunil and Sarah gobbled theirs, while Mrs Puri brought a spoonful of her bhelpuri to Ramu's mouth.

Mrs Rego asked: 'Why did no one come today from the Confidence Group to tell us it is over?'

'Mr Shah must be preparing the papers for his half-Shanghai. My guess is that he will send Shanmugham over tomorrow.'

Ramu chewed his food. His mother watched him, gently pressing the stray puffed rice to his mouth.

'Do you know everyone in Tower B got their final instalment last week?'

'So quickly?'

'Ahead of schedule, once again. Ritika phoned. This man, this Mr Shah – he does keep his word.'

Mrs Puri fed her son another spoonful.

'Do you know what *Kala Paani* means? They used to call the ocean that. People were frightened to cross it. Ajwani says we are all at the *Kala Paani* now. Mr Shah says the same thing. We must cross the line. The way he did, when he came to Mumbai without shoes on his feet.'

'How do you know this?' Mrs Rego's voice dropped. 'Did you meet him?'

Mrs Puri nodded.

'Did you talk about money?'

'No. He didn't try to bribe *me*.'

354

Mrs Rego looked away.

'It is a simple thing,' Mrs Puri said. 'And then this nightmare is over for all of us. We can phone Mr Shah at once. Before Shanmugham comes.'

'We already tried the simple thing. I didn't like it. Criminals inside my Society.'

Mummy smiled and wiped Ramu's mouth.

'There is an even simpler thing. Just a push. But it must be done *now*.'

Mrs Rego frowned; she tried to understand what her neighbour had said.

'Georgina! What are you doing in Bandra?'

A woman in a green dress was walking towards them; a tall, bald foreigner with a goatee followed behind her.

Introductions were made: the woman in the green dress was Catherine, Mrs Rego's sister, and the foreign thing with her was her American journalist husband, Frank. His articles appeared in many, many progressive magazines.

'We read about your Society in the paper, Georgina,' Frank said, addressing his sister-in-law. 'And your old teacher. In the *Sun*.'

Mrs Rego had not paid much attention to her plate of bhelpuri. Now she began eating.

Frank rubbed his hands. 'I know why he's doing this. It's a state-ment, isn't it? Against development. Against *unplanned* development.'

Mrs Rego ate bhelpuri. Mrs Puri stood up and faced the foreigner.

'He's not making a statement. He's *mad*.'

The American winced.

'No, I think it's a statement.'

'What do you know – you don't live in Vishram. Yesterday he was walking on the terrace. Round and round and round. With a Rubik's Cube in his hand. What does that mean, except: "I have lost my mind completely." And we hear him, don't we, my husband and I, from next door. Talking to his wife and daughter as if they were alive.'

Mrs Puri looked at Ramu. The boy was playing with Mrs Rego's children.

'No statement is happening here,' she whispered. 'Just madness.'

The plate of bhelpuri dropped from Mrs Rego's hand. She began to sob.

Catherine squatted by her sister and rubbed her back.

'Frank, did you have to mention that horrible man? Did you have to upset my sister?'

'What did I do?' The man looked around. 'I just said—'

'Shut up, Frank. You are so insensitive sometimes. Don't cry, Georgina. We'll get you another plate. Here, look at me.'

'I'm going to lose the money, it's not fair,' Mrs Rego sobbed. 'It's not fair, Catherine. You've trumped me again. You always do.'

'Oh, Georgina...'

Mrs Rego's children came to either side of her and held her hands protectively.

'Mummy,' Sunil whispered, 'Aunty Catherine's children are stupid. You know that. Sarah and I will make a lot of money for you, and you'll trump her again. Mummy, don't cry.'

An hour later, Mrs Puri opened the gate of Vishram Society for her Ramu. Mrs Rego and her children came in behind Ramu.

'All of Vishram Society is helpless before a bird,' Mrs Puri said, when she stood outside Mrs Saldanha's kitchen.

The crow's nest had come up above Mrs Saldanha's kitchen window; it had been showering twigs and feathers into the kitchen for days. Mary had refused to do anything; it would bring bad luck to toss the eggs down. 'I am a mother too,' she had retorted, when Mrs Saldanha accused her of dereliction of her duties.

Now the eggs had hatched. Two blood-red mouths opened out of little beaks and screeched desperately, all day long. The mother crow hopped from chick to chick and pecked each one consolingly, but they, with raised beaks, cried out for more, much more.

'We'll tell the Secretary to call the seven-kinds-of-vermin man,' Mrs Rego said, keeping her eyes to the ground.

This man, who worked near the train station, was often called to Vishram to knock down a wasps' nest or a beehive; he scraped it down with his pole and sprayed white antiseptic on the wall.

'Don't call anyone,' Mrs Puri said. She seized Mrs Rego by the arm to arrest her.

'We will do it right now. You watch.'

She took out her mobile phone and punched at the buttons. Ajwani was at home. He came down wearing a *banian* over his trousers and scratched his forearms: he lived directly above the nest, it was true, but on the second floor ...

'It is just a crow, and we are people,' Mrs Puri reasoned with him.

Ajwani remembered a long pole he used to clean cobwebs from the ceiling.

A few minutes later, he was leaning out of his wife's kitchen window, aiming the long pole at the crow's nest like a billiards-player. His sons stood on either side and guided his aim.

The Secretary came out of his office to watch. So did Mrs Saldanha.

Mrs Puri sent Ramu up the stairs; he was under orders to wait for her on the first landing.

'Do it quickly,' she shouted at Ajwani. 'The mother knows.'

Ajwani pushed at the nest with the pole. The crow flew up, its claws extended. Ajwani pushed again; the nest tipped over the edge, the two chicks screeching desperately. 'A little to the left, Father,' Raghav said. The broker gave a final nudge: the nest dropped to the ground, scattering sticks and leaves.

One of the chicks was silent, but the other poked its beak through the overturned nest. 'Why doesn't it shut up?' the Secretary said. Giving up on Ajwani, who had closed his window, the crow flew down towards her living chick. Kothari stamped on the fledgling's head, stopping its voice. The crow flew away.

Suddenly, someone began to scream from the stairwell.

'A simple thing, wasn't it?' Mrs Puri said.

All of them looked up at the roof: Masterji was up there, hands clasped behind his back, walking round and round.

A few hours earlier, he had been standing at his window: in the garden he saw Mary's green hosepipe lying in coils around the hibiscus plants.

Things, which had seemed so simple that evening at Crawford Market, had now become so confusing.

Something rattled against the wall of the kitchen: Purnima's old calendar.

Masterji searched among the crumpled clothes by the washing machine, picked a shirt that was still fresh-smelling and changed into it.

Out in the market, Shankar Trivedi was enjoying, in between the chicken coop and the sugarcane-crushing machine, the second of his daily shaves. His face was richly lathered around his black moustache. He held on to a glowing cigarette in his right hand, as the barber unmasked him with precise flicks of his open blade.

'Trivedi, it's me.'

The priest's eye moved towards the voice.

'I've been trying to find you for days. It's tomorrow. Purnima's anniversary.'

The priest nodded, and took a puff of his cigarette.

Masterji waited. The barber oiled, massaged, and curled the priest's luxuriant moustache. He slapped talcum powder on the back of Trivedi's neck – gave a final *thwack* of his barber's towel – and discharged his customer from the blue chair.

'Trivedi, didn't you hear me? My wife's death anniversary is tomorrow.'

'… heard you… heard you…'

The freshly shaved priest, now a confluence of pleasing odours, took a long pull on his cigarette.

'Don't raise your voice now, Masterji.'

'Will you come to my home tomorrow – in the morning?'

'No, Masterji. I can't.'

Trivedi drew on his cigarette three times, and threw it down.

'But… you said you would do it… I haven't spoken to anyone else because you…'

The priest patted fragrant talcum powder from his right shoulder.

The moral evolution of an entire neighbourhood seemed compressed into that gesture. Masterji understood. Trivedi and the others had realized their own property rates would rise – the brokers must

358

have said 20 per cent each year if the Shanghai's glass façade came up. Maybe even 25 per cent. And at once their thirty-year-old ties to a science teacher had meant no more to Trivedi and the others than talcum powder on their shoulders.

'I taught your sons. *Three* of them.'

Trivedi reached for Masterji's hand, but the old teacher stepped back.

'Masterji. Don't misunderstand. It's easy to rush to conclusions, but...'

'Who was the first man to say the earth went around the sun? Anaxagoras. Not in the textbook but I taught them.'

'When your daughter died, I performed the last rites. Did I or did I not, Masterji?'

'Just tell me if you will perform my wife's one-year ritual, Trivedi.'

The baby-faced barber, resting his chin on the blue chair, had been watching the entertainment. Trivedi now addressed his appeal to him.

'Tell him, *everyone* in Vakola knows that he is under so much mental stress. I am frightened to do anything in his place. Who knows what might happen to me in there?'

'Mental stress?'

'Masterji: you are losing weight, your clothes are not clean, you talk to yourself. Ask *anyone*.'

'What about those who smeared excrement on my door? What about those who are paying thugs to attack me? Those who call themselves my neighbours. If I am under stress, what are they under?'

'Masterji, Masterji.' Trivedi turned again to the barber for some support. 'No one has attacked you. People worry about your stability when you say things like this. Sell 3A. Get rid of it. It is killing you. It is killing all of us.'

I should have told my story better, Masterji thought, on his way back to Vishram Society. *Ajwani and the others have convinced them I am losing my mind.*

He saw Mary's drunken father, silver buttons twinkling on his red shirt, lying in the gutter by Hibiscus Society like something inedible spat out by the neighbourhood.

The first honest man I have seen all day, Masterji thought, looking down at the gutter with a smile.

He took a step towards the gutter, and stopped. He remembered that there was a better place to escape to.

When he got back to Vishram, he walked on the roof, turning in circles, wanting to be as far above them all as possible.

Mani, Ajwani's assistant, knew that his boss did not want to be disturbed. Standing outside the glass door of the Renaissance Real-Estate Agency, he had seen Mrs Puri and the broker talking to each other for over half an hour. Something big was going on in there; he had been given charge of keeping Mrs Puri's Ramu occupied outside the office.

On the other hand, it *was* a girl.

He pushed open the glass door and put his head in.

'Sir...'

'Mani, didn't you hear what I said?' Ajwani winced.

Mani just stepped aside, to let the boss see what had turned up.

Ajwani's frown became a pretty smile.

Though today she wore a black salwar kameez, it was the same woman who had come dressed in that sky-blue sari the day Shanmugham had delivered the details of Mr Shah's proposal.

'Ms Swathi. Sit down, sit down. This is my neighbour, Mrs Puri.'

The girl was almost in tears.

'I came looking for you earlier, sir. I have to speak to you now, it's urgent.'

'Yes?' The broker leaned forward, his hands folded. Mrs Puri sighed. She had almost convinced Ajwani, and then *this* happens.

The girl reminded the broker. He had helped her find a place in Hibiscus Society. She was supposed to move in today. He remembered, he remembered.

There had been a lift in the Hibiscus building when she had visited with him, but when she had gone there today, the lift was not working. It would not be repaired for three months, the landlord said. 'How will my parents go up the stairs, Mr Ajwani? Mother had a hip replacement last year.'

Ajwani retreated into his chair. He pointed a finger behind his head.

'I told you to worship Information, Ms Swathi. You should have asked about the lift back then. The landlord is within his rights to keep the deposit if you cancel the lease.'

She began to sob.

'But we need that money, or how will we go looking for another place?'

Ajwani made a gesture of futility.

'I suppose you're also going to bring up the matter of the broker's fee that you gave me.'

She nodded.

'Sixteen thousand rupees. Like the landlord, I have every legal right to keep it.'

Ajwani's foot left its chappal, and opened the lowest drawer of the desk. He leaned down and brought up a bundle of cash, from which he counted off 500-rupee notes. Mrs Puri stared.

The broker counted them again, moistening his right index finger on his tongue thirty-two times; then pushed the bundle of notes across the table.

'I'll phone the landlord. Go home, Ms Swathi. Call me tomorrow, around four o'clock.'

The girl looked at him, through her sobs, with surprise.

'A rare thing in this modern age, Ms Swathi. The way you take care of your parents.'

Mrs Puri waited till the girl had left, and said: 'This is why you never became rich, Ajwani. You waste your money. You should have kept the 16,000 rupees.'

The broker rubbed his metal and plastic rings. 'Women I did well with, in life. Money, never.'

'Then become rich now, Ajwani. Be like Mr Shah for once in your life. What you did today with a pole, do again tomorrow on the terrace.'

This was where they had left off.

'I'm not frightened,' Ajwani said. 'Don't think I am.'

About to speak, Mrs Puri saw Mani, and stopped.

The broker looked at his assistant. 'Go outside and play with

Ramu,' he said. 'You shouldn't leave the boy alone out there.'

Mani sighed. He stood outside the office and pointed at passing cars and trucks; Ramu held on to the little finger of his left hand. He was still sobbing because of the way the chick's head had been crushed under Kothari Uncle's foot.

After half an hour, Mrs Puri left with her boy.

As he watched the fat woman leave, Mani thought: *What* have *they been talking about?*

When he pushed open the glass door, he found the office deserted; from the inner room beyond the Daisy Duck clock came the noise of a coconut being hacked open.

Lying next to Ramu's blue aeroplane quilt, Sanjiv Puri, who had been drawing cartoons of lizards, white mice, and spiders, now began to sketch, as if by logical progression, politicians.

As he was putting the final touches to the wavy silver hair of his favourite, ex-president Abdul Kalam, he looked up.

The lights were on in the living room: his wife had come home with his son.

'Ramu.' He put down his sketchbook and held out his arms.

Mrs Puri said: 'Play with your father later. He and I have to talk now.'

Closing Ramu's bedroom door behind her, she spoke in a soft voice.

'You can't come to Ramu's pageant tomorrow.'

'Why not?'

'Stay late in the office. Have dinner there. Use the internet. Don't come home till after ten o'clock.'

He watched her as she went to the dining table, where she began folding Ramu's freshly washed laundry.

'Sangeeta…' He stood by her. 'What is happening that I can't come to my own home until ten?'

She looked at him, and said nothing, and he understood.

'Don't be crazy. If they do it, Ajwani and the Secretary, well and good. Why should you dip your hands into it?'

'Keep your voice down.' Mrs Puri leaned her head in the direction of *you know who*. 'Ajwani is doing it. Kothari is going to hide somewhere all day long – so if Shanmugham comes in the morning, he will not be able to tell him that the Confidence Group has withdrawn its offer. And unless their letter is not handed to the Secretary of a Society in person, they cannot say they have taken back their offer. That is the law. In the evening Ajwani will do it. I'll phone him when Masterji goes up to the terrace. That's all there is to it.'

'But if anything goes wrong… it is a question of going to *jail.*'

She stopped, a blue towel over her forearm. 'And living in this building for the rest of my life is *better* than going to jail?' She flipped the towel over and folded it.

Her husband said nothing.

Ramu popped his head out of his room, and Mummy and Daddy smiled and told him to go back to bed.

'My fingers still smell,' she whispered. 'That man made me dirty my fingers. With my own son's… He made me do that. I can never forgive him.'

Mr Puri whispered: 'But tomorrow is Ramu's pageant.'

'So it's perfect,' Mrs Puri said, pushing the towels to one side, to start work on Ramu's underwear. 'No one will suspect me on a day like tomorrow. I will have to stay back at the school hall to help dismantle the pageant. Someone will remember me. Someone will get the time confused. I'm not asking you to do anything. Just stay away from home. That's all.'

Mr Puri went to the sofa, where he slapped magazines and newspapers on to the ground with his palm; then he walked over to the kitchen, where he stripped things off the fridge door, and then he shouted: 'No. I won't do it.'

His wife stood holding Ramu's underwear against her chest. She stared.

'No.' He took a step towards her. 'I'm not leaving you alone tomorrow. I'm staying here. With you.'

Letting the underwear fall, she put her fingers around her husband's neck, and – 'Oy, oy, oy' – kissed the crown of his head.

Ramu, opening his bedroom door just a bit, gaped at the show of affection between Mummy and Daddy.

Mrs Puri blushed; she pushed the boy back into his room and bolted the door from the outside.

'He isn't in his room now,' she said, putting her ear to the wall to check for any sound. 'So he's still up on the roof, then. He went up there yesterday and he went today. He will probably go tomorrow too. Ajwani will have to do it then. Up there.'

'Kothari?'

'He will say what we want him to say. When it's all over. He promised me that much.'

Mr Puri nodded. 'It could work,' he said. 'Could work.'

The sketchbook on which he had been doodling lizards and politicians lay on the table; he tore out a page.

'Here. We should write it down here. What time he goes up to the terrace and what time he comes down. This will help us tomorrow.'

'Ramu! Stop pushing the door!' Mrs Puri raised her voice; the bedroom door stopped rattling.

'Write it down?' she asked her husband.

'Why not? It's how they do it in the movies. In the English movies. They always plan the previous day. Let's take this seriously,' Mr Puri said, as if he had been the one to come up with the whole idea.

He put his ear to the wall.

'His door has opened.' He turned to his wife and whispered: 'What time is it?'

So I have failed you again, Purnima. Masterji removed his shoes, went to his bed and lay down, his arm over his face.

He controlled his tears.

His shirt was wet from walking round and round the terrace; when he turned in the bed, it stuck to his back and made him shiver. A husband who survives his wife must perform her memorial rites. But all of them had got together to strip away even this final satisfaction from him.

He bit his forearm.

How obvious now that Mr Pinto had *wanted* someone to threaten him outside the compound wall that evening. How obvious now that he and Shelley wanted the money. How obvious that the Secretary had been lying all this time about responsibility and flamingoes; he wanted money. He had been cheating them for years; he had been stealing from the funds. How obvious that Mrs Puri wanted money for herself, not for Ramu.

He covered his face in his blanket and breathed in. The game he played as a child: if you cannot see them, they cannot see you. You are safe here.

Look down – he heard a whisper.

What is down there? he whispered back.

Look at me.

Under his blanket, Masterji felt himself sliding: trapdoors had opened beneath his bed.

Now he was again on the builder's terrace on Malabar Hill, watching the darkening ocean. He heard blows like the blows of an axe. The water was ramming into Breach Candy – into the original wall that held the tides out of the great breach of Bombay.

He saw its horns rising out of the dark water: the bull in the ocean, the white bull of the ocean charging into the wall.

Now he could see the original breach in the sea wall reopen: and the waters flooding in – waves rising over prime real estate, wiping out buildings and skyscrapers. Now the white angry bull, emerging horns-first from the waves, charges. The waves have come to the edge of the towers, and flooded into them. Muscles of water smash into the Brabourne Stadium and into the Cricket Club of India; a hoof of tide has brought down the Bombay University...

A finger snapped and a voice said: 'Get up.'

He opened his eyes; he was too weak to move. Again the finger snapped: 'Up.'

I cannot go back to bed. If I lie down, I will curse my neighbours and my city again.

He opened the door and went down the stairs. The moonlight pierced the octahedronal stars of the grille; it seemed as bright as the moon he had seen that night, so many years ago, in Simla.

Pinned by a moonbeam, he leaned against the wall.

The Republic, the High Court, and the Registered Co-operative Society might be fraudulent, but the hallways of his building were not without law; something he had obeyed for sixty-one years still governed him here.

He returned to his home; he closed the door behind him.

Opening his wife's green *almirah*, Masterji knelt before the shelf with the wedding sari, and thought of Purnima.

Low, white, and nearly full, the moon moved over Vakola.

Ajwani could not stay at home on a night like this. He had walked along the highway, sat under a lamp post, then walked again, before taking an autorickshaw to Andheri, where he had dinner.

It was past eleven o'clock. After a beer at a cheap bar, he was returning along the highway in an autorickshaw. The night air lashed his face. He passed packed, box-like slum houses along the highway. Dozens of lives revealed themselves to him in seconds: a woman combing her long hair, a boy wearing a white skullcap reading a book by a powerful table lamp, a couple watching a serial on television. The autorickshaw sped over a concrete bridge. Below him, homeless men slept, bathed, played cards, fed children, stared into the distance. They were the prisoners of Necessity; he flew.

Tomorrow by this time I will be different from all of them, he thought: and his hands became dark fists.

When Masterji opened his eyes, he was still kneeling before the open green *almirah*. Sunlight had entered the room.

It was a new day: the anniversary of Purnima's death.

My legs are going to hurt, he thought, searching for something to hold on to, as he raised himself up.

He walked over the underwear lying around the washing machine and went into the living room.

It was his wife's first anniversary, but Trivedi had refused to do the rites. Where could he get them done at the last minute?

As he brushed his teeth, it seemed to him that the face in the mirror, enriched by wisdom from the foaming toothpaste, was offering him a series of counter-arguments: so what if Trivedi said no? Why a temple, why a priest? Physics experiments could be done by oneself at home: the existence of the sun and the moon, the roundness of the earth, the varying velocities of sound in solids and liquids, all these could be demonstrated in a small room.

True, he acknowledged, as he washed his face and mouth at the sink, very true.

He cupped the weak flow from the tap in his palm. It seemed that water was a part of all Hindu religious ceremonies. The Christians used it too. Muslims gargled and cleaned themselves before their *namaaz*.

He clutched a handful of water and went to the window. Sunlight too was congenial to religion. He opened the window and sprinkled water in the direction of the morning sun. Something was usually said to accompany this sprinkling. People used holy languages for this purpose. Sanskrit. Arabic. Latin. But the words came out of him in English. He said: 'I miss you, my wife.'

He sprinkled more water.

'Forgive me for not being a better husband.'

He sprinkled the last of the water into the light.

'Forgive me for not protecting you from the things I should have protected you from.'

One drop of water had fallen on Masterji's fingertip; it glowed in the morning light like a pearl.

The iridescent drop spoke to him, saying: *I am what you are made of. And in the end I am what you return to.* In between there were puzzling things a man had to do. Marry. Teach. Have children. And then his obligations were done and he would become drops of water again, free of life and its rainbow of restrictions. Death said to Masterji: *Fear me not. Purnima your wife is more beautiful than ever, she is a drop of shining water. And Sandhya your daughter is right by her side.*

Something was usually done for others in remembrance rituals. When he had performed his father's last rites in Suratkal, they had left steaming rice balls on a plantain leaf for the crows.

He came down to the compound, where Mrs Puri was clapping to keep time for Ramu; with a gold-foil sword in his hand, the boy, whose cheeks had been rouged, walked four measured steps, swished his sword, and bowed before an imaginary audience. Masterji remembered: the annual pageant.

'Good luck, Ramu,' he said.

Ramu, despite his mother's stern gaze, thrust his golden sword at Masterji.

Ajwani woke up and found himself under arrest.

Two *samurai* had taken his arms in theirs. 'Tae kwon-do time, Papa' – little Raghav brought his fist right up to his father's face. 'You've overslept.'

In brilliant white outfits embellished with Korean symbols and a small Indian flag in the upper right-hand corner, the boys arranged themselves before the dining table in kicking-and-punching positions. Though not formally trained in the martial arts, Ajwani understood the basic principles of strength and speed well enough.

'Hey-a! Hey-a!'

The two of them kicked; Father watched from the sofa, yawning.

'Harder. Much harder.'

Then the three of them sat down at the green dinner table for a breakfast of their mother's toast.

Now in their blue ties and white school uniforms, Rajeev and Raghav lined up for the spoon full of shark liver oil that their father held out for them. Wetting his fingers at the kitchen tap, he wiped shark liver oil from each boy's lips and sprinkled his face to make him laugh.

'All right. Off to school.'

Ajwani's wife, a heavy swarthy woman, was frying something in sunflower oil in the kitchen. She shouted out: 'Will you bring some *basmati* rice in the evening?'

'If I remember,' he shouted back, and slapped his armpits with Johnson's Baby Powder, before putting on a safari suit, and shutting the door behind him.

Halfway down the stairwell, he stopped and did a set of push-ups leaning against the banister.

Some time after 10 a.m., Masterji returned from the market with a packet of sweets.

He walked past the gate of Vishram Society, down to the Tamil temple. He remembered it from the evening he had gone through the slums to see Mr Shah's new buildings.

The sanctum of the temple was locked, and two old women in saris sat on its square verandah, in the centre of which a tree grew.

He put the sweet-box before the old women. 'Please think of my departed wife, Purnima, who died a year ago.'

Ripping open the plastic packaging around the sweets the old women began eating. He sat on the verandah with them. Through the grille door with the shiny padlock, he could see the small black

Ganesha idol inside the dim temple, anointed with oil and kumkum and half buried under marigolds.

He watched the old women gobble; he felt their filling stomachs refuelling her flight. Their belches and grunts were a benediction on Purnima's soul. Through the grille door, he watched the Ganesha, a distant cousin of the red idol at SiddhiVinayak. He was a jolly god, Ganesha, always game for a bit of mischief, and when the wind blew Masterji thought he heard someone whisper: 'I've been on your side the whole time, you old atheist.'

A blind man sat outside the temple with a tray that held flowers of four colours, strung into small garlands. A few red petals had flown from his tray and floated on a sunken manhole cover that had filled up with black water. Masterji thought of the beautiful bronze tray with petals floating on it that he had seen at Gaurav's home.

Water buffaloes came near the temple, coated in dust and dung, their dark bulging bellies spangled by flies.

Leaning back against the wall of the temple, he saw, through the coconut trees, Mr Shah's two buildings. The work appeared to be complete: a continuous row of windows sparkled down the side of each building. Soon, catching the angle of the setting sun, the buildings would flash like side-by-side comets. He remembered the blue tarpaulin that had covered their structures when he had last seen them; that must have been in June or July. He became aware of the passage of time, and it occurred to him that the deadline had really passed now. The fifth of October.

'It is over,' he said softly. And then, he got up and said, in the direction of Mr Shah's two buildings: 'You have lost.'

The tree in the courtyard began to shake. A boy was up in the branches, while a girl held out her blue skirt to collect what he was throwing down.

'What are you doing up there, fellow?'

The boy smiled and half opened his hand, revealing three tiny green fruits.

'And who're *you*?' he asked the girl.

She spoke into her skirt.

'What was that?'

'Sister.'

Masterji closed an eye against the sun and looked at the boy. 'Throw me one, and I won't tell the priest you're taking his fruit.'

The boy let one of the fruits slip from his palm; Masterji caught and chewed on it. Citrus-like and sour, it reminded him of things he had once climbed trees for. That was before his thread ceremony in Suratkal at the age of fourteen, a full day's business of chanting Sanskrit in front of a sacred fire and blinking and coughing in the wood smoke, at the end of which a lean, geriatric, crow-like priest spoke to him the formulaic words of wisdom for coming-of-age Brahmin boys: 'This means no more climbing trees for fruit, my son. No more stoning dogs, my son. No more teasing girls, my son.' Then the priest had concluded by saying: 'And now you are a man.'

But that had not been true. Only now, at the age of sixty-one, did he feel like a man.

'Help us down, Grandfather,' the boy said, and Masterji steadied his waist as he climbed down the branches. The boy and his sister divided the spoils; Masterji watched and wished Ronak were here.

He thought of that evening at Crawford Market, when he had seen the light behind the buildings and pledged to fight Mr Shah.

But that fight was over. The deadline had passed, and that builder would go somewhere else. What was he expected to do from now on?

The residue of citrus on his tongue had turned bitter. He covered his face with his hands, and closed his eyes.

Mrs Puri applied mascara, fluttering her lashes to even the colour. In a corner, Ramu fluttered his eyelashes too.

Boxing with him all the way, Rum-pum-pum-pum-pum-pum, Mrs Puri led him down to 1B and pressed the bell.

When Mrs Rego opened her door, Mrs Puri stopped boxing with Ramu, and asked: 'Didn't you tell me you were going to your sister's place this evening? The one who lives in Bandra?'

'No... I didn't tell you that.'

Mrs Puri smiled.

'You *should* go to see her, Mrs Rego. And you should take my Ramu with you, too.'

'But… I promised the boys who play cricket at the Tamil temple I would take them to the beach.'

'This is a favour I ask of you as a neighbour. Have I ever asked you, in all these years, to take care of Ramu?'

Mrs Rego looked from Ramu to his mother, waiting for an explanation.

'Ramu has to be David, Slayer of Goliath, in the school pageant. I will have to stay back to help them remove the stage decorations until nine o'clock.'

'But Ramu can stay with me right here.'

Mrs Puri put her hand on her neighbour's shoulder.

'I want you to go to your sister's house. It's a simple thing, isn't it?'

The five-second rule. As children in Bandra, Mrs Rego and her sister Catherine had played it each time a chicken leg or a slice of mango had fallen to the floor. Pick it up before a count of five and you did not have to worry about germs. You would stay safe. She remembered this now.

Saying, 'I'd be happy to do this for you' – one, two, three, four – Mrs Rego closed the door.

'Be brave, Ramu. I have to leave you with Communist Aunty. Mummy must help the other Mummys clean the stage after the pageant – or who else will take responsibility?'

Ramu hid inside his aeroplane quilt and sulked with the Friendly Duck.

Sitting beside her son, Mrs Puri checked her mobile phone, which had just beeped. Ajwani had sent her a text message: 'Going city. Back 6 clock.'

She knew exactly which part of the city he was going to.

Falkland Road.

Her brother Vikram had been in the Navy, and in the mess they had been issued with bottles of Old Monk rum every week. It brought the heat into the blood. Men performing bold physical action needed heat.

In her mind's eye she saw Ajwani crouching on the terrace, now moving fleetfoot behind Masterji, until the time came for the push. Heat: a man needed it for these things. If he had to go to Falkland Road for his heat, then so be it.

An arm slid out from the aeroplane quilt and bunched the bangles on Mrs Puri's forearm together, until her wrist was plated with gold like a warrior's. She shook her arm, and the bangles trinkled down; the sweet music drew Ramu, beaming like sunrise, out of his quilt.

Up and down his mother's forearm he rubbed her golden bangles. Her flesh grew warm and the hairs on her forearm were singed from the friction.

Mrs Puri wanted to wince. She smiled and let her son continue to play.

Mumtaz Kudwa called her husband some time after noon to say she had overheard Mrs Puri asking Mrs Rego to take care of Ramu in the evening. And then the Secretary knocked on the door to say that no one was to leave the building after nine o'clock.

'What are they going to do to Masterji this time?' Kudwa asked his wife.

'I don't know,' she said. 'I thought they would have told you.'

'They always leave me out. They didn't tell me when they got the duplicate keys done… what do you think I should do – should I go to Sangeeta-ji and ask her what is going on?'

Mumtaz started to say something but stopped, and settled on the old formula: 'It's up to you. You're the man of the house.'

Typical, he thought, stroking Mariam's hair as he sat in his cybercafé, typical. A man has a right to expect his wife to make a decision for him now and then, but not Ibrahim Kudwa. As alone after marriage as he was before marriage.

On a corner of his table was the black helmet of his new Bajaj Pulsar. He wished he had listened to Mumtaz and waited until the deadline before buying the bike: if they didn't get the money now, how would he pay its monthly instalments?

If only you were older, he thought, bouncing Mariam on his knee. *If only* you *could tell your father what to do.*

He looked at the helmet.

Now he saw it creeping over his table again: the black swamp. He heard his neighbours standing behind him, and yelling for him to reach into it.

Little Mariam cried. Her father had banged his fist on his desk and shouted: 'No.'

Giving instructions to Arjun, his assistant, to double-lock the door, he shut his internet café and went home with his daughter.

Something very bad was going to happen to his Society this evening: unless he stopped it from happening.

After eating lunch in his office at two o'clock, Ajwani had taken the train into the city; he had brought along his copy of the *Times of India* real-estate classifieds to read on the journey.

He got off at Charni Road. Grant Road would have been closer, but he wanted to see the ocean before seeing the girls.

He crossed Marine Drive to the ocean wall and stood on it. Except for a rag-picker down among the tetrapod rocks, he was alone.

All his life he had dreamed of something grand – going across the *Kala Paani* to a new country. Like Vasco da Gama. Like Columbus.

'Just a push,' he said aloud. He practised pushing a phantom body off the ocean wall into the rocks, and then did it again.

At Chowpatty beach he crossed the road to stop at Café Ideal for an ice-cold mug of draught beer. Done with his drink, he was startled to find a phrase written all over the *Times of India* real-estate page: 'Just a push'. Ripping the paper to shreds, he asked the waiter to make sure it went into the waste bin.

Outside, he hailed a taxi and said: 'Falkland Road.'

Marine Drive is flooded with light from ocean and open sky; but a simple change of gear, three turns on the road, and the ocean breeze is gone, the sky contracts, and old buildings darken the vista. When you have gone deep enough into this other Bombay, you will come to Falkland Road.

Ajwani stopped the taxi, and paid his fare with three ten-rupee notes from a wad in his pocket.

'I don't have any change,' the driver said.

Ajwani told him not to worry. One and two rupee coins wouldn't matter after today.

He put the wad of notes back in his pocket, patted it, and felt better. Having money made things so much simpler, as one grew older.

There were friendly hotels by the Santa Cruz station and all along the highway, but it would do a man no good to look for pleasure where he might be recognized. In the old days – oh, five, six years ago – Ajwani went to Juhu and visited a pretty young actress there once or twice a month. Then real-estate prices went up in Juhu. Even those holes-in-the-wall became too costly for that actress and the other nice girls like her. They packed up and went north: to Versova, Oshiwara, Lokhandwala. Ajwani's trips grew longer. Then real-estate prices went up in the north too. The girls moved to Malad, too far for him. And that wouldn't be the end of it. Sooner or later a man would have to drive all the way to Pune for a blowjob. Real-estate speculation was destroying Bombay.

Thank God, Ajwani thought, *there will always be Falkland Road*.

Greying multi-storeyed buildings stood on either side of the road, each collapsing in some way. Some of the windows had been gouged out, and men in *banians* sat in the open holes, looking down. Ajwani passed dental shops with plaster-of-Paris dentures on display, dim restaurants as greasy as the biryani they served, and cinema theatres with garish film posters (collages of violent action and sympathetic cleavage) outside which young migrant men stood in queues, withering in the heat and the shouting of theatre guards. Muck was congealed in between the buildings, and spilled on to the road. As if summoned for contrast, a row of silvery horse carriages shaped like swans, the kind that took tourists on joyrides near the Gateway of India, had been parked by the rubbish. Neither the horses nor the drivers were around, but women leaned on the carriages, sucking their teeth at Ajwani.

He smiled back at them.

This early in the day, Kamathipura would be quiet, and the second floor of the discreet building behind the Taj Hotel would be closed, and Congress House might or might not accept gentlemen callers. But Falkland Road was always open for business. The women waited in bright blue doorways, squatted on thresholds, and stepping forward from the silvery carriages taunted Ajwani.

A girl in a green petticoat sat hunched over in a bright blue doorway; cigarette smoke rose up her face like sideburns.

He was about to speak to her when he heard metallic noise, and saw flashes of light behind the prostitute.

Smiling at the warm green petticoat to indicate that he'd be back, Ajwani took a few steps down the lane behind her brothel.

The bylane, like the others around the red-light district, was busy with the hammering of iron and the hiss of white-blue oxyacetylene flame. In an economy typical of the city, the metal-working district is packed into the mazy lanes around Falkland Road – the pounding of steel and sex combined in the same postcode. Ajwani had seen the metal-cutting shops in passing many times before.

Now he walked about the glaring and hissing workshops like a man who had stumbled into a new country. Outside one shop, the metal worker lifted up his rusty visor and stared at him.

Ajwani turned away from his gaze. He walked further down the lane. Strings of glossy ribbons led down to a bulbous green mosque at the end. An acrid industrial stench. Behind a chink in a blue door, a man in a visor squatted on the floor and seared a rod with a flame. Metal grilles for windows were stacked outside another shop. A worker stood tapping on the grilles; a customer in a grey suit was listening to him.

'… a flower pattern in the iron rods is normal, it's free. But this thing you want, two flowers joining together… I'll add two rupees per kilogram…'

'Oh, that's too much,' the customer said. 'Too much, too much.'

Suddenly both the worker and the customer turned and faced Ajwani.

He walked to the end of the lane. Right in front of the green mosque, he saw a buffalo tied to a tree; the restless head and horns of the animal emerged from the deep shade and then drew back into it.

A door opened in what he had thought was the mosque wall. A piece of corrugated iron roofing emerged from it. Two bare-chested men carried it in front of Ajwani, and he saw his own shadow ripple over the folds of iron.

He stared at the disappearing shadow; he shivered.

'It is not just a push,' he said aloud, and turned, to make sure the buffalo had not overheard him.

Ajwani sneaked past the workshops to the main road. Leaning on the horseless silver carriages, the prostitutes sucked their teeth for him as he left Falkland Road. His eyes full of oxyacetylene, his sinuses full of fumes, the broker staggered back towards Marine Drive.

He still heard hammer blows from the workshops that were far behind him; his nose still burned, as if reality had been brought red-hot right up to it. He stopped for breath. Ahead, foreshortened by the perspective, the massed buildings skidded like a single lightning bolt of stone and masonry towards Chowpatty beach. The plunge in the city's topography worked a corresponding effect in Ajwani's mind; all other thoughts fell away, isolating a lone enormous truth.

... *it is not 'just a push'. It is killing a man.*

A rubber ball struck the demon's face painted on the wall of the Tamil temple.

Masterji opened his eyes, and stood up in the shade of the fruit tree. He realized he had gone to sleep. As he rubbed his eyes, he heard a woman's voice booming: 'Rakesh: is that how to bowl? Don't you watch TV?'

Masterji hid behind the tree; he had recognized the voice.

'Yes, Aunty. Sorry.'

'I am not your aunty.'

Half a dozen boys converged around Mrs Rego. Sunil and Sarah were with her, and also Ramu, who was dressed in a red shirt, with make-up on his face and a golden sword in his hand. The pageant day must have ended. Why was Mrs Puri not around? Why had she left Ramu with Mrs Rego, of all people? But he no longer had any right to ask about their lives.

'... boys, a promise is a promise, I know, but I just can't go today. I *will* take you to the beach, and all of us will have sugarcane juice there. In the meantime I hope all of you have been staying out of trouble and...'

'Aunty, no trip to the beach *and* a lecture? That's not fair, is it?'

'I am sorry, Vikram. I will take all of you one day.'

The cricket game continued after Mrs Rego left. One of the boys chased the ball into the temple courtyard.

'Masterji,' he said. 'I'm Mary's son. Timothy.'

Taking the old teacher by the hand he brought him out to show the other boys. At once, two of them ran away.

'What happened?' Masterji asked.

'Oh, that Kumar, he's a strange boy. Dharmendar too.'

Timothy smiled.

'Will you take us to the beach, Masterji? Mrs Rego Aunty was supposed to take us.'

'Why do you want to go to the beach?'

'Why do you think? To play cricket there.'

'So go on your own.'

'Well, someone has to pay for bus fare. And sugarcane juice afterwards, Masterji.'

'Ah,' he said. 'Maybe I'll take you there one of these days. If you can answer this question: why are there tides at the beach?'

'No reason.'

'There is a reason for everything.' Masterji pointed to the boy who had been bowling at Timothy. 'What is your name?'

'Vijay.'

'Do you know the reason, Vijay?'

He picked up a red stone, went to the wall of the Tamil temple, and drew a circle above the demon's wide-open mouth.

'This is the earth. Our planet. In infinite space.'

Masterji saw shadows on the wall – he felt sweat and heat nearby – he realized that they had all gathered behind him.

'Our earth is that small?' someone asked.

About to reply, Masterji stopped and said: 'I can start a school here. An evening school.'

'Evening school?' Timothy asked. 'For *who*?'

The boys looked at one another; Masterji looked at them and smiled, as if the answer were obvious.

The sun had slipped in between two skyscrapers on Malabar Hill; the nearer of the buildings had become a flickering silhouette, a thing alternately of dark and light, like the lowest visible slab of a ghat descending into a river.

Ajwani sat on the sea wall of Marine Drive, looking at the tetrapod rocks below him and the waves washing around them.

He had been thinking for over an hour, ever since he had come down here from Falkland Road. It all made sense to him now. So *this* was why Shah paid Tower B ahead of time. To get everyone at Vishram desperate. This was why he did nothing when the story ran in the newspaper. He wanted *them* to do it.

'And making Shanmugham tell me his life's story,' Ajwani said, aloud, surprising a young Japanese man who had sat down by his side to take photographs of the city.

Ajwani thought about the details of Mr Shah's story. Now it seemed to him that something was wrong with the information. If Shah had come to Bombay with only twelve rupees and eighty paise, and no shoes on his feet, how did he manage to open a grocery store in Kalbadevi? There was a father in the village – he must have sent him money. Men do have a sense of responsibility to their first wife's sons. Ajwani struck his forehead with his palm. These self-made millionaires always hide a part of the story. The truth was as obvious as the ocean.

'It's been cat and mouse. From the start.'

And the cat had always been Dharmen Shah.

I'm trapped, Ajwani thought, as he walked on the ocean wall towards Churchgate station. Mrs Puri and the Secretary were waiting for him. He, more than anyone else, had moved his *nothing* Society to this point. He could not fail them now. He looked down and thought if only he could live there, by the crabs, among the rocks by the breaking water.

Inside the station, Ajwani paid five rupees for a white plastic cup

379

of instant coffee. His stomach needed help. All that industrial smoke from the metallurgical shops. Sipping the coffee, he walked to his platform; the Borivali local was about to depart.

Now he had industrial smoke *and* instant coffee in his stomach. He felt worse with each shake and jerk of the train.

He cursed his luck. Of all the things to pick up from Falkland Road – all the horrible names he had worried about for all these years – gonorrhoea, syphilis, prostatitis, Aids – he had to pick this up: a conscience.

'You are at the *Kala Paani*,' he told himself. 'You *have* to cross it. *Have* to be one of those who get things done in life.'

A fellow passenger was staring at him. Lizard-like, stout, thick-browed, massively lipped, the man clutched a small leather bag in his powerful forearms: his eyes bulged as they focused on Ajwani.

The lizard-man yawned.

When he shut his mouth, he had taken on the face of the managing director of the Confidence Group. In a moment the train compartment was full of Shahs.

'Fresh air, please. Fresh…' Ajwani moved through the crowd to the open door of the moving train. 'Please please let me breathe.'

Migrants had squatted on the wasteland at the edge of the tracks; they had turned it into a vegetable patch, seeding and watering it. Ajwani held on to the rod in the open door of the train. Behind the little green fields he could see the blue tents they lived in. The sight was chastening; his stomach wanted to call out to them.

He began to vomit on to the tracks.

The lights were coming on in the market as the Secretary scraped his shoes on the coir mat outside the Renaissance Real-Estate office.

'Come in, sir,' Mani had said. Ajwani had told him what to do when Kothari arrived.

He showed the Secretary past the Daisy Duck clock into the inner room and told him to sit on the bed.

'Your boss isn't here?' the Secretary said, looking at the empty cot. 'I was hiding in my mother-in-law's house all day long. In Goregaon. Near the Topi-wala building. I just got back to Vakola. Where is he?'

Mani shrugged.

'He isn't even picking up the phone. Maybe I should wait outside for him.'

'It's better that you wait here, sir, isn't it?' Mani's eyes shone with their usual half-knowledge of his master's dealings.

The Secretary sat on the cot in the inner room, looking at the wicker basket full of coconuts and wondering if the broker had counted them. A few minutes later the door creaked open.

'You?' Mrs Puri asked, as she came into the inner room. 'You're not supposed to be here.'

'I kept worrying about you, Mrs Puri. I came to check that you were all right,' the Secretary said.

'Better you leave us alone here, Kothari. All we want from you is an alibi.'

The Secretary of Vishram Society shook his head. 'And what of my responsibility to you, Mrs Puri? My father said, a man who lives for himself is an animal. I'm going to make sure you're all right. Now tell me, where is Ajwani?'

'In the city,' Mrs Puri said. 'Falkland Road.'

'On a day like this?'

'Especially on a day like this. That's the kind of man he is.'

'Let me wait until he comes back. It's my responsibility to do so. Don't tell me to go away.'

'You're not such a bad Secretary after all,' Mrs Puri said, as she sat on the cot.

Kothari kicked the wicker basket in the direction of Mrs Puri, who kicked it back, and this became a game between them. Someone knocked on the door of the inner room.

When the Secretary opened it, he saw Sanjiv Puri.

'What are you doing here?' Mrs Puri hissed. Her husband walked in, and along with him came Ibrahim Kudwa.

'He rang the bell and asked for you.'

'I know what is going on,' Kudwa said. 'No one told me, but I'm not as stupid as you think. And I know you didn't tell me because you thought a Muslim wouldn't want to help you.'

'Nothing is going on, Ibby.'

Kudwa sat beside her on the cot. 'Don't treat me like a child. Ajwani is going to do *something*. Tonight.'

The Secretary looked at the Puris.

'What's the point of hiding it from Ibrahim?'

'We know it's dangerous, Ibby. That is why we kept you out of it.' Mrs Puri reached for his forearm and stroked it. 'The only reason. We know you have Mumtaz and the children to take care of.'

Her husband moved protectively in front of her. 'Will you tell the police about us now?'

'No!' Ibrahim Kudwa winced. He slapped his breast pocket, brimming with heart-shaped antacid tablets. 'You're my *friends*. Don't you know me by now? I want to save you. How can Ajwani get away with this?' he pleaded with folded palms. 'Ram Khare will be watching from his booth. Someone passing on the road might see. Masterji might cry out. It's a trap – can't you see? The builder has trapped all of you. From the day he paid the money to Tower B ahead of schedule: this is what he wanted you to do.'

'And he's *right*, Ibby,' Mrs Puri said. 'That man walked into Bombay with nothing on his feet, and look at him now. And look at *us*. We should have done this a long time now.'

'Don't raise your voice,' the Secretary said. 'Speak to Ajwani when he gets here, Ibrahim. Me, I don't want the money. I just want to make sure that no one goes to jail. That is my sacred responsibility here.'

The lynx-lines spread wide around his eyes; he grinned.

He picked up the big crescent knife from the basket and scraped it against the nuts.

'Ajwani is an expert at this. I'm not quite sure how it's done.' Selecting a large coconut, which was still attached to the brown connective tissue of the tree it had been hacked from, Kothari held it out at arm's length: then he stuck the knife into it. Three hesitant strokes, then it came to him. *Thwack thwack thwack.* The white flesh of the coconut exposed; fresh water spilling out.

'Not for me,' Kudwa said, pointing to the antacid tablets in his translucent shirt pocket. 'Bad stomach.'

'Have it, Ibrahim. All of us are going to. It will cure a weak stomach.'

Kudwa had a sip, and then offered the coconut to Mrs Puri, who sipped and passed it to her husband. When he was done, the Secretary reached in with his knife, and carved out the white flesh of the coconut, which he offered to Mrs Puri.

'It's there, why waste it?'

'All right.'

Mrs Puri scooped the coconut flesh with her fingers, and passed it to Kudwa, who did the same, and licked the white slop off his fingers.

The Secretary pitched the coconut into the corner. Kudwa pointed at the knife that he had just placed over the coconuts.

'Is Ajwani going to do it with that...?'

The Secretary pushed the basket away with his foot.

'We don't know anything about it, Ibby. We're just here to give Ajwani some support.'

'That's right,' the Secretary said. 'We'll say we were here with him when it happened.'

They sat there, in the inner room: the chiming of the Daisy Duck clock from outside told them it was a quarter past seven.

Kudwa stretched his legs.

'What is that you're humming, Ibrahim?'

With sly fingers the Secretary pinched the strip of heart-shaped antacid tablets from the shirt pocket and examined them.

'"Hey Jude".'

The Secretary put the antacid tablets back into Kudwa's shirt pocket. 'What is that?'

'You don't know? How is it possible?'

'I'm a Mohammad Rafi man, Ibrahim.'

'Here,' Kudwa said. 'It's an easy song. Here, I'll show you.' Clapping his hands together, he began to sing.

'Voice is so beautiful, Ibby,' Mrs Puri said.

He blushed.

'Oh, no, no. It's terrible now, Sangeeta-ji. I don't practise. But you should have heard it in college...' Kudwa moved his hand over his head, to indicate past glories.

'Should I go on with "Hey Jude", or do you want something in Hindi?'

He waited for an answer from Mrs Puri. Standing at the door of the inner room, she was telling Mani: 'Close the outer door. And don't answer the phone for any reason. Do you understand?'

Returning after dark, Masterji stopped in the stairwell of Vishram Society; his red fingers reached for the wall.

By the banister on which his daughter used to slide down on her way to school (her father upstairs shouting: 'Don't do that, you'll fall'), he said aloud: 'I am starting an evening school. For the boys who play cricket by the temple.'

At once he felt something he had almost forgotten: a sensation of fear. 'Have to get checked for diabetes tomorrow,' he reminded himself. 'It's just a question of taking tablets and watching the sweets. You'll be fine.'

He kept going up the stairs to the fifth floor, where he opened the door that led to the roof terrace.

Firecrackers were exploding in the distance. *The wedding of a rich man*, Masterji thought. Or perhaps it was an obscure festival. Incandescent rockets and whirligigs and corkscrews shot through the night sky: Masterji put both hands on the short wall of the terrace. He heard a snatch of what he thought was band music.

'We beat Mr Shah,' he wanted to shout, so loudly that the people celebrating could hear, and celebrate louder.

He wished he could go to where the rockets were bursting: and soar over the fireworks, over Santa Cruz, over the churches and beaches of Bandra, over the temple at SiddhiVinayak and the darkened race course at Mahalakshmi, until he alighted at Crawford Market. There he would look for that bearded day-labourer and fall asleep by his side, adding to the numbers of those who were not alone tonight.

Mr Pinto did not hear the phone, but its ringing pierced through the cotton wool to reach his wife's more sensitive ears. She shook his shoulder until he unplugged his ears and reached for the receiver: it might be the children calling from America.

For an instant he thought the threatening calls were starting again. It was the same voice.

'Pinto? Don't you know me? It's Ajwani.'

Mr Pinto breathed out. 'You frightened me.' He looked at the clock. 'It's eight fifteen.'

('Is it Tony?' Mrs Pinto whispered. 'Deepa?')

The thin voice on the phone said: 'No one else is picking up, Pinto. It's all up to you.'

'What are you talking about, Ajwani? You're frightening me.'

'Do you know where I am? In Dadar. I can't leave the station. The hand shakes. It took me an hour to pick up the phone.'

'The Secretary told us to stay in bed and wear ear-cotton tonight, Ajwani. We are watching television. Good night.'

'... Pinto... tell them it's a mistake, Pinto. You must tell them it's a mistake.'

'What are you talking about?'

'Tell them not to do it. We can all live together in the building like before. Tell Mrs Puri. Tell the Secretary.'

Mr Pinto put the phone down.

'Who was that?' his wife asked.

'Do *not*,' he said, 'make me pick up the phone again tonight. Do not.'

He took the phone off the hook.

He and Shelley watched their favourite Hindi TV serial, in which the acting was so exaggerated, and the zoom-in camera so frequently used, that an absence of sound only mildly inhibited one's understanding of the plot.

Mr Pinto folded his arms in front of the TV and watched. On a piece of paper by the side of his sofa, he had written:

$100,000 x 2

and

$200,000 x 1

*

385

The Daisy Duck clock outside chimed nine o'clock. In the inner room of the Renaissance Real-Estate Agency, Kudwa was singing 'A Hard Day's Night', while the Secretary was slapping his thighs in time.

'Ajwani is not coming.' Mrs Puri stood up from the cot and straightened her sari. 'Something has happened to him.'

'So?' Kudwa stopped singing. 'It's over, isn't it?'

Without looking at each other, Mrs Puri and her husband held hands.

'We can't waste this chance, Ibby. It's for Ramu.'

'I can't let you two do it on your own.' The Secretary got up. 'I'll make sure no one's watching. That's my responsibility. And you, Ibrahim. Will you go to the police?'

Ibrahim Kudwa blinked, as if he couldn't understand the Secretary's words. 'You are my neighbours of nine years,' he said.

The Secretary embraced him. 'You were always one of us, Ibrahim. From the first day. Now go home and sleep.'

Kudwa shook his head.

'Nine years together. If you're going to jail, I'm going to jail too.'

It was decided that the Puris would leave first. The back door that led from the inner room to a side alley closed behind them.

Kothari's mobile phone rang a few minutes later.

'Masterji is on the terrace. Ram Khare is not in his booth. Come.'

They went out through the back door. They crossed the market. On the way to the Society, Kudwa said: 'Maybe we *should* ask him. If he'll sign.'

Both stopped. To their left, a paper kite had floated down and collapsed on the road.

The Secretary moved, but not Ibrahim Kudwa; the Hindu holy man was sleeping by the whitewashed banyan outside his cyber-café. A cyclostyled advertisement had been pasted over his head:

STRONGLY SCENTED PHENYL.
DISINFECTS. FRESHENS YOUR HOUSE.
BUY DIRECT.
170 RS FOR FIVE LITRES.

If only, Kudwa thought, *I could inhale the cleansing scent of disinfectant right now.* He looked up and saw the dark star from last Christmas over his café.

'Do you think… they expect me to come all the way to the Society?'

'What are you talking about, Ibrahim?'

'I mean, do Mrs Puri and Mr Puri expect me to come all the way? Or would they know I was being supportive if I came this far and went back?'

'Ibrahim, I expect you to come with me all the way. We have to make sure Mr and Mrs Puri are safe. We're not *doing* anything.'

The door of the cyber-café trembled. Kudwa realized that it had not been doubled-bolted from the inside. How many times had he told Arjun, someone could pick the lock from the outside and steal the computers unless he…

'*Ibrahim.* I need you.'

'Coming.'

With Vishram Society in sight, the two men were spotted.

'It's Trivedi. He's coming this way. We should go back.'

'He won't say a thing tomorrow. I know this man.'

Trivedi, bare-chested except for his shawl, smiled at the men, and passed them.

When they got to the gate, the Secretary looked up and said: 'He's *not* on the terrace.'

They unlatched the gate and tiptoed through the compound, the Secretary darting into his office for a few seconds, leaving Ibrahim Kudwa rubbing his hands by the noticeboard.

'What do you want that for?' he asked, when Kothari emerged with a roll of Scotch tape.

'Go into the office,' the Secretary whispered, 'and bring the hammer with you. It's sitting next to the typewriter.'

Mrs Puri was waiting for them at the top of the stairs. Her husband stood behind her.

'He just returned from the terrace and closed his door. You men took too long.'

'Do we call it off?' Kudwa asked. 'Another day?'

'No. Do you have the key, Kothari?'

The Scotch tape was not the only thing the Secretary had brought from the office. He inserted the spare key to 3A into the hole and struggled with it. They heard the sound of a television serial from the Pintos' room.

'Should we ask him, one more time, if he will sign?'

'Shut up, Ibrahim. Just stay there and watch the door.'

The door opened. Masterji had gone to sleep in his living room, his feet on the teakwood table, the Rubik's Cube by his chair.

Kudwa came in behind the others and closed the door. The Secretary, moving to the chair, cut a piece of Scotch tape and pressed it over Masterji's mouth.

That awoke the sleeping man. He ripped the Scotch tape off his mouth.

'Kothari? How did you get in?'

'You *have* to agree now, Masterji. Right now.'

'Think of Gaurav,' Mrs Puri asked. 'Think of Ronak. Say "Yes." *Now.*'

'Get out,' the old man said. 'All of you get out of my—'

The Secretary moved before he could finish the sentence: he cut another slice of Scotch tape and tried to stick it over the old man's mouth. Masterji pushed the Secretary back. Mr Puri stood stiff near the door.

'Kothari, don't touch him,' Ibrahim Kudwa warned.

Masterji, recognizing the voice of his protector, got up and began to turn in his direction.

'Ibby,' Mrs Kudwa said. 'Ibby.'

At once, Ibrahim Kudwa lifted the hammer he had brought from the Secretary's office, lunged forward, and hit Masterji on the crown of his head. Who, more from surprise than anything else, fell back into his chair with such force that it toppled over and his head landed hard on the floor. Masterji lay there like that, unable to move, though he saw things with clarity. Ibrahim Kudwa stared with an open mouth; the hammer dropped from his hand. *I should reach for the hammer*, Masterji thought, but the Secretary lunged and picked it up. Now he felt a weight on his chest: Kothari, pressing a knee on his torso, turned the hammer upside down and stubbed it on his forehead using both his hands. It hurt. He tried to shout, but he heard only a groan from his mouth. Now something, or someone, sat on his legs, and he lost control of them; he was aware that Kothari was pounding his forehead with the hammer again and again. The blows were landing somewhere far away, like stones falling on the surface of a lake he was deep inside. He thought of a line from the Mahabharata: '... King Dhritharashtra's heart was like a forest lake, warm on the surface but icy at the bottom.' Kothari stopped and took a breath. *Poor man's arms must be aching by now*, Masterji thought. He was sure he had never seen anyone move as fast as Kothari was moving with the hammer, except for the boy at the McDonald's on Linking Road when he lifted French fries from the hot oil, slammed them into the metal trough, and put the empty container back in the oil. Then the hammer hit his forehead again. 'Kothari. Wait.' Now Sanjiv Puri came from the bedroom with a large dark thing, which he lowered on to Masterji's face. When the dark thing touched his nose, Masterji understood. Yes. The pillow from his bed. It pressed down on his nose and crushed his moustache: he understood that Sanjiv Puri was sitting on it. His legs thrashed: not to free themselves, but to take him down to the bottom of the lake faster. He was in very cool and black water now.

'He's unconscious. Sanjiv, enough. Get up.'

Sanjiv Puri looked at his wife, who was sitting on Masterji's legs, and then at Ibrahim Kudwa, who was watching things with an open mouth.

'Quickly. You take the feet, Kothari will take the head,' Mrs Puri told her husband. 'Ibby, pick up that hammer. Don't leave it here.'

Kudwa, rubbing his forearms, stood still. 'Oy, oy, oy,' he said.

'Wait,' Sanjiv Puri said. 'First put some more tape on his mouth. In case he wakes up.'

Kothari did so. Then the two men lifted Masterji's body, and moved towards the door. Mr Puri winced: 'I stepped on something.' His wife kicked the Rubik's Cube out of their path.

She opened the door for the men, and checked the corridor.

'Wait for the lift. I've hit the button.'

'It never works, let's take the stairs, there's two strong men here. He has lost a lot of weight.'

'It was working in the morning. Wait.'

Mrs Puri jabbed the 'call' button again and again.

Sanjiv Puri had given up on the lift, and had begun moving with Masterji's feet (his end of the dazed body) towards the stairs, when the machine clicked – the whirls and wheezes began – and a circle of light moved up towards them.

His wife held the door open from the outside until the three bodies were in. The Secretary managed to reach the button for the fifth floor. The two men saw, in the round white light on the roof of the lift, three tiny dark shapes. Wasps, which must have flown into the light a long time ago: six undecomposed wings.

When they reached the fifth floor, Sanjiv Puri prepared to press against the lift door; but it swung open of its own accord. His wife, despite her bulk, had come up the stairs faster than they had.

While they brought the body out of the lift, she pushed open the door leading to the roof terrace.

'We'll never take him up that way,' the Secretary said, looking at the steep narrow staircase.

'One step at a time. You can do it,' Mrs Puri said, from above them. 'One step at a time.'

The two men put the body down and changed positions. Sanjiv Puri, the stronger of the two, took the head this time. The Secretary followed with the feet. One step at a time. Pigeons scattered on the terrace as they came out.

'Mrs Puri…' the Secretary panted, 'make sure no one is sitting down there in parliament…'

The wall of the terrace was three feet high. Mrs Puri looked down.

'He's opened his eyes. Do you have the hammer here?'

'No, I left it in the room.'

'Why didn't you bring it up with you?'

'You never told me to…'

'Oh, stop it,' Mrs Puri said. 'Get the work done.'

The two men staggered with the body, which had begun to squirm, to the edge of the terrace; on a count of three, they heaved it up and pushed.

'Why isn't it going over?'

'He's awake again. He's holding on to the terrace with his hand. Push harder. Push.'

Watching the struggle, Mrs Puri joined in, and pressed her back and buttocks against the stone that had blocked her happiness for so long.

Now, when he opened his eyes, he could not tell if he were dead or alive; these men seemed to be demons, though kindly, who were forcing his body to budge from some place between life and death where it was stuck.

And this was because he was neither good nor bad enough; and neither strong nor weak enough. He had lost his hands; he had lost his legs; he could not speak. Yet everything he had to do was right here, in his head. He thought of Gaurav, his son, his living flesh. 'Help me,' he said.

And then he realized that the thing that was blocking his passage was cleared, and he was falling; his body had begun its short earthly flight – which it completed almost instantaneously – before Yogesh Murthy's soul was released for its much longer flight over the oceans of the other world.

Down on the ground it lay, sprawled, in perfect imitation of a suicide's corpse.

Loose strands of hair fell down the sides of Kothari's bald head; he rearranged them into a comb-over.

'We have to go back and find that hammer, Mrs Puri. And where is Ibrahim? Is he still in the room? What is he doing there? Mrs Puri, are you listening to me?'

'He's still alive,' she said. 'He's moving down there.'

The Secretary was out of breath. So Sanjiv Puri ran down the stairs to the fifth floor, took the lift, and burst out of the entranceway. He stood by the body, turned his head upwards and shook it. The movement had stopped. It was just a death spasm.

A corona of dark liquid surrounded the head; Mrs Puri thought she saw things coming out of the skull. It was done.

'Scotch tape…' she hissed at her husband from the terrace. 'The Scotch tape on his mouth. Quick-ly. Ram Khare is coming back.'

A special night. He usually had a quarter of Old Monk rum in his room, but tonight he had gone into a bar and said: 'Whisky. Royal Stag.'

Why not? It was the evening of 5 October. The fight in his Society had to be over now. Even if you thought that the builder had delayed by one day, that was yesterday. Any man who gave his word that he would not extend the deadline would lose face if he did so after today.

The TV screen in the bar was playing a movie featuring Praveena Kumari, a famous 'sex bomb' of the 1980s, now making a come-back in a film called *Dance, Dance*. Ram Khare had never been a fan. Not curvy enough.

He had his whisky and asked for another.

The truth be told, he thought, *I was always hoping that Masterji would defeat the builder. Where would I find work at another building at my age?*

Now he was hungry.

A fine meal of chow mein, fried in a large black wok, at a street-side stand run by Gurkhas. Ram Khare sat on a bench next to the wok, and ate with a plastic fork, splashing a vivid green sauce and ketchup on the chow mein.

Done with his dinner, he washed his mouth and headed back to Vishram.

He had unlatched the gate and was walking to his booth, when he saw a human being lying near the entranceway of the Society.

Catherine D'Mello-Myer's flat in the Bandra Reclamation was a warm anarchy of left-wing academic journals and foreign toys.

Her three children and their two cousins had rampaged through the kitchen and the bathroom before she ordered them into the TV room, where they had turned on the Sony PlayStation.

Now she sat at the dinner table with her sister and the sweet imbecile boy holding his green sign saying 'NO NOISE'. His sword had become a piece of crushed cardboard on the floor.

Catherine had never seen her sister like this.

Mrs Rego sat at the table with her right hand lying on a black mobile phone.

Frank, Catherine's American husband, looked out from their bedroom. He gestured with his head towards the children screaming at their PlayStation.

She glared at him.

Some things men could not understand. Her sister had never done this before – come here at such short notice, bringing along her children and this neighbour's son.

Catherine knew she had never done enough for poor Georgina.

She understood that an important call was going to be made from that mobile phone. Her job was to take care of the children until the call was made, and Frank could go to hell.

'Come, Ramu,' she said, drawing the imbecile boy away from her sister. She touched him and withdrew her hand almost at once.

'Georgina,' she whispered. 'I think he's soiled his trousers.'

The boy parted his lips, and began to emit a soft, high-pitched whine.

Mrs Rego picked up her mobile phone and dialled.

'Is that you, Mrs Puri?' she asked, when the call was answered.

Catherine came closer to listen.

'No, it's Mr Puri,' a man's voice said. 'My wife will call you in half an hour. The police are asking her some questions – there has been an unfortunate incident at the building. Is Ramu safe?'

Frank, opening the door of the bedroom to send another message, saw Mrs Rego break down and sob, while her sister stood over her, patting her back and whispering: 'Georgina, now, now…'

Bowing to the golden Ganesha on the lintel, Shanmugham walked through the open door of his employer's home in Malabar Hill.

He heard Kishore Kumar's "Ek Aise Gagan Ke Tale" on a tape recorder.

The living room was deserted. A plate full of chewed crusts lay on the dining table; he recognized the marks of his employer's teeth on the toast.

393

The fragrance of *gutka* guided him to the bedroom.

Dharmen Shah lay in a nest of printed papers, scratching on a pad with a pencil. The plaster-of-Paris model of the Confidence Shanghai sat beside him near the bedside lamp.

'What?'

Shanmugham did not know how to say it. He felt a strange fear of incriminating himself with any word he might use.

Looking up from his calculations, Shah saw his assistant's hand rising up in a fist.

The fist opened.

'How?'

'He fell, sir. From the terrace. About one hour ago. They say it's suicide.'

Shah opened his red mouth. Eyes closed, he pressed his head back against the white pillow. 'I thought it would be a push down the stairs, or a beating at night. That's all.'

He caressed the soft pillow.

'I forgot we were dealing with good people, Shanmugham.'

Scattering papers, the fat man climbed off the bed.

'You drive back to Vakola. Find out from your connection in the police station what is happening with their investigation. I'll call the astrologer in Matunga and get an auspicious date to start the demolition.'

MUMBAI SUN

SUICIDE IN SANTA CRUZ (EAST)?
By a staff reporter

Mr Yogesh Murthy, a retired teacher at the famous St Catherine's School in the neighbourhood, allegedly committed suicide last night from the rooftop of 'Vishram' Society in Vakola, Santa Cruz (E).

While there is no suspicion of foul play in the matter, the Santa Cruz police said they are not ruling out any possibility at this stage. An investigation is underway.

It is believed, however, that the deceased had slipped into a state of extreme depression following the death of his wife almost exactly a year ago. Residents of the neighbourhood say that he had been progressively losing his mind under the pressure of diabetes and old age, withdrawing into his room, talking to himself, engaging in anti-social behaviour and fighting with his entire Society over a proposed offer of redevelopment, which he alone opposed. Dr C. K. Panickar, a clinical psychiatrist at Bandra's Lilavati Hospital, says he had shown classic symptoms of mental deterioration. 'Paranoia, passive-aggressive developments, and even schizophrenia cannot be ruled out given the subject's behaviour in his final days,' he suggests.

The deceased is survived by a son, Gaurav, who lives in Marine Lines, and a grandson, Ronak.

EPILOGUE

Murder and Wonder

The little dark man in the blue safari suit walked through the vegetable stalls, disappointed that no one looked at him this morning as if he were a murderer.

For nearly two months the watermelon and pineapple sellers had discussed how that broker from Vishram, Ajwani, the one who sat across the road in that little real-estate office with the glass door, had arranged for one of his underworld contacts to kill Masterji; no – how he had done it himself, tiptoeing into Vishram under the cover of darkness and lifting the old teacher up on his thick arms to the terrace. They would turn around to find Ramesh Ajwani there, always with a smile, saying: 'What is the price for brinjals today?'

And they would start to haggle with him: for being a murderer does not necessarily get one a better rate with the brinjals.

He had been the first suspect. Nagarkar, the senior inspector, had summoned him to the station the morning after the death; he knew that Ajwani had connections to shady characters throughout Vakola. (The kinds of clients he had bribed them to get clearance certificates for!) For half a day the inspector grilled him below the portrait of Lord SiddhiVinayak. But his story held. A dozen people remembered seeing the broker outside the Dadar train station at various hours of the night of Masterji's death; he was said to have suffered an attack of indigestion, and to have lain there, writhing and incoherent.

'If you didn't do it, then who did?' the inspector asked. 'Do you really expect me to believe it was suicide?'

'I don't know,' Ajwani said. 'I came home after midnight. I was not well. The police were already there.'

The Secretary was the next to be summoned to the station. But three witnesses put him in Ajwani's real-estate office at the hour of Masterji's death. One was Mani, the broker's assistant, and the other two were Ibrahim Kudwa and Mr Puri, two of his neighbours, both respectable men. Every resident of Vishram Society, it turned out, could prove that he or she had been somewhere else at that time. The only ones who were in the building when Masterji fell off the roof were an ancient couple, the Pintos, who seemed barely capable of either sight or movement.

The builder? Nagarkar knew that Shah was a smart man: too smart to become involved if he would be an immediate suspect. So Masterji became the prime suspect in his own murder. Many people, both in Vishram and in the neighbourhood at large, gave evidence that the teacher had been growing senile and unpredictable for a while. His wife's death and his diabetes had made him depressed. In the end the Inspector decided, since he did not like unsolved mysteries, that it must have been suicide.

Ajwani knew it was not. For one week he had not spoken to anyone else in Vishram. Then he moved his son and wife to a rental flat by the train station. He was not going to live with those people again.

How they had done it he was not sure. Maybe Mr and Mrs Puri had done it on their own; the Secretary may have helped. Maybe it was just a push. But no, some part of him knew that Masterji would have struggled. A born fighter, that old man. They must have drugged him, or maybe hit him; whatever they did, either because the skull cracked in the fall, or because the doctor who examined the corpse was incompetent or bored, nothing had been detected.

He came to the fruit and vegetable market twice a day, three times a day if he could. He bargained for carrots and guavas and abuse; this was part of his penance. He hoped that the vendors would surround him one day and thrust their fingers into his ribcage; then pelt him with tomatoes and potatoes and push chillies into his eyes. He wanted to go home stained and accused of murder.

For two months after his death, Masterji was a residue of dark glamour on the Vakola market, a layer of ash over the produce. Then other scandals and other mysteries came. The vendors forgot him; Ajwani had become just another customer.

He walked away from the market, hands behind his back, until he heard hammers chipping away at stone and brick.

Vishram Society was overrun by workmen like a block of sugar by black ants. The roof had fallen in; men sat on the exposed beams and stood all along the stairs, hacking at wood with saws, and hammering at walls and beams. TNT could not be used in a neighbourhood this densely populated; the destruction had to be done by human hands. The men who had been working on the Confidence Excelsior and the Fountainhead were now chipping, peeling, and smashing Vishram; the women carried the debris on troughs on their heads and dumped it into the back of a truck.

Every few hours, the truck drove down the road, and poured its contents as filling into the foundations of the Ultimex Milano. The metal skeleton beneath the paint and plaster would be sent to workshops around Falkland Road to be broken up and recycled. Even in death, Vishram Society was being of service to Vakola and Mumbai.

As each hammer struck Vishram, the building fumed, emitting white puffs from its sides, like an angry man in the *Tom and Jerry* cartoons that Ajwani's sons watched in the mornings. It looked like some slow torture for all the trouble that the building had given Mr Shah. Some of the Christian workers had wanted to save the black Cross, but it was gone, probably crushed into the foundations of the Milano. Soon all that would remain of Vishram Society would be the old banyan; and each time there was a wind, its leaves brushed against the abandoned guard's booth like a child trying to stir a dead thing to life.

Ajwani leaned against the tree and touched its trunk.

'Rich man! Where have you been?'

A tall and lean man, brushing white dust from his white shirt and black trousers, had come up to him.

'You haven't signed the Confidence Group papers,' Shanmugham said, 'and without it we can't give you the money.'

Ajwani stepped back from the tree.

Shanmugham raised a leg and patted white dust off his trousers.

'One and a half crores of rupees. All of you are now rich men, and what do I get, Mr Ajwani? Nothing.'

Mr Shah had not given him a bonus or an extra. Not even a pat on the head, not even what a dog would get for chasing a stick. All the boss had said was: 'Now I want you to make sure that the demolition does not fall one day behind, Shanmugham. Time is money.'

For months he had been the man handing out red boxes of sweets to the residents of Vishram: where was *his* red box?

Moving close to the broker, he lowered his voice.

'I've been thinking about what you said. That day in your inner room, when we sat with the coconuts. About how some clever left-hand men actually manage to...'

Shanmugham started. The broker was walking away briskly, arms swinging, as if he were about to break into a run.

'Come back, Mr Ajwani! If you don't sign your papers, you won't get the money!'

What was wrong with the man?

With one eye closed, Shanmugham looked at the old banyan's leaves: sunlight oozed through the dark canopy like raw white honey. He picked up a stone and threw it at the light.

16 DECEMBER

The lift opened: the chai boy stepped out into the car park with a tray full of teacups.

He stopped and stared.

The tall man in the white shirt was doing it again. Standing before his Hero Honda motorbike, he was talking into the rear-view mirror.

'Mr Shah, I know you told me you didn't want to talk about a certain event ever again, but yesterday I met that broker, and I...'

The tall man closed his eyes, and tried again.

'Mr Shah, the real story behind... I know you told me never to mention it again, but I...'

The chai boy tiptoed around him; he took his tray of morning tea to the drivers waiting at the other end of the basement car park.

A quarter of an hour later, Shanmugham stood before his employer. Giri was in the kitchen, cutting something to pieces.

At his work desk, with the poster of the Eiffel Tower behind him, the boss was signing each page of a bundle of documents.

'Did I ask you to come up, Shanmugham?' he said without looking up. 'Go down and wait for me. We have to go to Juhu immediately.'

The left-hand man did not move.

Shah looked up; he held a silver pen in his fingers.

'We just had a call, Shanmugham. Satish has been arrested. Doing the same thing with the gang. This time in Juhu.' He made a circular motion with his pen in his hand. 'They sprayed some politician's van. Giri is putting the money in the envelope. We won't be able to keep it out of the newspapers this time.'

Shanmugham said what he had rehearsed for nearly twenty minutes in the basement: 'Sir: in the matter of the murder at Vishram Society. I have been thinking about it for some time. It is not a suicide. In Vakola they say either Shah did it, or the neighbours did it. And you didn't do it, since I didn't do it. So the neighbours did it.'

Shah did not look up.

'The newspapers said it was suicide. Go down and wait. We must go to Juhu.'

Shanmugham spoke to the poster of the Eiffel Tower over his boss's head.

'The police might be interested, sir, if someone told them that the people in Vishram did it. They might reopen the case. Look at the photographs of the corpse more carefully. The construction might be delayed.'

The silver pen dropped on to the table.

Shanmugham shivered; in another room, Shah's mobile phone had begun to ring. Giri came in with the mobile phone, wiped it on his lungi, and placed it on his employer's desk.

Shah, his eyes closed, listened to the voice on the phone.

'I am on my way. I understand. I am on my way.'

He rubbed the phone on his forearm and held it out for Giri.

Giri stood in the threshold for a minute, looking at the two men. Then he went back to the kitchen to continue cutting his bread.

Shah's jaw began working. He started to laugh.

'Oh, you are a son of mine, Shanmugham. A real son.'

He tapped twice on his desk.

'You listen to me: there is already one body in the foundations of the Shanghai, and there's plenty of space there for another. Do you understand?'

Shah grinned. Shanmugham understood that he had one sharp tooth, but this man had a mouth full of them.

'Do you *understand*?'

Shanmugham could not move. He felt his smallness in the den he had walked into: the den of real estate.

'Shanmugham. Why are you wasting my time?'

'Sorry, sir.'

'Go down to the basement and wait in the car. We have to get the boy out of the police station.'

And Shanmugham went down to the basement.

At least, Shah thought, *I got six good years out of this one.* On the pad on his table, where he had written:

> *Beige marble.*
> *Grilles on windows. (Fabergé egg pattern: pay up to one rupee extra per kg wrought iron. No more.)*

he added:

> *Left-hand man*

He straightened his clothes in the mirror, spat on to a finger, checked the colour of his insides, and went downstairs.

Juhu. Two half-built towers like twin phantoms behind a screen of trees, neither vanishing nor growing into clarity.

Dharmen Shah was sick of buildings.

He turned to his son and asked: 'How many more times will you do this?'

'Do what?' Satish was looking out of the window of the moving car. He wore a light green shirt; his school uniform shirt, which he had changed out of, was in a plastic bundle by his feet.

'Disgrace your family name.'

The boy laughed.

'I disgrace *your* name?' He stared at his father. 'I read the papers, Father. I saw what happened in Vakola.'

'I don't know what you've read. That old teacher killed himself. He was mad.'

The boy spoke slowly. 'All of us in the gang are builders' sons. If you don't let us do these things now,' he said, 'how will we become good builders when we grow up?'

Shah saw a platinum necklace around his son's neck; the younger generation preferred it to gold.

Satish asked to be let down at Bandra; he wanted to eat lunch at

Lucky's. His father had taken his credit card from him at the Juhu station; now he gave it back here to the boy, along with a 500-rupee note.

Satish touched the note to his forehead in a *salaam*. 'One day, Father, we'll be proud of each other.'

On a pavement near the Mahim Dargah, Shah saw a dozen beggars, waiting for free bread and curry, sitting outside a cheap restaurant. Tired, lively, cunning, each dirty face seemed to glow. One blind man had his face turned skywards in a look of dumb ecstasy. Just a few feet away, a man with red bleary eyes, his head in his hands, appeared to be the most frightened thing in the world.

Shah watched their faces go past.

If only the traffic hadn't been so light that evening the old teacher came to the Malabar Hill house. If only he had met face to face with that teacher, the matter would have ended right then. Blood need not have been spilled.

So why had they not met?

He had a vision of a blazing red curtain and a silhouette moving behind it: when the red curtain was torn away, he saw the faces of the beggars outside his car. All his life he had seen faces like these and thought: *Clay. My clay.* He had squeezed them into shape in his redevelopment projects, he had become rich off them. Now it seemed to him that these shining mysterious faces were the dark powers of his life. *They made this thing happen. Not to get my Shanghai built. To get their city built. They have used me for their ends.*

One of the beggars laughed. A choir of particulate matter shrilled inside Dharmen Shah's lungs; he coughed again and again, and spat into a corner of the Mercedes.

Half an hour later, he lay shirtless on a cold bed. In the only place on earth where personalized service depresses you.

'We changed the size of the bed to suit your body' – the voice of the radiologist.

Doctors display such familiarity only with the chronically ill.

Face down he lay, the fat folds of his chest and belly pressed against cold hard cushion. An X-ray machine moved above him, taking pictures of the back of his skull.

The X-ray machine stopped moving, and the radiologist went into another room, grumbling: 'I don't know if I've got the pictures, since you moved…'

Shah, shirtless on a three-legged stool, waited like a schoolboy.

'I'm sorry. We didn't get the X-rays. You have five minutes.'

He came out into the outpatient waiting room of Breach Candy Hospital. Rosie was waiting for him, in her shortest shortest skirt.

'Uncle.' She clapped. 'My uncle.'

Her nose was still bruised, a pale strip of skin revealed where the bandage must have sat for days.

'I thought you weren't coming, Rosie,' he said as he sat down by her side. 'I really did.'

'Of course I wouldn't leave you alone in the hospital, Uncle.' Dropping her voice, she asked: 'Is the skirt short enough?'

The other patients waiting outside the radiologist's office stared at this fat man with the well-rounded girl in skimpy clothes with her arms around him. Shah knew they were staring and he didn't give a shit. Shameless in health, shameless he was going to stay in illness.

'It'll warm the whole hospital.'

'That's the plan, Uncle.' She winked. 'They keep the AC on so high.'

He whispered into her ear.

'You can go home, Rosie. A hospital is no place for a girl like you.'

Rosie didn't bother to whisper.

'My father was the son of a first wife. I never told you this, did I, Uncle? His mother died of blood cancer when he was eight. This country is full of first wife's sons who ended up as losers. I like being around a winner.'

She kissed him on the cheek.

The wetness remained on Shah's cheek and he recognized it for what it was: ambition. The girl didn't just want a hair salon, she wanted everything: all his money, all his buildings. All his money above and below the earth. Marriage.

He wanted to laugh – a girl he had pulled out of jail! – and then he remembered the story Rosie had told him. The actress and the Punjabi producer. 'Her blowjobs sing across the decades.'

How there is nothing small, nothing ignoble in life. A man may not find love in the sacrament of marriage but he has found it with a woman he coupled with on his office sofa: just as a seed spat out by the gutter pipe, sucking on sewage, can grow into a great banyan.

'Mr Shah?' A crooked finger summoned him back into the X-ray room.

You don't fool me, Shah thought, as the X-ray machine did its work again. *You're not going to save anyone.* This was just the bureaucracy of extinction: its first round of paperwork. The cold of the metal bed penetrated multiple layers of butter-fed fat; he shivered.

'Should I keep my eyes closed or open?'

'Doesn't matter. Just relax.'

'I'll close them, then.'

'As you wish. Relax.'

He could feel Rosie's fingers still warm on his own. He could smell her legs on his trousers. He thought again of the abandoned old mansion that he passed every day on his way down Malabar Hill, the green saplings breaking through the stone foliage. It was as if each green sapling were a message: *Leave Mumbai with Rosie, find a city with clean air, have another son, a better one – you still have time, you still have…*

Shah took a deep breath and closed his eyes.

… He saw the hawks again: circling with drawn claws, as they had been that sunlit morning in Doctor Nayak's home above the Cooperage, locked in battle, the most beautiful creatures on a beautiful earth.

The hawks faded away, and he saw an island in the Arabian Sea – saw it as he had once, years ago, on a return flight from London which was held up by congestion at the airport and flew in circles: down there, the city in sunlight seemed like a postage stamp struck in silver, precise and shining and so easy to comprehend. He saw it all, from Juhu to Nariman Point: Bombay, the Jewel in the Jewel in the Crown. He saw south Bombay and Colaba: so closely packed with mirror-clad buildings that the land glittered. He saw Chowpatty beach; the two green ovals of the cricket stadia; the Air India building and the Express building behind, and the towers of Cuffe Parade…

The plane turned to the right. Now he saw the city dramatically walled in by green-red cliffs and plateaux. The air on one side of the cliffs was dark blue and dense; on the other, it was clear. If a man crossed those cliffs, he would find clean air – he would breathe.

The mucus in his chest rumbled. It voted for the clean side of the cliffs.

Dharmen Shah moved the plane back to the dirty side of the cliffs.

The plane was over Vakola now. He saw his Shanghai, most silver among the silver towers; and next to it another Shah tower; and next to it...

His diseased body began to move, despite the radiologist's orders, on the cold bench, seizing more square inches for itself, dreaming, even here, of reclamation and warm space.

There had been another terrorist threat to the city, and the metal detector at the entrance to the Infiniti Mall in Andheri (West), installed months ago and left inactive ever since, was turned on at last.

It responded with such enthusiasm – beeping three times for each person – that every man and woman entering the mall became a high-risk terrorist threat. A quick frisking and opening of bags restored their name and good reputation, allowing them to ride the escalator to the Big Bazaar supermarket on the first floor, or the Landmark Book Store on the second.

'Thirty-six rupees for a plate of bhelpuri!'

Mr Kothari, the former Secretary of Vishram Society Tower A, sat down at a table in the atrium of the food court with a heaped plate of bhelpuri. Tinku, holding his plate in one hand, pulled a chair from an adjacent table and joined his father.

'It is a mall, Father, what do you expect?' He began to scoop the food into him.

'This place used to be just birds and trees.' Kothari looked about the atrium. 'Andheri.'

As if conjured by his nostalgia, a few sparrows flew into the food court.

His mouth full of puffed rice and diced onion, Tinku gaped.

'Look who's here, Father.'

'Who? Oh, ignore them. Keep eating.'

'Father, they're coming here.'

'A man can't even enjoy his bhelpuri. Which he's paid thirty-six...'

A piece of tomato slipped out of Kothari's mouth as he smiled; he sucked it back in.

'Forgotten your old neighbours already, haven't you?' Ibrahim Kudwa asked, as he came up to their table with little Mariam in his arms; Mumtaz, following him, was carrying two shopping bags. Kudwa dragged a metal chair over to their table.

'I was just telling Tinku it was time to give you a call – when look who turns up.'

'You're looking good, son.' Kudwa patted Tinku on the back. 'Healthy.'

The fat boy winced: he knew what this meant.

As Kothari petted Mariam's cheeks, her father asked: 'Where do you live these days?'

'Right here. Andheri West.'

'But...' Kudwa frowned. '... there are no flamingoes in Andheri West.'

'Flamingoes were for big men like my father. Those fellows are good enough for me.' Kothari pointed to the sparrows hopping about the food court. 'We are in the Capriconius Society. Behind the HDFC bank on Juhu-Versova Link Road. Good place. Good people.'

'They want Papa to be the Secretary there too,' Tinku said, as his father blushed.

'Some bhelpuri for you, Ibrahim? Or you, Mumtaz? A bite for Mariam.'

'Oh, no,' Kudwa said. 'I take three Antacids a day just to go to sleep. The wife has forbidden all outside food.' He looked at her with a smile. 'We have good people in our new Society too. In fact' – he pointed to one of the shopping bags his wife was carrying – 'I'm taking a gift for my neighbour's son. A surprise.'

He beamed with pleasure. He noted that Kothari was wearing a new gold necklace – he tried to remember if the man had ever worn gold in his Vishram Society days.

'But *where* do you live, Ibrahim?'

'Bandra East. We have a family shop in hardware. I became a partner with my brother. There's no future in technology, I tell you. Hammers. Nails. Screws. If you ever need any of these in bulk, please come to Kalanagar. Let me write down my address.' He turned to Mumtaz; putting her bags down, she took out a ballpoint pen and wrote on a paper napkin.

When she had done as her husband told her, Mumtaz put the pen down and looked at Kothari.

'Any news from the builder? The second instalment is already three weeks late.'

'I phoned his office and left a message.' Kothari folded the napkin with the Kudwas' phone number. 'If he doesn't pay this instalment and the next one on time, we'll go to court.'

'What a fraud that man proved to be. Mr Shah. We trusted him.'

'All builders are the same, Ibrahim, old-fashioned or new-fashioned. But the first instalment did come, and he did give us eight weeks' rent while we looked for a new place. He *will* pay. Just likes to delay.'

'Where is Mrs Puri these days, Ibrahim? Any idea?'

'Goregaon. Gokuldam. In that new tower there. Nice place, new woodwork. They've hired a full-time nurse for the boy.'

'That's the future. Goregaon. So much empty space.'

Kudwa shook his head. 'Between us, the boy's health has suddenly become much worse. I don't know what she will do if he... Gaurav comes to see her all the time, she says. He's become like a son to her.'

Kothari dug his plastic spoon into his food.

'And Mrs Rego?' he asked. 'Any word?'

'We were never close,' Kudwa said. 'The Pintos of course are living with their son. He came back from America. Lost his business there.'

'Everyone is coming back from America.'

Shifting Mariam to his left arm, Ibrahim Kudwa touched the table for attention.

'Ajwani refused to take any of the money, did you hear? Not one rupee.'

Kothari sighed.

'That man – all his life he was obsessed with money. Sat in his real-estate office with a bundle of cash in his drawer to feel rich. And then when he actually gets a windfall, he says no. A *nothing* man. *Pucca* nothing.'

Kothari ate more bhelpuri.

Mumtaz Kudwa picked up her shopping bags; her husband stood up with Mariam.

'Life is good,' he said. 'It is not perfect, but it is better with money.'

'You have said it exactly right, Ibrahim. Goodbye, Mumtaz. Bye-bye, Mariam.'

On the escalator down, Kothari went over the bill for the food he and his son had just eaten; his lips worked.

'... the bhelpuri was only twenty-six rupees, Tinku. They charged ten rupees for water. But we didn't have bottled water.'

'No,' the boy agreed. 'We didn't have any water.'

Stepping down from the escalator, he said: 'Let's go and get the ten rupees back, Tinku.'

'For ten rupees? All the way up?'

The two got on the other escalator and went back up to the food court.

'It's the *principle*. A man must stand up for his rights in this world. Your grandfather taught me that.'

Tinku, who was starting to yawn, turned in surprise: his unmusical father was humming a famous Beatles song and slapping the escalator with the back of his hand.

On any evening Juhu beach is overwhelmed by cricket matches of poor style and great vigour; on a Sunday, perhaps a hundred matches are in progress along the length of the sand. All face a fatal constraint: the ocean. Anyone who hits the ball directly into the water is declared out – a uniform rule across the beach. A good, honest pull-shot to a bad ball, and a batsman has just dismissed himself. To survive, you must abandon classical form. What is squirming, quicksilver, heterodox thrives.

'A million people are batting along this beach. Play with some style. Stand out,' Mrs Rego shouted.

She stood in her grey coat at the wicket, an umpire-commentator-coach of the match in progress.

Timothy, Mary's son, was batting at the stick-wicket; Kumar, tallest of the regulars at the Tamil temple, ran in to bowl.

Mary, sitting on the sand, the game's only spectator and cheerleader, turned for a moment to look at the water's edge.

It was low tide, and the sea had receded far from the normal shoreline, leaving a glassy, marshy in-between zone. Reflected in the wet sand, two nearly naked boys ran about the marsh; they jumped into the waves and splashed each other. The sunlight made their dark bodies shine blackly, as if coated in a slick of oil; in some private ecstasy, they began rolling in and out of the water, barely in this world at all.

Mary now saw a familiar figure walking along the surf. The bottoms of his trousers were rolled up, and he carried his shoes over his shoulder, where they stained his shirt.

She waved.

'Mr Ajwani.'

'Mary! How nice to see you.'

He sat by her side.

'Did you come to watch your son playing cricket?'

'Yes, sir. I don't like to see him wasting time on cricket, but Madam – I mean Mrs Rego – insisted he be here.'

Ajwani nodded.

'How is your place by the *nullah*? More threats of demolition?'

'No, sir. My home stands. I found work in one of the buildings by the train station. An Ultimex building. The pay is better than at Vishram, sir. And they give me a nice blue uniform to wear.'

The two of them ducked. The red ball had shot two inches past Ajwani's nose – it soared over the glassy sand and detonated in the ocean.

'Timothy is out!' Mrs Rego cried.

She saw Ajwani sitting alongside Mary.

He saw the hostility in her eyes – they had not spoken once since that night – and he knew at once, 'she too was in it.'

'Let me stay, Mrs Rego,' he said. 'It is one of the rules of Juhu beach: you can't say no to any stranger who wants to watch you play.'

Mrs Rego sighed, and looked for the ball.

The two boys who had been rolling about in the water now rushed towards the ball; it came back, in a high red arc, as the cricketers cheered. Up in the sky, a plane cut across the ball's trajectory – and the cricketers let out a second cheer, a sustained one.

The plane had caught the angle of the setting light, and looked radiant and intimate before it went over the ocean.

The game continued. Mrs Rego kept offering the boys 'tips' on batting 'with style'. Ajwani and Mary cheered impartially for all the batsmen.

The setting sun brought more people. The smell of humans overwhelmed the smell of the sea. Vendors waved green and yellow fluorescent wires in the darkening air to catch the attention of children. Particoloured fans were arranged on long wooden frames to whirl in the sea breeze, green plastic soldiers crawled over the sand, and mechanical frogs moved with a croaking noise. Small men stood with black trays of skinned peanuts warmed by live coals suspended around their necks; tables of coconuts and pickles were set up under umbrellas; boys bathed in their underwear and Muslim women took dips in sodden black burqas. Glowing machines talked to you about your weight and destiny for a couple of rupees.

The cricket game had degenerated. On the promise of merely burying Timothy in sand, Dharmendar and Vijay had proceeded to carve breasts and genitals in the sand over him, and had written in English: 'FUK ME'.

'You could at least spell it right!' Mrs Rego tried to look stern for as long as possible before helping the others to rescue the trapped boy.

The ocean was a brimming violet: twilight glowed over Juhu.

'All right, boys, collect the bat and ball and come here,' Mrs Rego shouted. 'It's time for a speech.'

'Speech? Why does there always have to be a speech, Mrs Rego?'

'We have to make a speech about Masterji. Do you think his son is going to remember him? We have to do it. In fact, *you* are going to start, Timothy.'

The other boys gathered in a semi-circle around Timothy. Ajwani sat next to Mary.

Timothy grinned. 'I once saw Masterji sitting under a tree near the temple. He was eating all the fruit...'

'Timothy!' Mrs Rego said.

The boys clapped and whistled: 'Great speech!'

'Sit down, Timothy.' Mrs Rego pointed to Ajwani.

'*You* speak now.'

'Me?' The broker wanted to laugh, but he understood that she was serious. Everyone sitting here – in fact, everyone in this beach – had had some involvement in the affair. His share was larger than that of most others.

Wiping the sand off his trousers, he stood up. He faced the semi-circle of four boys and two women.

'Friends, our late Masterji—'

'The late Mr Yogesh Murthy,' Mrs Rego corrected.

'... late Mr Yogesh Murthy, was my neighbour, but I don't have much information about his life. He was born I think in the south and came here I think after his marriage. Wherever he came from, he came, and became a typical man of this city. What do I mean by that?' Ajwani looked at the ocean. 'I mean he became a new kind of man. I think about him more now than I did when he was my neighbour.'

He hoped that they would understand.

Mrs Rego stood up, and everyone turned to her.

'Boys: I would like to say hip-hip-hooray for Mr Ajwani – for his fine speech. Now I want everyone to clap for him. Will you clap, boys?'

'Hip-hip-hooray! Aj-waaa-ni!'

'Boys, I have a few more words for you.'

'Don't you always?' – laughter.

The semi-circle shifted and moved so that Mrs Rego was now in its centre.

'Boys, where Masterji was born, where he studied – these things don't matter now. What matters is this. He did what he believed to be right. He had a conscience. No matter what people said to him or did to him he never changed his mind, and never betrayed his conscience. He was free to the end.'

'Enough, Aunty.'

'Shut up, and don't call me Aunty. Now: all of you keep quiet.'

And some of them did.

'Boys, some years ago I went to Delhi and met a man who had never seen the ocean in his life, and thought, what's a life like that worth? We will always have the ocean and that is why we live in the true capital of this country. All we need are a few more good men like Masterji and this island, this Mumbai of ours, it will be paradise on earth. As it used to be, when I was a girl in Bandra. When I see you boys sitting here before me, I know that there are future Masterjis among you, and this city will again be what it was, the greatest on earth. And so, gentlemen of the cricket team, so as not to keep this speech going on any longer, let us all stand up, and put our hands together, and give a hip-hip-hooray in memory of our late Masterji, whom we promise to remember and honour.'

'Hip-hip-hooray!' they shouted together.

The cricketers had been good boys and now they wanted their reward. A sugarcane stand had been spotted nearby.

'You too,' Mrs Rego said. Ajwani accepted. They walked in a group towards the sugarcane juice stand at the end of the beach. Mrs Rego, overriding the broker's protests, was paying for all the drinks. She counted heads so that she could order the right number of glasses. Suddenly she let out a shriek.

A lizard was running down her skirt.

'*Who* did that?'

Timothy and Dharmendar looked at each other, and everyone else giggled. Ajwani dispatched the plastic lizard towards the beach with a kick. Mrs Rego resumed counting heads.

'What will you do now, Mr Ajwani?' she asked, as she drank her juice.

'At first, I thought of leaving real estate entirely,' he said. 'But then I thought, there are honest men in this business too. Let me add to their number.'

With one eye closed, she looked into her glass, and then put it back on the stall.

'Is it true, what they say: that you refused to take the builder's money?'

He licked his lips and set his glass down by hers.

'At first. But I have a family. Two sons. A wife.'

A bearded man came up to the sugarcane juice stall; he peered at Mrs Rego and then smiled.

'You're the social worker who does good things in the slums, aren't you?'

Mrs Rego hesitated, then nodded.

'I've seen you in your office, madam,' the bearded man said. 'I too used to be from Vakola. I lived in a slum: it's where the Ultimex Group are now building their tower. Ultimex Milano.'

Ajwani and Mrs Rego peered at the bearded man. He was wearing a white Muslim skullcap.

'Are you… the fortunate man? The eighty-one-lakhs man?'

'By the grace of Allah, sir, you could say that was me. I don't have any money on me, now. Bought a two-bedroom in Kurla in a *pucca* building. A small Maruti-Suzuki too.'

'You don't look unhappy at all,' Mrs Rego said.

'Why should I be unhappy?' The fortunate man laughed. 'My children have never had a real home. Four daughters I have. Fate is good to many people these days. There's a man here in Juhu, living in a slum, who has been offered sixty-three lakhs by a real-estate developer to move out. He's a connection of a connection of mine, and I came to talk to him. About how to deal with these builders.'

The workers at the sugarcane stand had overheard, and now they asked the fortunate man for details; a nearby newspaper-vendor came to listen in. A fellow in a slum? Sixty-three lakhs? Nearby? Which slum? Which fellow? Are you sure it was *sixty*-three?

Mrs Rego and Ajwani watched the bearded man, who had freckles on his large nose, perhaps from measles, wondering if those were the marks by which fortunate humans were identified.

Done with their sugarcane juice, the boys walked from the beach to the main road. Vijay, revitalized by the juice, had caught Dharmendar in a head-lock.

Mrs Rego wished she hadn't had the juice: the sudden sugar, as it always did, made her feel depressed. She licked her lips and spat away what remained of the sweet juice – the finest compensation the city could offer these boys for the dreams it wouldn't make real.

'What will become of them, Mr Ajwani? Such fine boys, all of them… '

'What do you mean, what will become of them?'

'I mean, Mr Ajwani, all this talent, all this energy: do these boys have any idea of what lies ahead for them? Disappointment. That's all.'

The broker stopped. 'How can *you* say this, Mrs Rego? You have always helped others.'

She stopped by his side. Her face contracted into something smaller and darker with grief.

Ajwani smiled; the parallel lines on his cheeks deepened.

'I have learned something about life, Mrs Rego. You and I were trapped: but we *wanted* to be trapped. These boys will live in a better world. Look over there.'

'Where?' She asked.

A bus passed by with an advertisement for a film called *Dance, Dance*; autorickshaws and scooters followed it. When they had passed, Mrs Rego saw a group of white-uniformed *dabba*-wallahs with their pointed caps, seated in a ring, playing cards on the pavement.

'The light is not good. I can't see what you're...'

After a while, Mrs Rego saw, or thought she saw, what her former neighbour was pointing at.

Past the traffic, on the other side of the road, she saw the boundary wall of an old Juhu housing society, displaying three generations of torture devices: primitive coloured bottle-glass shards, stuck into the entire length of the wall, and over them a layer of rusty barbed wire with its ends tied into jagged knots, and over that, rolled into giant coils, a shinier barbed wire with large square metal studs, like she had seen in action movies around American military installations, less crudely threatening than the rusty layer but unmistakably more lethal. Behind these overlapping wires she saw banyan trees; all of which were hemmed in by the fencing; except for one greying ancient, whose aerial roots, squirming through barbed wire and broken glass, dripped down the wall like primordial ooze until their bright growing tips, nearly touching the pavement, brushed against a homeless family cooking rice in the shade; and with each root-tip that had beaten the barbed wire the old banyan said: *Nothing can stop a living thing that wants to be free.*

Vakola, Mumbai
March 2007–October 2009

419

ACKNOWLEDGEMENTS

Robin Desser at Knopf edited this novel and made it a better one.

I thank my uncle, Mr Udaya Holla of Sadashivanagara, Bangalore, for taking care of my interests for so many years.

I thank Drew MacRae, Ravi Mirchandani, Pankaj Mishra, Akash Shah and his family, Justice Suresh and Rajini, Shivjit 'Chevy' Sidhu, Vinay Jayaram, Vivek Bansal, William Green, Elizabeth Zoe Vicary, Professor Robert W. Hanning, Professor David Scott Kastan, Jason Zweig, S. Prasannarajan, Devangshu Datta, Sree Srinivasan, Robert Safian, Jason Overdorf and Ivor Indyk.